THE DIVINE ENGINE

EMBRACE CHAOS!

MICHAEL P. WILLIAMS

authorHOUSE®

AuthorHouse™ LLC
1663 Liberty Drive
Bloomington, IN 47403
www.authorhouse.com
Phone: 1-800-839-8640

Published by AuthorHouse 07/25/2014

ISBN: 978-1-4969-2826-9 (sc)
ISBN: 978-1-4969-2827-6 (e)

Any people depicted in stock imagery provided by Thinkstock are models,
and such images are being used for illustrative purposes only.
Certain stock imagery © Thinkstock.

This book is printed on acid-free paper.

Because of the dynamic nature of the Internet, any web addresses or links contained in
this book may have changed since publication and may no longer be valid. The views
expressed in this work are solely those of the author and do not necessarily reflect the
views of the publisher, and the publisher hereby disclaims any responsibility for them.

This book is dedicated to all of the people who have influenced or altered my life throughout the years. To my family and friends, The Creator and all of the lesser Deities I have worshiped throughout the years: H. P. Lovecraft, Philip K. Dick, Hunter S. Thompson, Derrick W. Dick, Matt Groening, Bill Hicks, Steven Wilson, and Edward Lee. And to my wife, Tina, for her unconditional love, patience, understanding, exceptional editing skills, and most of all for her guidance in helping me get this story out of my head. Thank you…

oOo
REVELATIONS

There is but one question. This question has been asked throughout the ages in a multitude of ways, for an infinite number of reasons. Scientists have been digging for the answer to this question for centuries, but they always seem to be looking in the wrong places. Just when they think they've got it all figured out something new comes along; something new to learn, to explore, to figure out how it all works, all the while forgetting one *very* important thing. Call it Karma, call it the Divine Plan, call it what you will it's out there, whether we see it or understand it... or not, *everything* happens for a reason.

Therein lies the question: Why? Why are we here, and where exactly, did *here* come from? Some people have figured it out though most have gone crazy, driven mad by one demon or another. It is my belief that a good percentage of the people who are labeled crazy and locked away are, in fact, as sane as you and I, if not *more* so. The only difference is that these so-called "crazy people" see reality in a way that *we* do not. Is that such a bad thing?

What is it that makes something real? There was a time when it was thought that what one could touch, smell, see and hear was all that reality consisted of. People were *murdered* for thinking outside of the box! Here's the thing that gets me: if the brain is capable of altering one's reality, how can we honestly say that the reality we see before us is what is truly here? There are people who live in another reality entirely, and to them, it's as real as the one we call home. With *that* possibility alone, how can we honestly say that we know what reality is? Is it because we "normal" people all see the same reality? No! It is a fact that we all see things differently; the basic story is still there but the details change. Or could it be that things really *are* different for each individual? Maybe the details *didn't* change and that is how *they* see reality? Could it be possible that we see reality as we do because that is how we expect to see it, that we, as a species, dictate our own reality? There is so little about the human mind that is actually understood, so who the hell is anyone to tell anyone else what reality is? Is it not what we make it?

My name is Marcus Quincy and I have Tourette syndrome. With this disorder, uncontrollable urges, cursing, tics, and panic attacks are just the tip of the iceberg. The effect Tourette's has on the human mind is far, far worse. My mind is constantly racing. So many thoughts, so hard to hold on to just one. It truly *can* be a curse... a curse to always be asking why. Why am I like this? Why are we here? What drives me to search for resolution to questions that refuse to be answered? Questions like, why is the subconscious mind *much* more dangerous? My mind likes to make me think about things I'd rather not think about. Rape, torture, murder... you name it, it's in there. I fucking *hate* myself for these thoughts and they thoroughly disgust me! I would *never* act on these urges, but it's amazing how thin that line is. How easy that line would be to cross, to let things go too far. It's also amazing that I never ended up a serial killer; I always used to say I was one more childhood trauma away from becoming the next Ted Bundy or John Wayne Gacy. Call me crazy if it suits you; hell, any doctor would certify me insane and lock me away if I told them *any* of this. Which brings me back to *why*. Why can't people just open their minds and say, "Hey, maybe this one's right?" Scientists everywhere back up their explanations with theories that work on paper but no hard proof, and never give one second thought to some "crackpot" who claims to know the truth. Why? Because they're afraid of finding out everything they've ever known is wrong!

People fear what they do not understand. We seek truth in knowledge, we theorize and hypothesize simply for the sole purpose of distracting us from our fears, immersing ourselves in numbers and equations to momentarily ease the pain of living in ignorance. Take a moment to contemplate the significance of numbers and why they play such an essential role in the grand scheme of things. Everything, all of reality, can be reduced to numbers. There are numbers that pop up in everyone's life more often than others. Over the years I've had a lot of jobs that required me to count large amounts of items every day. Day in, day out, certain numbers seemed to be more prominent than any of the others. Seven has always played an important part in my life. Along with my Tourette's, I've been graced with the tendencies of an obsessive compulsive, therefore, I often find myself counting my tics. They have *always* come in waves of seven. I, myself, have never put too much faith in the whole numerology thing. Yeah, I think there could be something to it, but I'm not sure I want yet another thing running my life; there are enough *people* out there doing a fine job of that as it is. Besides, two other very prominent numbers of mine are 420 and 666. Do these numbers destine me to become an evil stoner? Maybe *you* should decide; after all, I'm just another nut job looking to tell his story, right?

Now that we've established the importance of numbers, let us move on to patterns. Patterns play just as crucial a role in the inner workings of the cosmos as well as our daily lives. Spring, summer, fall, winter, get up, go to work, go to bed, get up, go to work, go to bed, GOD I *hate* patterns! Have you ever seen the patterns when you close your eyes? What I have always seen when I close my eyes are thousands of tiny black dots with halo's of color throughout my entire field of vision. I see them in the dark with my eyes open; I even see them in the daytime if the lighting is just right. I've done some research on this and it seems I am not alone. These *phosphenes,* as they are supposedly called (though the descriptions given and explanations as to their origin do not match what I and many others out there see) are always moving, up, down, horizontally, I can even make them change direction and color just by thinking about it, but no matter how hard I try I can *never* get them to stop moving.

Several years ago I started getting this constant ringing in my ears. Not so loud that I couldn't tune it out most of the time but it was *always* there. I went to several doctors but they all told me the same thing, my hearing was fine and it was all in my head. Over time, the ringing became more of a high-pitched electrical whine, like constant feedback blaring in the back of my skull. It was July Seventh of 2007 when I first noticed the tone changed, randomly shifting from one pitch to another. I was 25 years old and I had a beautiful wife and two lovely twin girls. It was around this time that I started experimenting with a few meditation techniques that I had read about online. If done correctly, these techniques were supposed to ease me into a lucid state of dreaming.

Dreams have played a very important role in the molding of my psyche. I could never remember much of my childhood before the age of seven, but I could *always* remember my dreams. There are several that have haunted me throughout my life. I can't call them reoccurring dreams, because each time I have one, it's always different from the last time in some way. Sometimes the difference is no more than the color of someone's eyes, other times the dream takes place somewhere else entirely. Then there are the words and phrases that are spoken or written on objects. There is one phrase that has *always* been in my dreams. Over the years it seemed to occur more often, sometimes in every dream for weeks on end. That phrase is, *"There are patterns in the lines."* I nearly drove myself mad trying to figure out what that meant. That's the funny thing about the brain; it likes to play tricks on you. Shouldn't there be an untainted bond between a man and his mind?

One of the many reoccurring characters in my dreams is a young teenage boy, thirteen, fourteen maybe. He wears faded blue jeans, a white t-shirt with the logo of a rock band called Triumph, and a blue ball cap turned backwards on his head. He follows me around repeating one phrase over and over, *"The sandman is looking for you."*

There are times when I close my eyes at night to sleep and the first thing I see is a face. It creeps the shit out of me! It lasts only a moment before the figure drifts off into the darkness, but while it's there I can see every feature clearly, every feature but his eyes, they are always filled with the black dots. It's not just the vision that's a bit unnerving, because there's a presence too; I can *feel* him there. I started calling him the Sandman in my late teens.

Back to the summer of 07'… I was meditating, trying to focus in on one of the countless number of images flashing around in my head at all times, but those damn dots kept distracting me! It was when I stopped trying and cleared my mind that it hit me…

I stood in a small hallway. I placed my hand on the wall, running my fingertips across fieldstone covered with a thick layer of gray paint. I saw a small window near the ceiling of one wall, no glass, just an opening framed with small tree branches. The hallway led to a large, empty room. Somehow, I knew I was in a church, and that I was not alone. I heard someone talking a few rooms away from me, or was he praying? I looked around and I realized I could no longer see the dots before my eyes and, like a fool I tried to focus in on them. I couldn't at first. It took a few seconds to find them and when I did, the image was gone but the dots remained; only now they were bright white pinpricks with black halos, and for the first time in my life they stood perfectly still!

Even now I remember the first time with remarkable clarity. Right away, I knew it was much more than a dream. For a brief moment I was somewhere else. Perhaps this realization is what prompted my access to the seldom-achieved goal of lucid dreaming. It was starting to come easy. I'd just lie down and close my eyes and let the images flow. They moved so fast, I had to learn to concentrate on one part of the image and not the whole. I focused in on the small details and the image seemed to slow, allowing me to see more as each image passed by until finally, my mind was able to read an entire vision. When this happened, I got pulled into the image, into the dream. As a young man I used to keep a journal next to my bed to record my dreams. Unfortunately, I lost my dream journal a long time ago, so as I once again began my journey into the world of dreams, I decided it was time to start a new one.

Journal Entry 3   Dream #6   7/7/07

I walked along a path in the woods, the setting sun offering little light in the shadows of the trees. I saw houses in the distance and heard laughter from a group of children playing somewhere out of sight. The path led behind a row of houses with fenced in back yards where the woods ended abruptly in pavement. Something about the place seemed… familiar. I stood in the street and looked around, wondering which direction to go. I heard the laughter once more and walked around a nearby house to find several children playing a game I had never seen before. There were five young girls around the age of six or seven, they held hands and giggled as they walked slowly in a circle around two telephone poles buried deep in the ground. Binding the two poles together was a sort of rope that looked like it was made out of cotton, adorned with offerings of shiny gold jewelry in the shape of human organs. Atop the poles, which stood about ten feet high, was a sixth young girl the same age as the others. I realized then that all of the girls were twins. The child atop the pole sang a song that I could not hear as she dropped rose petals down onto the girls below.

Off in the distance, a small group of adults sat talking on the porch of a nearby house. There were four of them, two men who appeared to be twins (they both wore matching outfits), and two women, all in their late twenties. I couldn't see the men's faces; they were a blur, like a smeared painting. Of the four of them, for some reason, I only saw the face of one. She was an attractive woman with shoulder length dirty blonde hair. Something told me I knew her. The other woman's face I never really saw, and though she always kept her long dark hair, her face would change every couple of seconds, barely enough time to take in all of her features. As I drew closer, the blonde woman called to me.

I shook hands with all but the blonde, who wrapped her arms around me and hugged me, then kissed me on the lips. Not a sexual kiss, just a friendly one. I don't know how I knew her name, but I did. Her name was Julia. The twins were Mark and Mike, and the face-changing brunette was Carlie. How did I know these people? I decided to ask some questions, but Julia was the only one to talk to me, as the others conversed among themselves. Unfortunately, as conversations in dreams can be, this one started out making *very* little sense.

"Did you see the pumpkin burning?" Julia asked.

"No," I said.

"How could you not, it was huge!" she exclaimed.

"I must have been asleep," I answered, confused.

"Sleep, what's that?" Julia teased.

"So, why can't I see the twins' faces?" I asked bluntly. Julia ignored the question and began humming a childhood lullaby I couldn't place. "Why does Carlie's face keep changing?" I asked next, and Julia sort of gave me an answer, she said, "Because it's not ready to come out yet." What did she mean by that?

Mark, Mike, and Carlie turned and entered the front door of the house. Julia took my hand and led me in. The outside of the house wasn't bad, a modest two-story farmhouse, but the inside... The inside was like an old Victorian mansion! A massive, dark cherry staircase wound its way up to the third floor, though from the outside, the house had only two levels. Julia tugged on my arm and pulled me up the stairs. She stopped on the second floor and led me down the hall to a door that stood open. Mark, Mike, and Carlie were sitting on a large wooden four-poster bed with green curtains hanging down on all sides. The front was drawn open and I watched them playing a game of cards that seemed to melt in their hands. I sat down in a large chair in the far corner of the room. Julia picked up a coffee mug from the nightstand and sat in a chair on the opposite wall. She held the mug up to her nose for a moment before taking a sip.

"To answer your question, Marcus, why you see my face and not the others," Julia paused for a moment and smiled. "You see what you want to see."

"I see you the way I do because I *want* to? What the hell does that mean?"

Mark, Mike, and Carlie looked up from their game but said nothing. I looked back at Julia and in the moment I had looked away, her face changed. I was now looking into my wife Anna's beautiful green eyes! I looked at the others and saw Carlie's face... sort of, it still changed, though I now recognized every person she became. People I knew, some I had met only a single time. And the two men, Mark and Mike… I was now looking at two identical versions of myself. I woke up…

Dreams have always intrigued me. I've read books, articles, you name it, on dreams and their possible interpretations, but I just don't buy the explanations given. Saying dreams are the mind's way of working out problems is no different than Fraud's phallic cigar; it's all a bunch of bullshit! Sorry Sig., but if you're *thinking* dick you're going to *see* dick. *You see what you want to see!*

While dreaming, there are times when virtually *everyone* has had the epiphany that what is going on around them is not real, but why is it so easy to forget, to find yourself immersed in this world once more with no idea that what is happing to you is not real? How can it *not* be real? If the mass's view of reality relies on the fact that we all see things the same way, then think about this: everyone dreams, therefore, dreams *must* be real. Let's face it, dreams have a way of screwing with us on so many levels, the rules that apply in the so-called "real world" are not the same set used in the world of dreams. Nevertheless, they *are* rules, and rules can be bent. It took three months of practice through trial and error before I honed my skills enough to not only bend the rules, but break them…

Journal Entry 95   Dream #2   10/31/07

I walked down a crowded city street. The throng of travelers consisted of thousands of laughing children dressed in their Halloween costumes, toting sacks of candy. Every child wore a red raincoat over his or her costume, some wearing the hoods. The costumes were all well made, each more horrific than the last. All manner of bizarre creatures passed me by on both sides, and from my vantage point (I stood a good two feet taller than any of the children), I saw the crowd stretching out for miles in all directions. I looked up at the buildings where I saw hundreds of adults standing on the balconies and rooftops. Some were pointing at me and shouting, though I could not hear what they were saying. One of the children bumped into me with his overstuffed sack of... The sacks that were once filled with candy were now filled with treats of another kind... If you're Jeffery Dahmer, maybe...

Blood dripped down the side of the sack, smearing the hip of my jeans. I turned and saw an arm sticking out of the top of the kid's bag, the severed end spurting as the child skipped down the sidewalk. Severed heads and limbs bulged from the bags, and one child even had a torso, deprived of its limbs, stuffed into the sack he carried over his shoulder. The laughter changed. I looked around me and saw that it wasn't just the laughter, the costumes no longer contained children; these creatures were real! Razor sharp claws and teeth clicked as the monstrosities stopped and stared at me. Some of the bastards were even licking their lips! I could now hear the cries from the balcony as the creatures tore at their raincoats with fierce claws and teeth, sending shreds of red plastic through the air in all directions. I took the advice of the cries from the rooftops and ran like hell!

A woman on a balcony waved to me from across the street, she shouted something inaudible and pointed to a large dump truck parked below a fire escape. I sprinted across the street and scaled the truck, looking back on the army of creatures. If I could get up there, so could they. I jumped off the truck and opened the door to the cab. After releasing the brake, I scrambled back up top and dove for the ladder before the truck lurched forward and careened down the hill toward a shopping mall. The truck crashed into the wall of the building with a terrible thud, followed by an even more terrifying sound... the sound of screams as the creatures entered the mall through the hole in the wall and began feasting on the people hiding inside. I closed my eyes to contemplate what I had done, and when I opened them, I got my first good look at the woman. It was Julia, or Anna, or whoever she was.

"I know I'm dreaming, so why am I afraid?" I asked.

"Seeing is believing," she replied.

"So what?" I questioned. "If I close my eyes they'll go away, they're not really there?"

"Oh, they're there all right, and they can and *will* kill you," Julia cautioned. "Dreams have rules, Marcus. When you come here there are mechanisms in place to insure that, if something were to happen to you, you would instantly be brought back to your reality. Because you are here and fully aware that you are dreaming, Marcus, you can die here." That was news I hadn't expected.

"What happens to a person's body in their reality if something happens to it in the dream realm?" I asked. "The body would suffer any injuries it obtained while in the dream state, thus killing the physical body as well," Julia answered flatly.

"Then what happens to our consciousness if we die in the dream world?" I asked.

The dream changed and I found myself standing on a cliff, maybe twenty feet wide, narrowing down to a four-foot wide ledge overlooking an endless abyss. Julia stood out on the ledge looking down into the darkness. Overhead, clouds flashed, speeding by as if watching the sky on time-lapse in multiple colors of the spectrum. It was dark and everything was cast in an eerie blue glow.

Julia turned to look at me. "You ask too many questions, Marcus," she said.

"I have plenty more to ask." This is how she responded: "You will get answers in time, Marcus, the Seraphim will show you the way. You have much to learn, which is why I look as I do, things are not as they seem here, remember that. Nothing is as it seems. Why did you release the brake on the truck?"

I did not know why I had done so. By trying to save the people on the roof, I had killed the ones in the mall. "You have learned an important lesson, Marcus. Changing things has consequences. Remember that." It was then that I woke…

Although she did not look like her, Julia *was* my Anna. There's that connection you have with the ones you love; it *was* my wife! We talked the next afternoon, Ann and I, about dreams mostly. I always loved our conversations; we would talk about the coolest things. Out of the blue, we could get on any subject and by the end of the conversation, we had talked about science, religion, cooking, friends we hadn't seen in years, Robert the Bruce, where cell phone technology was heading, and finally…dreams. Anna said she had never put too much thought into the origin of dreams and that she never questioned the scientific explanations given. Here we go with theories again. Theorists don't even know what causes dreams, never mind what they mean. I have had some truly disturbing dreams throughout my lifetime that have defied explanation or interpretation. Sure, if someone wanted to, they could draw their own conclusions and try to tell me what the dreams had meant, but that's what the dreams had meant to *them*, not me…

Journal Entry 121   Dream #4   11/17/07

I stood in a field of the greenest grass I had ever seen in my life. The field sat on a plateau high above the forest below. I saw other levels of grassy fields, like a giant set of steps climbing the side of a large mountain that rose up into the clouds before me. I crossed the field and began to climb the rocky ledge until I reached yet another field. Once again, I crossed the field and climbed, only to find that I must do it all over again. When I reached the seventh plateau, the field was shrouded in a blanket of fog. As I walked, it dawned on me that I had reached the layer of clouds. The field ended abruptly before a large stone wall carved into the mountain. I looked up and saw two pinpricks of light flickering high above me in the bank of clouds. It was time to try and break the rules. I closed my eyes and pictured myself standing in the field with the mountain before me. I saw myself rising up into the clouds, focusing on the fires burning on the cliffs above. As I neared the flames, I opened my eyes to find myself on a wooden platform leading to a large, walled city. It felt more like I was transported there than anything. In any case, I was there, so I walked across the platform to the city gate.

I walked up to the massive door and knocked seven times. I don't know why, I just did. There was a loud bang from the other side of the wall, followed by an even louder rumble from within as the door inched its way open to reveal an abandoned courtyard. Another door opened at the base of a large turret rising into the sky. I crossed the courtyard, entered the door, and began to climb. A large stone staircase wound around the inside of the turret, ending before a single wooden door. When I opened the door, I found my dream Anna sitting on a large sofa in the middle of an elaborately decorated room. I looked at Julia and said, "We meet again."

"Sit," she said. "We need to talk." I sat next to her and she took my hand. "I know you can do this, Marcus," she said. "I know you have the strength to make it."

"What are you talking about?" I protested in ignorance.

"I can not tell you any more than I already have without jeopardizing everything, and I fear that this may be the last time I will see you. Know that I have always loved you Marcus, and I always will. I will say some things to you that I don't mean, but please know that I am truly sorry my love. You did the right thing." It was hard to look past the face, but it was her underneath, it was Anna.

"I know it's you, Anna," I said, squeezing her hand in mine. "Why won't you show me your face?"

"I already explained that I could say no more…"

"Then don't speak," I said. I pulled her into my arms and looked deep into her eyes. I saw my face reflected back at me a thousand times and I kissed her. She wrapped her arms around me and returned my kiss passionately. As our lips parted she let out a sigh and said, "I never could hide from you, Marcus." I woke up…

1⅂1
EVERYTHING IS CONNECTED

MULTIVERSE

I was kicking back in my recliner one night, off on one of my "vegetative meditations", when I began to feel a pulling sensation inside my chest. The first time I felt it I thought I was having a heart attack. After a while I began to suspect it was anxiety or panic attacks. It was during one of these episodes that it first happened. I focused in on the "ringing" in my ears because I wanted to see what time it was and *bam*! It was like getting sucked into a wormhole. When I found the "ringing" in my ears, those dots, or whatever they are, started exploding into swirling patterns. I felt myself plummeting in the darkness, the only light coming from the patterns around me. My descent suddenly stopped and I felt the G-force of the initial impact before being drawn back, as if pulled by an invisible bungee cable. This, in turn, caused me to hurl (I thoroughly enjoyed cleaning *that* mess up when I finally returned to my reality). I looked around. Patterns once more exploded into a wave, like watching the after effects of a stone thrown into a pond and the soft ripple of waves flowing outward. As the ripples moved further away from the center I began to see the patterns more clearly.

I watched as each pattern turned into an image. The best way I can think to describe it is this: Remember those pictures that are made up of smaller, individual pictures? Mosaics, if I'm recalling things correctly. If you look at the smaller images, the larger image is obscured, start with that. Each individual image was a memory, thousands placed tightly together like an infinite photo album within the minds eye, turning upside down, rotating, left becomes right, up becomes down. Then I heard a voice, it took a few seconds to realize that it was my own, I said, "There are patterns in the lines." As I watched the images changing, I noticed that some of the lines in the pictures were fixed, regardless of which way the images were facing. These lines are what created the larger image, I know that now. Unfortunately, I did not get to see what the larger image was, because as soon as I became aware of it, I was pulled back to consciousness as if someone did not want me to see it.

I say someone, because it was about this time that I began to suspect I was being followed. The first time I became aware of it I was sitting in my car, in traffic, on my way home from work. One minute I could see perfectly fine, the next it was like my eyes had crossed. Everything was out of focus, blurry, I was seeing double. The silhouette appeared in the middle of the road a few car lengths ahead of me. All I saw was a dark, blurry, human-like form, more a shadow than a solid figure, but it just stood there. I don't know how to explain it but I knew it was staring right at me. The car behind me hit its horn. I shook my head and my eyes focused, and when I looked, the person was no longer in the road. This was the first of many encounters with the shadow figure; sometimes it seemed I couldn't go anywhere without seeing it out of the corner of my eye. Were these paranoid delusions or was I just plain losing my mind? By that point I was beginning to suspect that there was an "I Love Me" jacket somewhere out there with my name embroidered on it... and I knew the padded cell with my ass print on the floor would soon follow.

I'll skip ahead to the summer of 2008. It was the eighth of August when everything changed, one minute I had a semi-normal life, the next... I had another episode, just like the one before. The same pulling sensation, the dark tunnel, the patterns, the nausea... at least I didn't toss any chunks that second time. When the pulling stopped, there were waves but no patterns, only darkness. When the last of the waves faded out, I was left alone in the middle of a vast nothingness. I wasn't sure if I had a body there, and even though it felt as if I did, I saw nothing. Then I noticed the ringing, it was no longer coming from inside my head, but emanating from deep within the vast nothingness around me.

I followed the sound until I noticed the ringing grow louder with each step I took. I saw a faint light ahead of me and picked up my pace until I was within a few hundred feet or so. I could not see exactly where the light was coming from, only what was being illuminated. It was a person, hanging upside down, arms outstretched in a parody of crucifixion. The closer I got, the more distinct the details of the figure became. His long white hair seemed to defy gravity, flowing up and over his shoulders. I began to suspect who this person was, though in my visions the figure had always been dark, here the creature's skin was a brilliant white, as if this person's flesh were pure light! When I got within a few yards of the man of light, I knew he sensed my presence. At once, I was drawn closer, pulled in a spiral by some unseen force until I was standing face to face with the creature. I saw its features *very* clearly, and recognized them. This was the face I had seen when I closed my eyes, the presence I felt watching me in my dreams. The Sandman!

I had never seen the creature's eyes until now… The eyes… they shone brighter than the rest of his body which seemed impossible, but that wasn't the weird part. There were patterns swirling where the iris should be, three conjoined figure eights repeatedly turning themselves inside out. I backed up a few feet while the thing just stared at me. I held my hands up into the light but I saw nothing. There was no trace of my corporeal body. I looked back to the face in front of me. "Who are you?" I asked.

"I have many names." The creature spoke with two distinct voices, one male and one female.

"Just give me one," I said.

"I am Ma Hua Ra," he announced as if this name should mean something to me.

"Is the Sandman among your many names?" I asked.

"Yes," he answered. *"There was a time when the mind was innocent, not ruled by hatred and fear. It is I who would guide the children through their dreams until they were no longer afraid."*

15

"Where am I?" I questioned.

"Somewhere you should not be, not yet. But you are *here and I must know why."*

"Where exactly *is* here?" I asked.

"You are in the Nexus."

"The *what*? Am I dreaming?"

"That is for another time. First, I must know why you are here so soon." All at once, everything went black, my stomach turned as my head spun, and as suddenly as it started it stopped.

I sat up, not sure what to make of what had just happened. I pulled the sheets back, allowing the air from the ceiling fan to cool my skin and calm my nerves. I took a deep breath, let my body sink back into the bed, and exhaled. "Quinn, are you alright?" It was Anna.

"Yeah, I'm fine," I lied. "I was just having a dream."

"Are you still having the headaches?" she asked sympathetically.

Poor Anna, I wish I had told my wife what was happening to me, but at the time I thought it was best to keep it to myself. When you start to doubt your own sanity you don't want to spread it around. No… that's something a man keeps to himself!

"Yeah," I answered. "I'm still having the headaches."

"Everything is going to be just fine, Marcus Quincy, we'll get through this." Anna rested her head next to mine on the pillow and softly kissed my neck. I remember thinking for a while before falling asleep, thinking about what the future held for my family, my children, and for humanity. Almost a year went by before I would see Ma Hua Ra again, but a great deal occurred in the meantime. My visions escalated, becoming more frequent, more severe. By that point, each day had become an adventure. Each day things around me changed. It could be a detail as insignificant as the color of someone's tie, and at other times, people just disappeared into thin air. Sometimes they would reappear a few seconds later, but other times I never saw them again! Do you now see why I doubted my sanity?

Anna has and always will be my anchor, the one thing that binds me to this reality. I'd do anything for her and our girls, including lying there half naked on a damned uncomfortably hard examination table for hours on end. Anna kept insisting that I see another doctor. So I saw one after another, after another, and Anna kept pushing me to keep going, to find out what was wrong. So there I was, in yet *another* doctor's office, getting yet *another* head scan. As soon as my body went into the machine, everything went black.

I recognized the emptiness around me; I was in the Nexus. I heard nothing but the ringing in my ears and it *was* in my head this time. "Ma Hua Ra," I called out, deciding to make him come to me.

In a flash of static, he appeared. "Why am I here?" I demanded.

"I do not think you are ready for that answer."

I knew it wouldn't be easy, so I decided on a new line of questioning.

"What *is* the Nexus?" I asked.

"The Nexus is a singularity, the point where all realities merge."

"Realities?"

"Yes," said Ma Hua Ra, *"the multiverse, as your kind calls it. The sensations you have been feeling and the nausea, they are a side effect of tuning."*

"Tuning?" I had no idea what in the hell this creature was talking about.

"Each reality," explained Ma Hua Ra *"has its own wavelength. The ringing in your head, it changes tones, yes?"*

"How do you know this?"

"It is my purpose to know. Time is of the essence. The ringing?"

"Yes," I said, "the tones change."

"As I have told you, each reality has a wave length, a tone, if you will. With practice, you will be able to tune into whichever wave length you desire." The light emanating from Ma Hua Ra suddenly got dimmer. *"We must go; our time here is up. We will meet again when you are ready."*

"When will that be?" I asked.

"Soon," said Ma Hua Ra. As these words were spoken, his light grew brighter until all I saw was white. Gradually, the outside world crept back in and I heard the doctor telling me to relax.

"Just lie back Mr. Quincy, we're almost through."

"What's the matter, Quinn?" Anna asked from outside the chaos of my thoughts. "You haven't been yourself from the time we left the doctors office. You know, you should talk to Dr. Spencer about the depression." I only half listened as she drove. My mind was still adjusting to what had happened.

At that moment, I almost let my fears slip. "It's not that," I objected. "I'm not feeling too well, that's all."

The tone of her voice had given away what she was feeling. She was worried… worried about me, worried about *us*. "We're going to be just fine, Anna Quincy," I said as I leaned my head back and closed my eyes. "We'll get through this."

Thankfully, Anna spent the rest of the drive home concentrating on traffic and left me alone with my thoughts. I wanted to tell her everything but I couldn't find the words, not without it sounding like I'd lost what was left of my mind. Hell, part of me was still telling myself that I had. Could these things really be happening or was Ma

Hua Ra just a figment of my overworked imagination? Could it be, as I had been suspecting for a while, that I was schizophrenic? I thought about these things as I rode home, turning my conversations with Ma Hua Ra over in my mind. I was looking for clues to satisfy myself, to let me know that I was not insane.

It was seven thirty in the evening on the fifteenth of July 2009 when we arrived home. Anna paid the sitter for watching the twins and then took them upstairs to get ready for bed. I was looking forward to some sleep myself. My eyelids were heavy and it was getting hard to focus. I decided it would be best if I went to the bedroom to lie down, so I poured myself a glass of soda, grabbed my cigarettes and made my way up the stairs to the bedroom. Halfway up I began to feel light headed; I reached for the railing to steady myself as I awaited the return of my equilibrium. Something wasn't right. The pulling in my chest began and I stumbled on the stairs. The light in the hall began to flicker, or so I thought; it was my vision that was giving out on me. I made my way to the bedroom by touch and memory alone, and I had barely made it to the side of the bed when my legs gave. I fell onto the bed, but for some reason, the bed was not sufficient enough to break my fall.

When my vision returned I stood up and looked around. I was in a poorly lit parking garage filled with cars of all makes and models, most of which I had never seen before. I glanced around, trying to gain some sense of where I was, but I saw nothing that looked familiar. Starting off in the distance, the car's headlights began to turn on. They flickered to life one by one until all of the headlights were illuminated and I stood bathed in the blinding glare. Without warning, car horns and alarms began to sound off throughout the parking deck, until all were blaring out a deafening symphony. I tried to focus on the ringing in my head, the "wavelengths" Ma Hua Ra had spoken of, but with all of the noise it was useless so I stood my ground and waited. A strong feeling of déjà vu hit me hard; there was something about that place… The next thing I knew I felt a sharp pain piercing through my body, like I was being torn into pieces! The last thing I saw was a shadowy figure stepping out into the light. When I came to, Anna was at the bedside.

"Quinn? Are you ok?" I looked up at Anna. It took me a few seconds to realize that I was still alive. She knelt down to pick up my glass and used the towel slung over her shoulder to soak up the soda I had spilled. "What happened?" she asked.

"I was having a dream," I answered, confused.

I sat up, looking for my cigarettes. Anna had a strange look on her face.

"Quinn..." Her beautiful eyes glared at me as she spoke. "You just walked in here half a second ago... never mind..." Anna turned and made her way back to the bathroom where the girls could be heard splashing and yelling. I pulled a smoke out of the pack and lit it. I inhaled long and slow. What the hell was happening to me?

After the girls were tucked in for the night, Anna and I finally got to talk. According to her, what had seemed to me to last several minutes, had actually taken place in a matter of seconds. Anna told me that she had just leaned her head out of the bathroom as I was closing our bedroom door, and that was when I screamed. My heart began to race just thinking about it again.

"So you're telling me you were having a dream while walking into the bedroom?" Anna asked, just a little *too* sarcastically.

"Maybe I *was* sleepwalking... I don't know," I responded nastily, defensively.

"Quinn," Anna said, "I can't help you if you won't tell me what's going on!"

"What do you want me to do, Ann? I don't know what's happening to me any more than you do!"

At least here I was not lying. I truly did not comprehend what was happening to me. That would take some time. Who knows how long it would take for a healthy mind to absorb such things, but mine?

That night, as I lay in bed listening to the ringing in my head, I noticed that there was no longer just one tone, there were *several*. I tried to tune in to one as Ma Hua Ra had suggested. It took a number of tries, but I finally caught one. It was like riding a roller coaster on steroids, twists and turns pulling my body in ways it was never meant to go. When the ride was finally over, there were two things that caught my attention. One: I stood in the middle of the street, cars screeching and honking as they swerved to avoid me. And two: I had tits! I felt them bouncing as I tried my best not to become road kill. My hair was blonde, barely shoulder length, and I saw it sway from side to side as I ran. I couldn't see my image in any of the storefront windows, for some reason, all of my reflections were a blur. Looking around, I quickly realized where I was. It had been a while since I'd been to Boston but I recognized the city skyline with ease.

Out of the corner of my eye, I caught a glimpse of a dark figure moving through the crowd. I turned and followed. The figure had long dark hair but I could make out little more. He was a shadow among the crowd of pedestrians, when he walked, he seemed to move in slow motion, and randomly shifted forward several feet, as if skipping ahead in time. Something didn't feel right; maybe it was the way the air chilled as I passed where he once had walked. The man was dragging something on the ground behind him, the large object rested effortlessly on his left shoulder. He looked back at me through the crowd and turned into an alley. I followed, but stopped just shy of entering. On the ground was a stack of newspapers spilling out from a street vendor's stall. I was stunned by what I saw; *my* picture was on the cover! But how could this be me? The headline read: "Man found slain in parking garage." The article went on to graphically describe how the man had been found in nine pieces scattered about the garage. There was a grainy photograph of the crime scene that failed to show any details of what had taken place that day, but I did however, recognize that it was the *same* parking lot from my earlier vision. I took the paper, folded it under my arm, and entered the alley.

All at once, the sound of metal scraping on concrete filled the air around me. The creature stepped out of the shadows and I saw it clearly for the first time. He looked just like Ma Hua Ra! But unlike the Ma

Hua Ra that I had previously encountered, this creature's skin was black and shiny, illuminated in its own way. He lurched forward, sparks flying all around as his burden dragged across the pavement. He came at me fast, and before I had time to react, the blades were in me. His weapon looked like a sword with five edges like a star; it had a long handle, and when the handle was pulled back and cocked like a shotgun, the blades extended out in five directions, slicing me into pieces...

The sound of screaming entered my conscious mind; it was Anna. I looked up at my reflection in the bathroom mirror and I saw my wife standing in the doorway behind me. In my right hand I held a steak knife streaked with blood; in my left, I held the chunk of flesh that I had just carved from my stomach.

I had plenty of time to think about things during my stay in the hospital. I spent the rest of that first night under suicide watch, as the doctors had deemed my wound to be self-inflicted. The nurses came and went throughout the night, with drugs and soothing words. I didn't see Anna again until the following day. When she came in to see me she was holding a blood-splattered newspaper. Anna held up the paper so that I could read the headline: "*Man found slain in parking garage.*"

"Where did this come from?" she asked.

"That..." I don't know why I did it, but I lied. "Troy had it made up as a joke."

There she was, holding the evidence in her hands, but something inside told me to keep my mouth shut. I ended up spending over a week in the hospital recovering. Anna was at my bedside most of the time, but I knew her mind was elsewhere. On several occasions, I asked her what was wrong, but she always evaded my questions. "You think I'm losing it, don't you?" I asked.

Anna stared at me for the longest time before replying.

"We'll get through this, Marcus." She let go of my hand, rose, and left without saying another word.

I think a part of me died that day.

Sure, Ann and I had some fights, and some vicious ones at that, but I had *never* felt a distance between us like I did then. I remember the first time I set eyes on her; there was *always* something special about Anna. I'd known her since childhood and I knew she had a crush on me, but for some reason I had never let it go anywhere. Sometimes, you just *know* that this is the one. Maybe that's what scared me away. There is no greater feeling in the world than that of when love is new. You're so damn happy and the two of you feel as though you are connected in every way, so that the two become one. That is the one time in your life when you *truly* feel at peace with yourself and everything around you, when the problems in your life and in the world just melt away. I have always believed that *true love* should be mankind's ultimate goal, but unfortunately, the real world always comes crashing back in. People will *never* find inner peace with the world as messed up as it is. It's just another hand we get dealt in the game of life. We deal with whatever shit bomb explodes that particular day, pick up the pieces and start over. I caught on quick to that lesson in life, especially with my condition. I know that's what made me push Anna away all those years, but when I saw her that first day on the job all of the feelings from the past rushed in and everything seemed new again.

I remember watching Anna bounce around the room energetically and being *so* damn cute. Her long red hair was pulled out through the back of a baseball cap and she wore a pair of tight blue jeans with a white button-down shirt that pulled tightly across her killer rack. Man, she was smokin'! I'd run into Anna a few times in the past and had thought about telling her how I felt, but she'd always been in a relationship, and the timing had never seemed right. I often wondered back then if we would ever meet under the right circumstances. That particular day I had waved to her, and when she saw me, she instantly bounded over in my direction. Anna and I had lunch together that day and I finally told her how I felt about her. It just so happened that she was not in a relationship at the time, and the rest as they say, is history. Several years later, there I was feeling sorry for myself while stuck in a hospital bed, thinking back through our lives together wondering where the *fuck* things went wrong!

On my last night in the hospital, Ma Hua Ra came to *me*. I sat in front of the hospital room's single window looking out over the parking lot. I heard a slight crackling sound behind me, and when I turned, he was there.

"It is time," said Ma Hua Ra. *"You must begin your journey."*

"Journey to where?" I asked.

"You will begin your journey with death. Seek it out and embrace it."

"Death?" I questioned.

"Deaths with no apparent cause," Ma Hua Ra continued with a disgusted look on his face, as if ashamed I would dare question him. *"Only* then *will you find the path leading you to the truth. Only* then *will you begin to understand your destiny."* Before I could say another word, Ma Hua Ra was gone.

Anna picked me up from the hospital the next morning, saying nothing to me the whole ride home. As the days passed, the distance between us continued to grow. Anna got up and left for work in the mornings before I climbed out of bed, and she worked late every night, not getting home until well after nine. I tried to talk to her but she always walked out of the room. As soon as I could sit in front of the computer for any length of time without hurting, I began the search as Ma Hua Ra had instructed.

I looked for days before finding anything of interest. It seemed that all the good stories were well hidden, maybe on purpose, maybe not. I found a twenty-eight year old woman in Burlington, Vermont who had died from drowning. She was fully dressed and her clothes were dry when she was found, yet her lungs were filled with water. Her husband and children had been out of town at the time and there was no apparent sign of forced entry. The case remained open. Further digging led me to a thirty-year-old man who had been found dead in his home in Riverside, California. The official cause of death was a bullet wound to the heart. X-Rays showed the slug within the muscle yet there was no point of entry. I found other cases too, once I knew how to search. It was almost like something had led me to them. Since I was not going back to work for at least a month, I decided to go investigate a couple of the cases that weren't so very far away. I withdrew some cash from the savings account that I shared with Anna, made arrangements for the care of the twins, packed as lightly as I could, and hopped into my car. Sure, I knew Ann would be pissed, but hey, as the saying goes, all is fair in love and war.

My first stop was in Hickory, North Carolina where, in 1999, a twenty-two year old man had died from blunt force trauma to the head. The only problem was, although the man's skull was split almost in two, there were no marks whatsoever on his scalp. I talked to a few of his family members, but it was his brother who gave me the most useful information. He said that he was there when the incident occurred, that his brother had seemed to be having some sort of seizure, screaming "No... no", before falling over dead. This roused my curiosity to a new level.

My second and final stop was in Knoxville, Tennessee where, in the spring of 2005, twenty-one year old Elizabeth Patton had died of complications from a surgery that had never been performed. Doubting that I would be able to get my hands on the autopsy report through official channels, I decided to contact the family under the guise of writing a book about bizarre deaths. I spoke to several family members on the phone and got pretty much the same story from all of them; the so-called complications from surgery did not exist. I was eventually able to convince Mr. Patton to let me stop by so that I could talk to him in person.

The house was in a quiet neighborhood on the outskirts of Knoxville, just far enough away from the highway and close enough to the mountains to almost forget you were in the city. Elizabeth's father answered the door. I was surprised at how much he looked like an uncle of mine, so similar in fact, that this man could have been another of my father's brothers. He invited me in to a hallway filled with framed photographs. A picture of Elizabeth's mother showed that she had been a pretty woman once, but grief had long since taken its toll, ravaging her former beautiful features into a mask of pain. There was a young boy in the photographs, as well, Elizabeth's brother, or so the man said. I saw the young boy sitting on the swing in the back yard through the window as I talked to Mr.

Patton. Elizabeth's father told me that there was nothing strange about his daughter's death, as it was a simple case of heart failure and the media, as they often do, had exaggerated the situation. I thanked him for his time and left empty handed. When I reached my car, the boy from the back yard ran around the side of the house and stopped in front of me. Without saying a word he handed me a large manila envelope, smiled, then turned and ran into the shadows of the tree lined yard.

When I got back to my hotel, I emptied the contents of the envelope on the bed. Inside I found a scanned copy of the coroner's report, several pieces of paper ripped from a diary or journal, a medallion of the Virgin Mary, and a hand written note from the boy containing a brief explanation. The note was written quickly in the typical chicken-scratch style of a child his age, the message simple:

Please don't tell Mom and Dad I gave this to you and please don't use our names in your book. I hope you can make more sense of this than me. The diary pages are really weird! My parents don't believe the doctor's report. They seem to think my sister was on drugs before she died, but I know she wasn't.

I placed the boy's note down on the bed and began to read through the seven-page autopsy report. There were a few points of interest that caught my attention. First, as the boy had stated in his note, the postmortem toxicology screen had come back negative, as did the screens for heavy metals and poisons. The second point of interest was the cause of death. It *was* listed as heart failure, but as to the reason for this the examiner was at a loss. Although there was no evidence of external injury, her heart was simply *not* in the chest cavity. I decided to turn my attention to the diary pages in hopes of making more sense of things. The pages were dated March 9th to the 14th, of 2005, the last week of Elizabeth Patton's life.

3/9/05   8:30 pm

It happened again. I wasn't going to write about it but I don't know what else to do. I woke up this morning and went downstairs

26

for breakfast before catching the bus to campus, expecting the usual morning ruckus created by my little brother, but he wasn't there. It's not like Michael to miss breakfast, so I went up to his room and when I opened the door… It was my brother's room all right, the same angled ceiling, the same windows, but all traces of him had disappeared! It was the same all over the house! All of his favorite movies, gone! His drum set out in the garage, gone! It was replaced with a brand new VW convertible and I'll be pissed if I ever find out it was mine! I saw that my baby brother, pain in the ass though he is, was even missing from the pictures hanging on the walls!

The first time it happened it wasn't this extreme. It was last Friday as I left the house to catch the bus. I've taken that bus for a year and a half and it has always been red and white. When a blue and silver bus pulled up and everyone just got on it, no questions asked, I have to admit I was a little confused. So I got on the bus and rode it to school. Kevin, from my journalism class, sat next to me. We were talking and I started to feel a little sick when, right in front of my eyes, his tie changed color! From black to red, just like that! Then, when I got off the bus I looked back over my shoulder, and the bus had changed colors! It was red and white, just like it always was. I decided not to say anything to anyone about this, not even write it down on these pages, but after the second time it happened, I felt that I just had to do SOMETHING!

Tonight when my parents got in I asked them where Michael was. They told me that I had no brother and looked at me like I was crazy or something, and the nausea came again. Just as it was passing, Michael walked down the stairs into the living room and everything was normal again. The pictures, his drum set, his room, all as they had been, just like the bus changing colors. What is going on? Am I losing my mind? I will pray tonight that the lord will show me the way.

I couldn't help but notice the similarities between what Elizabeth Patton had described and what I had been experiencing. It seemed I was not alone in my search for the truth. Even then, that early in my journey, I had the answer to my first question. I was *not* insane.

3/10/05   10:17 pm.

Someone followed me home from school today. It was weird. I knew I was being followed because I could *feel* this person, like we were somehow connected. I only caught glimpses of a vague presence and it was strange! I couldn't tell if it was a man or a woman, because no matter where the figure stood, it was always in the shadows. I ran to the bus and got on, sat all the way in the back, and waited. The bus filled up, the doors closed, and we pulled away. When I got off at my stop and began walking home, I started to feel this person again. I turned and she was there! Her hair and skin were as black as night. She was beautiful... and terrifying! I could not look away from her eyes and the patterns swirling within them. Then, just like that, she was gone! I ran home, wanting to write all of this down, but I couldn't. I am terrified! In her eyes I saw my own death and she was the reaper. I need to think about this. I need to pray!

3/11/05   6:35 pm

I saw the woman again in my dreams last night. This is going to sound crazy, but I watched her murder someone! Why didn't I do anything to help? Her eyes... I think they might be sixes, three of them, constantly moving, collapsing in on themselves. Not once did her eyes leave mine as she lunged at her helpless victim with a huge, five bladed sword! I know how this sounds but it's the truth! As the victim lay dying, the dark woman held up her head so I could see the woman's face... and it was me!

I couldn't go to sleep after that, afraid of what I might see in the next dream. Is this some sort of test from God? I have prayed every night since the beginning of my strange experiences, but I still receive no answers. Help me Lord; help me to make sense of these things!

3/11/05   9:20 pm

I told mom what has been happening to me. Can you believe it? She actually had the nerve to accuse me of doing drugs! I now know that I will not get any help from my parents, and I don't dare tell any of my friends for fear of being ridiculed. I am utterly alone… and scared as hell! I felt the dark woman following me again today. I did not see her but I knew she was there. She is *always* there! She'll be coming for me soon. I can feel it. I see my death every time I close my eyes. I'm going to talk to Father McLeod tomorrow. Maybe he will be of more help, or at least tell me why God refuses to answer my prayers. Please Lord, I need your guidance now more than ever.

3/12/05   7:27 pm

Father McLeod told me that I need to accept the circumstances I have been given and that God has a reason for putting me through all of this. He said it is up to me to figure out what I am supposed to do. I can't take this for very much longer…

03/13/05   2:39 am

I just awoke from the most horrific dream. Father McLeod was giving his Sunday sermon and was standing in front of the lectern when the dark woman suddenly walked up behind him. She began to touch Father McLeod, running her hands up and down his body, and he seemed not to notice, he just continued with his sermon. The dark woman slid her hands down his pants and began to stroke him. Father McLeod just went on talking like nothing was happening! Then, without warning, he grabbed her wrist, pulled her hand from his groin and, twisting her arm back, he forced the dark woman into the altar. Father McLeod pulled down his pants, bent the dark woman over, and entered her. Still his sermon continued! He spoke a little more loudly, with a little more excitement, as he neared climax and screamed, "Praise the Lord!" as he came! Why me Lord, oh please, why me?

03/14/05   12:02 am

"I know your name!" A man shouted that from the other side of a door as I watched the dark woman murder me again tonight in my dreams. I watched as she inserted her hand into my doppelganger's chest, leaving no wound or even a mark, and pulled out her heart! The dark woman looked at me and smiled as she took a bite out of my twin's heart. She wiped the blood from her lips with the back of her arm and said, "You're next, my darling, you're the last." I looked down at myself lying on the floor for a brief second and, when I looked back, the dark woman had gone. In my dream, I held myself as I took a final breath. With her last ounce of energy, my dying twin gave me the pedant she wore around her neck…

The final page of Elizabeth Patton's diary was not dated. Instead, she had drawn a picture of the necklace and written four words in capital letters that had been traced over several times in different colored pens. It read: I BROUGHT IT BACK! I reached for the necklace to examine it. There didn't seem to be anything unusual about the medallion. It was just a simple silver pendant, oval in shape, approximately three inches tall, with the Virgin Mother standing with her arms out to her sides. I studied the image for a while but found nothing interesting about it. The chain on the other hand, wasn't really a chain, not for a necklace anyway. It was one solid strand of gold about a quarter of an inch thick, yet it was as flexible as any linked chain. There did not appear to be any clasp and the pendant was suspended by a thin wire wrapped several times around the necklace. The edges were round but the sides were flat and, on one side, the chain was polished smooth and seemed to change color with the light. The other side was flat but not polished, and there were small notches cut into the metal all the way around, marring the surface. My mind was on overload. I placed all of the items back in the envelope, turned out the light, and fell asleep dreading the eight-hour drive home.

222

BALANCE

CHOICES

According to religious theology God created man in one day, but who is to say that one day on *His* timescale is not a *billion* years for mankind? From the time the Creator planted the seed of life until the time we walked upright and used logic to solve problems could *easily* have passed by as quickly as a day for an omnipotent being. Scientists say they have an open mind but when a new theory comes along that goes against the knowledge that they hold sacred, a crusade to pick it apart and prove this new theory wrong invariably ensues. Look at that, science and religion going hand in hand.

It doesn't matter whether we crawled out of the oceans or we got kicked out of the Garden of Eden. What matters is that we *are* here. And since we've been here our race has thrived on two things, the ability to weave fantastic and outrageous tales, and the ability to believe such stories. Humans need to believe in something *so* badly that we blindly follow anything or anyone who promises a possible explanation as to why we are here. The premise had worked for Catholicism for centuries and science has taken over in an attempt to explain what religion had failed to justify. It's not like the Catholics didn't have it coming. During the crusades the Church tried to wipe out *any* trace of an explanation other than the one they offered. Should we be surprised then to see science doing the same thing today? Newton taught us that for every action there is an equal and opposite reaction. What is jokingly referred to as "Murphy's Law" tells us that anything that *can* go wrong *will* go wrong. This is *very* important in understanding the answer to why things happen. Things happen because they *can!*

I drove back to North Carolina the next morning thinking about what I'd read in Elizabeth Patton's diary pages. I finally knew for certain that there was at least *one* person out there who had seen the things I'd seen, felt the things I'd felt. Piecing together my experiences with those of Elizabeth Patton's, only one answer made sense: alternate realities, which brought to mind how asking "why not" is oftentimes the answer, as *well* as the question. Logic demands that, when faced with a problem, the easiest way to find and fix that problem is to figure out what it is *not*. We *have* to ask this question. So, alternate realities? I can buy that. I understood then why Ma Hua Ra had sent me in that direction. I understood that, if a person were to die in another reality, they would die here as well. That was the same thing Julia/Anna had told me during one of my lucid dreams.

When I arrived home that evening, Anna's Camero was in the driveway, an indication that she had not worked late, as had become her norm. When I got inside she was putting away groceries, so I asked if she needed any help. To my astonishment, Anna just said no and went back to what she was doing. I decided to confront her. "Did you even *notice* I was gone?" I asked.

"Why would I?" Anna fired back. "You do it all the time. Even when you *are* here, you're not. Two can play at this game you know. If you hate it that much there's the door, but the boys are staying here!"

"Boys?" I ran to the children's room. I opened the door and, to my utter and total surprise, sitting on the bed were two seven-year-old twin boys! The nausea that came with the reality shifts, the Ma Hua Ra's "tuning", hit me, so I closed my eyes and took the ride. When I opened them again, Tara and Tori, my *girls*, were sitting on the bed playing checkers. They looked up at me and asked if I wanted to play, their hearts in their eyes. I told them I couldn't just then and promised to play with them real soon.

Entertaining the theory of alternate realities had seemed just fine when I was thinking about the concept, but actually flopping between realities was a little harder to get used to. I needed to be careful, and I needed to remember that the reality shifts could happen at any time. When I returned to the living room Anna looked me in the eyes for the first time in weeks. "Tell me you're all right, Quinn," she said. "You're not looking too good. Come on, let's put you to bed." Anna put her hands on my shoulders and softly nudged me up the stairs and toward the bedroom door. She pressed against my back and wrapped her arms around me as we walked. When we reached the bedroom, Anna helped me out of my clothes and climbed into bed beside me. "Where *were* you?" she whispered softly. "The girls and I have been worried sick! I hope you find what you're looking for, Marcus, and I want you to know that I'll stand beside you, but *please* tell me the next time you feel the need to leave like that." Anna kissed me on the lips, gathered me in her arms, and I drifted off to sleep.

I went to work the next day only to be thrown off the property and charged with trespassing. It seems I had never been employed there. While sitting in the holding cell at the jail, waiting on Anna to come bail me out, I felt the nausea again and thankfully the ride was much smoother. When it passed, I was thrown back from a jolt of electricity. I looked up from the floor to find that I was once again at work. Smoke poured from the open control panel and my wrist wouldn't stop twitching. I decided then and there that it would be best for me to not leave the house for a while. The remainder of that day went by without incident, and by the time I got home and finished eating supper, I was so exhausted that I showered, smoked a cigarette, and then climbed into bed. As soon as consciousness left me, Ma Hua Ra arrived.

"Have you come to terms with the notion of alternate realities?" he asked.

"Yeah," I replied, "I think I have, but there's still something bothering me. I've always held a strong belief that our paths are laid out before us, and it's up to *us* to find the clues that lead us down the roads we're supposed to travel. I guess I'm still trying to figure out where a multiverse fits into it all."

"*The multiverse is an essential part of the Divine Plan, Marcus. Without it, a predetermined course for mankind would not work. If the history of mankind was predetermined at the moment of creation, choice becomes obsolete. That is why so many people have turned their backs on the idea of a Divine Plan. However, there is one connection that mankind has not made.*"

"What is that?" I asked.

"*Humans were given free will to make their own decisions, to* choose *their own path. The multiverse compensates for these choices. An infinite number of realities for an infinite number of choices.*"

I had never thought of it that way, but what Ma Hua Ra had stated made perfect sense.

"So, why *did* God give man free will?" I asked.

"*Well,*" Ma Hua Ra paused to choose his words. "*He* had *to. In nature, there are no choices. I am sure you will agree that, while alive, plants are unable to make choices, yet they* can *learn. And they are able to do this why? Because Chaos reigns supreme.*" Ma Hua Ra's inner light increased a few watts as he said this. "*If not for Chaos life could never exist, species could not adapt and life would simply die out. Free will is* also *Chaos at work.* Everything *happens because of Chaos.*"

"Then what *is* chaos?"

"*Chaos is everything God is not.*"

"Then who, or what, is *God*?" I was getting frustrated. My face, if I even had one in the Nexus, twitched uncontrollably.

"*God is everywhere and everything. I am sure you have heard that saying at least a few times in your life. Correct?*"

"Yeesss," I answered sarcastically.

"According to scientific theories, the Big Bang created the universe out of a vast nothingness, but what did that nothingness consist of? What was contained in the space the universe was born into? That original nothingness created a whole, Marcus. Absolute zero is not zero, it is one, and that one is God. In the beginning, there was nothing but energy, nothing but God. Like a cell, God divided into two positive charges, drawn together, yet forced apart."

"I thought God was one," I interrupted. Ma Hua Ra simply continued in his usual 'holier-than-thou' tone. *"Remember, the combined nothingness creates a whole. This combination was in perfect balance, locked in a stalemate like two black holes, each unable to absorb the other. In order to create the conditions needed for life, God created the Divine Engine to reverse the polarity of one of His charges. One would become Chaos, the other remained God. Think of God as a magnet that is positively charged. What then becomes of the negatively charged portion?"* Ma Hua Ra paused and watched as I contemplated this. Then it came to me. "If Chaos is the opposite of God, the negative force would be drawn to the positive."

"Correct," said Ma Hua Ra. *"With the charge reversed, the two opposites were attracted to one another, with the electrical charge from their collision initiating the first Big Bang. These events* must *take place in order for life to last long enough to get a foothold in the multiverse. God and Chaos* must *exist as one."*

"But doesn't that still make two?" I asked.

"At least two forces are needed to create one. Yin and Yang, positive and negative, good and evil, one cannot exist without the other. There must always be opposites. There must always be two. Tell me, Marcus, do twins run in your family or in that of your wife?"

"Mine." I answered.

"How often?"

Ma Hua Ra's question created a new connection in me, and I knew why I was special, why my mind works the way that it does. My parents were the first branch on the Quincy family tree to have only one offshoot. For twelve generations of Quincy's, the firstborn had *all* been twins, until me, I was an only child. "Chimerism," I answered. Did Ma Hua Ra smile?

"Correct again, Marcus, the condition that occurs when two separate embryos merge in the womb to become one child. Normally this only occurs in cases of fraternal twins, but with you, Marcus, an embryo split to become identical *twins, but later merged together to form one fetus. This is much like the combined nothingness, separating and rejoining to becoming one."*

"Ok," I said, just a *little* taken aback. "So how literally *can* the Bible be taken?"

"The truth is there, if one knows where to look. Remember, the Bible was written by many men; men who needed to find explanations for the things that they did not understand or, worse yet, did not want the masses to know. A great deal of information was written out of the Bible by religious leaders of various times and faiths, based on those leaders' fear of losing their grip on the masses. In all actuality, if one were to take all of the religions scattered across the globe and combine them, one would be closer to the truth than any one religion can claim to be."

"So if God and Chaos are one, good and evil are one and the same?" I don't know why I kept pushing him; maybe I *was* still questioning my sanity a little.

"Yes and no," Ma Hua Ra casually answered my *obviously* stupid question. *"The impact of opposite forces left a void made up of both positively and negatively charged matter and dark matter; this is the multiverse. Positive dark matter is what scientists call dark energy. Positive dark energy expands, like the vast empty regions of space, while negative dark matter contracts, creating black holes. Positive and negative coexist on every plane, but there is only one place where they exist simultaneously. Where then, do you think matter goes when it is pulled into a black hole?"*

"The Nexus," I answered.

"*Correct! Matter is turned into energy and absorbed into the Nexus which, in turn, gives birth to new universes, new realities.*"

"Then where exactly *is* the Nexus?" I asked.

"*As I have told you, the Nexus is a singularity. It lies between the positive and negative forces of God and Chaos. The Nexus is what links the multiverse together.*"

"How so?" I asked.

"*The multiverse is within everything, Marcus; even the smallest particles are a gateway to other realities.*"

"But where *are* these other realities?" I queried.

"*The multiverse is much less complex than scientists make it out to be. What is called your galaxy, the Milky Way, is in all actuality the entirety of your universe. Each galaxy that can be seen through a telescope is, in fact, another universe, a copy of the Milky Way if you will.*"

"Then why do they all look so… different?" I asked.

"*Even perfect copies do not always look the same, Marcus. Remember, it is* not *what you see with your eyes, it is what you* know *in your heart.*"

"Wait a minute," I interrupted. "What the hell does *that* mean? And why are the galaxies moving through space?" There were too many questions and not enough answers. It's rather difficult to let go of everything you've ever known.

"*It is not only space we move through, Marcus, it is also time. Scientific theory dictates that all galaxies are moving away from the center of the universe where the Big Bang took place when, in fact, they are moving away from the first reality created. Dark Energy then takes hold and the multiverse continues to expand, making way for new realities, new choices.*"

"What about colliding galaxies," I asked. "How is *that* possible?" I was becoming increasingly annoyed by Ma Hua Ra's arrogance and his obvious superiority complex, so I continued to interrupt with my own questions.

"When choices are made, realities may split. Choices can also be made that cause realities to merge; therefore, choices made in alternate universes can create the same outcome in both universes. If the realities contain enough similarities, then choices made and their resulting outcome can cause the realities to merge."

"But doesn't that take millions of years and wouldn't the collision destroy most of the galaxy?" I asked.

"No," said Ma Hua Ra. *"Time slows at the speed of light, this has been established. When the light from a star passes through the event horizon of a black hole it is, in fact, traveling through negatively charged dark matter, this further slows time and thus decreases the speed of light even more. And then we have dark energy. Within the empty regions of space, time does not exist. There are galaxies that you see in space that haven't even been born yet. What you perceive to take a million years occurs instantaneously, without the inhabitants of the colliding realities even noticing. Of course, things are going to change and, although the combined realities of the once separate universes will look different, most of the people will be unaffected, as if the universes had always been one."*

My head was starting to throb, it was a hell of a lot of information to try and absorb.

"Back to the Nexus," I said. "How am I able to find it?"

"The answer is within your mind, Marcus. Your consciousness has the ability to enter the Nexus and travel throughout the multiverse at will. This travel is common. Every time you dream you are traveling through the Nexus."

"So my dreams are someone else's reality?" I asked.

"More like reflections *of someone else's reality."*

"Is that why dreams are so… weird?"

"No, there are random events continually occurring that go unnoticed, things that most don't see, even in your *reality, Marcus. This is Chaos at work."*

"Why don't we see these things?" I asked.

"Because you choose not to. Circumstances are worsening; soon, Marcus, you will not be able to look away from the truth. Balance must *be restored. The balance which was once present until something…* unexpected *happened."*

"Unexpected? Now what the hell does THAT mean?"

"The inhabitants of Eden were shielded for some time until…"

"Wait a minute!" I interrupted loudly. "How did we get to *Eden?*"

"… The seven deadly sins were set free to roam the multiverse."

Ma Hua Ra's voice boomed in the blackness around us as he stood before me, silent and motionless, the only movement in his eyes. The swirling figure eights sped up, twisting and unfolding at incredible speed.

"The tree of knowledge of good and evil." I finally said, understanding what Ma Hua Ra was telling me.

"Correct again, Marcus. The Bible was accurate in its telling of man being expelled from the Garden of Eden, though it was more out of necessity than punishment. Man was sent off into the multiverse, to live on planets where evolution had come to a dead end, thus sparking human life in these alternate realities, where human life had not yet begun."

"So *that's* why they can't find the missing link!" I jokingly exclaimed.

"I apologize, Marcus. There is much you need to know and the time is drawing near."

Before I could get a word in to question his statement, Ma Hua Ra continued.

"Eden's inhabitants called the fruit from the Tree of Life the Godivel fruit. Far from your standard apple, the Godivel is a highly hallucinogenic fruit. It still grows in some realities, though the remaining versions are not nearly as potent as the fruit from the tree in Eden. All modern drugs are a derivative of the Godivel fruit."

"Wow! My high school health teacher *was* right; drugs *are* evil!"

"Not quite," said Ma Hua Ra. *"Drugs are knowledge. Some drugs allow the use of parts of the brain that lay dormant. This knowledge can sometimes bring about advances in evolution, but it can also lead to destruction. Visionaries and healers from all civilizations have used hallucinogens derived from close relatives of the Godivel fruit to reach a plane of existence outside of their reality in an attempt to understand or improve the world around them."*

"So was it *really* Eve's fault?" I asked.

"Adam and Eve and the Tree of Knowledge are two separate stories," Ma Hua Ra stated smugly. *"If you must know, it was a young boy who set these things in motion. The inhabitants of Eden were given everything, provided they lived without the ultimate knowledge. Eden's inhabitants were told by God not to eat from the Tree of Knowledge, but they were not told why. God did this for a reason. For centuries, the citizens of Eden lived happy, peaceful lives, until Chaos found them. God knew this would eventually occur. Having never been exposed to Chaos, it was essential that humans ate the fruit and that is why God provided the Godivel tree, as it held the knowledge they would need to survive elsewhere. Man's succumbing to the temptation of eating from the Tree of Knowledge was God's way of knowing that sin had arrived and it was time to close Eden. Eden's inhabitants were not capable of surviving the closing, so God cast them out into the multiverse."*

"But there *has* to be more than that," I said. "Why do we not have access to that knowledge now?"

"Everything fades with time, including knowledge. Although knowledge may fade, it continues to reside somewhere deep within the brain. Some drugs give limited access to forgotten knowledge, but these drugs have been diluted far too much; it would take the Godivel in its pure form to open the encoded information. This was also a part of God's plan, for humans were destined to return to Eden one day."

"So why do some of us still know these things? Why is it that we only find the truth by leaving our reality or through dreams?" I asked.

Ma Hua Ra, impatient now, barked, *"The conscious mind may not see what is truly occurring, yet the subconscious mind does see these things. While dreaming, it is the subconscious that is in control, thus enabling one to know things, to do things that are believed to be 'impossible' in the 'real world'. In actuality, there is no difference between the dreaming world and the world one occupies while awake. Some people, like yourself, have learned to see these things that go unnoticed because of an anomaly."*

"My Tourette's," I said.

"Correct, Marcus. I have noted that you are coming along nicely in your attempts at tuning."

"If you call bouncing around uncontrollably 'coming along', then yeah," I said.

"My apologies. This 'bouncing' is a sort of defense mechanism, necessary to avoid difficulty." Ma Hua Ra paused, pondering his next statement. *"For the moment, it would be best that you not spend too much time in one place. It makes it too easy for you to be found."*

"Who's looking for me?" I demanded. "And what about Elizabeth Patton? She went through the same thing! How many more of us are out there?"

"What makes you you?" he asked me.

"What does that have to do with…?"

"I'll make it easier for you," Ma Hua Ra cut in before I could finish. *"If you were in another body, would you still be you?"*

"I suppose…"

"What if you grew up in another body, say, a female?"

"I guess I'd be different but… Are you trying to tell me that Elizabeth is me?"

"She is a part of you."

"How is that possible?" I protested. "We're in the same reality; how can she be me?"

"We are all branches on the cosmic tree. Some have branched off far enough to become a new identity. These new identities then branch off into other realities, including your own. In each reality, there can be several versions of each person. In your case, Marcus, you grew up as Elizabeth Patton in another reality, thus shaping you into a separate personality. The Elizabeth here is not technically you, as she is of a separate bloodline. Remember, things happen for a reason."

"I just wish I knew the purpose of all this," I said exhaustedly.

"The purpose is simple," Ma Hua Ra casually replied. *"The upcoming celestial alignment marks the end of a cycle, Marcus, and a choice must be made."*

"What does this have to do with me?" I asked suspiciously.

"You, Marcus, have been chosen as the new savior It is your destiny to reconcile the multiverse."

"Savior? Reconcile the multiverse?" I asked, stunned.

"That is all you need to know for now, Marcus. Embrace Chaos, make a choice!"

"And if I refuse?"

"It is simple, you succeed or you die. You may refuse the task, but doing so will not change the outcome. It is up to you to save all the species of the multiverse from the evil that wishes to take hold. I will give you twenty-four hours to provide your response."

In a flash of static, Ma Hua Ra was gone.

Twenty-four hours! That pompous, overbearing, omnipotent being had demanded that I make a life-altering decision in twenty-four fucking hours? There was so damn much cruelty in the world and this bastard expected *me* to save it? *Why?* Why is that cruelty is more than tolerated, it's *accepted*. We call *this* human nature? Is it some remnant from our past, the "pack mentality" to get rid of the weak? Why would we evolve a need to do this? It made no sense! Just one more hole in the theory of Evolution. When put in this perspective, suddenly evil, or the devil, or even Chaos, didn't sound like such a strange idea.

Over the years I had grown to hate the outside world, it made me sick to see the shit that goes on in the world that people had just turned their backs on. Look at murder. Hearing about someone dying in a violent manner used to shock people, but now we hear about two or three murders a day as if it's no big deal. And what is so disgusting is that violence truly is *not* a big deal anymore, because people *are* used to it. And *why* are we used to it? The media. It wasn't always this way; in the past the media was much less likely to report on a murder case unless it involved a celebrity or a serial killer. Now, we only hear about the bad stuff that happens in a day's time. Oh, sure, the nightly news might be capped off with a "fluff" story so as not to go out on a sour note, but the rest of the news is nothing but death, suffering, and crime. Shouldn't the *real* crime be that corporate media reports that shit because it's what makes money? People *want* this garbage! Why?

The media, the government, corporations, all tell us what we need and just can't live without. They tell us they're trying to make things easier for us, but what they are doing is dumbing down the human race. Telling us what to think is another way for the bureaucrats to control the truth. Our forefathers must be rolling in their graves at having to see our current leaders fucking everything they built right in the ass. Don't get me wrong, I *love* America, I love everything that this country once stood for. Unfortunately I'm no longer sure what that is. Even *God* has been taken away from us. I'm so tired of hearing people bitch about the word God! You can't pray in school because someone might get offended. Our children can no longer say the Pledge of Allegiance because the word God is used. What's next, the National Anthem? Our courts and federal buildings were ordered to remove anything depicting the Ten Commandments from the premises, when those ten little rules were what all of our fucking laws were based on to begin with! Why do people bitch about such petty things anyway? Do they have nothing better to do than to sit on their collective asses thinking about who's going to offend them next? Meanwhile, they're the ones bitching about *their* rights and *their* religious freedoms. What the fuck about *my* rights and freedoms? Why do we let people get away with this shit? Can you now see why I had such a hard time with this decision?

Aside from religion, most of the problems in the world today stem from a lack of tolerance toward other races and cultures. There are no innocent parties here, as racism takes many forms. I've used the dreaded "N" word more times than I'd care to admit. Making a word taboo, especially one as derogatory as the "N" word, changes the manner in which it is used forever. The word becomes used purely for the reaction it receives. The only way to change the reaction is to stop saying the fucking word! That goes for every*one,* every *race*! I know there's bigotry out there and there always will be. If people are so damn tired of being stereotyped then they should *stop doing stereotypical things!* This goes for *every* race and culture! You may call *me* racist for some of my previous comments, but I'm not. I'm more of an equal opportunity bigot; I hate everyone *equally.* I'm sure that there's someone out there right now saying that I have no idea what it's like to be black, or red, or Asian, or Irish, or *whatever*... well, guess what? Growing up with Tourette's was no fucking picnic either! I know what it's like to be discriminated against, to be mocked and ridiculed. I know what racism feels like but I dealt with it.

Since I was brought up Catholic I know the role the Middle East plays in religious history. Even in the theory of evolution, all life is said to have begun in that same general area, and there *is* history there for *all* races. The Middle East is one of the most religious regions in the world and has also historically been one of the most unstable due to the constant infighting between the various religious factions. Imagine that, religion equating to violence. Why? Because no one likes to be proven wrong. I'm not saying that Middle Eastern religions promote violence; it's more that the only time we hear about anyone promoting those religions is *through the use of* violence; again, blame the media for *that* one. We have to accept that we are all *one* species and we are *all* immigrants. Even the Bible tells us that the sins of the fathers are *not* the sins of the sons; when do we finally learn this and stop killing ourselves off?

I struggled on a daily basis with the fact that my daughters were growing up in a world that just kept getting worse by the second. What were things going to be like for them when they reach my age? If things don't change, and I mean soon, this world is heading for a bleak and dismal future. Therein lies the crux of my problem. Why should *I* be responsible for the destiny of mankind? Why should I do anything for a world that had turned its back on me decades ago? I tried to think of the good things, and there were many, but the evil in the world outweighed the good immensely. But then I thought of Tara and Tori, my beautiful girls, and my Anna… If I had the power to change things, shouldn't I do so, even if it was just for them? If I could have the slightest chance of making the world a better place for them to grow old in, then how could I possibly refuse to take on the task Ma Hua Ra had thrust upon me? Just because the world had shit on me my entire life it did not mean that I had to lower myself to the same level as the assholes that'd made my life a living hell; I was *better* than that. As I lay in bed with this final thought in my head, I fell asleep.

DECISIONS

I've spoken of the patterns in my life, my visions, my dreams. There were certain visions that I saw repeatedly, most notably the one that consists of eyes, just the irises, with no surrounding white area. Sometimes it was one eye in great detail; other times it was thousands of eyes throughout my entire field of vision. I never understood the significance of why I had visions of eyes until my dream that night.

The dream started out just like before. I stood in the field, looking up at the grass and stone staircase leading to the castle. I closed my eyes and focused, and within moments I was standing in the courtyard. I climbed the tower and relived my conversation with Julia/Anna up until the moment before I kissed her. I was looking into her eyes and time stood still around us. I saw everything at the same time, a moth hung motionless in the air behind me, drawn to a torch with flames that looked like luminous ice. Before me I saw my image in Anna's eyes reflected back at me a thousand times and I realized that it was not only *my* reflection. Each face was different, each face an individual person. Mine was there, but there were many others as well. The twins' eyes were there, as were our entire extended families, close friends and co-workers. There were people that I'd seen on a regular basis, like the clerk at the convenience store and the gas station attendant at my regular stop. The deeper I looked, the more eyes I saw, as if I were seeing every set of eyes that Anna had ever looked into. As *my* eyes came across the familiar features of my own reflection, the face staring back at me spoke. It said, "This is how God sees."

Now that I was awake and twitching like a tweak on meth, I got out of bed, trying not to disturb Anna's slumber. It was then that I realized I was not in the reality I'd initially fallen asleep in. The now familiar blackness of the Nexus surrounded me, and I knew that the time had come for my decision.

"All right, Ma Hua Ra, you bastard," I shouted, "I've made my choice!" My cry was answered with a crackle of static.

"You have made the correct choice, Marcus. I see inside your heart and your answer beats loudly. And before you ask, yes, the dream you just had has everything to do with the path you have chosen."

"So, you gonna' tell me?" I smarted off.

"The eyes are the windows to the soul. This phrase, so eloquently put, is difficult to accept as being coined by a human. What did you tell yourself in your dream, Marcus?"

"This is how God sees," I answered.

"Each time you make eye contact with another person, Marcus, a connection is made. From that point on, you will always be connected with anyone your gaze rests upon in some way. You can use this to your advantage. Concentrate on the target and you will learn to see what they see, as God is able to see."

"So God *does* see all."

"Yes, Marcus, but remember, there are positive and negative forces everywhere. As God can access the connection, so can Chaos. You have one week to find a safe place to hide your body where the least amount of eyes can see you. While on your journey, your body is vulnerable and must be protected at all costs." Ma Hua Ra stopped and cocked his head as if straining to hear a distant noise. *"We must go; I will find you in one week."*

I woke up instantly with a skull-splitting headache. I turned on my side and watched Anna as she lay next to me dreaming what I hoped were pleasant dreams. I lay awake for the next hour thinking about my family, my only anchor to this reality. I gathered Anna close to me, thinking thoughts of how she was in danger because of me and that, even now, as she lay next to me wrapped in whatever scenario that was playing out in her mind, her life could be in jeopardy. How could I protect my family where they were most vulnerable, in their dreams? This in turn led to thoughts of what the dark woman was capable of doing to my wife, to the twins. How could I even attempt to stop something I didn't understand? How *does* one stop the end of all existence? It was the fall of 2009 when I decided to let go, to pull anchor. Ma Hua Ra had given me one week to figure out what it was that I was supposed to do. As I was pondering my destiny I must have fallen asleep because, the next thing I knew, I was standing in a cemetery that stretched out as far as the eye could see.

The pale white moonlight fell from above, bathing the graveyard in its soft glow. In that moment I was reminded of a poem I had heard somewhere. The verses came clear in my mind as if I had just memorized them moments ago.

> *As I sit on this hillside I watch the clouds chase the sun*
> *As it runs for the cover of the horizon*
> *To elude the impending darkness of nightfall*
> *I see blades glistening in the moonlight*
> *As the grass dances to the symphony of the wind*
> *I hear leaves and crickets*
> *And the deafening echoes of the silence of nightfall.*
> *Moonbeams, Death-dreams, Terror-screams*
> *Oh, how I love the sounds of the night!*

I walked in the direction of the moon, and as I walked, a memory slowly worked its way out from deep within my brain. I'd had this dream before! I was seven years old and I remembered writing the poem down in my journal. The memories came rushing back to me; I reached down, pushed open the gate, and began to walk up the hill.

As I approached, I saw a fire burning and I heard the old man talking. He was reciting the end of the poem. "...Oh, how I love the sounds of the night! It's so good to see you again, Marcus!"

I knew he could not see me from where he sat by the fire; I knew this because the old man was blind. I remembered his eyes from my earlier dream and they were strange. His irises were dull brown beneath a milky white cloud, and his pupils... They were not solid, more like a halo that seemed to cut through the cloud with a deep black clarity, and there were three lines extending outward through each iris, in the shape of an inverted Y. I walked down to the fire pit and sat beside the old man.

"How old are you now, Marcus? How long has it been?"

"I'm twenty-eight." I said. "It's been just over twenty years."

"Seems like yesterday to me," the man muttered to himself, turning to face me.

"So to what do I owe the honor of your presence?"

I thought about this for a second. Why *had* I gone there? I didn't feel as though I had chosen my destination, not at first. "You're the one with the all-seeing-blind-eye," I said. "You tell me!"

"I cannot. The answers you seek are with me in the past, not the here and now."

I thought about this as well; what was he trying to tell me?

"Where is the here and now?" I asked.

"A long time from when you need to be." The old man returned his gaze to the flames, and as he did this, the scene before me lost focus and reality shifted.

When my vision returned I stood in the middle of a field, the scene before me awash in daylight. Hundreds of large round bales of hay lay scattered across the barren pasture in all directions. Beyond the field on a distant hill I saw a large farmhouse. I focused in on the house with my eyes, my body jolted, and I landed on the front porch I had been looking at from the field. At least half a mile in the blink of an eye, I just *had* to learn how to control that! I knocked on the door but there was no answer. I turned the knob. It clicked open and I walked inside.

My search of the first floor ended in the den where an old television, the kind in the wooden cabinet with legs, played an old black and white western which softly filled the room with light and noise. Finding no one in the house, I returned to the entranceway and headed up the ornate stairway to the second floor. My hand slid across something warm and wet on the wooden banister. I looked down at my open palm, only to find it smeared with freshly spilled blood! I climbed the stairs and entered a long hallway that stretched out the entire length of the house. Light streamed in from the window placed on the far end of the hall, its blinds open. There were three doors on each side of the hall. Each door stood open, daylight spilling into the hallway from all but one. I followed the trail of blood on the hardwood floor to the last room on the left, the door that did not emit any light. When I entered the room I felt a sort of electrical charge in the air and the smell of copper clogged my nose. The hair on the back of my neck stood up and tingled as I crossed the room and looked out the bedroom window. A full moon bathed the back yard with a light so bright that it blocked out all of the stars, turning the sky a hazy gray.

I turned and saw a man wearing a pair of green and black flannel pajamas sitting on the floor in a darkened corner on the left side of the room. He sat with his arms crossed and resting on his knees, his head nestled in his arms. The man didn't answer me when I said, "Hello?" I reached out and pushed against his left shoulder and the man fell to his side, sprawling out across the floor. His face was badly mangled and unrecognizable, the front of his shirt drenched with his blood. His throat had been cut. I stood up when I heard someone whistling as they slowly climbed the stairs. I listened to the footsteps, the tread heavy, like a man carrying something. He reached the top of the stairs and continued down the hallway, still whistling his song. What *was* that song? He carried two teenagers, one over each shoulder, a boy and a girl. I watched as he threw them down onto the floor of the room I stood in. The unconscious children tumbled across the floor, landing at my feet. I looked up and stared in disbelief at what I saw. Standing in the doorway, covered in blood, wearing a tool belt filled with instruments of torture was… *me*!

I watched as the other me pulled a large knife out of his belt. The knife was covered in blood; some fresh, some so old it looked like hardened rust. This other me reached down with his free hand and picked the boy up by his short blonde hair. Consciousness returned for the boy and he struggled to get free as the bastard me effortlessly slit the teen's exposed throat. I lunged at this other me, ready to tear his head off if that's what it took to stop this madness, but… I landed on the floor after passing right *through* him! The madman looked down at me and smiled, or so I thought. The smile, in reality, was for the young girl who lay sobbing, curled in a fetal position on the floor behind me. I screamed every obscenity I could conjure at this crazy version of me as he reached right through me and lifted the girl up by her hair. He looked into her little terror filled eyes with hunger, even as he slid the knife across her throat. I watched helplessly as he carelessly, cruelly, kicked the children into different corners of the room. He posed them to his liking in their respective corners, then walked over to the door and closed it, revealing yet another corpse. Just as the children had been arranged, so was the mother, who was hidden behind the door. She, too, had had her throat slit. My evil persona walked over to the shell of the father and sat it back up so that it was arranged as it had been when I'd first entered the room. The bastard resumed his whistling, walked to the center of the room and…

In an instant, I was startled awake. I looked at the clock; it was three a.m. Anna was asleep beside me, tugging at the blankets. I let her have them and got out of bed, grabbing my cigarettes as I slipped out of the bedroom and into the reading room where I opened the sliding glass door that led to the second floor deck. That was one fucked up dream! Sure, I've had thoughts about it, but I didn't think I was actually capable of the unspeakable acts I had witnessed in my dream, but *seeing* them, *watching* myself murder an entire family… *That* was a little much for me. These thoughts, in turn, made me think about the dream journal I had lost as a child, how it had just seemed to vanish one day. When I'd asked my parents about the missing journal, they had almost convinced me back then that the journal never even existed, that I'd made it all up. I still had a lot of random thoughts running through my head, so I put out my smoke and went inside to sit down and sift through what little I could remember of the days before my journal disappeared. I was fifteen when I'd lost my journal; I knew that much, but I couldn't remember exactly when it was.

I heard the bedroom door open with a snick, interrupting my thoughts, and Anna appeared in the doorway wearing a small blanket and nothing else. "Are you okay?" she whispered.

"Fine, just couldn't sleep, as usual," I told her gently.

Anna slowly, sinuously, walked over to me, letting the blanket slide off her shoulders. As she stood before me, she used her hands to seductively explore her exposed flesh, caressing neck and thigh with equal fervor. Anna slid her fingers into her sex, laying it open, exposing its inner beauty, slick with her juices. "Fuck me, Marcus," Anna whispered as she slid her fingers in and out of her now swollen sex. Now, how could I turn *that* offer down? Anna quickly slid my boxers down to my ankles and climbed on top of me like a flame climbing a tree in a forest fire. There was no foreplay that night, which kind of bummed me out; having watched her fingers caress one of my most favorite places, my tongue got a little bit jealous. My wife impaled herself as soon as she straddled me in my chair, gasping her pleasure as she slid her warm wetness all the way down. Now, any other warm-blooded man would have been living solely in the moment, but not me, oh, no… *that's* when it came to me, my damn random thoughts intruding on the moment. The recollection came rushing back just then and I remembered waking up on the morning of October thirteenth 1996 to find my first dream journal missing. It was already well past midnight the night that Anna seduced me. That night was October thirteenth 2009.

I looked up and saw that Anna was no longer on top of me. I was still being fucked, but it was the dark woman who was riding me like a cowgirl, the female Ma Hua Ra described in Elizabeth Patton's diary pages. The dark woman's hand shot out for my throat, her fingers tightening around my neck.

"Tell me where it is!" she hissed. From under the couch, zigzagging lines of black light began to spread out across the carpet, growing wider and brighter. All at once, there was a loud sucking sound, like a giant vortex opening beneath the floor. In the spaces between the black light, the floor began to crumble away, and for a moment the reclining chair seemed to hover over the abyss, and then plunged downward.

The bitch wrapped her legs around me and tightened her grip on my neck.

"Where is it?" she screamed over the sound of the vortex. *"The journal, tell me where it is!"*

Was my first dream journal what the dark woman had been seeking all along? What was in that journal that could be so important to her? Suddenly, I was no longer falling, and the dark bitch was no longer anchored to me by hand and cunt. Realities had seemingly, once again, shifted without warning.

When my vision cleared, I stood behind some bushes in a darkened back yard. I recognized my surroundings instantly and stepped forward, emerging from the confines of the shadows to stand in front of my childhood home. All of the lights were out and the house looked dark and cold. At the same time however, it was welcoming me, inviting me inside to warm my bones and bathe myself in memories. I crossed the yard and entered the unlocked side door, crept to the front of the house, and quietly climbed the stairs to my bedroom. Funny, I remembered every creaky stair, every loose floorboard, and how I had avoided them when sneaking in at three in the morning. I put my hand on the doorknob of my old bedroom and stopped, holding my breath as I opened the door.

There I was in bed, fifteen years old again and sound asleep. I looked at the nightstand. It was there, a faded green notebook, my dream journal. I tiptoed across the room and reached for my book of memories. As soon as my fingers touched it I was pulled somewhere else.

I sat in the living room of a house familiar to me, yet, at the same time, utterly alien. It was *our* house, Anna, the kids and mine, but all of the carpets and furnishings were different. A large mirror hung over the fireplace, so I stood up to check out my reflection. It was me, at least the me that I knew back then. My head flooded with memories as I sat down on the couch and began flipping through the pages of the journal. I'd decided at that moment to start at the beginning and just read it straight through, hoping I would learn why my childish dreams were so important to the dark forces I was beginning to encounter more and more often. The pages were filled with dreams I'd had on a reoccurring basis throughout my life. I skipped through those and read on. There were dreams about women, several starring Anna, but one in particular caught my attention. As I read through my description of her, I became more and more convinced that it was my dream Anna, who had gone by the name of Julia. I had described her to the smallest detail on the pages before me. The way she spoke, the way she moved, the smell of her skin and breath. I realized then that, the more memories we gather throughout a lifetime, the more we forget things. I understood that these memories are not gone, simply misplaced in the darkest corners of our minds, waiting. Waiting for that one thought, phrase, sight, smell or touch, to trigger the memory and pull it back into the conscious mind. Once again, I was reminded of the connection of two, the conscious and the subconscious minds working together, yet independently, to create one personality with numerous sets of memories. Why hadn't the dreams I'd had of Julia/Anna triggered the memory of this dream on their own?

I resumed reading my first dream journal. As a teen, I'd stood and watched as a giant pumpkin much taller than I, was lit by a man on a ladder. The pumpkin had been hollowed out and filled with leaves and small branches that were soaked in what smelled like kerosene. I stopped reading, something wasn't right. Either I was remembering things wrong or this was *not* my journal. As soon as I had made this discovery, something hit me hard, like being kicked in the chest. The journal slid from my fingers and fell to the floor. I saw something moving in the shadows of the room's darkened corner and knew instantly that it was the dark woman. I could feel her eyes penetrating me through the blackness.

"How did you do it?" the creature whispered. *"How did you break the illusion?"*

The dark woman was after something, a memory in my head of a dream I had as a teenager. I was not prepared for this encounter. I knew what the creature was capable of and I doubted I would come out alive if it were to attack, but she just stood there.

"I know you're afraid, Marcus; you needn't be, not if you give me what I want."

"What *do* you want?" I asked.

"The map, give us the map!" the dark woman hissed. I could feel the room chill as her anger rose, sending a shiver through my body. I had no idea what she was talking about and the dark woman seemed to sense this because her anger subsided and she once again spoke in an even tone.

"The information is there, Marcus. You can access it with our help."

She slowly inched her way closer to me.

"Yes, Marcus, let us help you." As she said these words her voice deepened and her body began to transform. Her muscles expanded, her height increased. Before my eyes, the creature changed from female to male. I knew I was screwed. I had the feeling that I wasn't going to be given a choice, that the information would be extracted from me one way or another, so I decided to strike first. I slid my feet back against the couch and pushed off, lunging at the dark creature. He tilted his head back and laughed as I hit him and went right through... or was it *into* him?

I once again stood in the back yard of my childhood home. The vile creature's laugh still echoed in the darkness around me as I heard a scream coming from my open bedroom window. I sprinted across the yard and pushed the door open, not caring how much noise I made that time. I hit the stairs at the front of the house and took them three and four at a time. I rounded the corner to the doorway of my bedroom and froze. My fifteen-year-old self stood in the middle of the room with a terrified look on his face and a glistening blade to his throat. Once again I stood face to face with my murderous counterpart, but this time when he stared back at me, he *could* see me; he *knew* I was there. My evil twin's eyes went to the journal on the nightstand, and then focused back on me. When his eyes shifted to the journal a second time I took a chance, for I knew I would not have another. I dove for him fast and hard, but I wasn't fast enough. His knife opened my teenaged self's throat with one quick motion of the wrist. He let the teenager fall to the floor and lunged for the nightstand. He held the journal in one hand and pointed his knife at me with the other. It was a big knife, the blade at least eight inches long. The blood from the knife scattered through the air as my evil half waved it back and forth. I looked down at the boy clutching his throat as he lay on the floor dying. My evil self laughed a familiar laugh and I could feel the anger rising in me. My lungs filled with it until they burst and I screamed, *"Nooooooo!"* and time stood still.

I looked around the room, at the gruesome scene stopped by time. My young self lay in a fetal position, hands to his throat. He looked dead. The other me, my evil counterpart, stood there with that stupid fucking grin of mine on his face. The knife no longer moved from side to side, hanging motionless in the air, as did the droplets of blood exiled from the blade. There was a sound that I vaguely recognized and I turned to find *my* Ma Hua Ra standing over the teen's body. His light filled the room, removing all shadows. *"Very good, Marcus,"* he said with a smile.

"I did that?" I was stunned!

"Yes, Marcus, you are moving along much more quickly than anticipated."

"How? How did I do *that*? And what *is* all of this?" I motioned to the scene that was now standing silent and still. "And the dark woman, what does she/he/it want from me? Is this really happening or are you just fucking with my head?" I was starting to get a little pissed and my shoulder started to twitch. Funny, I thought I'd lost that tic a long time ago.

"This is *happening Marcus. I can only hold off their influence for so long, so I will be brief. The dark woman is my negative half."*

"Why do I see it as both a male and a female?" I interrupted.

"You see me as you want to see me. I allow you to come to your own conclusions whereas my negative self uses deception to sway your perceptions."

"The prince of lies, the origin of the devil," I said.

"Yes. As I am of God, She is of Chaos. Everything in God has an opposite in Chaos, linked together by a point in the Nexus. Each reality exists in both God and Chaos as well as the multiverse. Heaven and Hell, with the known universe in between. Every living soul occupies all three. Your point in the Nexus is, shall we say, much stronger than most. This allows you to draw energy from both God and Chaos directly. This ability affords you a few… powers. You will learn how to use these powers in time."

Ma Hua Ra stooped at the boy's side and took the child into his arms.

"Will he die?" I asked. "If he does, what happens to me?"

"What is done, is done," Ma Hua Ra said as he stood, the teen cradled in his arms. *"This does not affect you as you are, Marcus. You are dreaming; this is* not *your reality."* Ma Hua Ra's inner light slowly increased in intensity, shining brighter and brighter as he spoke, washing out the scene around us.

"You now know where to look, Marcus," he said. And he was gone.

I sat up in the chair, my heart beating in triple time. I looked around the reading room for some sign of deception. Everything appeared to be normal, but I knew how deceptive appearances could be.

333
CHIMERA

SHADOW LAKE

I opened the bedroom door and heard Anna softly snoring. I climbed into bed beside her and lay there thinking, letting everything that I had experienced explode inside my head at once. So much had happened since all of this started and I could hardly decide where to begin to sort things out. I thought about the dream with Julia and the pumpkin and how something just wasn't right. In the vision provoked by the dark woman the pumpkin was just an ordinary jack-o-lantern, but not so in the original dream. Just seeing the journal in my travels had jogged my memories, even if the information the journal contained had not been entirely correct.

I vividly remembered the original dream then, and I remembered the pumpkin. It *was* a jack-o-lantern of sorts. It had a deformed caricature of a face carved into its skin that, when I approached, I realized was three separate faces joining to make one. The instant the kindling inside the pumpkin was ignited, the images that were missing in the vision induced by the dark woman appeared, radiating a brilliant white light. I searched for patterns involving events in my life at the time of a reoccurring dream, but I came up empty. So, how was I supposed to get my brain to understand that I needed to see something I had missed over a decade ago? As usual, my mind was way ahead of me. I fell asleep and began to dream.

I heard laughter. A group of four men walked ahead of me on a dark path that twisted its way through an even darker forest. I followed them. The men walked single file, the first and last in line each held a torch, creating two rings of light around them in the shape of a figure eight. I tried to stay close and silent on the dark path but I could see nothing, like the woods did not exist at all and I was following the men through a dark void where only their torches held solid ground to walk on. I stumbled through thorns and briars, silently cursing as a small tree branch smacked me in the face, barely missing my left eye. It was difficult keeping up with the men, my vision was blurry from allergies and tears. I know the four men must have heard me in the woods behind them but they never turned around for they were on a mission, determined to deliver their payload on time. Each man carried a sack over his shoulder, two had sacks full of leaves and two had sacks full of sticks and twigs. I saw light up ahead of the men, and I heard more laughter followed by a cheer as the men emerged from the canopy of trees into a large crowd awaiting their return. I hung back in the woods a bit to watch. The path led to a dead end street and in the middle of the road, surrounded by a crowd of onlookers, stood a six-foot tall pumpkin. The men placed their sacks at the bottom of the gourd and laughed amongst themselves. Two stepladders emerged from the crowd and were quickly handed to the men. The ladders were set up on either side of the pumpkin and two of the men from the woods began to climb. Both pulled out large knives and began to pry out the giant stem. It took the combined strength of both to wedge the chunk out and hand it down to the two men waiting below. They gently placed the stem on the ground and then handed each man on the ladders a sack of leaves. When the sacks were emptied, one of the men on the ladders pulled a bottle out of his coat pocket and bit the cork. He pulled on it with his teeth until it popped free, then spit the cork into the opening on top of the pumpkin. The man took a quick swig of the sharp smelling alcohol before passing it to his comrade on the other ladder. He reached for the bottle, took a swig, and dumped the rest into the hollowed out pumpkin. The two men then climbed down and took their place in the crowd.

The two remaining men each climbed a ladder and emptied the sticks and twigs into the pumpkin one sack at a time. When the task was complete, one of the men took a bottle out of his pocket and uncorked it. He took a hit and passed the bottle to the remaining man, who also took a swig before dumping the rest of the alcohol on top of the sticks and leaves. The men climbed down, removed one of the ladders, and joined the crowd. Someone new stepped forward and climbed the remaining ladder. He pulled out a box of matches and carefully selected one. Deciding this was indeed the match, the man struck the stick across the side of the box and dropped the flame into the pumpkin. The innards quickly ignited with a great *whoosh* and the images appeared.

After about fifteen minutes, the crowd began to thin and, in thirty, the street was empty. I quietly moved closer, careful not to wander too far out of the woods. I recognized some of the images on the pumpkin; I saw a spear and some sort of lens, a small map of Egypt, what looked to be Alexandria, and another image of the Ark of the Covenant. I saw a half circle, a figure eight, and a square. The rest of the images were strangely shaped objects that could be anything. I did my best to memorize each and every image and its place on the... Was it a map? The dark woman had said she was looking for a map. The pieces seemed to be parts of a whole but parts to what? The questions continued to crowd my mind as the dream continued. "Lovely evening for a fire," a voice called out from behind me. I turned to find Julia slowly walking out of the woods. "Where did you come from young man? We don't get many visitors around here anymore."

This was the first time I noticed my age. I was in my early teens when I originally had the dream.

"Where is here?" I asked.

"Why, Shadow Lake of course. Say, what's your name?"

"Marcus," I answered. "Are you sure you've never seen me before?"

"Don't be silly! It's a pleasure to meet your acquaintance, Marcus. There, now we *have* met." Julia reached out and took my hand. "Come, Marcus, I want to show you something."

This wasn't part of the original dream, but I decided to go along with things anyway. We stuck to the outskirts of town, walking just within the tree line to avoid the crowds and festivities. We came to a path in the woods and Julia stopped, letting go of my hand. She reached for one of a dozen machetes that were stuck into a nearby tree. Julia pulled the machete free and turned to me.

"Keep close and don't be afraid," she said, then turned and slowly walked down the darkening path.

I followed behind as she'd instructed, not saying a word. Once in the woods the light faded quickly. Julia stopped and bent down to pick something up from the ground. It was a three-foot long stick that looked like some sort of torch. Julia put the tip of the stick to her lips and blew. The tip ignited and we now had fire to light our way.

The trees and underbrush seemed to close in on us as we walked down the trail that was presently barely wide enough to call a path. Julia handed me the torch.

"It doesn't take long for things to grow back out here," she said.

We continued to walk down the trail in silence for a while until she stopped again.

"Come here, I need light." Julia tugged on my arm until I was standing by her side. "Now hold it up." What I saw were some of the biggest vines I had ever seen, it looked like the trail was blocked by thirty-foot long dangling anacondas. Julia was good with the machete; she knew just the right angle to hit the vine and to hold the blade, obviously, she had done this before.

"It's not much further now," she huffed, almost out of breath.

"Let me take over," I offered, and reached for the machete.

"No!" Julia yelled, raising the blade too high for me to reach. "No outsider has *ever* been here before, we have to be careful!" Julia refocused her attention on the vines.

"How did you get here, Marcus?" she asked as she hacked away.

"I don't know," I lied. "I can't remember."

"Well, there's only two ways here, that's the bridge or by boat; Shadow Lake is an island. *There!*"

The last of the vines fell away, exposing a large clearing in the middle of the forest. Julia took the torch from me and placed it in a hollowed out log that was buried upright in the dirt and stone. She set the machete down on the ground next to the torch and turned to me.

"This is the exact center of the island," she said. "All around life thrives, but here... nothing grows here. It's because of *that*." Julia pointed to a large indentation in the soil at the center of the clearing. I walked closer and saw that the disturbance in the soil was much more. The surrounding earth crumbled away into a vast hole in the ground.

"How deep is it?" I asked.

"No one knows. You can drop anything down there and not hear it hit, *ever*! No splash, nothing. There have been stoves, refrigerators, even a car was dropped down once but you never hear..." Julia's words were stopped cold as a voice boomed from within the dark pit.

"*Julia,*" the voice commanded, "*Give him to us!*"

"Run, Marcus!" Julia screamed. "Run, before it's too late!"

I watched the expression on Julia's face change from terror to joy as she reached for my arm, her fingernails finding purchase and digging in hard.

"You heard what it said!" Julia laughed a wicked laugh and shoved me into the pit.

The blackness of what I somehow knew to be the Nexus surrounded me. I caught a glimpse of something swimming through the darkness, waving like the tail of some great sea beast. I could barely see the form of the creature, it stayed far enough back so as not to be seen as much more than a shadow, but still it was *huge!* "What are you?" I yelled through the blackness.

The creature answered through my thoughts in a voice as dark as my surroundings.

"I am Legion." It boomed.

"That's just the kind of answer I would have expected from an *amateur*," I taunted the beast. "Yeah, yeah, you are Legion, you are many. I'm human and there's a shitload of us, too!"

The creature roared and moved a few yards closer, long enough for me to see some of its features, then quickly retreated into the darkness. Its "body" consisted of dozens of human-like figures intertwined, limbs passing through each other like smoke. Each silhouette twisted and writhed in agony, while their faces screamed out in pain. Three of the heads on the front of the creature merged into one terrible face.

"We are Mille Umbra," it boomed from the safety of the darkness. *"Why are you here?"*

"You tell me! You're the one who had Julia toss my ass down here in the *first* place!" I yelled.

The creature's many forms twitched and shook; it seemed the Umbra was getting angry again.

"You know things…" The Umbra paused to contemplate its words. *"There are thoughts I cannot penetrate; what are you hiding?"* The creature moved closer, circling around me in the darkness.

"I'm not hiding anything."

"Lies!" the Umbra screamed. *"No matter, we will know you in time."*

The tones in my head started ringing loudly, the volume turned up to eleven. When the ringing abruptly stopped, I no longer heard the creature in my head. My vision began to return but it was still obscured by the "dots". I heard someone crying and I vaguely made out the shape of a woman kneeling. I must have made some sort of noise for, the next thing I knew Julia leapt up and ran to me excitedly screaming.

"Marcus! I'm so glad you're alive!" She pulled me into her arms and sobbed.

"Julia, I'm fine," I said, pushing away from her. I turned and pointed into the abyss I had so recently returned from. "I need you to tell me everything you know about that hole and what's in it."

"I will," Julia whispered, "but not here."

With the machete once more in hand, Julia led me back down the path. I watched in awe, as the vines seemed to grow back before my very eyes as she hacked away until we were once more on the edge of town. Julia returned the machete to the log with a swipe and a thunk. "This way," she said. It was late and the streets of Shadow Lake were virtually empty. We entered a courtyard leading to the town square, walking past a rusted cannon that had its end cemented shut. We made our way across the deserted square and turned into an alley beside the local tavern. The alley led around the back of the building and into a fenced in baseball park. We climbed the fence and walked to the entrance on the far side.

"Why do I feel as though I know you?" Julia asked as we crossed home plate. "I know I've never seen you before, but…"

"Maybe you haven't seen me *yet*." I said. "Maybe you dreamed of me and your conscious mind just doesn't remember."

"I don't dream," Julia stated flatly. "What about me, Marcus, do I look familiar to you?"

I thought about lying to her but she seemed to be playing a crucial role in events surrounding my life. "I've dreamed of you several times throughout my life," I revealed and waited for her reply.

Julia laughed. "You can't be more than fifteen," she said. "How much life can you have lived?"

"You wouldn't believe me if I told you," I said, holding the gate open for her.

"What *I* believe just might surprise you," Julia snapped back as the humor of our conversation faded. "They sure seem to surprise everyone else around here," she sighed.

The house we stood before was not the same as it had been in the dream with Julia, the twins, and the face-changing girl. This was a more modest house, and this time the interior matched the exterior. The two-story house had a less extravagant entranceway, but still, it had a nice feel to it. I followed Julia down the hall and into the kitchen; a good-sized room filled with 1970's era appliances. The countertops were marble and the hard wood floors had been stained a lighter shade of cherry than the entranceway. On the other side of the room I saw a doorway leading into a large dining room with built in glass cabinets lining two of the walls. A sturdy oak table and chairs sat in the center of the room on top of a spiral woven rug. Julia lit the pilot on the stove with a match and set a large cast iron kettle on to boil. She crossed into the dining room and flipped on the light switch. "In here, Marcus. Come, have a seat."

Julia pulled one of the chairs out for me to sit in and took her own. "The water will take a few minutes to boil," she said as she placed her elbows on the table and rested her chin in her hands. "So, are you going to tell me about your beliefs?" Julia waited only a brief moment, and when I did not reply right away, she continued talking. "Belief is a scary thing, Marcus. It can cure and it can kill. It can make men strong and it can make them weak. It can dictate *every* aspect of a person's life and it can even drive some people crazy. Why *does* it have such a hold on all of us?"

"Because we *need* to believe in something," I stated.

"Right, but why? And what if you had the answer? What would you do with that knowledge?"

"I doubt anyone would really care," I answered.

"Precisely! We *have* to believe, not caring how or why. As for me, I *do* believe in God, but my God is much different than most. At the same time, my God is *all* Gods."

"I'm with you so far," I said. "Our beliefs are more similar than you think."

"Then you are cursed, Marcus. Belief was God's final curse on man. For us to *need* to blindly follow anything, be it God or something else." Julia sat back, folding her hands on the table in front of her.

"God's final curse? I asked. "Does that mean He is in hiding, that God no longer has anything to do with what goes on in the world around us?"

"In hiding, yes, but God still has influence over us. God still loves us, even if God is not in complete control."

"Chaos reigns supreme." I found myself repeating Ma Hua Ra's words to Julia. "I noticed you don't refer to God as a he or a she," I stated.

"God is neither male nor female," Julia stated sternly. "God is three, God is the Chimera."

The kettle of water on the stove began to whistle as the steam escaped.

"You know more than you should," Julia said as she rose and walked into the kitchen. I followed.

"What do you mean by Chimera?" I asked. "God, Chaos and the Nexus?"

My query hung in the air, while the sound of the kettle's whistle slowly faded. Julia turned and looked me in the eyes. "You're scaring me, Marcus. How do you know these things that are in my head, why are you truly here?"

"For the pumpkin," I answered honestly.

"Do *you* see them too? I thought *I* was the only one!" Julia's face turned ashen with this admission.

"She sent you, didn't she?" Julia asked sheepishly, her hands shaking as she prepared her coffee.

"Who?" I queried.

"The Woman of Light." Julia could only be talking of one person. Ma Hua Ra.

"You've seen her?" I asked.

"Only once, when I was a child. I saw her in the woods before that hole opened, before things... before *people* started to change. The Woman of Light told me that she would send someone to me one day, and I was to give that person something. That I was to give them..." Julia walked over to me, bent down, and kissed me on the forehead. "This..." The room began to spin and everything went black.

REALITY SLIPS

My vision came into focus and I tried to sit up. I couldn't! It seemed that I was strapped to a bed. I tried to speak but nothing came out. Somehow, I managed to make a sound approximating a moan. "Marcus?" a surprised voice sounded nearby. "You're awake!"

My beautiful wife Anna's face smiled down on me and I forced out the words, "What... happened?"

"I found you unconscious on the floor, Quinn. You've been here... You've been in..." Anna paused, and then finally said, "You've been in a coma since the middle of October!"

"What day is it? How long has it been?" I asked, shocked.

"It's February third, 2010." Anna whispered. "It's been over three months..." Anna's voice trailed off into sobs as she rested her head on my chest and softly cried.

"Time flies when you're having fun," I sighed, "What are the straps for?"

The door opened and one of the hospital staff entered the room.

Anna quickly stood and said, "He's awake, can we take the restraints off now?"

The nurse walked to the side of the bed and shined a flashlight into my eyes.

"I'll see what the doctor says." The nurse turned and left the room.

Anna rose, straightening out her blouse. "The phone doesn't work in here," she said. "I'm going outside to call the girls and tell them you're awake." Anna picked up her purse from the floor and kissed me on the lips. "I'll just be a few minutes," she said. "I love you, Marcus." I listened to Anna's heels clicking off down the hallway until the elevator dinged, and then she was gone.

I closed my eyes briefly, only to open them again as someone else entered the room. He was an older man, sixty maybe, wearing a white lab coat and a stethoscope. The doctor, I presumed.

"How are you feeling, Mr. Quincy?" he asked with a fake smile.

"A little confused and thirsty as hell," I replied. "And I wouldn't mind being able to sit up,"

The nurse again shuffled into the room and offered the doctor a chart. The man studied the pages intently before closing the folder and handing it back to the nurse. He checked the instrumentation on the beeping, clicking machines and shined a light in my eyes to examine my pupil dilation.

"Remove the straps," he said. "I'll be back down in half an hour to check on him."

The doctor stood and left the room. The nurse removed the straps and handed me the control to the bed. "Press the red button if you need anything, hun." She smiled and left the room.

I messed with the controls for a while, trying to get the bed in the most comfortable position. I heard Anna walking back down the hall, the clicking of her heels in time with my heartbeat.

"No more straps," I said, and sat up as she opened the door.

Anna threw her arms around me, pulling me close, holding me tight. She sobbed as though her heart were breaking. "I was so afraid," she whispered, moving her hands to my face and looking deep into my eyes. "I love you, Marcus Quincy. Now and forever." Anna smiled and kissed me.

"So, why the restraints?" I asked.

"You were having seizures, or fits or something. The doctors think it might be night terrors." She didn't sound too convinced. "I need to get home and cook dinner for the girls," she said. "I'll call you after I get them into bed, you should have a working phone in here by then. I have the next couple of days off, so I'll be here first thing in the morning." Anna bent over and kissed me once more. "I love you, Marcus. I'll be dreaming about you."

I sat in bed thinking about Anna's kiss for a few minutes after she left. Then I remembered the other kiss; the one Julia had given me. When Julia had kissed my forehead, something happened. The map on the pumpkin that I had memorized suddenly flashed inside my head in great detail, each image coming to life and spinning, moving so fast that they began to hum. The hum turned into a whine and then distinct tones, each of these tones seemed to correspond with an existing tone in my head, marking its location. I could *feel* the tones inside my skull. The door of my hospital room opened once more and the doctor stepped in, pulled a stool over next to my bed, and sat. "So, what's the diagnosis?" I asked.

"I'm not sure yet," he said cautiously. "Your wife tells us you don't have a history of night terrors or seizures. I think it would be wise to kept you in here for a few days, give you some time to rest."

The doctor stood and left the room, but remained outside my door, speaking to one of the nurses.

"Make sure someone is monitoring him all night," he said, "we don't want a repeat of Monday. One nurse with a broken jaw is sufficient, don't you think." The doctor chuckled and retreated down the hall, his shoes squeaking on the tiled and polished floors. My door opened again and the nurse entered.

"I overheard what the doctor said. Who did I hurt?" I asked.

"A third shift nurse named Catherine; it's about time someone *popped* her!" The nurse giggled as she pushed buttons on the monitors and adjusted the flow of meds through the tube in my arm. "It's kind of peaceful around here with her gone, nice and quiet."

"Well, at least tell her I said I was sorry."

"Oh, don't be. But I will, I'll tell her." She smiled once more and left the room.

I awoke that next morning vaguely remembering a dream I'd had the night before. There was a knock on my door and a nurse entered. This nurse was short and round, with long dark hair and a constant scowl on her face. She examined the printouts and adjusted the equipment before turning to speak to me.

"Someone will be up soon to get you prepped for your scan," she said, and left the room.

About half an hour passed before the door opened again, this time to a smiling Anna. She held up a vase of flowers, walked to the window, and placed them in the sunlight that streamed into the room.

"They're from my office," she said. "My boss sent them to the house this morning."

Anna sat in the chair beside the bed and took my hand.

"They're coming to take me for some tests," I said. "Don't know what kind though."

Anna stroked the back of my hand with her fingers.

"I'll find out when they get here," she said. "If you don't mind, I'll stick around for the tests, at least until its time to get the girls." Anna rose. "I need a coffee," she said. "Can you have anything?"

"I'm fine," I answered. Anna smiled and left the room. When she returned, she was talking to someone as they walked down the hall. The door opened and Anna walked in with a young man dressed in hospital scrubs. "They're taking you for an MRI. He said I could come down and watch." Anna held the door as the man wheeled my bed out into the hallway. We entered the elevator and the doors shut with a hiss.

"What are they looking for?" Anna asked.

"Anything out of the ordinary," was the young man's reply.

"There's plenty of that in *his* head," Anna joked with a smile.

The elevator door opened with a ding and I was wheeled out into the labs.

"I just had an MRI not too long ago…" I began to say.

"They want to compare this one to the first one," the intern interrupted, "before they decide what to do next."

Two young women from the MRI department had me transfer to the table of the doughnut shaped machine. One woman exited the room while the second placed a plastic brace around my head so I could not move. "We have seven images to take, Mr. Quincy," the remaining woman said. "The tests will last three to fifteen minutes each, so you need to lay perfectly still." She covered me with a small blanket and left the room. I heard a soft hiss, a click, and then, "Lie back and relax, Mr. Quincy." The voice came from a speaker somewhere inside the room. The MRI machine buzzed to life with a soft whir and I was pulled into the confines of the centrifuge. The humming inside my head made it hard to think. I could make out seven tones that were louder than the rest, but there were more just beneath the surface. I thought about the images on the pumpkin from my dreams, there were forty-nine in all.

"Just a few more minutes Mr. Quincy." The voice cackled over the speaker. Any longer, I thought to myself, and my head is going to explode. Now *that* would make a pretty sweet image on the MRI!

My entire skull throbbed in unison with my heartbeat as I patiently waited for them to finish the tests. The machine stopped humming and the table slowly slid out. The two women returned to the room and helped me back into the bed I was brought down on. One left immediately, while the other opened a small panel on the back of the machine and started pushing buttons. Two men dressed in blue uniforms covered in dirt and grime entered the room, one talked to the young woman while the other began tinkering with the MRI machine. He wasn't in a very good mood. "There ain't nothin' wrong with this goddamn thing," the man grumbled. "I just did a PM on it last week."

When I returned to my room, Anna was there with the girls. My children climbed on top of the bed screaming, "Daddy! We're so glad to see you daddy!" I hugged them both tightly, not sure if I would ever get another chance to do so. Tori kissed me on the cheek and giggled.

"When are you coming home, daddy?" she asked.

"Yeah," added Tara, "when are you coming home?"

"I don't know sweetie, maybe your mom can find out for us."

Anna shifted in her chair and smiled a fake smile. Something was wrong.

"Take care of daddy," she said as she stood up from the chair. "I'll be back in a few minutes."

Anna left the room and the girl's attention returned to me.

"Can we watch T.V. for a while?" Tara asked.

"Sure, honey." I handed the remote to the girls and the television instantly came to life, filling the room with sound. I tightened my grip on the twins, one in each arm, when suddenly I was fighting to keep my eyes open and I was losing the battle, my lids were just too heavy and I was losing my grip on the girls. Somehow, I lost hold of them all together and passed out.

Wide-awake, I sat up and looked around the room. The girls were no longer with me. I looked under the bed, searched behind the curtains and in the bathroom, but they were gone. The only sound in the room was the soft buzzing of the television, the sound of white noise. Were there voices in the static, too? I couldn't make out what the voices were saying but I thought I heard something, almost like a chant, repeated over and over again underneath the static hiss. I reached for the door and the room went black. The static coming from the television had changed, dropping several octaves. The rumble of deep bass rattled the speakers and shook the vase on the windowsill, sending it crashing to the floor. I turned and looked at the television, the screen had gone from white to black static. I reached for the door… "Marcus!" The voice rumbled through the speakers.

I turned and saw myself on the television, the girls sat on his lap as he stroked their hair and spoke. "Don't worry," he said. "I'll take good care of them. Raise them as my own. Teach them as they *should* have been taught from the beginning." The other me smiled and looked down at Tara.

"Isn't that right sweetie?"

"Whatever you say, dad," the child responded sarcastically.

My twin looked back up at the camera and spoke. "We're waiting for you, *daddy*, come and find us." Glass and sparks flew everywhere as the screen of the television blew out. I pulled the IV from my arm and ran out the door.

The hallway was deserted. There were no patients in the rooms and no nurses at their stations. Where to go now? The elevator dinged and the door opened. I climbed aboard and pressed the button for the lobby. The doors closed and the elevator began to move up. I heard music coming from a speaker somewhere. It sounded distorted, like a cassette tape being eaten while played. The Elevator stopped on the top floor and the doors opened into yet another deserted hallway. I searched every room, finding them all empty, until I came to a door with an electronic lock requiring a key card, which I did not have. A small bank of LED's on the lock changed from red to green and the door clicked open. Someone had opened the door, but who? I looked around and saw no one. I entered the hall and spotted a door to my right with a blank plaque and a sliding shutter that, when opened, revealed a window. The first three rooms were empty, but when I reached the door to the fourth, there was a name on the plaque. It read *Jacob Chant*. I slid the shutter back to find the window streaked with bloody handprints. It was so covered in blood that the figure moving inside the room was only a shadow, but still, he must have seen me. The man lunged for the door, his hand on the glass further smearing the blood. When the man used the sleeve of his shirt to clean some of the blood away, I saw his face and the source of the blood. "It's in the eyes!" he screamed over and over. "It's in the eyes!"

I saw then that his eyes had been gouged out, as if he had dug them with his own fingers, and in the process, taken out large chunks of flesh around his eye sockets.

"They know where I am!" The man screamed. "They see through your eyes!"

Right in front of me, the crazy bastard jammed two fingers into his left eye socket, up into his brain, and he fell dead to the floor.

The next two rooms I peered into were empty but the third had a name on the door. The plaque read *Marcus Quincy*. I pulled back the shutter and saw nothing but blackness. For a moment, I thought the window might have been painted black, until I saw something move inside. All of the rooms I had seen so far were the same size, approximately ten by ten, but what I saw moving in that room was much further back, swimming through the darkness like some alien eel. It reminded me of what I'd seen in the abyss in Shadow Lake but much, much bigger. I put my forehead to the window and blocked out what light I could with my hands, scanning the darkness within.

Something hit the door hard, shoving me backward across the hallway. There was a flash of white as my skull hit the wall like a melon hitting pavement. I slid down the wall and sat, too stunned to think. I looked up at the door, surprised to see it still intact, and saw a face I recognized staring at me through the glass. There were many more heads this time, so it took the creature a little longer to form into one being. I wasn't sure if this was even the same nightmare I had met in Shadow Lake, but it was most *definitely* a member of the same species... the Mille Umbra. It watched me with its empty eye sockets and smiled, its razor sharp teeth, which seemed to grow out of the shadows making up the creatures mouth, glistening in the light from the hallway. ***"They are my soulssss, Marcussss,"*** the Umbra hissed.

The creature had claws to match its teeth, claws it was using to etch something into the glass.

"Who are you?" I screamed. The Umbra said nothing. When it had finished, the creature looked up at me with a hideously deformed smile on its many faces. The creature had carved three letters into the glass. ***"Yesss,"*** the Umbra hissed. ***"I am Iraaa..."***

"Enough small talk, where are my girls?" I demanded.

The creatures face began to come undone, twitching and shifting until its shadowy forms were set free. "How do I find them?" I screamed.

"This is not your dream, Marcussss." The Umbra retreated into the darkness and stopped, looked over its many shoulders, and said, **"You are in himmmm and heee isssss in yoooou."** I watched through the window until the figure was no longer in sight. What did it mean? Then it hit me... I was in my *other's* dream. And that would mean that he was...

My body jolted and I awoke to find my hands around my daughter Tori's neck. Tara screamed as three rather large men rushed past her and dove for the bed. They were trying to pull my arms back as a nurse desperately attempted to pry my hands loose from my baby girl's throat. I relaxed my muscles and let the men take control of me. I knew that it was not *me* hurting my daughter. I *knew* that! But my beautiful Tori... *she* did not. How could I expect my seven year old daughter to comprehend what even *I* had difficulty understanding? I saw the look of pure terror in her eyes, damning me, *begging* me to stop. I saw all of this in her eyes in the first moments I was back in my reality. The thought of what happened that day still pisses me off and hurts like hell at the same time. There was a moment when I first returned to my reality, before my mind had time to comprehend what was happening, that it *was* me choking my daughter. I will *never* forgive myself for that. And for Tori to have to live her life thinking that her own father would do something like that to a child he is supposed to love unconditionally... For *that* alone, that *bastard* me would pay!

I felt a sharp pain in my arm as someone injected me with some sort of drug. Whatever it was it worked fast. My body went numb and my vision faded to black. When I emerged from the drugs I was in a darkened room, the straps once more tying me down to the bed. The room was too dark to see anything and all I could hear was the clock ticking away on the far wall. How long had I been out? Was I even awake? I had learned by then to ask myself that question often. I heard a noise from somewhere in the room, was it a cough? "Who's there?" I croaked. My query was answered with a whimper and a sob.

"Anna?" I pleaded, "Is that you?"

"How *could* you?" It was Anna's voice all right, full of hurt and outrage. I didn't know where to start so I chose to tell her everything then, about the visions of the dark woman, about Elizabeth Patton's journal and the multiverse. I even told her of the Ma Hua Ra, of the battle between Good and Evil, balance and Chaos. Then I had to explain to her about me, about Good Marcus and Bad Marcus. I finished my story with God and what I knew at that point of my part in the Divine Plan.

"I love you with everything that I am, Anna! *Please* believe what I'm telling you! I'm doing this for *you*… for you and the girls. *Everything* is for you and the girls!"

I'd laid myself bare to my wife, as I should have done years ago when all of this started, and waited for her response to my pleadings. The foundations of all that I had known and built suddenly came crashing down around me. The invisible clock of time ticked away, my head throbbing with every move of the second hand. Finally, Anna got up and opened the door.

"I *hate* you," she whispered, and then she was gone.

I thought of nothing but Anna for the rest of the night. I relived our encounters as children and our courtship as adults, our wedding and the births of or children. Throughout the night, the doctors and nurses came and went, each face as unfamiliar as the last. Nothing mattered to me anymore. Not the world or the people in it. Not God or Chaos or even the annihilation of all reality. Nothing mattered at that very moment but my family. I had just hurt, no make that *devastated,* all of the people I loved the most. Why did I always wait so damned long to do the right thing? Out of fear I had hidden the truth from my wife. That mistake had caused the outcome I had been so afraid of. Why hadn't I seen this in time?

I actually slept that night. There were no dreams, no visions, as if my mind had been wiped clean. I awoke the next morning to the blinding glare of the rising sun. I was still strapped to the bed and could do nothing but close my eyes to block out the glare. I felt around for the controller with my hand and my finger caught the cord. I pushed the button on top and waited.

"What kind of rat bastard puts a bed in front of a window facing east?" I growled as the door opened.

"Oh, that would be Mrs. Catherine." The nurse spoke with a thick southern drawl. "You remember, the nurse whose jaw you broke?"

"Guess I deserve it," I said with grudging embarrassment. "Could you at least close the blinds?"

"Sure thing, Mr. Quincy." The nurse strolled over to the window and fumbled with the cord until the blinds rolled down hard, landing on the windowsill with a metallic clank.

"Sorry 'bout that hun, but now that you're awake, the doctor will be in to see you soon."

She placed my chart on the door and left.

The television hummed in the background. It was on one of the news channels, CNN or Fox, my vision still too blurry from the drugs to make out the call sign. A female reporter was standing in a cemetery in the middle of a downpour, the rain coming down so hard it looked like the umbrella she was holding above her head might collapse at any given moment. There was a news ticker on the bottom of the screen, no doubt informing the public where this was taking place, but I could no more read that than the call sign. I still had the controller in my hand so I turned the volume up.

"*...The groundskeeper heard a sound and went to investigate. What he found was this sinkhole here behind me...*" The camera moved to the right, showing a small sink hole approximately six feet wide. The camera, equipped with a light, peered down into the hole, showing nothing but blackness. I couldn't help but be reminded of the abyss of my dreams; the hole looked like a smaller version of the pit in Shadow Lake. The image changed to a rugged looking man in his mid to late sixties. He had a long white beard and wore his hair, which was even longer, in a ponytail. He looked like he had just climbed out of a lake; his face, hair, and clothes were soaking wet and covered in mud. The reporter pointed her microphone at the man who said in a garbled Southern accent *"...I's heard a sucking sound acomin' from outs in the yard, so I's decided to investergate. That's when I comed across that hole over yonder. Weirdest thing I ever did seen."* The image cut back to the reporter, who was now under the shelter of a nearby tent as she continued her narrative. *"Some time this week excavation teams will be out here to try and recover the body of Elizabeth Patton who died back in 2005 under mysterious circumstances..."*

Someone took the remote from my hand and switched off the TV. I looked up to find my family physician, Dr. Bruce Spencer, standing over the bed. He flipped through my chart; reading the things that only doctor's and nurses seem to understand. "It's good to see a familiar face," I said.

"I have you set up for another MRI this morning, Marcus, and then we're going to move you somewhere a little better equipped to deal with your condition."

"And what exactly *is* my condition?" I asked.

"That, my friend," Dr. Spencer put his hand on my shoulder, "is the question of the day. Now all we need to do is find the answer."

"I don't think you're going to like what you find," I said.

"Maybe not, but I hope I can help you accept the outcome, Marcus, whatever it may be. They'll be right in to take you down for your MRI." He placed the chart back on the door and left.

What could the dark forces possibly want with the body of Elizabeth Patton? That question worked its way through my brain as two nurses came in. They injected my IV with some more drugs, and then went to work on getting my bed ready to move. The questions inside my head were building. How could I stay one step ahead of the forces working against me when they knew everything that I knew? My anxiety was starting to go through the roof and my tics were getting harder for me to control. The hospital went by in a blur as I was wheeled down the brightly lit hallways. My thoughts again turned to Anna and the girls. What was happening to them?

I tried tuning into one of the tones buzzing around in my brain but there was too much noise in my head. The drugs hit hard, and I lost track of where I was supposed to be. I might have been in an elevator for a while, but when the drug haze settled in I found myself in another room. Whoever had brought me there was gone or out of my line of sight. I heard movement from the other side of the room but my body was numb from the drugs and I could barely move my head. As my gaze fell upon the cot on the other side of the room, the man reclined on it sat up. I saw his face and recognized him as he looked at me and smiled and said, "It's in the eyes." The last time I had seen his face it had been covered in blood and void of eyes and… in my visions! My head moved more freely now and I could see the entire wall, as well as the man in the bed that had just spoken to me. I looked at the mirror on the wall and the reflection in it, there was no one in the room but me. Was this just another vision, was that even *me* in the mirror? My bed began to move once more and I was in the new room. One of the technicians slid me into the MRI, things were better inside the machine, the soft humming soothed my head that time. I was completely relaxed until someone yelled, "There is *nothing* wrong with it!"

I was taken to a new part of the hospital at some point. My straps were removed and I was left alone. I could not see the clock in the room but I could hear the damn thing ticking. It was like someone hitting me on the head with a hammer every time the second hand moved, and it ticked 1,800 times before I was able to get up out of bed and pull the damn thing off the wall.

"What are you doing?" a nurse I didn't recognize asked as she entered the room.

I had forgotten I was on a new floor, that these people didn't know me.

"Sorry," I said. "My head is killing me and the clock was driving me crazy."

The nurse retrieved the clock from my hand and placed it back up on the wall.

"Now, get back in bed and I'll get you something for your headache," she said and then left.

I climbed back into bed, my thoughts returning to Elizabeth Patton. I hadn't even noticed the nurse return until the needle was in my arm. She said something to me but I ignored her and she left. I was still focused on Elizabeth. What were those sick fucks doing with her body right now? My mind ran wild, and let me tell you, I have a sick, *sick* mind. The door opened again; can't these bastards leave *anyone* alone? Dr. Spencer walked in and took a seat in the chair next to my bed.

Several years ago, Anna had struck up a friendship with her then new office mate, Lori, who just happened to have a husband who was a doctor. The doctor was also a pretty good guy. Before the girls were born, Ann and I had spent the occasional weekend exploring the Outer Banks of North Carolina with Bruce and Lori in the good doctor's boat. We maintained a pretty good friendship until two years ago, when Lori was diagnosed with an inoperable tumor. Lori had handled the news well, however, Bruce did not. How could he? Bruce had said he couldn't stand going to work any longer, that he was tired of making other people healthy, while he could do nothing but watch as the woman he loved withered away. Anna and I didn't see Bruce for six months after the funeral. He'd told us that he and Ashley, his and Lori's daughter who was two years older than the twins, were going up north to spend some time with family. They eventually came back, and Bruce opened up the doors to a new office, but he was never the same after Lori died. We'd still talked, and occasionally went out for dinner, but it had been hard to get Bruce motivated to do something other than work.

"I'm glad you're here, Bruce," I said sincerely. "These other doctors can't seem to figure out what's wrong with me."

"What makes you so sure that I can?" Dr. Spencer asked with a smile. "Look, Marcus, to tell you the truth, I'm at a loss. We're *all* at a loss. Listen, my brother's coming down here for vacation, he'll be in this weekend, and I want you to talk to him."

Bruce's brother, Andrew, was a highly respected psychiatrist with a private practice in upstate New York.

"I take it you've talked to Anna." I said.

"Have you been having these delusions long?" he asked me.

I thought about protesting; after all, my *sanity* was in question. But seeing as how I was hospitalized because the powers that be thought that I'd tried to kill my daughter, I figured it was best for all involved to just keep my mouth shut and play along.

"For a couple of years," I said. "So tell me, Bruce, what did the head scans show?"

"They were..." the doctor paused, searching for the right word. "Inconclusive."

"*All* of them?" I shouted. I shouldn't have pushed Dr. Spencer; I could tell he was getting irritated, maybe because he was out of explanations, or maybe because he didn't have any to begin with.

"We'll figure this out." Dr. Spencer stood and turned for the door. "I'll stop by to check on you later. And *please* consider talking to Andrew." I told Bruce that I would, and he left.

LETTING GO

Just after lunch they let me out to mingle with the other patients in the "activity room". Most were so doped up they weren't any good for conversation, while others would gladly talk... and talk... about nothing mostly, trivial thoughts, obsessions and crazed ranting seemed to be the topics of the day. There was one man who stood out as not quite as crazy as the rest of the patients. He sat by himself in a corner of the room where even the sunlight wouldn't go. He knew I was watching him but he pretended not to notice. The man had an intense look on his face and he was completely engrossed in what his eyes were studying, which appeared to be the floor. Every now and then he would glance up and scan the room. What was he looking for? The man's eyes met mine and he motioned with his head that it was safe for me to come closer, inviting me to join him. "I'm Marcus," I said as I approached.

"Hunter," the man replied. He motioned for me to take a seat in one of the empty chairs and, as I approached, I saw what he had been glaring at so absorbedly. His eyes had not been cast on the floor as I initially suspected, but upon a book sitting on his lap, although how he was reading it in the dark I did not know. Hunter closed the book without marking the page and sat back in his chair.

"What you in for?" he asked.

"Psychotic behavior and schizophrenic visions, you?"

"Pretty much the same thing," Hunter replied with a chuckle. His smile faded when the door opened and two individuals in uniforms entered. The pair consisted of a man in his mid fifties who had Admiral's bars and a younger woman with short blond hair and insignias that I couldn't readily identify.

"Who are they?" I asked.

"Old friends," Hunter said as we both stood. He inhaled deeply. "I *smell* them on you!" he screamed as he lunged for me. "Who sent you?" Hunter's hands were on my neck. The other patients rushed around the room yelling. "Who sent you?" Hunter demanded again.

Two large men in hospital attire rushed over to pry him off of me. Hunter was still screaming at me as they dragged him off down the hall and through the doors. "Which one was it? Which one sent you?"

After Hunter was taken away, I reached down and picked up the book he had been reading from. It had fallen face down on the floor when he dropped it to grab my throat. The book was bound in black leather with gold writing that read New Testament. I stuffed the book in my pocket and approached the Admiral, who was arguing with a nurse on the far side of the room.

"It was him you were here to see, wasn't it?" I asked. "Hunter?"

"I never forget a face, Mr.?" The Admiral waited patiently for my response.

"Quincy, Marcus Quincy, and you are?" I offered him my hand.

"Admiral Forsythe." He took my hand and shook it, applying just a little too much pressure.

"As I was saying, Mr. Quincy, I never forget a face, and I've seen yours before. Are you an acquaintance of Mr. Hunter's?" Although we had finished with the obligatory handshake, the Admiral still held my hand gripped tightly in his, no doubt trying to show his superiority.

"Sorry, just got here today. This is my first time out amongst the general population. Insanity *is* rather underrated; you should try it sometime," I remarked sarcastically. "So are we done holding hands then?"

"For now," The man said as he let go of my hand and turned to continue arguing with the nurses.

I walked rudely in between the Admiral and the charge nurse. Her ID read Nurse Garland; she had been receiving the brunt of the Admiral's verbal assault. "Can I go back to my room now?" I asked.

She turned to me and smiled. "Sure, Mr. Quincy." She took my arm and led me off down the hall and through the doors. She thanked me for rescuing her before leaving me alone in my room. I pulled Hunter's bible out from my pocket and opened it. In faded ink, the words "To Thomas, Love Mom," were written inside the cover.

I skimmed through the pages of what appeared to be a standard version of the New Testament, finding nothing out of the ordinary. As I was about to close the book the power went out and an alarm blared throughout the hallways of the hospital. In the seconds before the emergency power kicked in I saw the pages of the book change. On the darkened pages there were passages written in glowing red ink. Symbols that I did not recognize, written in a language I did not know. When the lights came back on, the pages in the book returned to normal. I later found out that Thomas Hunter had made his escape during the power failure, killing five members of the hospital staff in a needless spree of violence. What did he know, and who did he think he could smell on me?

I closed the blinds and pulled the curtain shut before turning out the light and opening the book I'd tucked under my pillow. It was too dark to read, but I could still make out some of the passages. I needed more darkness so I stepped into the bathroom and closed the door. I opened the book, not sure what I would find, but there they were. The glowing symbols filled the pages and I got to see them more clearly this time. One by one, each symbol randomly shifted its position on the page, but the number of symbols that made up a word always remained the same.

I heard a knock on the bathroom door. "Marcus, are you in there?" It was Dr. Spencer.

"Yeah, I'll be out in a sec."

I flushed the toilet and opened the door. Bruce stood at the window looking out over the parking lot; he'd opened the blinds but had not turned on the light. I slipped the book under my pillow and sat down on the bed. "I talked to Andrew," he said without turning to face me. "He wants to see you tomorrow morning."

"Tomorrow's fine," I responded, and then asked, "What do you know about Thomas Hunter?"

Bruce looked me in the eyes for the first time. "You know I can't tell you anything, Marcus, and even if I could, you wouldn't be happy with what little I know." Dr. Spencer sighed and placed his hand on my shoulder. "I'll talk to you tomorrow," he said. The doctor held his hand there for a moment longer and then turned and left the room.

I spent the rest of the afternoon watching TV and praying for Anna to call or stop in, but she never did. The nurses came and went, the faces changed, the programs on the television changed. The only things that remained the same were the almost incoherent thoughts racing around in my head. I didn't care what time it was, or even what day. I just wanted it all to stop, the beeping of the monitors, the beating of my heart. The only thing I didn't mind was the constant flow of some really good drugs that were making it incredibly hard for me to think. This was a *good* thing, for the thoughts in my head were not ones I wanted to have, in fact, they weren't even mine. But whose thoughts were they? It was also about this time that I noticed the dots behind my eyes were becoming visible on a full time basis, not just when I was having a vision or trying my hand at "tuning." They were *always* there, day *and* night, closing in on me, beginning to obscure my physical vision.

I heard the nurse talking to someone outside my door. "Sorry, visiting hours are over," she said. I couldn't hear the rest of the conversation but it sounded like I had a visitor.

"Hello, Marcus," the man said as he opened the door, walked across the room, and took a seat in the chair next to my bed. It was the Admiral, no longer in uniform, but still no less imposing.

"I told you I never forget a face," the Admiral said to me as he handed me a photograph. "It was taken just outside Los Alamos, New Mexico on the morning of July 16th, 1945," he said. I looked at the grainy black and white photo. It showed a group of soldiers posing in front of a large steel tower that was surrounded by sand in all directions. There were twelve men in the photograph, seven standing and five kneeling, I scanned the faces and was amazed to find two solders that I recognized. One of the men in the back row showed striking similarities to the Admiral, a close relative no doubt, and the other solder... the second solder from the right in the front row... looked just like *me*!

I handed the photo back to the Admiral and said nothing, but the thoughts came fast and furious. Was that me in the picture or was it my evil twin? Could it be another me entirely? And what did the Admiral think of this? Did he think the man in the picture was a relative, or did he think it was me, even though the photo had been taken over sixty years ago and the man in the picture looked just as I did today? The Admiral placed the photo into his shirt pocket and sat back in the chair. I decided I would use this situation to try and find some answers to the questions running around aimlessly within my head.

"Tell me about Thomas Hunter," I said. Admiral Forsythe looked at me long and hard before replying.

"If that's the way you want to play," he said. "I took Mr. Hunter under my wing several years ago, thinking I could exploit his talents."

"And what might those be?" I asked.

"Let's just say he knew things," Admiral Forsythe grudgingly stated.

"I can live with that answer, but tell me, if he's so important to you then why was he *here* instead of a military facility?" I asked.

"Thomas Hunter is not a man who can be held in captivity very easily or for very long, as you have witnessed."

"Then how did you get him in here?" I questioned.

"I didn't put him here," he said. "This was a voluntary commitment."

"Then he could have left at any time?" I asked. He nodded and that told me something very important about the man named Thomas Hunter. "If he could have left at any time, then why did he kill five people escaping from here?"

"Murder is in his blood," the Admiral replied, which told me something important about the Admiral as well. How could he let a man he knew was capable of such acts roam freely? He seemed to sense my question and gave me an answer before I could voice my thoughts.

"I can no more control Mr. Hunter than you can control the delusions in your head. I've read your file, Marcus; you and Mr. Hunter have much more in common than you think."

"What do *you* know about my delusions?" I demanded. "And how the hell did you get a hold of my file?" Admiral Forsythe ignored my questions.

"We are all pawns in a game on a cosmic scale, Mr. Quincy. I have spent my life looking for a way to win at this game; unfortunately, I haven't even figured out most of the rules. Time is running short. Something is about to happen that will change all of our lives forever. Perhaps it is *you* that can shed some light on this for *me*."

"I'm not quite sure what you're talking about," I said.

"Maybe not at this moment, but you soon will. And I hope you can find it in your heart to keep me informed on what you have learned. I do not yet know the significance of this," the Admiral patted the photo in his pocket with the palm of his hand, "and I am now quite sure that you also know nothing of this. What I must do now is wait and see which side you chose to play for. Make your choices wisely, Mr. Quincy, and remember, you have friends if you chose to acknowledge them." The Admiral got up and left without saying another word.

It was well after ten o'clock on that night when I picked up the phone and called my house, only to hear my own voice talking to me from the answering machine. I could hear the girls playing in the background and I missed my life even more. The life I had before the dreams, before the visions, before Ma Hua Ra. I hung up the phone wondering where my family could be at that hour, almost afraid to hope that they were on their way to see me. I remembered the nurse's, "Sorry, visiting hours are over," comment to the Admiral and knew that I wasn't going to see my family that night. I switched off the television and closed my eyes. The ringing in my head was loud that night, louder than I had ever remembered it being. I tried to tune into a single tone but it was no use, as I wasn't able to clear my head of thoughts long enough to catch one. I suspect that it was the drugs fogging my mind but maybe not. At least I had the images behind my eyelids, and the patterns. It wasn't long before sleep overtook me and I began to dream.

I stood on a cliff overlooking the ocean. The sound of the surf crashed against the rocks below, filling the night air. There was a steady breeze coming in off of the sea, blowing back my hair and whistling through the rocks as it made its way up the face of the cliff. When the wind died down, the whistling remained. I knelt down at the edge of the cliff and scanned the rocks below, spying several caves high above the ocean. One opening was only about twenty feet from the top of the outcropping. I examined the rocky ledge, decided it was worth the risk, and began to climb down to the mouth of the cave. When I reached the opening I'd seen from above, the whistling stopped, and I was left with nothing but the darkness to guide me.

Without thinking, I reached out in front of me and opened my hand, palm up and out. The cave instantly filled with light that had radiated from my palm and out through my fingertips! "That's a new one," I mumbled aloud. Further back in the cave, I saw two passageways leading off in different directions. I closed my palm, extinguishing the light in my hand and walked forward, letting fate choose my path. I walked until I heard the crackling of leaves and tinder engulfed in flames and I saw a faint flickering of light on the walls of the cave ahead. As I approached, I saw that the cave had another entrance, and what I saw outside the cave surprised me. Sitting in front of a fire was the blind old man from my dreams. He was writing with some sort of quill in a small leather book. "Hello, Marcus," the man greeted me, but when he spoke it was not with one voice. I stepped out into the night air and saw four additional men sitting around the fire. The men were *identical* in every way, and all were writing in their own books. "Sit, Marcus," they said, and motioned for me to take a seat beside them in unison. I took a place beside the old man I had first seen from inside the cave. The pages of his book, as well as the others, were filled with the glowing red symbols of Thomas Hunter's Bible. I have to admit it was a little strange to see a symbol that had just been written instantly move to another location on the page.

"What language is it?" I asked.

"It is the Divine Language," they answered.

"Why do the symbols move?"

"Do they?" The five asked. The old man I'd seen in my travels before followed up with, "You will understand what is written in time."

"How will I make the symbols stop moving?" I queried.

"You must name the book," the old man said before returning to the writing of his tome. Before I could say another word, the nausea and the spinning told me that the conversation, as well as the dream, was over.

I awoke in the darkness of the hospital room. The light from a distant streetlamp filtered in through the blinds. I got out of bed, reached under the pillow and pulled out Thomas Hunter's Bible. As before, in the light, the book was a perfectly ordinary Bible. I closed the blinds on the window, sat down on the bed, and opened the book. The room was instantly illuminated by the soft red glow of the symbols, the Divine Language. The old man had told me to name the book, but I knew little about Thomas Hunter, so I took my time studying each image before turning my attention to cracking the code. The symbols were grouped together almost like words, but there were no sentences, no paragraphs. There was no punctuation whatsoever, just groups of words. I looked for common symbols, but there were an endless variety of images, and far too many symbols for any alphabet I could comprehend. There was no way for me to crack this code, but there *was* something compelling in the images. There was a pattern, a single symbol, followed by two more. The next grouping was made up of three symbols, the next of four, and so on. The last grouping was nine symbols long, and then the pattern repeated itself. I was about to give up and close the book when I got out of bed and stepped on something. What I picked up was a thick black magic marker, the permanent kind that gives you a good buzz when you open the cap. I didn't care how it got there but I instinctively knew what I must use it for. I started on the upper left corner of the wall with the window overlooking the parking lot, and began to draw each symbol to find out just how many there were.

Moonlight turned to twilight and slowly the bright red symbols on the pages of the book began to fade. I had covered all four walls of the room with the symbols, and had even written on the floor and ceiling, on every piece of equipment, the clock on the wall, the curtains and blinds, even the sheets on the bed. When the sun began to rise and the room had begun to lighten, I took the book with me into the bathroom to continue sketching the images. When I was finished, there was only room for one more symbol on the bathroom mirror. I gazed into my own reflection looking back at me through the empty space.

I heard someone moving around on the other side of the bathroom door. The shocked nurse stared at me as I stepped out. I'm not sure if it was the symbols or my nakedness that drove her off, but the nurse darted out of the room. I put on my robe and sat on the bed waiting to see what would happen next. As I'd suspected, the goon squad burst through the door and hauled me off down the hall. The bastards filled me with even more drugs and one of them gave me a cheap shot to the ribs. I lost all control of my legs from the drugs. The men had given up trying to carry me, as they started dragging me down the hall by my arms. The goon patrol took me through a door with an electronic lock and down a hallway. I had been there before, sort of. As they dragged me down the hall I saw the familiar shutters and plaques on the doors. One of the assholes slid a card on a door that had my name on it. The door opened and I was pushed inside, left to lay helpless on the floor in a puddle of my own drool.

When I regained consciousness it was to the sound of someone snapping his fingers, an orderly, trying to bring me around. My vision was blurry from the dots, so bad that it was hard to focus on the room with them swimming in front of my eyes. I was in an *"I love me"* jacket, sitting in a chair in front of a large particle-board table, the kind you set up outside for a family gathering. The table divided the small room in half, stretching across and touching both of the otherwise empty walls. I was blocked in on one side of the room, with my ankles cuffed and chained to a large eyebolt that stuck up out of the floor. Once he was sure that I was awake, the orderly exited through the door, leaving me staring at myself in a large mirror that covered the far wall. A mirror that I knew allowed someone to watch back from the other side.

A door slammed shut somewhere nearby and the door to my room opened.

"Hello, Marcus; it's good to see you again, though I wish it could be under better circumstances."

Andrew Spencer, brother to my family doctor, shrink extraordinaire, walked across the floor and took the empty chair on the other side of the table. He placed a large bundle of files and papers down in front of him. "You look remarkably awake for the amount of drugs they've pumped into you, not to mention the lack of sleep. I've looked over your handy work, Mr. Quincy. You were *very* busy last night."

He took out Thomas Hunter's Bible and placed it on the table next to the folders.

"This does not belong to you. The staff says it belonged to one Thomas R. Hunter."

"Yeah," I said. "He dropped it when he attacked me; I never got a chance to give it back."

Andrew Spencer sat up straight in his chair and pulled the book back with his hand, sliding it off the table and into his coat pocket. "I've spoken to your wife and children," he said. "Beautiful little girls by the way; no doubt there are wondrous things ahead for them." He was trying to get me to react; I just sat there. "I've also heard what your doctors, my brother included, have to say. Now it's *your* turn, Marcus. Tell me what *you* think is happening to you."

I thought to myself, *what the fuck, what do I have to lose?* I'd been instructed by Ma Hua Ra to find a place to hide my body and the psych ward was as good a place as any. Besides, something inside told me I needed to tell my story one more time.

I spoke of God and Chaos, Ma Hua Ra and the Mille Umbra, and even about my evil twin. Dr. Spencer sat there digesting it all with a look on his face that was impossible to read. Then I told him what was to come, about the Tree of Knowledge and the Divine Engine, and the choice I had made. He smiled when I finished my story, but said nothing, making me wonder what he was thinking. Probably something like "this is the most fucked up person I have *ever* met!" Dr. Spencer did nothing but smile as he pushed the stack of folders across the table. "What's this?" I asked.

"Your head scans," the doctor said. "Go on, take a look."

He pulled out the first image and I couldn't believe my eyes. It was my most recent MRI, a view down through the top of my skull. Starting at the center of my brain and radiating outward to my frontal lobe was a bright white spiral. Andrew flipped through the rest of the images and I saw they were all the same.

"What does this mean?" I asked.

"The beginning of something wonderful!" the doctor responded with a smile. Did he always smile?

"Who are you?" I then asked.

Andrew leaned forward, pulled back the stack of folders in front of him, and stood up. He picked the bundle up and raised them into the air, then let the files go. The film folders only made it halfway down before being caught by some invisible web, where they hung motionless above the table.

"You have used this power before," Andrew said. "I can feel it in you."

Dr. Spencer was right. It was *I* who had stopped time after the slaughter of my teenage self. I just didn't know how I'd managed it. Dr. Spencer sat back down in his chair as the folders hovered just above our line of sight. "My true name is Animus," he finally said. "I am Mille Umbra."

I pushed back against the wall, falling out of my chair when the chain on my leg pulled tight.

"Relax, Marcus," Dr. Spencer chuckled. "I will not harm you. While in this body my true self cannot emerge. I have *some* power, but not much. It seemed a fair trade at the time in order to lead a normal life."

I relaxed and listened as he told his story.

"After I was banished, there was nothing to do but watch. How I longed for a chance to enter the multiverse and truly live. Then I found a way. Every soul passes through a point in the Nexus that connects it to Heaven, Hell, and the multiverse. I discovered that one in my condition could 'catch a ride', so to speak, with a soul on its way to the multiverse. I was born in this body, I grew up in this body, and as far as everyone is concerned, I *am* Andrew Spencer. Born September seventh, nineteen sixty-four in North Hampton, Massachusetts to Rodger and Audrey Spencer. I have one brother, one niece, and a beautiful daughter. You see, Marcus, I am *not* your enemy. There is a reason we met, a purpose. Everything is connected in some way. I could not see it at first, but my role in this is clear now. Please, stand." Andrew stood and I did the same. He reached across the table with a hand that created its own electrical charge. Arcs of current jumped between his outstretched fingers and leapt from his fingertips as he touched my chest. "I'm sorry, Marcus," he said, "but this *must* be done."

When Dr. Spencer pulled his hand back I couldn't move. I was as frozen in time as the folders floating above the table in front of me. I could do nothing but watch and listen.

I heard a voice speaking a language I did not understand, was the voice mine? A terrible pain filled my head and worked its way down my spine and through my limbs, filling my entire body. My veins turned black and pulsed as the agonizing pain took form inside me, trying to escape. It seeped out of my pores and through my clothing in a black cloud, forming a man, another version of me. I watched as my twin stepped forward to the edge of the table and spoke.

"Animus," my twin said viciously to Dr. Spencer. "Ira is here to destroy you as promised,"

Another black form erupted from my twin's chest, it was a knee, then a leg, and a foot placed itself on the table. I watched as another black form completely emerged from the body of my twin and stood up on top of the table, towering above Andrew Spencer. This new being was a female with skin and hair as black as night; it was the dark woman of my dreams.

"I cannot lay hands on an Umbra and Ira cannot fully enter the multiverse," she said as she walked along the table, pushing the folders aside with her hand, stopping only when her toes hung over the edge on Dr. Spencer's side. She looked down on Andrew and laughed. *"It is a pity I can not kill you myself,"* she said. *"My body is only the vessel of your destruction, Animus."* When the dark woman said the creature's name, a long thin tentacle shot from her mouth and wrapped around Andrew Spencer's throat. Two more tendrils extended outward to bind his wrists. The dark woman opened her mouth wider, expelling a black mist into the air. This mist formed the familiar features of a Mille Umbra, complete with the razor filled mouth and the bottomless pits of its eye sockets. It spoke.

"Your time has come, Animussss."

"I will not fight you, Ira; I am ready to die." Andrew Spencer stated this coolly, without fear.

"I would be glad to oblige," it said as it pulled Dr. Spencer closer with its shadow tentacles.

"I have been waiting for this moment for a long time. Let me taste my sweet rewards."

Ira pulled Andrew's face closer and bit into the soft skin of the doctor's cheek. Andrew did nothing, not even scream, as the flesh was ripped from his face and spat out on the floor. ***"The meat beneath isss so much ssssweeterrrr,"*** the Umbra said, sinking its teeth into Andrew once more, tearing deeper into the doctor's face. The Umbra swallowed the meat and then went to work on Andrew's neck. Blood pumped from the wound as the artery was severed, splashing across the table, walls and floor. Andrew turned his gaze to me and smiled as I watched the last remnants of light in his eyes fade and then he was gone. Andrew's body slumped, hanging from the mouth of the beast, while the Umbra sucked out the last drops of blood before releasing its hold on the corpse. The dark woman and my twin vanished as Andrew Spencer's body fell to the floor with a thud, followed by the folders crashing to the table as time returned to normal.

The only inch of my new room not covered in padding was the small rectangle of the window on the single door. Faces peered in through the glass every now and then, but I didn't pay them much attention; besides, I couldn't make out much more than indistinct shapes; the dots had virtually blinded me by then. Being blind didn't bother me either; my mind was still going over what had happened to the doctor and to me. My *other* half had stepped right out of me, for fuck's sake! I needed to clear my mind and focus on the task at hand, but thinking was difficult. The vast quantities of drugs constantly flowing through my system had taken their toll. I could barely move under my own power, so I closed my eyes and let the patterns and visions take me wherever they may. First, I was in a building that looked like a school, and then I was outside somewhere. The next location was dark and I could smell the ocean, then everything went black.

My head went silent for the first time in a long time; I heard and saw nothing, not even the dots. I felt insignificant in the vast nothingness around me, like I was truly alone for the very first time. A sudden noise told me that my ears still worked. There was the crackle of static and then the voice of Ma Hua Ra.

"So here we are at last. Are you ready to begin, Marcus?"

I turned toward the voice but saw nothing, just blackness.

"Remember, Marcus, you do not need your eyes to see. You must simply... feel. Let your senses take over, your mind will adapt." My mind

told me that blind people do this all the time. They can simply *feel* objects near them, so why, then, had it been so difficult for me to grasp the idea of seeing without eyes? *"You must be ready to let go,"* said Ma Hua Ra. *"Focus on nothing but me."*

It was starting to work. I was beginning to feel my surroundings. I could tell where there was empty space and where Ma Hua Ra stood.

"Excellent! Focus on my voice, Marcus. When the ringing returns to your head, you will notice one tone is louder than the rest. This tone will help you find Eden. Once this task is complete you need only think of your desired destination and the proper tone will reveal itself to you."

The world around me grew brighter and I could make out a shadowy form where Ma Hua Ra stood. His form turned from black to white as color slowly returned to my world, like watching a sunrise through a rain-streaked window.

"Wonderful, Marcus, you are now free of your eyes."

"What happened?" I asked. "What *are* the dots?"

"Another defense mechanism, they are there to cover what should never be seen, truths that should never be known."

"So what happens now?" I questioned, curious as to how I was supposed to begin the task of saving the world from itself.

"Now you must find Eden and eat the fruit from the tree. Only then will you gain the knowledge to complete the Divine Engine and return balance to the multiverse. I will be there when you need me, Marcus. Now go... fulfill your destiny."

Ma Hua Ra was gone, but he'd left me a gift. As promised, the ringing had returned and one tone was much louder than the others. I focused on this new tone and prepared to enjoy the ride.

444
EDEN

FAITH

I found myself in a cemetery, bathed in a familiar glow of moonlight. This was *not* my destination, as I still had the tone ringing loudly in my head. But *something* had brought me there, so I closed my eyes and tried to shift up the hill. I felt an immense energy repelling me like the shockwave from an explosion, the concussive force pushing me from my destination. I flew backwards through the air and hit the ground hard, knocking the wind out of me. I lay in the grass for a moment to catch my breath, dazed from the impact and wondering what had just happened. I stood and stumbled up the hill and through the woods, following the sound of the old man's voice as he spoke. I silently circled the fire through the tree line located to the right of the cave and peered out through the branches. I saw then who the old man was speaking to and suddenly understood why I was unable to shift. I was already there.

"Come in, Marcus," four voices called to me from inside the cave. I slipped through the trees and the shadows to where the light from the fire could not penetrate. The four identical old men stood within the cave, listening intently to the fifth old man who was presently talking to my childhood dream-self by the fire. "It is time for your first lesson, Marcus." The four old men said in unison, mimicking the conversation going on outside.

"L-l-lesson?" The words fumbled from the lips of the child.

"Yes, my boy, I must teach you to jump strings."

"Jump *what?*" the boy asked.

"The *tones*, Marcus, you must learn to jump between the *tones*. Each point in the Nexus, be it a person or a star, is connected to all realities by a string. Most people are only connected to realities that *they* are a part of but *you*, your connection is much stronger, granting you access to every Nexus point in *every* reality." I saw the confusion on the boy's face and remembered it well. The first time I'd had this dream, the words that were spoken had made little sense, but now that I was there again, the pieces were coming together. The old man had told me to seek him out in the past if I wished to find answers, but until then, I hadn't figured out the proper questions to ask.

"While riding a string to a destination," the five old men continued, "you may need to alter course, jump to a different Nexus point, but this can only be done at the correct time on the correct tone. You must jump in time to the songs of existence."

"How am I supposed to know when *that* is?" My lips moved with the boy's.

"You must learn the music, Marcus. Music, much like the multiverse, is made up of vibrations and patterns. While jumping strings you must know where you are and where you are going at all times. Just as each Nexus point in any given reality has its own tone, each reality has its own 'song'. If you jump from a string as you tune, you *must* remain within the current destination's reality, jumping to the next tone in the song. Each reality's song consists of patterns repeated over and over again. It doesn't matter where in the pattern you jump but you *must* choose the correct timing and tone."

"So how do I learn the timing of the songs?" This was *not* the question I had asked as a child, but I was older and wiser. When the four old men answered my question, it was not the same as the conversation that continued outside.

"You will hear the songs as you tune," said the four. "The louder the tones, the closer the reality. Pay attention to the tones, Marcus, and you will know what to do." The tone given to me by Ma Hua Ra resounded within my head, pulling me from the cave on the hill. When I tuned I listened, becoming aware of the tones in the background and how they *did* form patterns. I just needed to learn how to sort them out.

When the ride was over, the string that Ma Hua Ra had given me dumped me out on a cliff overlooking an ocean. I scanned for openings in the cliffs below and found none, as I was not on the other end of the cave where I had left the five old men. I stood on the cliffs and took in my surroundings; it was nothing like using my eyes. For starters, I saw *everything*, three hundred and sixty degrees all at the same time. I saw that the world around me was dieing. I saw threadbare pine trees off in the distance, across a vast field of decay. The trees were a good mile away but I saw each individual needle as it swayed in the breeze. I saw an object shining in the distance to the north, a large copper fish sitting above two arrows, both facing south. It was a weathervane shimmering in the setting sun, mounted atop a large stone building with a single chimney. I shifted from the cliffs to an open doorway and instantly recognized my surroundings. The cold gray walls, the single window in the wall, no glass, just a hole framed with small tree branches. I listened, and before long, I heard a man sobbing from somewhere in the building.

I followed the sobs through the empty chapel to a back room, where in the corner I saw an open trap door. "Hello?" I called out as I descended into the darkness down a narrow stone staircase.

The sobbing stopped and a dark figure appeared in the doorway, holding up a large double barrel shotgun.

"Who's there?" the man demanded.

"My name is Marcus," I called out.

"Where did you come from?" The man paused as he cocked the gun and took aim. "How did you get here? You can't be here, *He* told me I was alone!"

"*Who* told you that?" I pressed.

"The Morning Star, the Prince of Lies. Did *He* send you?" the man shouted as his anger rose and his trigger finger began to twitch.

"No," I answered in a calm, even voice.

The man's anger subsided and he began to sob.

"What happened here?" I asked.

"Lucifer tried to break me," the man said, "to make me denounce my God. But I would just as soon die than deny the Lord my devotion, and the beast *knew* that. So He cursed me with a hellish plague, and I was forced to watch everyone I cared for, everyone I loved..." The priest paused for a moment to hold back the tears. "He made me watch them die!" he said. "I came here to this church in hopes that I would be far enough away that some *one,* some *thing,* could survive. But I was too late. The children and the elderly were the first to die; humanity was wiped out in a matter of months. The animals went next, and soon all of the trees, all of *life* will be gone... all but me." When the man finished speaking, his chin dropped to his chest and his shoulders slumped down dejectedly. "Come," he said, "sit with me and talk."

When the man raised his head and lowered his weapon, I saw the collar he wore around his neck. My instincts had been correct when I originally had this vision; the man *was* a priest. I followed him into a room filled with stacks of boxes lining all four walls. The boxes overflowed with ID's and driver's licenses that were piled so high they spilled out onto the floor. The priest turned to me and I saw his eyes, cold and foggy, as he was obviously blind. Still, his dead pupils seemed to follow me as I moved farther into the room. "Please, take a seat," he said, motioning toward an old wooden chair in the center of the room. "I spend far too much time in that thing as it is."

I stepped past the priest and took a seat in the chair.

"I spend every day in here praying, I pray that all of these people," the priest raised his hands to the boxes around us, "will be forgiven. I memorized most of the names in my first few years alone here, but my memory is not what it used to be."

"So tell me, father, how long has it been since you've delivered a sermon?" I asked.

A puzzled look came over his face before he answered. "Must be close to ten years now," he said as he scratched his matted gray hair. "Would you like to hear one?" he asked excitedly.

"Yes," I answered, "I would."

"How rude of me," the father said. "I have not yet introduced myself. I am Father Anderson Clark, but please, call me Andy."

"Okay, Andy," I said, "let's hear your sermon."

When Father Clark spoke, it was with the wit and grace of a man twice his age, and the passion of a man half his age. I saw before me a man with a fire burning in his belly, the fire of youth, from a time when he'd still had hope that humanity would find its way, and stop turning a blind eye to the evil that surrounds us every day. Anderson recited his sermon from heart, the words perfect and clear. Not once did his voice crack or stutter.

"Where… is… God? People come to me and they say, 'Father, how can God let there be so much evil in the world? Why does He let people starve and children die? Where was God when *this* happened? Where was God when *that* happened?' What I tell them is simple. I tell them that, if they have to ask this question in the first place, then there is another question that they need to be asking. And what is that question? That question is, simply, do you *truly* believe in God? If one doubts that God is there when things happen, then it is one's *faith* that is truly in question. For me, God is everywhere. We *must* embrace this idea, reach deep down into our souls to the place where God resides. We must pull Him up to the surface, spread Him throughout our bodies and release

Him out of our skins and into the world around us. We must believe that *we* are part of God and God is part of *everything.* We... are... all... one, yet we *strive* for individuality, often taking things to the extreme, trying to stand apart. Is that really so bad? If the body is simply a vessel, then what is wrong with sprucing it up a little bit? Absolutely nothing, but we forget... We forget that what is on the outside does not matter. The Bible says that when Adam ate from the Tree of Knowledge of Good and Evil that his eyes were opened. What did this mean? It means that Adam saw with his *eyes* and not his soul. Over the centuries, what we see with our eyes has distracted us from what we are supposed to see within ourselves, that we are all connected, that we are all one. Until we can embrace this ideology, we cannot *truly* believe in God. We must always remember that He helps those who help themselves, and He lives in those who truly believe. The good Lord put us here for a reason; who are we to judge what that reason is? My message is simple: enjoy the ride and try not to take what we see around us so seriously. It is what's on the *inside* that counts, not what everyone else thinks of us. Rather, it is all about what *we* think of *ourselves,* for this is individuality in its purest form. To be one with oneself is to be one with God." Father Clark stopped and looked at me. "Would you like me to continue?"

After everything this man had been through, without a single shred of doubt, he still believed. How could God let someone like this suffer? Father Clark was a modern day Job, a shepherd without his flock. And his punishment was eternal loneliness. "You haven't always been blind, have you?" I asked.

"I have sinned, Marcus," he answered. "When the Prince of Lies came to me as a woman and seduced me, I broke my vow to God. There is no need to ask His forgiveness. He knows what happened and that what is done is done. I refuse to question my destiny." The priest's face grew somber and he spoke in a lower tone. "I spend my days here praying, Marcus, because at night *she* comes, making me do things that should never be done... Doing things to me that..." Father Clark's voice trailed off into sobs.

"The sun is setting," I reminded him. "If that's the case, I'd rather not be around when *she* gets here."

The priest wiped his eyes and sniffled. "You are a wise man, Marcus," he chuckled, and then continued. "One morning I broke. I asked God for *one* thing. I asked Him to make me blind." Father Clark suddenly changed the subject. "Tell me, Marcus, what brings you *here* of all places?"

"You," I answered honestly. He gave me a rather strange look at first, but then his face changed.

"You've been here before, I remember now. Without my sight, some of my other senses have become a little more sensitive, perhaps part of my punishment for asking?" Sadness washed over the priest's face as the words fell from his lips. I took his hand in mine. "You'll be considered a prophet one day," I said.

"To whom?" he asked, barely able to speak through a fit of laughter.

"There are others out there to spread your wisdom," I said. "I'll help you if I can."

Father Clark's laughter quieted and he looked at me with his dead eyes, a look of puzzlement on his face. "You would do that for me?"

"Yes," I said. "But first you must tell me about Eden, the *real* Eden."

After standing for so long, the priest's legs began to buckle and he stumbled, trying to regain his balance. I reached up and took hold of his arm to steady him.

"Here, sit." I stood and helped him into the chair I had vacated.

"Thank you, Marcus." He looked up at me with his unseeing eyes. "You must not tell me what you need to know, *she* will punish me enough as it is. If you are meant to know the truth, then look into my eyes, Marcus, and take your chances." For a brief moment the priest's eyes turned clear, his irises changed from dead gray to an ice blue and his pupils dilated. In that moment, I saw everything. Father Anderson's entire life played out before me in a fraction of a second, from the first time he had opened his eyes in his mother's womb to the sermon he had just recited. I felt his pain as the world around him died, his shame as he was defiled night after night by the dark woman, and I also saw Eden. I heard three distinct tones in my head that joined to create one beautiful harmony. As soon as the tones merged I felt their pull, my body tingled and my head spun. "I must go," I said. "And I *will* find a way to help you."

Father Clark smiled. "You already have," he said, his voice fading as I tuned to the sound of Eden.

ELYSIAN FIELDS

I saw flowers of every color imaginable, like a giant canvas painted in every style, every medium. I inhaled the sweet fragrance of the fields and my body tingled when the flower's petals caressed my skin. I saw a statue of a woman in the distance, carved from one large pillar of white stone. Tucked beneath her crossed arms, the blades imbedded in the stone base at the statue's feet, was a strange sword that I had seen before. The "psycho scissors" wielded by the dark creature in the alley. The statue stood upon a pedestal, high above the vast field of flowers, and just below where sword met stone, was a plaque that read *Dionia*. For a moment, everything went fuzzy and when my vision returned, I stood in front of the statue of a female Ma Hua Ra.

"*I am Dionia, guardian of the Elysian Fields,*" the statue said as the swirling figure eights in her eyes doubled in speed. "*Only the pure may enter.*"

Well, I guess that ruled *me* out. "What do you consider pure?" I asked.

"*Come closer.*" Dionia uncrossed her arms and placed her hands on the handle of the sword, slowly pulling it loose from the stone. I was close enough that, if she'd wanted to, she could have sliced me in half before I even knew what hit me. "*You are touched, Marcus.*" She relaxed her muscles and let the blade slip into one hand. "*To be pure is to be without doubt. Do you doubt yourself, seven?*"

"Seven?" I questioned.

"Your eyes," she said. *"They tell me you have doubts about your destiny. Four trials await you, Marcus. All will be lost if you cannot empty your mind of doubt."*

"I was told that humans couldn't survive in Eden after the closing. How am I able to be here?" I asked.

"As I have said, you are touched. The blood of the Divine flows through you. Unfortunately, you may not use your power here. Lose your doubt, Marcus, or all will be lost and you will remain in the Elysian Fields forever." Dionia crossed her arms around the blade handle, once again taking the pose of the statue. *"Remember,"* she warned me before returning to stone. *"There must* always *be two."*

I listened to the "songs" in my head as I walked through the chest high field of flowers. There were far too many to try and remember every pattern and every tone, so I simply listened. After walking for some time, I saw a massive dark forest in the distance, and a path leading into the woods. I picked up my pace, and without warning, the ground below my feet began to descend. Soon the flowers were up to my neck and, before long, they were over my head. The thick canopy blocked the light, but I could still see my surroundings. I saw the stems of the flowers rising from the ground like cables attached to the world above, ridged, yet at the same time, soft and delicate. Once in a while I saw a stem vibrate for a brief moment, then it would be calm and still. The earth beneath my feet was a deep black and I left a trail of footprints in the soft, moist soil. Nothing grew there but flowers. There were no insects crawling through the earth, on the stalks or, come to think of it, none on the flowers above, either. I had traveled so far below the surface that I could no longer see the flowers above me, only the ridged stems that had towered over me like… strings? For some reason, my mind had made this connection; maybe it was because the songs still played in my head, maybe because each time I saw a stem vibrate, the vibration corresponded with a tone. I walked through the perfect rows of stems until I came to a large rock wall where the flowers simply stopped and I began to climb. I climbed until I saw something above me, something that grew out of a large crevice in the rocks. It looked like some sort of weed. When I reached the ledge, I saw that the crevice was more like a small cave, maybe teen feet wide by ten feet deep. Jagged leaves and vines grew out in all directions, but stopped just outside of the perimeter of the cave. I climbed into the opening, and there, in the center of cave, covered in giant leaves and wrapped in a rope of weeds, was a woman... a dark Ma Hua Ra. Just as Dionia had warned me, *"there must always be two"*...

The creature knew I was there but said and did nothing; it just stood and watched me. I took some time to study this creature. On the outside, she appeared to be identical to the females I had seen so far, but I could feel that she was *not* the dark woman I had encountered before. I stood so close to her that I got a good look at her eyes. Elizabeth Patton had been wrong; her eyes were not sixes, they were *nines*! Three nines, like the eights in Ma Hua Ra's and Dionia's eyes, constantly collapsing inward and reforming again. She wanted to speak, I felt that too, but she remained silent. Cautiously, I walked forward, expecting something to happen. I knew what these creatures were capable of and deceit was definitely among their repertoire.

The vines that bound the dark woman grew out of the ground and wove themselves tightly around her legs, crawling up her belly to her breasts, pinning her arms to her side. I saw why she did not speak; one of the vines had made its way into her mouth and down her throat. Her eyes followed my every move, but the look in them had changed. Was it panic or fear? When I had looked into the priest's eyes, I had watched his life play out before me, but with the dark woman, there was nothing. Nothing but the swirling nines. The last time I had been in the presence of the dark woman I had been afraid, but not this time. This was most certainly *not* the same creature I had encountered in the past, just as the statue of the white woman was not the Ma Hua Ra who had offered me guidance.

I reached up and took hold of the vine that had invaded the dark woman's mouth and tried to pull it out. It was no use; the vine seemed to have wrapped itself around something inside of her. A stream of black liquid trickled down the creature's chin and her face twisted in pain as I tugged one last time before letting go. She bit down, grinding her teeth until the vine gave, and swallowed.

"We... have known you, Marcus," the creature said.

"And who are *we*?" I asked.

"The Ah Me Ra," she smiled. *"It's been a long time since that name has been uttered here."* The dark woman closed her eyes and inhaled deeply.

"Ah Me Ra," I said the words aloud, as if trying it out. "What does it mean?"

"It means the Voice of Chaos, Marcus. It sounds familiar, doesn't it? We are the tones in your head, the Ah Me Ra and the others."

"Others?" Was she talking about the other dark woman? "Who is she?" The creature knew of whom I was speaking, that much was apparent, but she stayed silent. Already, the vine was inching its way slowly toward her mouth. She pushed at it with her chin a few times before giving up and turning her head to the side.

"Lilith," she mumbled through the vine as it slid over her tongue. *"Are you familiar with the story?"*

"Yes, Adam's first wife. But I thought Lilith was human?"

"You shouldn't... believe... everything... you read." The thick vine had succeeded in finding her mouth once more; it crawled down her throat and into her stomach, leaving her without a voice. She ground her teeth into it again and swallowed. *"Lilith was the first, and you're going to love this, Marcus, the true name of Adam is* Ma Hua Ra... *The Voice of God."*

The dark woman laughed as the vines crawled up my legs, wrapping themselves every which way. Her laughter was soon muffled as the vines found her lips and parted them, her throat penetrated and defiled once more. I pulled at the vines on my legs, but they were too strong and I could not break free. A million thoughts clouded my mind. The dark woman, Lilith, was Ma Hua Ra's *wife*? Have I been lied to? Was I just a pawn in a game much larger than I had been aware of? Why had Ma Hua Ra not told me these things, and more importantly, were the words of this woman even true? Dionia had warned me of my doubts. The vines continued to creep up my chest, panic was beginning to set in and my senses started to fail. The vines reached my face, covered my mouth, nose and eyes, and all I could do was listen to the muffled laughter of the dark woman as the blackness overtook me.

A startled cry and a sudden sharp pain in my hand replaced the laughter and then black turned to white. "Marcus Quincy, *stop* making that noise this instant!" Whack… another sharp pain.

I saw the Sister standing before me, waving the yardstick in my face as she spoke.

"I said *stop*! The devil has a hold on you, young man! You can make that noise all you want while you rot in Hell but *not* in my classroom!" I could not move my limbs to stop the nun from doing what came next. Her free hand sliced through air, slapping me hard on the face. I couldn't move my head, but I didn't need to; I saw the children in the desks behind me as they laughed and mocked me. The Sister reached up, grabbed my ear between her fingers and yanked me out of my seat. Books fell to the floor with a thud and papers scattered about, a pencil rolled under the Sister's foot and she stopped to grind it beneath her heel. All of the children laughed as she pushed me out into the hallway. "Get out of my class room, you rotten little turd. Go see Father Matthews right this instant!" She slammed the door and I stood there for a few moments, listening to the bitch as she tried to quiet the class. I turned and walked down the hall, listening to my shiny brown shoes clack on the marble floor and echo across the brick walls. I was about six or seven years old, first or second grade, I couldn't remember clearly. I did, however, remember the way to Father Mathews' office.

I knocked on the door and waited for a reply. "Come in," he called out, followed by a hoarse cough. I opened the door to a room filled with smoke. Father Mathews sat in a large chair behind a larger oak desk, his huge ass wedged tightly between the armrests. He must have weighed about two hundred and fifty pounds, and everything he did he did slowly, every movement leaving him winded and breathless. Too much food, too much booze, and too many cigars had turned a forty eight year old man into a walking time bomb. He looked nearly twice his age; his gray hair had already receded to the top of his head, exposing a large vein that throbbed when he got angry. The children had a running bet on when it would burst and he would collapse dead onto his desk. Jimmy Vassar had won the bet, as his guess had been five years from that day, though no one had ever paid up.

"Sit down, Marcus," he said with the cigar shoved in the corner of his mouth.

"What have you done now young man?"

"Nothing, Father," I answered.

"Don't lie to me son. Do you know what happens to liars? There's a special place in Hell for liars, boy." He paused for effect, or was it to catch his breath? "Disrupting class again, were you?

"Yes sir." If you didn't give him the answer he wanted, father Matthew's made certain that your life became a living hell.

"Making your little *noises* again, were you? You must not let the devil control your actions, boy. *You* are in control."

"I'm sorry, Father," I said, "but God is in control of my life, and if this is how He wants me then I cannot apologize for that."

"This is *NOT* how *He* wants you!" Father Mathews roared, sitting up straight in his chair, looking at me with those eyes of his.

Father Matthews was always watching; he seemed to have the amazing ability of making every child in a room feel as though his eyes were on each and every one us. No one was really afraid of the Father, as he was far too out of shape to be any sort of threat, but his eyes were feared by all. The way he looked at us… it wasn't lust in his eyes, it was something else, it was *hunger*! We would catch him sometimes, licking his lips, the look on his face ravenous, like we were everything to him at that moment. He could swallow us whole and slowly digest us like a snake, only to shit us out under his desk and welcome the next victim into his office. "If God truly loved you boy," Father Mathews said. "He would not make you suffer. Now get out of my office, go apologize to Sister Margaret and do *not* let me see you in here again today. I mean what I say young man."

"Yes, Father." I got up and left quickly, hopefully quick enough to avoid the inevitable…

"Oh Marcus…" He let the moment hang, waiting to see if I would turn or leave. You *never* leave, no matter how bad you wanted to, because he would always find you… He could always *see* you.

"Yes, Father?" I paused, waiting at the door.

"I think you need to see Father Stephens after dinner tonight."

"Yes, Father." I turned and pulled the door shut behind me.

Father Stephens was a counselor of sorts. He had no real background or education in the field; he was simply a man who liked to be around young boys. I'm not going to go into the details about what happened to boys during visits to his office; let's just say Father Stephens liked to play a lot of games. I went back to class and took my seat. No one even looked at me, and before I knew it, it was dinnertime. The food was supposed to be some sort of meat loaf, but tasted more like rat, accompanied by some flavorless chunky mashed potatoes and beets. I fucking *hated* beets! When dinner was finished, I had to go see Father Stephens. He would be waiting.

The room was dark, as it always was. In the center were two chairs facing one another, between the chairs stood a tall pole with a bright bulb on top that cast a circle of light on the floor. Father Stephens always stood in the darkness with his back to the door when we arrived, and it had taken a few years before I realized just what he had been doing. "Take off your socks and shoes and sit," he said.

Father Stephens was in his late twenties and he kept himself in shape. While the other priests let themselves go and were fairly easy to get away from, Father Stephens was not. He could be seen every day after classes out on the field running laps. He didn't drink, didn't smoke, and enjoyed none of life's vices but one. "Disrupting class again, Marcus?" He didn't give me time to answer. "Sister Margaret tells me you were making those noises in your throat again. You know *I* don't mind when you make those noises, Marcus, but that bitter old woman just doesn't understand." He sat down in the chair directly in front of me, reached down, and lifted my feet up onto his lap. "Do you want me to tickle them, Marcus? You look like you could use a good laugh." He didn't wait for a reply, but softly trailed his hand across the bottom of my foot, slowly moving his fingers harder and faster. He wouldn't stop until we laughed. We learned to laugh; things were fine if we played along. If we defied the Father, he would get angry, which led to violence. So, we played along. The phone in the back room rang, as it always did. He placed my feet back down on the floor and got up, disappearing into the room and closing the door. My eyes went to the corner of the room where the tiny red light flashed. Then I did something I had never done before, proving that this was much more than a memory. I got out of my chair and walked over to the red light in the corner of the room, knowing I was looking into a camera. I knelt down in front of it, looking directly into the lens. I saw *through* the camera, through the cables to a small TV in another room. Everything I saw was from the perspective of the television. I saw Father Matthews looking down at the screen just as he was getting ready to hang up the phone. "He's *not* in the chair!" Father Matthews yelled into the receiver.

The white woman, the Cherubim Dionia, had warned me of my doubt, and this little trip down memory lane was a reminder of my doubts about God. The Tourette's was bad enough, but to have to go through what Father Stephens had done to me and countless others? Stronger minds have snapped for much less. I was lucky. I was one of the few to make it out of that sort of childhood with my mind mostly intact. Sure, my brain's still fucked up as hell, but it works in its own weird way.

I had doubted the existence of God for years, until one day I said to myself, 'if there *is* no creator, then what's the point?' There *has* to be some sort of intelligent architect or all life means nothing, and I simply refuse to believe that. There is no doubt that *something* created us, but no one can seem to agree on what that something was. If you take away the stories and myths, we all believe in the same thing. Why then, must we wage wars in the name of our beliefs? We blame everything but the true source of the problem… us. Every time man gets introduced into the equation things go to hell. So, if we can't believe in man, who *can* we believe in? That is why even just the notion of a God is important. Without the belief that there is something more, there would be pure chaos. Evil does not need a face when its presence is felt everywhere, because the fewer people that believe in something… *anything*… the greater the hold Chaos has. I may not have followed any one religion in my beliefs, but I have always believed, and I have believed in *something* long enough to not doubt the existence of some sort of God, and *that* is what truly matters. Believing in something gives you the ability to look at the evil and chaos around you and say no, that will *not* be me, I will *not* let myself travel down that path. I had a choice. I chose to believe that I *could* overcome my doubt, and I *could* succeed. At that moment, my trip into the past faded and the vines fell away, floating out into the field of stems, and carried off on some invisible current. The dark woman no longer laughed as I turned to leave and continued my climb to the top of the rock wall; she just stared at me as she had before my vision, and once again there was fear in her eyes.

REALITY DIVIDED

I followed the path I'd initially spotted from the field of flowers into the forest. It started out as fine sand, maybe a stone here, a root there, then I saw the bones. The more I walked, the more there were, until the path I was walking on was nothing but a road of bones. The forest grew darker with each step, the trees clustered closer together, their roots and branches entwined. The shadows fell an impenetrable black, leaving nothing before me but an empty void. I stopped to think. I had no power there and nothing to light my way. A sudden scream echoed through the canopy of trees, it sounded like a child. Another terrified child screamed out in pain, then another, and another. All of the cries from the forest were children, some even sounded like infants! I looked around in the blackness but saw nothing, and then light. I watched as the bones began to shine, slowly illuminating the path ahead of me.

The path opened up into a large circle of glowing bones. In the center of the circle stood another statue of a female Ma Hua Ra holding the blades. Beyond the statue, two paths branched off in opposite directions. The statue opened her eyes and she spoke.

"I am Aryania, guardian of the Tainted Forest. Tell me, Marcus, what is it you fear the most?"

"That I'm not being told the entire truth," I answered honestly.

"The fruit from the Tree holds the truth of which you speak, but you are not yet there, Marcus. Do not worry; in time you will have the answers you seek, but first you must confront your fears. Beyond lie the Two Paths of Darkness. Both are dangerous and both will take you to Hell. Chose wisely, Marcus."

Aryania smiled and returned to stone.

I walked around the statue and a figure appeared before me on the path to the right. We both stopped. I moved forward, he moved forward. I moved to the center, directly between the two paths, and another figure appeared, this time on the path to the left. Two identical versions of me. I knew this was an illusion, that these were not paths at all, they were more like mirrors. I found that if I stood in just the right spot, I could see the statue reflected behind me in each image. Both reflections of me would follow my every move, but they were not *quite* identical. In one reflection, I had blood on my face, and in the other I did not. I was no longer sure this was an illusion, because, standing just yards away, I could *feel* them. One reflection felt like the real me. The other one, the one on the right, the one with blood on his face, did not. But I *had* felt his presence before as I watched him butcher two young children in a farmhouse, and as I watched him murder my teenage self. I needed to know more about this bastard, and knowing that I was most likely making the wrong choice, I stepped into the reflection on the right and into a new memory.

Blood streamed from my arm, gushing bright red from an open wound. One of the cat's claws was still embedded in my skin, tugging painfully at my flesh as the feline struggled to free its paw. I held the palm of my hand against the side of the animal's face and pushed it down hard into the concrete.

I remembered this incident; I was nine years old at the time. I had been sitting on the street corner petting a stray cat, it was even purring, but then it went crazy and started biting and clawing at me. I had been angry, *really* angry; up to that point in my life I had never felt such a rage. *That* was the first moment in my life that I had wanted to kill. Something inside me had wanted that cat dead and I remembered how close I had come to giving in to my feelings. In *my* reality, I had let go of the cat and it ran off, but it seemed that I was no longer in my reality. *Crack...* The cat's skull snapped beneath my hand and blood poured from the cat's eyes as one of them slipped out between my fingers, looking up at me from the top of my hand. I let go of the limp animal and wiped my hand off in the grass next to the sidewalk. This had been *his* first kill. I felt everything that this version of me was going through, the fear, the excitement, the rush from what he had just done. That was truly a defining moment in my life, the moment when realities split and *he* had been born. It was the beginning of summer; I was in public school, once again living at home instead of boarding at the Parochial school. Things were good for the next couple of years. My parents were trying to work out their problems, each in their own way. I stood and looked down at the dead animal, hit play on my Walkman, and began walking home listening to Marillion's 'Childhood's End'.

A small path wound its way through the woods of a five-acre lot, a shortcut that would take me within a couple blocks of my house. In the center of the patch of woods there was an old building that used to be a slaughterhouse; some of the old equipment was even still inside. It had been a great party spot for the older kids, and during the day it was usually empty, but not that day. I saw a boy on the second floor, looking down into the rusty old blades of a large meat grinder. There was no power in the building, as the lines had been taken out years ago, but somehow the machine started. Chips of rust flew through the air as the blades started to spin. A rusted metal staircase took me to a catwalk on the second floor. The boy turned and looked at me once before he stepped in. He didn't even scream.

I remembered seeing his face before, but for the life of me, I could not recall his name. I took the stairs down to the front of the machine where a steaming pile of dark red meat lay in the dirt, chunks of bone and clothing scattered throughout. I heard a sigh and turned, knowing there was someone hidden in the shadows. "Who's there?" I called out.

"Come, Marcus," a voice whispered from the shadows, a female voice, another dark woman. She was laid out on a long stainless steel bed, her wrists and feet strapped to pegs. *"Set me free,"* she whispered.

"I'm not afraid of you," I said.

"If you don't set me free boy, you will be."

"No, I think I like you just the way you are."

"Silence!" the woman screamed. *"You will do as I tell you..."* she pulled her hands free from the restraints and sat up, *"or you will suffer the consequences!"* The dark woman reached down and loosened the straps on her ankles, setting them free. *"What is it you fear, Marcus?"*

I felt her in my head, digging through my memories.

"You two are not as different as you think. Your minds are remarkably alike."

"I don't kill things for fun," I screamed at the woman, "I don't murder children!"

She swung her legs off the table and sat, smiling at me. *"Yes, Marcus, you do."* She pushed off of the table and stood before me. I was lost in her blackness. The world around me faded and then...

There was a large sack on the ground before me, something inside of it was moving. I looked up at my grandfather's house and heard the celebration going on inside. It was his seventy-fifth birthday and it would be his last. I thought about throwing the sack in the pond or setting it on fire. Then I thought about an old wood chipper out beyond the barn on the other side of the garden. I whacked the sack a couple of times with a two-by-four until it stopped moving, then hefted it over my shoulder to find the chipper.

I knew that I was ten years old in this memory, but I did *not* recall this happening. In *my* reality, I had been inside during Grandpa's party. The party lasted until eight thirty; that's when Grandma noticed that Dusty was missing. Dusty was a wiry haired mongrel, somewhere between a terrier and a retriever, ugly as hell but a very sweet dog. He had never been found. This was the work of the dark woman; she was making me live this moment in *his* time. She had asked me what I feared and here was my answer: what I feared the most was becoming what my other had become.

I pulled the cover off and checked the gas gauge on the old chipper. "We're in luck boy," I said to the dog as he flopped about within the canvas sack, "we've got gas." The key was in the chipper, and I reached up and turned it, listening to the gears grind to life. I smiled as the blades whined, singing their song just for me. I reached down and untied the sack, letting Dusty's head poke out. I retied the sack around the dog's neck, just tight enough to keep it from slipping off. I wanted to see the dog's eyes as it was pulled into the chipper. I hefted the sack and dropped it in, Dusty howled as he was sucked inside, the blades grinding his poor flesh. I heard myself laugh as the dog's eyes popped and his face fell apart when the blades took it in... Fast forward...

I stood in the woods with the kid from the meat grinder. I remembered his name then, it was Aaron Radcliff. My friend Jim had always said that the A.R. stood for Ass Rag. In other words, we were never friends, so why was I there with him? I was eleven years old when he disappeared. Everyone said he had run away, but Aaron was found in the woods a week later after shooting himself in the head with his daddy's gun. As I relived my other's memory, I watched Aaron lift up his shirt and pull out a gun tucked into his pants. Aaron pointed it at me and started laughing.

"I wouldn't shoot ya, man" he said. "Here check it out."

He handed the gun to me. I was surprised at how good the weapon felt in my hands as I held it up to Aaron's face and pulled the trigger. I tried to stop myself from doing it but I had no control over the scene playing out around me, or within me. I searched my other's thoughts but found no remorse or regret as I reached down and took the dead boy's hand, placed the gun in it, and walked away. I began to see a pattern, this reality, *his* reality, was close to mine, and there appeared to be some sort of bleeding through of events. So I wasn't surprised to find myself at my next destination.

I stood outside the School of the Holy Trinity. There was one door in the back of the school that was always unlocked. I climbed the fence and made my way through the flower garden and into the building. The emergency lighting was on and the hallways were cold and silent, the slightest movement echoed louder than a siren. I took off my shoes and slipped into Father Mathews' office where he kept a spare key to his dorm room. I fished through the desk until I found the key and then left the office, heading straight for the staff dormitory.

I found the room, unlocked the door, and quietly stepped inside. I saw a light flicker in the room ahead and paused, Father Matthews should have been in bed by then. I reached into my back pocket and pulled out a short, thick, heavy piece of wood, something that looked like an old coffee table leg. I crept down the hall and stopped when I saw the source of the flickering light. The image on the television screen brought forth a flood of emotions, first anger, then hatred, and then rage. I saw a boy bent over a large wooden desk, Father Stephens behind him humping feverishly. I knew the boy on the video; he was the younger brother of one of my classmates. I saw the look in the child's eyes and remembered the pain and humiliation. I stepped closer and peered around the corner and into the room. Father Matthews sat naked in a chair with his back to the door, his eyes occupied with the television. I stepped closer and saw that he was not alone. Father

Stephens was on his hands and knees before his superior, his face buried deep in Father Matthews' lap, the rolls of fat almost engulfing the eager priests head. I crept up behind the chair and raised the table leg up into the air, letting it hang there, savoring the moment, and then brought it down onto Father Mathews' skull. The large man lurched forward and I heard a muffled cry from the priest's groin as he fell sideways out of the chair and on to the floor. Father Stephens managed to remove his mouth with a wet pop just before a stream of semen shot up into the air as the fat man shot his load. Father Stephens looked up at me sobbing as I held the table leg high and swung down hard, planting it right between the bastard's eyes. Blood gushed from a large wound, covering the priest's face. I pulled back and swung again, and again, I tried to block out the horrific scene, the blood, the screams, but it was no use. I had no choice but to continue bashing in Father Stephens' face with a coffee table leg. I knew what it felt like to kill and I wanted to give it back, I wanted to throw my weapon to the floor and void my stomach of its contents, unfortunately it was not my stomach.

Father Stephens' pleas turned to gurgles and then silence, but I only swung harder. I continued swinging until there was nothing left of the pedophiles head but a bloody mass of meat and bone. Father Matthews was beginning to wake up, his whimpers and moans rousing me from my blood rage. I sat down on the Father's chest and placed the table leg on the floor before pulling out a small pocketknife. I opened the blade as Father Matthews lay twitching on the floor, gargling through blood and bile as he tried to speak. I knew I didn't have long, soon the priest would be dead and it would be too late. "No more watching for you," I said as I drove the knife into one eye, and then the other. I wanted to do it while he could still see.

What is it you fear, Marcus? The question kept running through my head. I fear myself… and what I am capable of. From the death of Father Mathews on, this other version of me made a lot of choices that I would not have. I watched him grow up, through his teens and his twenties. I watched him grow smarter, and much, much darker. His mind went places I had forbidden mine to go, places vile and sadistic. My other had a lot more trouble controlling his Tourette's than I did. I guess it was a small price for him to pay; he was cruel and he was good at it. No one *ever* saw him take his victims.

I saw the first time he met Lilith. She'd made love to him as many women, all he had to do was say a name and she would morph into that person instantly. She promised him power, more power than he could feel in the moment of the kill, power he could *not* refuse. I watched as Lilith taught this Marcus the art of murder. There were dozens of victims, dozens of perfect crime scenes. Oh, how he loved it when there was more than one, their collective fear providing him with an indescribable rush. In his own mind, he was *God.* No one would ever catch him, Lilith had promised him that. Then she introduced him to Ira... to *Wrath.* I knew these things as my *other* knew them. Every memory he had, I now had access to, and one of them scared the shit out me. He was planning to kill Anna, *my* Anna... and he planned to make my children watch before he turned his knife on them. Maybe there *was* something I feared more than myself. My family would think that it was me who'd done these terrible things and I could *not* let that happen. Fuck the consequences; my family was *not* going to die that way! I had to concentrate, I had to move on. The sooner I got out of there, the sooner I could get to my family!

The visions of my other finally stopped and I was back in the slaughterhouse. The dark woman was no longer in my head, but once more stood before me. I grabbed her by the throat and choke slammed her down onto the steel table. She must not have expected my actions, for she said and did nothing to stop me. The restraints found her limbs as if called somehow to do so, wrapping themselves around her ankles and wrists, drawing tighter until she stopped struggling against them. I turned to leave and saw that the pile of Aaron was no longer on the ground. Suddenly, the room began to shake. The mortar between the stone blocks began to crumble, screws unwound themselves from objects, everything was coming apart. Piece by piece, the building rose into the air, until I was left standing on the glowing path of bones in the forest beyond the Elysian Fields.

I walked down the path until I came to another circle, and a third white statue. This statue faced away from the path forcing me to walk around to the other side. There was nowhere to go from there, no path ahead to follow, the only way out was the direction I had just come from. As I turned to face the statue, the white woman spoke. *"I am*

Lourkie, guardian of the Dark Place. You are doing well, Marcus, but your path only becomes more difficult from here."

Lourkie tilted her head back and opened her mouth as if wanting to tell me more. A black substance appeared in the corners of her mouth, quickly spreading across her face and down her body, turning every inch of her black. Before the metamorphosis could be completed, Lourkie succeeded in spitting out her words. *"Control your anger, Marcus."*

Her voice dropped several octaves and she spoke once more.

"Yes, Marcus, control it if you can."

The dark woman who now stood before me, laughed as the bones at my feet began to crumble into dust and drift away, leaving me suspended for a moment over a seemingly bottomless pit. The walls of the tunnel were engulfed in flames and every ten feet was a circle of thick chain, like the kind attached to the anchor of a large ship. My moment of weightlessness was over and I plummeted fast, the heat of the flames singing my skin on the way down.

I saw the bottom of the pit and it was coming at me fast. As I descend, I realized it was not the bottom I saw at all, but a 90-degree curve in the tunnel of flames. Somehow my body stayed in the center of the tunnel as I whipped around the corner and then went flying in a new direction. I saw a bright white light ahead of me then, it came from a small glowing ball. Around the glowing sphere were six rings of chain that criss-crossed one another. I heard laughter and felt a presence behind me, moving faster than I was; it was Ira! I turned, mid flight, so I could at least know when he was going to attack, but I somehow made it to the sphere before he did. Ira came to an abrupt stop at the end of the tunnel, his shadows shifting until a face was formed.

"There isss no essscape," Ira hissed. **"Join usss Marcusss, and nothing will happen to your family."**

"Right, I'm supposed to believe *that*?"

"Believe what you like, but know that you will die heeere."

Ira floated just inside the tunnel, not making any attempt to enter. I felt the power of this creature and it was much stronger there, its voice no longer a whisper.

"Fuck you!" I screamed. "If you want me so bad, come and *get* me!"

I bellowed the challenge, hoping my hunch was correct. Ira's forms shifted again; Wrath was preparing to do something, but what? Then I saw the Umbra relax.

"You are correct, Marcus. I cannot enter this place, but I do not have to."

Ira was in my head, searching my thoughts, taunting me with what he knew about my other.

"Such a pity it was not you who chose Chaos."

"Yeah, too bad you're stuck with a second rate hack, huh?" I could sense Ira's anger rising.

"He is more powerful than you know, more powerful than the rest."

"The rest?" I became intrigued with this little gem Ira had dropped.

"There are more of your other; five others for you to discover," Ira smirked.

"Five?" I pondered this for a moment before continuing.

"It doesn't matter, my other is weak. I've seen it. He'll lose control... *you* will lose control of him."

That statement pissed Ira off. The Umbra moved closer to me for a moment, but quickly backed away. "Where am I?" I demanded.

"You are in Chaos. The sphere behind you contains a singularity. This singularity is my chance to get home and you, you will not stop me."

"Where does it go?" I reached out to touch the singularity.

"NO!" the creature roared. The chains around the singularity began spinning, almost taking off my fingers. *"We are playing by my rules today, Marcus!"*

My head immediately filled with visions. There were so many memories, stretching back billions of years. I saw the birth of the multiverse and the rise of the Mille Umbra, and I now understood the importance of the singularity. In a flash, I knew its origin, its purpose. The singularity was Elizabeth Patton's. Her body was stolen from the cemetery in my reality, her singularity brought to Chaos to serve Ira's needs. "You're lying!" I screamed as I lunged in the creature's direction.

Something inside told me to stop before I touched the Umbra.

"Yes... you know more than you think you do."

Ira was correct. I instinctively knew that if I touched the creature in any way I would become another of the shadows that writhed within the Umbra's dark form. I stepped as close to the creature as I could and looked into the pits that substituted for its eyes.

"I can still stop you," I said.

"It is already too late." Ira laughed, a vile sound, as his heads formed into their best impression of an evil grin. *"Here is my gift to you..."* Once again, my world became dark and things began to spin.

I stood in the living room of my house. The sun streamed in through the windows. I started walking to my children's room, or rather *he* did. I was not really there, I simply saw through *his* eyes again. He opened the door to an empty room. My other then went to *my* bedroom door, pushing it open slowly and quietly. Anna was stretched out across the bed softly snoring. Always a light sleeper, she began to stir and her eyes fluttered open. "Marcus? Is that you?" Anna raised a hand to block the sun and used the other to rub away the sleep from her eyes.

My other attacked quickly, his hands around my wife's throat.

"Where are the girls, bitch? Where are the *fucking* girls?"

"Marcus!" Anna screamed. "What are you doing… how did you…"

Anna gasped for air and I could do nothing but watch as the scene played out before me. I couldn't even close my eyes… *his* eyes. Anna's eyes rolled back into her head and she fought less, her consciousness fading. He let her go when she stopped moving and searched the room for something to tie her up with. My other pulled open drawers, scattering the contents haphazardly until he found Anna's socks and nylons. He went back to the bed and punched at the tongue-and-groove backing of the headboard until a piece on each side was knocked out. He then grabbed Anna's wrists with his bloody hands. He bound her tightly, the nylons strung through the broken wood, my wife's prone body face up on the mattress. He stuffed a sock in Anna's mouth and wrapped another pair of nylons around her head to secure the gag, but left her legs untied. He *wanted* her to fight back!

I watched as my tainted self unbutton Anna's jean shorts and slide them off her body, her panties following suit. He pushed the clothing onto the floor as he fished a large folding knife out of his back pocket. My other climbed on top of my wife's stomach, straddling her with his thighs. He pulled the material of her shirt tight and cut the fabric from the neck down. I felt his excitement growing as Anna began to regain consciousness. He slid his blade under Anna's bra directly between her breasts and pulled up quickly, making the cups open like a flower. He trailed the knife around the side of her breast and up to her nipple. He pinched the nipple then, stretching it out, and drove the point of the knife into the areola. Anna moaned in pain and her eyes opened as he pushed the knife through to the other side. He let go of the nipple and started rocking the handle of the knife side-to-side, tearing the tender skin. Anna tried to scream through the gag, but could make no sound.

"Where are the girls?" he asked again, his voice cold and frightening. Anna's eyes filled with fear, tears streaking both sides of her face.

"No matter," he said with a smile, "I'll get to them in time." My other removed the knife from Anna's nipple and began carving on what remained of her right breast. I watched him carve six symbols from the book in a circle. He completed his work by slicing off the nipple, popping it into his mouth, and squishing it between his teeth for my wife to see.

Anna knew he was going to kill her... that *I* was going to kill her. She brought her knee up and slammed it into his back, knocking the wind out of him. He reached behind him to grab one of Anna's legs and slid his body back until he sat on her knees. "You're gonna' pay for *that*, bitch!" The bastard pulled Anna's legs apart and threw the knife he'd used on the floor. He reached for another knife, a *bigger* knife, the one he had used on the family at the farmhouse. He pulled it from the sheath strapped to his leg and held the blade up for Anna to see. The bastard smiled and lowered the knife. He slowly trailed the blade up the inside of Anna's thigh and rammed the knife into her vagina hard. Blood poured from the wound as he raped her with the eight inch serrated blade. "Has your pussy had enough yet?" My other grinned as he withdrew the blade and brought it to his lips. He licked the blood from the knife, then spat it out onto her stomach. He reached between her legs and pinched the vulva together, slid the knife down and cut. He picked up the desecrated flesh, displayed it like a trophy for a moment, and then placed it to his lips, licking the bloody meat and laughing. "I bet you like that," he said. Anna just sobbed.

My other, only having just started his grisly task, got down to the serious work of defiling my wife's once lovely body. Slowly, painstakingly, he etched out more symbols until the entire front side of her body was covered. The sheets were soaked with blood and Anna had stopped crying. Her mind, unable to absorb the atrocities that she believed her husband was committing, had shut down. She was mercifully passed out when he positioned the tip of the blade over her belly button, placed both hands on the top of the handle, and thrust. Everything went white... then black, and I heard Ira laughing once more.

"Do you like what you see? She thinks it was you, Marcus… she thinks it was you…"

Ira continued to cackle. I wanted him bad, I wanted to rip him to shreds but I knew this was not possible. I made a vow to myself that somehow I was going to make the fucker pay for killing my wife! I had always been good at pushing my anger aside when it got to be too much, but unfortunately, my anger always led to depression. Depression was my way of shutting everything down so that I could retreat inside my mind. That wouldn't have been a bad thing if I could've chosen what part of my mind to take refuge in, but I couldn't. I fell into the worst parts of my psyche, reminded of things I'd thought I'd forgotten, things I'd *prayed* I'd forgotten, and all of the evils in the world suddenly became intolerable.

TWO TREES

The scenery around me changed, but I didn't care. I wanted nothing to do with the outside world; all the imagery I would ever need was right there inside my head. But much to my dismay, the outside world insisted on making itself known. *"I am Ahnjizi, guardian of the Path to Eden."* The statue of the white woman forced its image into my head, demanding that I see. The statue stood in a large courtyard at the foot of a great mountain with two massive peaks that rose up into the clouds above me. Carved into the rock was a staircase leading upward. The night sky was dark and full of clouds. Lightning flashed in the distance. The wave of thunder rumbled by above my head and the statue continued to speak. *"You are almost there, Marcus. Eden lies within your grasp."* Ahnjizi pointed to the staircase but it was hard for me to concentrate. Images of Anna sobbing, begging for me to stop kept intruding.

"Why did she have to die?" I pleaded to the statue.

"It could be worse," she answered. *"See the fate of your children if you do nothing…"*

My head was filled with the worst images imaginable. I witnessed my baby girls being simultaneously raped and devoured by some sort of demons and other atrocities I simply could not wrap my mind around. *"This does not have to be, Marcus. See your children if you succeed."*

The visions changed to two teenaged girls sitting on a hillside, watching a sunset. They were holding hands and laughing. The image became blurry. The girls moved apart and then back together, forming one person as if I had seen double and there had always been only one girl. This vision unnerved me a lot.

Tara and Tori are among the smallest percentage of twins, as they are mirror images of each other. Tara was left handed, Tori right; their hair even parted the opposite way. Had my vision meant that one of my children would not survive in the future? *"You must overcome your despair, Marcus. You* must *continue!"* Ahnjizi was right. I had lost my wife, but my girls were still alive. I stood and faced the statue.

"Well chosen, Marcus. Now go. Fulfill your destiny." As before, the lifelike image of the woman faded, leaving me alone with the statue.

Thoughts of Anna still dominated my mind as I climbed. Memories, experiences, things we'd done, and things we'd meant to do. Our first kiss, long before we were in love. I cursed myself for keeping silent about my feelings for her all those years. A decade had been lost because of my stupidity, a decade that Anna and I could have shared together. Would things have fallen apart between us had we not waited? My thoughts also dwelled on Tara and Tori, my children. Where were they, were they still safe? I silently begged God for the chance to see them again, to find them before my *other* did. My thoughts drifted to the many ways I would make him pay for what he had done, each thought more splendidly delicious than the last. Then there was Ira. How do you kill what you cannot touch? How do you destroy pure anger… pure hatred… pure *wrath*?

The top of the mountain should have been getting closer, but it wasn't. For each step I took, two were added on to the top. My body was exhausted, my mind not far behind, and I had just about pushed myself as far as I could go. Man, I wanted a cigarette bad! It's probably a good thing I did not have one, as I'm sure the good lord would frown upon someone smoking in his garden. I took one more step and I fell, my body rolling backwards down a dozen or so steps, each blow to the head bringing me closer to unconsciousness. I sat up and my eyes grew wide at what I saw; by falling backwards I was now closer to the top! I stood up, faced the top, and stepped backwards down the mountain. With each step back I was moved forward three or four at a time and, before I knew it, I arrived at the top of the stairs.

Carved into the mountain where the two peaks joined as one, was another large courtyard, about a mile wide and a mile deep. Great columns were carved into the stone that surrounded the courtyard as if they alone held up the mountain. The ground before me was covered in short blue grass, the lawn littered with thousands of statues surrounded by small flower gardens. I saw a stone path made from the same white stone as the statues. The path wound its way to the other side of the courtyard, where there were two massive towers carved into the mountain flanking a huge iron gate. The towers were topped with spires that reached up into the sky, with a single window near the top of each one. As I stepped onto the stone path, the road before me began to glow. All of the statues lit up and two pinpricks of light ignited in the lone windows at the top of each of the towers.

The illuminated statues surrounded me as I walked. They were the Ma Hua Ra, the angels. Each statue had its own plaque with a name on it, names I'd heard before, like Uriel, Mikhael, and Sariel, but there were other names, like Akklfmoor and Rbdcklur, which were virtually unpronounceable by a human. One statue in particular on the other side of the courtyard near the city gates seemed to speak to me, and I was compelled to learn who this statue represented, but I could not yet reach it. When I arrived at the center of the courtyard I stopped, dropping to my knees before a statue unlike the rest, a statue that was carved from a different stone, darker, almost a bronze color with a slight hint of light radiating from within. The statue was of a human… the statue was of *me*! And holding each of the statue's hands, by its side, were figures that looked like my Tara and Tori. These girls were older, in their late teens, just like the vision I'd seen compliments of Ahnjizi prior to climbing the mountain. I bowed my head and cried, awed and overwhelmed with the blessing bestowed on me by God. When I'd composed myself, I looked around and saw that my statue sat in the middle of a large circle of stone. From this circle radiated seven paths, each leading to the iron gate on the far side of the courtyard.

I heard a sizzling and a loud *Crack* in the distance. Two beams of light shot out from the tower windows above and crashed to the ground just a few yards in front from me. The twin beams cut into the earth and scorched the soil, while plumes of smoke drifted up into the sky. Each beam began to dance, slicing wildly through the air like downed power lines, striking everywhere. None of the seven paths were safe to travel. I noticed a peculiar thing though; the arcs of light never *once* hit a statue! My mind raced, scrambling to find a way across the courtyard. I needed to reach that gate!

As the thought entered my mind, another thought intruded, seemingly coming from the statue that had beckoned me earlier. *"Trust in yourself, Marcus. Use what you have learned, use what you see."* Use what I saw? All I saw was light and statues. How do I use light? I considered my other option, the statues. The closest statue was the likeness of the girls and me. I placed my hand on Tara's shoulder and stopped to think, what was the voice trying to tell me? I reached up and touched the face of my statue, and when my fingertips should have been touching stone, I felt nothing. My fingers *disappeared* into the face! I reached out to touch Tara's statue again and nothing odd happened, my fingers touched stone. I had the same experience with the likeness of Tori. I moved behind the statue of myself, thinking... *use what you see...* and stepped onto the base of my statue... and *into* it!

The stone crumbled away as I pulled my hands free from the statues of my girls and stepped down. I didn't waste any time choosing a path, I simply walked forward. The arcs of light danced all around me as I crossed the courtyard, but never struck me as I'd presumed they would. The courtyard ended at a massive staircase, which was a half circle of stone carved into the mountain, rising up to the gate. The lights in the towers went out and the arcs bouncing around below disintegrated. Slowly, the glow of the statues around me faded, all but one. The statue I stood within crumbled and fell to the ground in a large pile at my feet. I turned to face the statue of *my* Ma Hua Ra. The plaque on this sculpture read Gabriel. "Thank you," I said, and the light inside Gabriel's statue went out.

Protruding from the tower wall on the right side of the gate, I saw a large crank. The gears creaked and moaned and ground to life as I turned the handle, while the gates to Eden slowly inched open. I entered the city and wandered the streets, marveling at the architecture of the buildings, most of them defying at least one of the laws of physics. There were buildings a block wide and twice as tall that rested on no more than an eight foot wide cylinder with a heavy steel door. What was in those buildings? There were no windows that I could see, just lots of columns, spheres, and angles. The streets seemed to be made from the same material as the buildings, an odd gold metal that reflected light in a rainbow of colors with each step I took. Well past the city gates, I began to feel two separate forces drawing me in the same direction, drawing me to the center of the city. One of the forces was unfamiliar, yet somehow felt safe, while the other force was dark, filling me with dread. *There must always be two...*

When I reached the heart of the great city, I stood before a building that was completely out of place. It looked like Jefferson's Monticello, built from wood and mortar except for the great dome, which reflected a rainbow of colors radiating from the light bouncing off of the buildings around it. I crossed the street and entered the odd-looking building. Once inside, I found some sort of library, with endless rows of bookshelves filled to the brim with books of all shapes, sizes, and colors. There were books bound in plastics and metals, leather or some sort of animal hide, and then there were others that appeared to be bound in human skin. I counted five stories in the building, each stuffed with bookshelves like the first floor. I climbed the stairs to the third floor, not really sure where I was going. The pull was stronger there and I found myself wandering through endless rows of books with no titles. Every now and again I pulled one out, opened it, and read a few lines, as long as the book was written in a language that I could comprehend, which very few were. Still, I was curious. The ones I *could* read were filled with stories of the divine, prophets telling of their visions. Rounding the last corner, I found myself totally and utterly lost. Who am I kidding; I was lost long before that! But at least I was getting close; the forces pulling me grew stronger with each creak of the floorboards.

I stood before a wall with thousands of holes cut into it. Each hole was only a couple of inches wide and a couple of feet deep, and each hole contained a rolled up scroll. I randomly pulled out a scroll, and found it to be a map of the city. Some of the buildings were missing, but it was still fairly accurate in its depiction. The forces that had drawn me there were now pulling me in different directions… I let the dark bitch wait. The comfortable force pulled me to the right, to a hole in the wall a few yards away. Standing on my toes, I reached up and withdrew another scroll. It was rolled awkwardly, and was a lot longer than I had expected. It slipped out of my hand and fell to the floor, rolling out and forming a large circle. In the center of the map was a mountain with two peaks. Drawn around the mountain was a circle of black, then a forest, then a field. Carved into the mountain was a vast stretch of land that would one day hold the city of Eden. There were notes scrawled all over the map, but it was two lines, right next to each other, that caught my attention. *Tree of Life* and *Tree of Knowledge*. I spread out the first map next to the scroll and tried to get my bearings. Looking at the round map there was no way of telling which side of the peaks the entrance was on, so I marked both possible locations on the smaller map of just the city, and rolled it back up. I let the dark force draw me to another small hole and another map. I gagged from the smell as I unrolled it. Marked on the map, with fresh shit, was an X, and underneath that were the words *'you should have opened me first.'* The X lined up with one of the locations I had marked on the first map. I unrolled the smaller map, circled the mark, and tried like hell to find my way out of the library.

I stepped into the street, opened the map to get my bearings, and walked. I was quite sure the dark force was sending me in the wrong direction but still, something inside me told me to go where I was being led. There had been so many thoughts in my head lately that it was difficult for me to know for sure which ones were my own. A lot of the thoughts *were* things that I thought about, but not at times or places that should make me bring up those memories. I needed to stop letting my mind drift and concentrate on where I was going, but it was no use, there was no stopping the thoughts once they had begun.

As I walked, I kept seeing things, people, even though I knew that no one was there. I had to remind myself that it was my own reflection on the metallic surfaces of the buildings and streets, but these images still caught me off guard as my thoughts raced. There were times when I saw two or more reflections at once, coming from different angles. I knew the light in this place could do some strange things, like throwing shadows in multiple directions, but reflections, *too?* When I reached my destination, I stood before a large oval building about four blocks wide and, according to the map, stretched back another twelve blocks. The building was *easily* a hundred stories tall, and from where I stood I only saw one way in. About a third of the way up the front of the building was a single, windowless door.

Eight large octagons of stone were embedded in the earth far below the doorway. When I stepped on the first one, it began to rise into the air, and by the time I had crossed it, the next stone had risen to the same level, waiting to carry me up further, an elevator of sorts. I continued to watch the stones rise out of the ground below me, while the earth, compacted tightly to the stone from centuries of pressure, crumbled away and fell back down onto the blue grass. I saw seven separate reflections of the stones rising on the side of the new building, and seven reflections of me as I climbed. One of the reflections wore a white shirt, while the one I wore was black. In another, the shirt looked red; in fact, the reflections *all* wore different colored versions of the same clothing. As I crossed the final stone, it stopped even with the bottom of the door I'd seen from the street. There was no handle, however, so I placed my palm on the metal door. The door was warm to the touch. The heat traveled up my fingertips and into my arms; soon, my entire body was filled with the sensation. The door hissed and pulled back a few inches, then flew up, much like a garage door. On the other side I saw a lush field. Across the field was a hill, and on that hill stood two trees growing about ten yards apart.

One tree was just a little bit taller than the other, its trunk and branches white and filled with shiny green leaves and a luminescent white fruit that resembled a lemon. The smaller tree was much darker, its trunk wider with the roots wrapped around its base before burrowing into the ground. Its leaves were deep purple with black veins and the bark was dark green. The tree bore a black fruit that looked like a small eggplant. *"I thought you'd never get here,"* a female voice called out. I didn't see her there at first, sitting among the roots of the smaller tree. The dark woman was masturbating and apparently enjoying it quite a bit. *"The Tree of Knowledge of Good and Evil. Yes, Marcus, you have finally arrived."* She held out her unoccupied hand as a dark fruit from the tree dropped to the ground. *"Here,"* she said as she caught the fruit and held it out to me. *"Eat."* She sighed in pleasure as her fingers began to stroke her nether regions more quickly. *"Or..."* her fingers began to move quicker still, *"you could choose..."* her breathing became more labored, *"the fruit from the Tree of Life... and save the one you love. You can stop your other, Marcus... your wife does not have to die."* The dark woman's eye lids began to drift down as she became lost in a sea of pleasure, her words coming out in choppy, breathless pants as she drew closer to orgasm. "Lies," I whispered.

"No, Marcus... eat from the Tree of Knowledge... and see that I am telling the truth... there is a way. But you can only... choose one... you can only... taste the fruit from... one tree." The dark woman placed the Godivel fruit to her lips and licked the skin, which was so soft her tongue sank in, allowing her to suck out the juice. *"Deliiiiicious..."* she moaned.

"I bet it is; how does the other one taste?" I asked, both horrified and captivated by the woman and her self-pleasuring.

"Try one and see." Her fingers moved faster still, her breath heaving in and out with short gasps. I reached up into the Tree of Life and plucked out one of the glowing fruits, placing it under my nose, I inhaled. Its fragrance was sweet, making my mouth water. I looked into the light emanating from the fruit and saw a form, a person. "Marcus... Marcus..." she called out and I clearly saw her face then; it was Anna. I pushed the fruit away and held it out in offering to the dark bitch.

"You want a bite?" I offered sarcastically.

"No... thanks... they're...too filling." The dark woman was approaching her climax. I drew the white fruit back to my lips. *"Yes... Yes..."* She began to grind her hips, arching her back upwards. *"Yes, Marcus... Yes..."* I opened my mouth as though to bite down.

"Yeeeessss…" she moaned, her fingers franticly moving in rhythm with her hips. I bared my teeth, drew the fruit inside my mouth… then stopped. *"NO!"* The dark woman screamed. I withdrew the fruit from my mouth and threw it at the creature. *"You bastard!"* She shrieked and scrambled to get out of target range of the glowing fruit. I reached up and pulled another fruit from the Tree of Life.

"You *did* lie to me, you whore! You've never tasted this fruit! *Why?*"

"I do not need to, for I am eternal." The dark woman's tone became haughty, snide. I slowly walked toward her, tossing the glowing fruit from hand to hand, taunting her.

"But you're not *alive*, not like me."

"Why would I want to live like such pathetic beings, blindly following anyone with power? You humans are all alike; you all think you are better than everything else, you all think you are special. You're an afterthought, a mistake! Life is a virus that takes over and destroys everything it comes into contact with. Your kind does not deserve to live!"

I placed the glowing fruit in my pocket and reached for the delicacy from the Tree of Knowledge of Good and Evil. I held the small black fruit in my hand and drew it to my lips. All of the lights went out in the branches of the Tree of Life when I had made my choice. I took a bite and all hell broke loose.

5S5

THE ENGINE

INTERROGATION

My hands were cuffed behind my back and they hurt like hell. I was strapped into some sort of chair, my arms behind me, and my legs bound tightly. I was back in the hospital, in a room like the one Dr. Spencer/Animus had died in. I saw two office chairs five or six feet away from me, and a flat-screen television and DVD player on a stand to my left. Admiral Forsythe was talking to an attractive brunette in her early thirties. She wore a badge and a gun, with an ID on the pocket of her blazer that said she was FBI. The Admiral took the seat on the left and said, "Welcome back, Mr. Quincy, open your eyes."

On the wall behind the chairs I saw a calendar that read November 2010. Could that be right? Had my trip to Eden taken that long? The FBI agent took her seat, placing a large leather purse on the floor next to her feet. The woman had mysterious eyes, sexy and penetrating. They were even sexy when she was nervous, like she was that day, though she usually wasn't that type of woman. What did she have to be nervous about? Every time she looked at me I saw things about her life, what she'd had for breakfast, her last date, what day her cycle started. Her memories were fragmented and she was missing days, sometimes *weeks,* of her life. I guess I had sort of expected something to happen right away in Eden, that I would bite into the fruit and instantly know everything, but that was far from the case and it was seriously screwing with my brain. There were parts of the FBI agent's mind that stayed a mystery to me, but the Admiral was another story. His thoughts, his memories, I saw those *completely*.

Admiral Forsythe had led an honorable life, but over the years, his job had required him to do some questionable things. He'd been through a lot, he'd *seen* a lot, and because of that he drank. It seemed that I had misjudged the Admiral during our previous encounters; he was a good man who did what he had to do for God and country.

"I'm here with Agent Mira Stark of the FBI," the Admiral began, but before he could continue the woman interrupted. "I'm investigating the deaths of Andrew Martin Spencer and Anna Parker Quincy," she said, "your wife, Marcus. Now open your eyes!"

The woman was getting angry. I ignored her.

"I can see just fine, Robert," I said.

The Admiral looked at me suspiciously. "Did Hunter tell you my first name?" he asked.

"No."

"What else do you know about me, Marcus?"

"This is *bullshit!*" Agent Stark interrupted. "I've been waiting over three months to talk to this piece of shit and all he wants to do is play fucking games!"

"I know why you let a psychopath roam the streets," I finally answered the Admiral.

"What's he *talking* about?" Agent Stark burst in, she obviously knew nothing of Thomas Hunter.

"That is *classified* information, Mr. Quincy," said the Admiral, but he was looking at Agent Stark. It just pissed her off even more. The admiral continued, "If you must know, Mr. Hunter's whereabouts had only recently come to my attention. I was in the process of transferring him to a more secure facility."

"You're afraid of him," I cut the Admiral off. Now *he* was getting pissed. It was good to see that I hadn't lost my touch. Agent Stark reached down and pulled a disc out of her purse; she opened the plastic tray and handed it to the Admiral, who slipped it into the DVD player and hit the play button. He held up the remote and turned on the TV.

"Open your eyes, Marcus. Agent Stark has something to show you..." I opened my eyes and both of their jaws dropped. "...What happened to your eyes?"

Agent Stark pulled a small compact mirror out of her purse and opened it in front of my face. That was the first time I had seen my eyes since the "dots" had taken over my vision and Ma Hua Ra had opened up my true eyes. I had seen these eyes before on an old man... on *five* old men. The inverted Y shape, the halo of black around a dead white center, I saw it all in great detail. The halo was broken in three spots and there was no inverted Y, what I saw in my eyes were three sevens circling each dead iris. I didn't know what to think just then, but at least I finally understood why Dionia, the Guardian of the Elysian Fields, had called me Seven. I heard a blast of static from the TV speaker and the video started.

"Where are the girls? No matter, I'll get them, in time."

"You *bastards!*" I screamed. And once more, I was forced to watch my Anna die.

Agent Stark went to the door and opened it. She conversed with an orderly on the other side for a moment and then shut the door. "We placed your house under surveillance after the death of Dr. Spencer, Marcus. We thought you might have had an accomplice on the outside."

"Isn't that an invasion of privacy?" I spat.

"*Fuck* privacy!" Agent Stark screamed. "Your wife is *dead* and *you* want to bitch about *your* rights?"

The door opened and a young nurse I recognized entered the room pushing a small cart. Nurse Garland wheeled the cart around the television and stopped directly behind me. She pulled out a small flashlight that looked like a pen, clicked it on and pried my eyes open with her thumb and forefinger.

"What the hell?" She dropped the pen and let go of my lids. "I've never seen *any*thing like this."

Nurse Garland took a deep breath, retrieved her flashlight, and began to examine my eyes anew.

"No response at all," she said. "There's *no* way he can see!"

"Does someone want to tell me what the *hell* is going on here?" Agent Stark's voice changed, just a little, but it was there, her accent shifting from Midwestern to somewhere in New England, upstate New York or western Massachusetts. She was pacing again. "On the morning of August second, 2010, you were found in a locked room with the body of Dr. Andrew Spencer. It looked like someone had *eaten* his face, yet you were leg cuffed to your side of the table, and even though the room was covered in blood, *you* didn't have a drop on you! Now, the video taken of the session was damaged and all we could retrieve was the audio. What were you saying, Mr. Quincy? Were you speaking in tongues? Are you going to tell us the devil made you do it?"

Agent Stark's mind raced and her thoughts jumped worse than mine. I stared into her eyes as she spoke, digging through bits and pieces of memories. I was trying to find my girls.

"Now, on the morning of August sixteenth we lost the video feed from your house and when we arrived, we found your wife butchered, Mr. Quincy. We were able to retrieve the footage from the hard drive and now we even have *you* on video *committing* the crime, yet somehow you were *here* in a *coma* the whole time? We can't find any record of you having a twin, but…"

"Where are my girls?" I demanded. Just then a single tone rose inside my skull and I knew I wouldn't be able to hold on to this reality much longer.

"The girls were with Agent Stark at the time of your wife's murder," the Admiral explained.

"You didn't answer my question," I said. "Where… the *fuck*… are… my… *girls?*"

"Calm down, Marcus." The Admiral stood and slowly walked toward me. "Social Services has temporary custody of the children until a suitable placement can be found. Don't worry, Marcus, they're in good hands." The Admiral looked over his shoulder. "Are you going to pace back there all day or are we going to get on with this interview?" Without a word Agent Stark crossed the room and took her seat.

"So, Mr. Quincy, are you going to tell me who this person is that murdered your wife?" Agent Stark spoke with the midwestern accent again. I decided to push her buttons.

"Who does it look like?" I asked.

"It looks an awful lot like *you,* Mr. Quincy!" I felt her rage for a brief moment and then calm; Agent Stark was good. "You may not be able to see, Mr. Quincy, but I know you can hear, so you're going to want to pay special attention to this."

The Admiral passed the remote to Agent Stark, who fumbled with the volume.

The speakers on the television hissed out a loud crash and a lot of yelling, the me on the screen placed his hands up in the air and dropped the knife he'd used to butcher my Anna, who lay in pieces throughout the room. The screen went black but the audio continued. *"How did you* do *that? Don't come any closer, I will shoot.*" It was Agent Stark's voice, and then mine. *"You'd shoot an unarmed man?"*

"I said stop!" Agent Stark screamed over the static in my head. Then I heard *my* voice again.

"No, you said don't come any closer. That doesn't imply that I have to stand still."

"Stop!" Agent Stark screamed again. There were several bursts of gunfire, then silence. Agent Stark, the one in the room, spoke. "I only turned for a moment, to check on the other agents at the scene. I saw him raise his bloody hand, dripping with *your* wife's blood, Mr. Quincy, then all of the other agents passed out, all but me. He took five rounds to the chest before he dropped. I don't know how, but when I turned around, he was *gone!*" Agent Stark paused to clear her mind of the memory. "While you were taking your little nap I had the doctors look you over. There were no signs of any gunshot wounds. Now, Mr. Quincy, are you ready to tell us who this bastard is?" Before I had time to come up with a wise-ass remark, a terrible ringing in my head resounded and in a great flash of light I was pulled from the reality. I heard Agent Stark yelling. "Get someone in here," she called out. "He's having a seizure!"

I stood in the blackness of the Nexus and looked around. A sudden static discharge crackled and a flash of light left my vision a canvas of white. A pinprick of light appeared in front of me, much brighter than its surroundings. The light grew in size and shape, turning into a halo and expanding outward. When the halo reached the size of a basketball it seemed to melt into the form of a human. The liquid light spread out like a cocoon and then dimmed, leaving behind the solid form of a Ma Hua Ra.

"Why didn't you tell me who you really were?" I asked.

"You already doubted your sanity, Marcus. If I had told you I was Gabriel, an angel, what do you think you would have done? Besides, I am not technically an angel. Angel is simply a term given to the Ma Hua Ra by humans."

"I don't know," I said, "I don't know what I would have done."

"I *do*," Gabriel said, *"and we would not be standing here at this moment in time. Must I remind you that everything happens for a reason?"*

"What about *Anna?*" I asked angrily. "I need to know *why* she had to die!"

"You will know the answer to that soon enough, Marcus, but I will tell you this, there was *a reason."* Of all the answers Gabriel could have given me, *that* was not the one I had expected.

"Well, if you couldn't tell me then," I said, "tell me now. Tell me about Lilith, about yourself and your kind." Gabriel stood motionless and said nothing, then for a brief moment, like his consciousness had momentarily left his body, he was gone... just as suddenly he returned, took a deep breath, and spoke. *"Very well, Marcus, I will tell you. The Ma Hua Ra, the Voice of God, and the Ah Me Rah, the Voice of Chaos, were God's second creation. Long before man, our kind resided in Eden until it was time for humans to evolve and us to leave."* I sensed a bitterness in Gabriel's voice as he told me this, did his dislike for mankind run that deep? *"We chose a planet on the outer rim of the first universe created and called it New Eden, but* you *call this planet Earth. Lilith was a good person once, and we had* many *children. She always bore twins, one of each, one dark and one light, to maintain balance."* Gabriel's voice trailed off as the memory carried him away. He was silent for a moment before continuing his explanation. *"It was shortly after the closing of Eden and man's introduction into the multiverse, that Lilith discovered power. She* loved *to be worshiped, found the adulation intoxicating."* Gabriel almost sounded regretful, as if yearning for a chance to do things over again. *"Mankind flocked to Lilith like sheep, following her every word. It was I who was given the task of killing her, the death of her mortal body causing her to ascend. She became much more powerful, but she would not be able to gain access to the multiverse. The Ma Hua Ra and the Ah Me Rah were then allowed to reside in the reflected multiverses of God and Chaos,"* Gabriel explained distastefully. *"But some chose to stay behind in the company of man. The Ah Me Rah that kept themselves hidden are very proficient in causing chaos. They allow Lilith to gain access to the multiverse as she needs."*

"Are the hidden Ah Me Rah the Mille Umbra?" I asked. He didn't answer my question.

"You have come a long way in your understanding, Marcus, but your journey is far from over. You must learn to harness your power and control your emotions… most of all, your anger. I must warn you, Marcus, that you can do nothing to change events, past, present, or future, or the Divine Engine will not work for you."

"Yeah, about that… how will I know what the pieces are and, more importantly, does it come with assembly instructions?" I was overwhelmed and confused, still grieving over Anna, but still able to make light of my situation.

"So good to see you've kept your sense of humor, Marcus. You will know what to do when the time comes, and know that we will see each other again if need be. Now go, and remember, God is with you." Gabriel's voice faded and a single tone that I instantly recognized reached out. The string pulled me from the Nexus and hurled me off through space and time to recover the first piece of the Divine Engine.

REFLECTIONS

The sun trickled down through the branches, leaving patches of light scattered across the path. The ringing in my head had stopped and I heard birds in the trees calling out for their mates. I walked, wondering who or what I would run into this time around. I had plenty of time to think while I walked, and I was pretty sure that that was the purpose, to give me time to think. I relived every moment of my journey to save mankind thus far, wondering if I could have done something differently, and why I had never tried to tell Anna what was happening to me. My wife would have believed me in the beginning, when this had all started, if I had only told her the truth. I *know* she would have believed me eventually. But I had let things go too far, I had waited too long and now I could do nothing. Sure, I could save all of humanity, all of existence, but I couldn't save my *wife*? If anything was going to make me snap it would have been this thought, but for reasons unknown,

I kept my sanity. Maybe that was the point, Anna's reason for dying. There were times when I had wanted to end it all, when I simply wanted to be nothing. But now I wanted to live, I *needed* to live. I needed to make things better... for my children... for everyone. I had to focus. I had to remember that all things happen for a reason. I couldn't go back and change things even if I wanted to... and I did. I wanted to say fuck everything for the chance to hold the woman I loved in my arms just one more time, to tell her that I loved her one more time. But changing *one* thing would change *every*thing. I'd had my one and only chance back in Eden, just like the dark woman had said. I don't regret my decision. I knew that changing my past would undo *everything,* and I knew... I knew there would always be *time.*

When I wasn't going over *my* thoughts, I contemplated the significance of the other thoughts in my head, the memories I had never created. There were a lot of memories of a life with Anna where we never had children. Then there were other memories where the twins were boys, and still more where Anna and I only had one child. In some of those memories that single child was a boy, in others, a girl. I could only find one memory not my own where Anna and I'd had twin girls, if only briefly. In that memory, Anna died during childbirth and the girls were stillborn. Were these memories from another life, or memories from another *me?*

My journey had led me to a bridge that crossed a large stream. There were markings carved into the posts in a language I shouldn't have known, yet somehow comprehended. I stood on the bridge for a while, watching the water rush by below me and the reflection of the clouds pass by overhead. They moved in opposite directions. I began to think about the dreams I'd had when this all started, the dreams of Julia, the dreams of Anna, and the dreams where they were the same woman. In those dreams she *knew* I wasn't crazy. I remembered her saying, *"Know that I have always loved you and I always will. I will say some things to you that I don't mean. Please know that I am truly sorry, my love, you did the right thing."* Anna had said this to me in a dream long before her death. Time is a funny thing. All's well and good when it's constant, but once you step outside of the multiverse, time means nothing. Remember, time does not move forward, *we* move forward through time. The dream could easily have been her telling me goodbye. I watched my tears fall into the stream, disrupting the current briefly before disappearing forever. I was now a part of that stream, and I would go wherever it took me, see whatever it saw. I made a wish as the next teardrop fell. I wished that I would one day be able to say goodbye to my wife and my children.

Two elderly women walked cautiously across the bridge. As I turned to face them, they screamed and chanted a prayer in that language I shouldn't have understood, and ran back in the direction they had come. I was pretty sure I wasn't the first Caucasian they had ever seen, or I doubted they would have approached me at all. It took a second for me to understand why they had fled. It was my eyes. If I could help it, I would have to remember not to let them be seen. I resumed walking and thinking, not even sure where I was going. Part of me just wanted to lie down in the grass and lose myself in my head.

"Why do you not?" said a voice from behind me. When I looked, I saw a man sitting beneath a tree, I don't know how I'd missed him as I passed by, but he was there.

"Excuse me?" I said. Was he reading my mind? And how the hell was I speaking his language?

The man kept his eyes closed and his body still as he talked. "I do not read minds," he said. "I read emotions. You do not need eyes for that."

"Believe me," I replied. "I know what you're talking about."

"Do you? I sense conflict within your heart, conflict *I* have felt in the past. If you truly do not need your eyes to see, then come... sit with me."

I took a seat on the other side of the tree, our backs separated by the trunk.

"My name is Marcus, Marcus Quincy"

"I am pleased to meet you, Marcus Quincy. My name is Siddhartha. You must sit with me and wait."

"Wait for what?" I asked.

"I do not know," Siddhartha said calmly. "Perhaps we will find out together?"

I had never thought I'd find myself sitting under a tree talking to Buddha, but then again, a lot of things had happened recently that I never thought could.

"You are on a quest, as am I," said Siddhartha, breaking the silence in a melodious and soothing voice. "Perhaps we may help one another. What is it your heart desires, Marcus Quincy?"

"For an end to all of the stupidity, the hatred, the jealousy…"

"These things will *always* be present," Buddha counseled.

"Not if I can help it," I shot back.

"Then you have already discovered the means to complete your task." He was right; I *had* found what I was looking for. I knew that I had not come to be there by accident. Hell, the notion of accident and coincidence had gone out the window long ago. I was there for a reason.

"You wouldn't happen to have something for me, would you?" I asked.

"Of course," he answered. "I have much to offer."

"To be honest," I said. "I'm not even sure what it *is* I'm looking for. I don't even know whether it's an object or not." I had an image in my head from a pumpkin, just a half circle of light, not much to go on.

"I have nothing physical to offer you, Marcus Quincy, only my wisdom. Are you sure it is I whom you seek?"

"Yeah," I said, "pretty sure."

"Here then …" Buddha reached behind him and placed something next to my leg.

"It is all that I possess," he said, "but you are welcome to it."

I picked up the object and turned it over in my hands. It was a shiny metal bowl, gold in color, but extremely lightweight. I turned the bowl on its side and it made a half circle, just like the image on the pumpkin. "Thank you," I said. "What is it?" Buddha seemed unaffected by my lack of knowledge.

"It is called a singing bowl," he answered.

"What does it do?"

"It sings." Siddhartha laughed for a moment. "Strike something against it and see."

I picked up a stick and tapped the rim of the bowl. It made the sound of a thousand beautiful voices singing simultaneously. The voices slowly merged to form a tone, matching the tone in my head that had led me there. "I have never heard it do *that* before. It truly *does* belong to you. Tell me Marcus, Do you believe one man can make a difference?" Buddha queried.

"Yes," I said. "Yes, I do."

"Thank you, Marcus, thank you."

"No, thank *you*, Siddhartha," I said "Thank you for enlightening me."

DEATH AND REBIRTH

Now that I had collected the first piece of the Divine Engine, what was I supposed to do with the pieces as I gathered them? It's not like I was some video game character who can shove a bazooka in his backpack, so… what to do with the bowl? I decided to leave the decision up to fate. I listened to the tones in my head until one caught my attention, and I tuned in. I didn't try to locate my destination; I simply let the string carry me.

I was spat out onto a wooden platform on top of a mountain, looking out over what remained of a cloudless blue sky. The sun was setting over the tops of the trees below me and the shadows were quickly spreading. Soon even the sky would be dark. I knew this place and I knew it well. Shamans from a local Indian tribe were said to have come there long ago in search of spirit visions. I had traveled there once before on a vision quest of my own, a vision of a future with the woman I loved. This was where I had proposed to Anna. I placed the singing bowl under the wooden platform and covered it with leaves before sitting down on the rocky ledge and letting the memories wash over me. It wasn't long before my thoughts were replaced with sound through a single tone. I took a deep breath, pushed the memories of Anna aside as best I could, and caught a ride on the string leading me to the next piece.

I stood on a large stone surrounded by a river of molten earth. I felt no heat, but saw the effects of it on the rocks around me as they slowly melted, becoming one with the red river. Smoke bellowed from the ground making it impossible for me to see more than a few feet around me. I concentrated hard on the smoke, willing it to clear and, much to my surprise it obeyed. The smoke dissipated and I saw a man standing on the lake of lava. As the man walked forward, the ground behind him solidified, and life began to grow. Red and black turned to lush green foliage. Forests grew and mountains formed, and still he walked forward. The man drew closer to me and I saw his face for the first time. Every possible combination of features imaginable sped by at fantastic speed, making his face a blur. This man was everyone; *he was creation*!

The trees around us grew at an alarming rate until they blocked out the sunlight completely. The man cocked his head, looked me up and down with a puzzled look on his many faces and said, "You are the same, but you are different." My first thought was of my evil twin. *You but not you…* I had heard this before. "Yes," he said, seeming to grasp some hidden meaning. "Death and rebirth, both are constant in all of Chaos *and* with God."

"He was here, wasn't he?" I asked.

The man looked puzzled again, but only for a moment. "Ah… he does not know."

"What? Who are you?" I asked.

"I am either a God who became a man or a man who became a God," he chuckled under his breath, "above all else, I am a teacher."

"You said I was the same, but different. What did you mean?"

Without warning, as if the sky had opened up, it began to pour leaves as the trees shed their blanket of green. The grass and plants on the ground before me began to decay, the bark on the trees melted and crumbled like ash, floating away until there was nothing left but a vast field of death. I watched the ground beneath my feet slowly turn from green to black to red until we stood once more on an ocean of lava. I knew that I needed to stay calm; the fact that this man was not answering any of my questions certainly didn't help. "You seem to know a lot more about what's going on than I do," I said. I took a moment to breathe. "Please, all I'm asking for is your name."

"You may call me Laud Agni," the man said. First Buddhism and now Hinduism; I felt that I *must* have been in the right place.

"I'm looking for something," I said. "All I know is it that it looks like an infinity symbol, a sideways eight."

"The artifact *was* here," the man said. "But no longer."

"Where did it go?" I asked.

"I gave it to you but not you."

"You gave it to *him?*" I was beside myself thinking that a madman had a piece that I needed to save the world.

"No," the man said, "I gave it to *her.*" Laud Agni lowered his head and closed his eyes. "Your arrival here can mean only one thing… She *will* be remembered."

"You're talking about Elizabeth Patton, aren't you?" I hastily questioned.

Laud Agni opened his eyes and smiled, then everything around me went black.

When my vision returned I looked around. Laud Agni was gone and I no longer stood on a lake of lava. I was in a room I'd never seen before. The walls were a light wood paneling that matched the hardwood floors, a wooden ceiling fan slowly rotated above my head. There was a fuzzy purple couch along one wall and a small stand holding a television along another. A few paintings hung in frames on the walls and there was a vase of roses on the coffee table in front of the couch. Something inside told me this was the last known location of the divine object before it was lost. Spying a drawer in the coffee table, I pulled it open, and inside I found a small photo album. I sat down on the couch to see what the pictures could tell me. The first photo was of a small dog, a puppy that looked like a boxer. I flipped to the second page where there was a photo of an elderly couple, holding hands and smiling. I turned the page to find yet another picture of the couple, but this time, there was someone in the photo I recognized. It was Elizabeth Patton. I heard a sudden loud noise from behind a closed door at the end of the hallway, a thump and a muffled scream. I placed the photo album down on the coffee table and got up to investigate. As I reached for the knob I heard something slam into the other side the door. It sounded like the bed. I tried to force the door open, but it was no use. From within the room I heard voices, a male and a female talking at the same time. "*I know your name!*" I screamed, but before the word "Lilith" could leave my lips, something hit me hard, like a force pushing me out of that reality. I focused on my destination… the string was taking me home.

I was in *my* house in *my* reality, but the house was empty now, containing no furniture, no appliances, just nothing. I pictured it as it had been and saw Anna lying on the couch in front of the fireplace sleeping. I saw the girls playing in their room and Anna again in the shower. Anna was in our bedroom, too… in pieces. I slammed the bedroom door shut, backed up against the wall and slid to the floor as the tears came. I didn't want to remember her like that, ever… but it was always there, the image burned deep in my psyche just waiting to be released… to *make* me remember. I focused my thoughts on the good times I'd had with my girls, and with my wife. I got up and walked to the sliding glass door that led to the back deck. I stepped outside and I saw the girls playing on the swing, Anna swimming in the pool. As I took my trip down memory lane, I listened to the tones in my head and thought about where to find my personal property. I was beginning to suspect that I had one of the pieces to the Divine Engine in my possession all along, so I concentrated on Agent Mira Stark until a single tone grew louder and I caught my ride.

RETRIEVAL

I appeared in the middle of a dark highway, blinded by headlights as a car careened toward me. I didn't even have enough time to move before I heard the brakes lock and the vehicle hit me, crumpling around me as I stood my ground. The back end of the car lifted up into the air and crashed down hard as the vehicle came to a dead stop. I watched Agent Stark's face as the airbag deployed and I saw the terror in her eyes before recognition set in. I was undamaged, but the same could not be said for Stark's Government issued sedan. I climbed up onto what remained of the hood and hopped down by the driver's side door. The airbag lay limp, but Mira's chest continued to slowly rise and fall. I looked in the back of the car and saw the envelope containing Elizabeth Patton's belongings lying on the floorboard. I saw the thick gold chain slipping out of the top. I leaned in through the back window to retrieve the envelope and was about to back out of the car when I heard a click. Agent Stark had her gun to my head. She looked over the dashboard at the hood of her car and saw that it was crumpled down the middle like a V.

"My car's... totaled... and you don't... have a scratch... on you." Mira spoke through shallow breaths. "How can that be?"

"I guess I'm lucky," I said. "Look, I just came for my stuff." Agent Stark looked at the envelope I held and, keeping the gun to my head, she climbed out of the open drivers side window. Mira tried to stand and her legs buckled. I reached out to steady her and she grabbed my arm, pulling me down to the ground with her. Her gun hit the pavement and discharged harmlessly into the woods. Mira rolled over and struggled to her feet. I managed to get the envelope with Elizabeth Patton's belongings stuffed down the front of my pants and covered with my shirt before her focus returned to me.

"Get down on your knees... and put your hands behind your head." Agent Stark was badly hurt, her face was bloody and bruised from the impact and she seemed to be nursing a broken rib. She held her gun with both hands, but it was shaking. I did as she'd instructed and got down on my knees. Mira shoved the gun in my face, the barrel wavering just inches from my nose. I wondered how long it would take for her to pull the trigger. "I don't know how you were able to keep it a secret," she said. "But the jig is up. Did his wife find out, is that why you killed her? You knew you couldn't be blamed for it as long as your brother was in the hospital." Agent Stark was referring to my physical body, which was safely tucked away in the psychiatric ward of a North Carolina hospital.

"He's not my brother," I calmly stated.

"Don't *fuck* with me!" Agent Stark pushed the muzzle of the gun into my forehead.

"I know you want to kill me," I said, "but you really shouldn't."

Mira laughed. "Why shouldn't I? Besides, who would care?"

"The little girl in the backseat of the car that's heading this way, *that's* who would care!"

"There's no..." Mira began to say when she saw headlights flood the road. The driver hit his brakes as his car came around the corner, but as soon as he saw Agent Stark's gun pointed at my face, he accelerated and sped off down the road. "Well, that takes care of that." Mira smiled as she tightened her finger around the trigger.

Another set of headlights lit up the road, followed by flashing blue lights. Agent Stark relaxed her trigger finger and took one hand away from the gun. She pulled out her badge and held it up into the floodlight of the Virginia State Trooper's car. The cop stepped out of his vehicle, placed a cowboy hat on his head, and drew his pistol from its holster. "You wanna' lower your gun, ma'am?" he said.

I looked into the trooper's eyes and his life flashed within my head. The nametag on the cop's uniform read Officer Stancil, but everyone called him Jimmy. "Ma'am?" the officer repeated.

Mira stared blankly at the cop for a moment before responding.

"I'm Agent Mira Stark of the FBI and this man is wanted for the murder of his wife and doctor."

"No way! I read about that on the news! The guy offed some rich shrink at a hospital down in Raleigh or somethin'." It appeared that Jimmy was well informed.

"Or *something*," Mira responded in a sarcastic tone. "So, you gonna' call for backup or maybe an ambulance?" Mira's head spun, she reached for her car to steady her balance and continued speaking. "Is the back of your car secure?"

"Why, it sure is, Ma'am. And don't you worry none, help is on the way. Here, let me take care of that piece of shit for ya'."

Mira leaned in close to my ear and whispered, "Guess you *are* lucky, Markie."

Officer Jimmy jerked my arms behind my back and cuffed me, almost pulling my shoulders out of their sockets as he hauled me up from my knees and dragged me to his car. The trooper shoved me up against his squad car, placed one hand on the back of my neck, and slammed my head down hard onto the hood. Mira was trying to walk and fell. It seemed my luck was still holding, as Officer Jimmy gave up his search of me before it even started. Opening the back door of his cruiser, he pushed me inside, then slammed the door shut and ran to Agent Stark's aid. I thought about the handcuffs being gone and they obediently opened and fell from my wrists. I pulled the envelope out of my shirt and emptied its contents onto my lap. The medallion and Elizabeth's diary pages slid out, but there was more, including a file on Elizabeth Patton. I looked out of the window and saw Officer Jimmy standing in front of Mira's car with a stupid look on his face. Agent Stark had a phone to her ear. I placed *my* ear against the glass and listened. "Yes, this is Agent Stark. I need to speak to Admiral Forsythe. Tell him it's urgent." She slowly walked over to Jimmy and stood beside him, looking at the damage to her car.

"You sure you weren't drinkin' tonight, ma'am?" the young cop questioned.

"*Yes,* Officer Stancil, I am *sure* I haven't been drinking tonight. Would you like to test me?" Agent Stark was obviously still in her sarcastic mode.

"Why no, ma'am, you're in no condition to be performin' no field sobriety test. Why don't you just sit on down here and wait for the ambulance to come check ya out."

Mira was still waiting for the Admiral to answer. "Come on!" she muttered impatiently.

"*Hello?*" I heard the Admiral's voice over the phone.

"Yes, Admiral, Agent Stark here."

"*I was just getting ready to call you. I'm holding the records from Marcus's birth in my hand. Do you have any idea what Tetragametic Chimerism is?*"

"No, sir," Mira responded with a puzzled look on her face.

"It's a condition where two embryos fuse together and become one fetus at some point during gestation. Marcus had a twin, but it's inside of him and always has been." The Admiral sounded matter of fact.

"So you're saying there's *no* possible way he could have a twin?" Mira queried.

"I've talked to the doctors present at his birth myself, Agent Stark. There is no way that Marcus has a twin."

"Then *please* tell me Marcus must have *somehow* escaped the hospital," Agent Stark demanded.

Admiral Forsythe laughed. *"Sorry, Mira, but I'm looking in on him right now. He just suffered a massive seizure not but a few minutes ago. He's sleeping quietly now."*

Agent Stark hung up the phone and stumbled toward the squad car. I removed Elizabeth Patton's last diary entry from the stack of papers and placed the rest of the pages, the file, and the medallion back in the envelope. I read the first few lines from the journal entry I'd kept out of the package... *"I know your name. Someone shouted that from the other side of a door as I watched her murder me again tonight..."* By the time Mira had reached the car, I had tuned and was long gone.

The dark woman sat on Elizabeth Patton's stomach, straddling her torso and pinning the poor woman to the bed. I knew right away where I was, *and* the identity of the dark woman. It was Lilith, and me, well I just sat in the corner of the room watching. Reading the pages of Elizabeth's diary had allowed me to see through her eyes, to relive the moment as her. I was in the body of the Elizabeth Patton who had written the journal. I watched the Elizabeth on the bed jerk wildly as she struggled to break the invisible bonds that kept her arms bound to the bed. Lilith laughed out loud and rode the bucking woman, yelling *"Yee Haw"*. Elizabeth screamed and stopped moving. Lilith relaxed and sighed, tracing her fingertips over her captive's lips, caressing her neck and shoulders, then moving on to Elizabeth's bare breasts. Lilith threw her head back and moaned as a long, thin tentacle emerged from the dark woman's navel. The tendril slithered across the soft skin of Elizabeth's stomach like a thin black snake, moving slowly to her breast. Lilith, meanwhile, placed her fingertips on Elizabeth's breastbone and pushed in. I watched her fingers sink into the exposed flesh. Lilith pushed harder when her fingers touched bone and her hand sank in to the wrist. The dark woman whispered, *"Phey lop J'Frie,"* and quickly yanked her hand out. Lilith held up Elizabeth Patton's still beating heart. The dark bitch looked at me and smiled as she placed the muscle to her lips and licked the blood that slowly dripped down the side from an open ventricle. Lilith parted her lips and took a bite. She wiped her lips with the back of her arm, looked at me and said, *"You're next, my darling."* Lilith vanished and I rushed to the side of the bed. Before Elizabeth expelled her final breath, she took off the necklace she wore and gave it to me. Her hands here shaking and I wasn't able to grasp the chain before it fell to the floor, and when I reached down to pick it up I stopped cold. The chain of the medallion was lying on the floor in the shape of a figure eight! The pain and the ringing in my head grew in intensity and I was abruptly pulled from Elizabeth's memory.

The string led me to a hill overlooking a large courtyard were a crowd had gathered to watch some sort of game. I still had the envelope with Elizabeth Patton's belongings in my hand, so I placed the medallion around my neck, rolled up the envelope, and stuffed it into my back pocket. From the look of the crowd below me, I was somewhere in Central or South America, several centuries in the past. I stood and watched the game for a moment. The courtyard consisted of two stone walls running parallel to each other. Halfway down the courtyard I saw a vertical stone ring, a "hoop" of sorts. Using only their lower bodies, the men were trying to get some kind of ball to go through the "hoop". It was dark, so the tops of the walls were lined with torches, and beyond the walls I saw a vast stone structure rising into the sky. The top of the temple was illuminated with bright white light radiating from the rising moon, casting a blanket of light down the great staircase that led to the bottom of the temple. A young boy, ten or eleven maybe, emerged from the trees and spoke. "You have returned," he said. The boy opened his mouth to call out, to get the attention of the crowd below us, leaving me no choice but to scoop him up in my arms and press the palm of my hand to his lips.

"No one must know I am here," I said to the boy. The fear left the child's eyes and he nodded. I removed my hand from the child's lips and let him go.

The boy backed away slowly with his head bowed. "I am ta-b'a-hi. How may I serve you, my lord?" He stopped a few yards back and fell to his knees.

"I'm looking for something," I said. The ringing in my head was connected to an image of a lens. In the back of my skull I felt a sharp pain, like something being driven in fast and hard… then I heard the thought. It was a single word. "kimi", I said, repeating the word spoken within my head. The boy looked at me and nodded. "What does it mean?" I asked.

Ta-b'a-hi pointed down into the courtyard and took my hand. "Follow me," he said, leading me down a narrow path. The boy stopped before stepping out into the light and turned to me.

"Death head," he said, "Kimi means death head."

The child pointed to the men on the court. One man hit the ball with his knee, like a soccer player, trying to get it to go through the stone ring. The ball tumbled through the air and was hit by another player. As the ball passed through the moonlight, I could see that it was not a ball at all, but a human head. The onlookers cheered as the second man hit the "ball" through the ring. The crowd ran onto the court and grabbed one of the men from the opposing team, shoving him out in front as thy escorted the players off toward the temple cheering.

"What are they doing?" I asked.

"He is the captain of the losing team," explained ta-b'a-hi. "He will become the ball for the next game." The boy ran out onto the court and retrieved the head, then stuffed it under his arm and ran back to me. He held it out with both hands and dropped to his knees. "Here, my lord." I took the head from the boy and turned it over in my hands. The skin was soft and springy, like there was something rubbery underneath. The man's lifeless eyes looked up at me, his mouth open wide as if trying to speak. What would he say if he *could* speak? And what the hell was I going to do with a human head? Was the lens I needed in the man's eyes? Somehow, I doubted it. The skull of the severed head seemed to be just a little too small, so I turned the head upside down and stuck my hand up into the neck. The inside of the head was stuffed with some sort of elastic material, but inside the material, I felt something wrapped in cloth. I stretched my fingers to reach around the object and pulled. It moved some, but not much. I pulled on a flap of skin hanging down below the head's jaw, trying to stretch the flesh enough to fit over the object inside. Slowly, the skin tore up the side of the face allowing me to slide the cloth covered object out. I unwrapped the delicate material to find a crystal skull. When I turned the object over, I noticed the cranial plates on the back of the crystal could be removed. I pulled them off to find yet another object hidden inside. It was a six-inch piece of curved glass. I held the lens up to the light cast by one of the torches and watched a rainbow of color explode out of the other side. "Thank you," I said to the boy. "I must go now." Ta-b'a-hi's eyes opened wide as I disappeared in a flash of light.

THE OTHERS

I found myself at what I began to call "Anna's Bridge". I placed the lens and chain into the singing bowl beneath the wooden platform before spending a while looking up at the stars. So many stars... so many realities; I could *hear* them. Billions of nine toned melodies repeated their endless patterns as I lay on the platform watching the heavens slowly pass by above me. It's easy to lose track of time while traveling throughout the multiverse, and it didn't help that every time I returned to my reality a significant amount of time had passed. I heard a loud boom and the sky filled with light. It was July the Fourth, 2011. The show lasted about half an hour before culminating in a not-so-grand finale. When the fireworks ended, I sat up and pulled out the envelope containing the rest of Elizabeth Patton's belongings. I took out the bundle of papers and sorted through the pages, pulling out the ones that caught my attention. Elizabeth's file indicated that she'd had a brother named Michael, but another page told me that he'd died at the age of six after getting hit by a car as he got off the bus from school, one week to the day after Elizabeth Patton had died! There were photos of Michael in the file, too. It was the same boy who had sat on the swing in the back yard as I spoke to Elizabeth's father, the same face that smiled at me as he'd handed me the diary pages, the chain, and the medallion. The ringing in my head grew louder, and I swore I heard other tones too, ones that never used to be there. These new tones were a deep bass, not like the high tones that had been in my head until then. My body jolted as the ringing grew deafeningly loud and I was pulled from the mountain.

I knew where I was going before I even got there. I shifted to the top of the hill with the cave where the five old men were waiting for me. Ten eyes stared back at me that looked just like mine.

"I want some answers," I demanded.

"We imagine you do," the five replied in unison. "You want to know who we are. Well, we are *you*, Marcus." I tried to read them, but it was no use, I saw nothing but my own life flashing before me.

"How do I know you're not *his* other five?" I asked.

"We are you and you are us," they said. "The others you speak of are no more."

"What happened to them?" I asked suspiciously.

"Your dark half killed them," said the man closest to me. "Listen, Marcus, remember the pumpkin? There were a *lot* of images on it."

"Forty nine," I said.

"You're not the only *you* out there looking for the pieces to the puzzle," said another, "so remember, you're not alone in this search."

Okay, so there were at *least* five of me out there looking for the pieces to the Divine Engine; maybe I *would* have enough time.

"You know, you could have saved me a headache and just told me that I had one of the pieces," I said.

"The time was not right," they explained, "and you already knew too much."

"So tell me, just how many of me *are* there?" I asked.

"There were seven of us once, hence the eyes. Victory will come at a cost, Marcus, as I'm sure you are already well aware. Fear not, my friend, you *will* see this through to the end."

The words echoed within my head as everything went black and before I could say another word I was ripped from the spot.

6Б6
HELL

FRIEND OR FOE

My body was numb and my heart raced. "Marcus, are you still with us?" I was back in the hospital but something was still pulling me, threatening to extract me from this reality at any moment. The force drawing me wasn't one of the pieces of the Divine Engine, the tone wasn't right. It was a deep bass, a dark tone. I knew that when I left the hospital I would have no choice but to follow the string, and I would have to be ready.

Admiral Forsythe looked down at me as I lay on the gurney. "Come on, Marcus, don't leave us yet," he said. Was that concern in his voice? There were three other people in the room with him, two doctors and a nurse. "Sir, I'm going to have to ask you to step back." One of the doctors put his arm out and pushed the Admiral back a few feet. "He's doing fine, we've got him." When I opened my eyes, the two doctors in my room looked at one another. The Admiral remained silent. "Look," one doctor said to the other, "he's tracking us. Do you think he can actually *see* with those things?" My restraints snapped and fell to the floor; the doctors backed up against the wall and the nurse screamed and ran for the door. I sat up and spoke to the Admiral. "Tell them to leave."

Admiral Forsythe turned to speak but the doctors had already fled.

160

"I'm not going to hurt you," I said.

"You're sick, Marcus. Your delusions have taken over your life."

"They're far from delusions, Robert, and you *know* it!" I snapped.

"Yes… yes, Marcus. The call I received from Agent Stark was an eye opener. I suspected that there was more going on here than meets the eye."

"Why are you so interested in me anyway?" I asked.

"Fear," was how the Admiral answered.

"Would you care to elaborate on that?" By then I was tired of all the bullshit that I'd been fed from so many different sources and I just wanted some clear-cut answers.

"People are afraid of the things they do not understand," the Admiral explained. "It is my *duty* to assure the public that there is nothing to fear. I always have my eyes open for… the unusual."

"Ah, but Admiral, are you willing to open your *mind*?"

"I have seen things that defy rational explanation…" The Admiral paused as the memories took hold. Through his eyes I watched them play out as he spoke. "…And, on occasion, when there's enough proof to back it up, I'm willing to believe in something that does not make sense to me."

"Good," I said, "then sit." The Admiral pulled up a stool and sat down next to the bed.

"Do you believe in God?" I asked.

"With all the evil I have seen there *has* to be something more. And yes, Marcus, I *do* believe in God. I go to church *every* Sunday."

"Then maybe you'll believe me enough to make sure, personally, that nothing happens to my girls. He'll be coming for them."

"Are you ready to tell me who *he* is?" the Admiral asked.

"He's me in another reality, one where things turned out differently. That's all I can say for certain at this point."

"Okay," replied the Admiral, "then why does he want to kill your family?"

"I don't know…" But I was damn certain that I was going to find out.

"Alright," said the Admiral. "Now tell me about this…" He pulled Hunter's Bible out of his coat pocket and held it up. "It was found on the body of Dr. Andrew Spencer."

"Yeah… Hunter must have dropped it when he attacked me."

"I find that hard to believe, Mr. Quincy. I have *never* seen Mr. Hunter without this book somewhere nearby." The Admiral was right; the book was Thomas Hunter's most prized possession. I decided to ignore the Admiral's comment and throw him some bait.

"I'm sure you've been keeping track of my file since I've been here," I said. "The night before Andrew Spencer died there was an incident."

"Yes," the Admiral nodded. "The symbols drawn on the walls of your room, where did they come from?" He seemed a little too eager for an answer.

"The symbols were from Hunter's bible," I said.

"I've looked through the book, Mr. Quincy, there are *no* such symbols." The Admiral flipped through the pages of the Bible as he held it before my face. The dark tone in my head had finally won the battle and reality was slipping fast. I couldn't resist the opportunity to shake some of the smugness out of the Admiral, so before I tuned and caught the next string I said, "You might want to try reading it in the dark sometime."

INTO THE ABYSS

I focused on the string to see where it was taking me and things weren't looking too good. I saw what lay in wait for me at the end of the string and I knew it was a trap. The glistening blades of the Umbra's teeth clanked together, the metallic tone resonating in tune with the string. I concentrated on the tone, trying to find the string's location in this realities song. Ira laughed a wicked laugh, his open mouth awaiting my arrival. I listened to the pattern repeat twice, hoping I would have enough time to jump before the tone came around again. I was close, too close. Three tones remained before my destination.

The thoughts of the Mille Umbra were forced into my head. *"You're mine now!"* it told me. Two… One… I jumped.

I stood in a parking lot looking out over a city in ruins. Smoke poured from the high rises in the distance and flames leapt from the windows of most of the nearby buildings. The tones in my head were different; they were *all* on the low bass end, no treble to be heard. I saw a crowd of people up ahead, at least a hundred. I shifted to the front of the crowd to see what was going on. Things were in total chaos. People were cutting themselves trying to get through the window of an electronics store to grab the merchandise, but it was no use; as soon as they touched something it began to dissolve. I watched a woman slit her throat on the storefront glass as she fell trying to run out with a melting computer.

"This way!" someone yelled. "I know where there's more!"

The crowd surged off down the street, leaving behind a dozen or so trampled corpses. I chuckled to myself, thinking Hell must have a special place for the idiots who spend days camped out in front of a store just to get their hands on the "next big thing". I looked up at the street sign in front of me. Marcus Street. I followed it to the end and took a left on Quincy Avenue. The street ended abruptly at the entrance to a subway station. I entered the revolving door into a large room with a high glass ceiling. The roof of the building was so covered in soot that, even if the sun *had* been shining, it could not have been seen. The subway station had been looted long ago, anything of value having long been torn from the spot.

I took the stairs down to the waiting platform and sat on one of the long wooden benches. A bare bulb hung from a cord above my head; somehow the lights worked down there. As I waited for something to happen, I reflected on what the five old men had told me. *There were seven of us once...* and my eyes, the sevens. I had dreamed of others being killed, murdered by the Ah Me Rah, so there *must* have been more of us. Why was Lilith killing us off? And why was she killing off Elizabeth Patton's others? I felt that I was close to answering those questions and more.

I heard a rumble in the distance and the squealing of brakes. The platform shook as the train came to a halt, an open doorway stopping directly in front of me. I stood up, walked inside, and cautiously searched the car until satisfied that I was alone. The doors on each end were locked, so I took a seat across from the exit and waited for something to happen. The exit door hissed shut and the train lurched forward. The lights outside the window passed by faster and faster like a strobe light, filling the car with pulses of light. I heard the door at the front of the train open and I saw a woman cautiously enter. She stood in the open doorway, nude and covered in cuts and bruises, yet I still recognized her. "Elizabeth Patton," I called out as I stood. She tried to hide her nakedness with her arms and hands, but she was too weak to hold them up. Her hair was a mess and both of her eyes were deep black with splotches of red. She stood there sobbing and asked, "Do I know you?"

"No," I answered. I could not trust that this was actually her; after all, she was *not* here of her own free will. I took off my shirt and threw it to her. "My name's Marcus. Any idea where this train goes?"

"No," she said. "I woke up on a platform with no exit. There was nowhere else to go but on the train."

"How long have you been here?" I asked.

"I lost track after two weeks." Elizabeth continued to sob. I wanted to comfort her, but she was too nervous, too twitchy. I was afraid to get close to her. When Elizabeth pulled my shirt over her head, I noticed the knife in her hand. She saw me eying the blade and held it up. "I didn't make these cuts," she protested, holding out her arms, revealing even more gashes. "It's for protection."

"From *what*?" I questioned.

"Your worst nightmares." Elizabeth took the seat behind me and let out a sigh. "You're the first *person* I've seen since I got here," she said.

"Person, huh? So, how'd you get through the door? I just checked and it was locked."

"They open randomly... and there's *usually* something nasty on the other side." Just as Elizabeth said this, the door on the back end of the car hissed open. I stood up and walked to the door while Elizabeth followed closely behind. We passed into another empty car, the door slamming shut tightly and locking behind us. The car's windows were tinted dark, allowing no light from the tunnel to penetrate. In the darkness I saw a small gift-wrapped box on the floor. I motioned for Elizabeth to stay behind me as I knelt down to check it out. Something inside was moving around. I pulled on the bright red bow and watched the ribbons slide off onto the floor. I pulled back the lid to find...

"What is it?" Elizabeth called from behind me. "I can't see."

Inside the box was the still beating heart of Elizabeth Patton and pinned to it with a tack was a post-it note that read:

The last is always the sweetest...
Just as God made her...
Right now I'm feeling a little stuffed...
So I think I'll eat it later...

Lilith

The beating of the heart in the box increased in both volume and intensity, each thump causing the heart to leap slightly higher until the muscle soared out of the box and into the air, freezing mid-flight.

165

The large exit door beside us suddenly hissed open, and the train car filled with light from the fixtures mounted to the inside of the tunnel. The heart hovered before us, its beat increasing to an incredible speed, matching the timing of the lights on the tunnel wall that passed by the open door like a strobe light, dark-light, dark-light. I looked back at Elizabeth, but she was gone, my shirt now lying on the floor where she had been standing. *"Ticket please,"* a voice called out from behind me as I pulled the shirt over my head.

I turned and stood to find myself face to chest with a large man. He wore a blue hat with a patch on it that was too covered in oil and blood to read. He wore a dirty blue coat over what I first mistook to be a red shirt, but I quickly realized that the man's skin was missing from his neck down. I looked up at his face. Starting at his chin, strips of skin were missing in patches, a half inch of muscle then a half inch of flesh and so on, leading up to his forehead. A half inch wide vertical strip of skin remained intact down the center line of the man's face, while each ribbon carved from the man's flesh was pulled behind his head and nailed into the back of his skull. *"Ticket please,"* he repeated. Blood dripped down his chin as the words gurgled from his partially lipless mouth.

"Sorry," I said as I reached out for Elizabeth's heart that still hovered in the air before me, "I don't have one." The man raised a large blood-spattered axe into the air above his head and began to laugh.

"I was hoping you would say that," the man gurgled as he lunged at me with the weapon. I plucked Elizabeth Patton's heart out of the air and jumped through the open doorway. I landed hard and rolled. At the trains present speed the fall should have hurt like hell, but I felt nothing. I stood and brushed the dirt from my clothes and made sure the heart was still beating. I started to place it in the right pocket of my pants, but had forgotten about the fruit from the Tree of Life I'd put there in Eden, so I stuffed the heart into my other pocket. It felt kind of weird beating against my thigh and on any other occasion I might even have enjoyed it.

I listened to the train rumble off into the distance, leaving me stranded before a vast field of glowing green orbs, each approximately the size of a bowling ball. The spheres emitted a bright green light that surrounded a black core. They seemed to float about four feet above the ground and were tethered to the desert floor by thick chains held down with iron spikes. There must have been millions of them, stretching back to the horizon where the black dirt met the red sky. A shadow moving through the field behind me drew my attention from the orbs and I saw a young girl, her dress covered in blood. As soon as the child knew she had been seen, she darted off into the field. The girl was roughly the same height as the tethered orbs, which made it difficult to see where she was going. I had to watch the spheres for movement in order to keep track of her as I followed her. Suddenly, everything stopped moving. I looked around in every direction, but there was no sign of the young girl. Off in the distance, to my left, I saw movement. I shifted to the spot and as soon as the girl saw me, she was gone again. She had *shifted*! But she left me something... a tone. I tuned into this new string and followed. I tried to focus on the child's destination, but somehow she was able to block me. The young girl looked over her shoulder at me and smiled, then I watched her vanish completely. As I arrived at the spot where she had disappeared I was pulled from the string.

I found myself standing on a large metal platform suspended between two giant towers with twin spires rising into the murky red sky. Two large metal rings hovered above my head about a foot apart and I saw nothing holding them in place. Each ring was attached to a chain, one hanging from each tower, forming a V above my head. For what purpose this monstrous contraption was designed I could not conceive. "I want to know *one* damned thing!" demanded a tiny female voice with a British accent. The young girl stepped out from the shadows of the tower. "Why did you kill Andrew Spencer?" she asked.

I recognized her at once. "I've seen you before," I said. "You and your sisters were playing a game in a dream I had once."

"I don't *have* any sisters!" she screamed angrily, "Now answer my *fucking* question!"

"I..." The child cut me off before I could answer.

"Did your *other* kill him, then?"

I could have easily said yes, but it wouldn't have been the truth. Sure, my other *had* been part of it, but...

"No..." I said. "It was Ira."

The young girl stared at me for a while, her body tense; she looked nervous. I could see nothing when I looked into her eyes and I wondered what was going through her head. "I believe you," she said. "To kill a brethren is an unspeakable act; Ira *must* be punished."

"How *do* you kill an Umbra?" I asked. My head buzzed from the tone rumbling in the back of my skull. I tried to hold on to the reality long enough for an answer, but the force pulling me away was much stronger than the ones I'd experienced thus far. Before I was pulled from that reality, the girl spoke. "The living must be reunited with the dead," she said.

SIRNIB

"Excuse me, mister." I stood on a pier, overlooking a large pond. "Excuse me, mister." Behind me was a scrawny young boy around eight or nine years old in tattered and ragged clothing. "Wow, you have *really* cool eyes! You gonna' eat that?" He pointed to a cooler packed with ice containing three large catfish. "They're not mine," I said.

"Good!" The boy dove at the cooler, knocking it over. Two of the fish fell back into the water, but he held on tight to the third. I watched the boy shove the fish into his mouth and swallow it whole.

"I'm sorry," said the boy, "but I'm *sooooo* hungry. Don't you worry, sir, I wouldn't try to eat *you*! Besides, you're *much* too big."

"I appreciate that," I said. "Where exactly *am* I?"

"Just got here, huh?" The boy seemed disappointed but quickly cheered up. "I've got thirty-six hours until I leave, so I'm goin' to the city. Wanna' come?"

"Sure, why not." We left the pier and started walking along a muddy dirt road. "My name's Marcus."

"I'm Sirnib," said the boy.

"How old are you, Sirnib?"

"I don't know; I've been here a *long* time."

The look on his face told me he didn't want to talk about his age. Sirnib just stared at the ground while he walked. The road was at least ten feet wide, but it did not look like it had ever been driven on.

"Is there any other way to get around or do you always have to walk?" I asked.

"Oh sure, there are *some* vehicles, but they're hard to come by, and they cost you an arm and a leg for a ride, sometimes *literally*!"

"What about shifting?" I wondered if I could take someone else with me when I shifted.

"Huh?" The boy had a blank look on his face.

"Teleportation? Moving an object or person from one place to another?"

"Oh no, that only happens when you jump. Well, there *is* one other place. You'll see soon enough."

"Jump?" I asked.

"Boy, you *are* new here."

"Again, where is *here*?" I asked.

"Well, better you hear it from me, I guess." The boy stopped walking and turned to face me.

"You died, buddy; you're in Hell." Part of me had already known that.

"So how do things work around here?" I asked.

"Well, most of the realities aren't *that* bad, but there are some... Let me tell you, you pray you won't be there long. But those are mostly the inner realms, where you don't jump as much, if at all..."

"So you *jump* between realities?" I asked. "Is it random? I mean, you said that you knew how long you have before you jump again."

"It's just more of a feeling," he said. "I've been doing this a long time."

"So there's no pattern to your jumps?" I asked.

"No, it's random, but the jumps *do* seem to happen at the most inopportune times. You're never at any one spot for the same amount of time," explained the boy, "but you *do* go to the same places every now and then. Shit, I'm sure there are realities that I've never been to..." Sirnib stopped speaking to watch some sort of strange animal wandering down the road ahead of us. It sort of resembled a dog with no skin, having six legs, and all of its muscles exposed and covered in large thorns.

"Oh man, I am *sooooo* hungry," Sirnib moaned.

"You're not going to try and eat *that* are you?" I nearly puked at the thought.

The animal was almost as big as Sirnib. He called the creature over and it approached with its head lowered, then nuzzled against the boy's leg, leaving a dozen or so deep cuts on the child's exposed skin.

It happened fast; one second Sirnib was talking to the dog in a soothing voice and the next, the animal's head was in the boy's mouth, leaving deep gashes on Sirnib's lips. The kid's mouth stretched around the animal's shoulders as he swallowed it like a snake. The dog's tail stuck out of the boy's mouth like a red cigarette hanging from his lips. I just *had* to think about that, didn't I?

"Ow! Those things *hurt*," Sirnib complained while he rubbed his stomach.

"Then don't eat 'em," I said.

"But I'm *sooooo* hungry," he whined.

"Say, they don't happen to have cigarettes here, do they?"

"You're in luck, buddy." Sirnib pulled a pack out of his pocket and held it out to me. "Now, if we only had a light. It's been over three days since I've had a smoke myself. Three days with no damn fire. Kind of ruins Hell's reputation, doesn't it?"

I pulled two cigarettes out of the pack and handed it back to him. Touching the tips of them together, I twisted the cigarettes against one another and they lit.

"How'd you do *that*?" Sirnib yelled.

"I'm magic," I said. I handed him one of the smokes and we walked down the road for a while in silence, enjoying the nicotine buzz. "So tell me, what happens to people here?" I questioned.

Sirnib responded, "It depends on how bad you were in your lifetime. Most people just spend their afterlife jumping between realities, never able to call one particular place home. Other people get stuck in their realities, and let me tell you, there are some pretty nasty places to get stuck in. And then there are the people who've done the most vile of deeds, or pissed off one of the Dark Ones; either way, *they* get stuck in a loop, destined to repeat the same act over and over again for all eternity."

"That would suck," I said.

"Sure would," gibed Sirnib.

"So what do *you* know about the 'Dark Ones'?" I asked.

"Nothing I can tell you. They *know* when you're talkin' about 'em, so we shouldn't." When Sirnib spoke there was fear in his voice. Sirnib stopped and stood for a moment, staring at a fork in the road. To the left, the road wound into the nearby mountains, and to the right, the road disappeared under a canopy of large trees.

"I thought you said you knew where we were going?" I taunted.

"Shhhh." Sirnib placed his finger to his lips before pointing into the thick grass between the roads where a mass of white fur moved about. Sirnib dove at the creature through the tall grass and hauled it to the ground. It was big, about the size and shape of a horse, with the hair of an Afghan hound.

"Are you going to eat that thing, *too?*" I questioned.

"No, stupid, *this* we ride… *then* we eat it." He climbed up onto its back and the beast stood.

"I thought something like this was a bit too big for you to eat," I said, recalling what the boy had told me when we'd met.

"So, I lied," Sirnib said and smiled. "Now get on."

I climbed onto the creature and the boy coached the animal down the path and into the forest.

"I can eat anything and not gain any weight," said Sirnib. "Weird, huh?"

"Yeah, if that's what you want to call it." I began to feel Elizabeth Patton's heart beating in my pocket, its rhythm increasing with each stride of the creature. I'd forgotten it was there. Out of nowhere one of the Dark Ones appeared on the road ahead of us. It was Lilith. The bitch was like a fucking plague!

"I *told* you we shouldn't be talking about them," Sirnib snarled. "Why did I bring it up? Stupid! Stupid, stupid, stupid!" Sirnib slammed his head against the skull of the beast we rode upon and the creature reared back, knocking us both off. Sirnib, not about to disappoint me, dove on the creature and gobbled it up. "What the hell did you do *that* for?" I screamed at the little monster.

"Hey, it might have gotten away. Besides, I'm not gonna' watch a perfectly good meal run away, not when it could be my last!"

Lilith continued to stand before us on the road about twenty yards away.

"Stay behind me," I told Sirnib.

"Oh, you don't have to worry about..." It was too late; he was already gone. Sirnib reappeared, floating in the air before Lilith. She reached up and took hold of the boy's throat as I slowly walked forward.

"*Stop!*" Lilith held her prize up high. "*Come any closer and this pathetic child dies.*" I stopped where I was. "*You have something of mine; might I suggest a trade?*" Lilith purred.

"Yeah, like you're not going to kill him anyway," I said. The heart in my pocket began to beat faster, like it might burst at any moment. I had to do something and I had to do it fast. I shifted beside Lilith and grabbed Sirnib, then shifted again and caught a string. I couldn't believe I had pulled it off! I could feel the kid in my arms; he was still with me! Once I had time to think about things, however, our escape seemed just a *little* too easy.

LOO RIN

"What the fuck was *that*?" Sirnib stumbled to the floor. "And now... and now *this*..."

We stood on a twenty by thirty foot platform that was suspended in the air. I looked over the edge and saw platforms below us, like a giant set of stairs leading down into the clouds. They went up from our platform too, into the red sky. Sirnib's voice interrupted my observations.

"We're goin' up, right?"

"Sorry, something's telling me to go down," I said. Sirnib didn't seem too pleased with that idea.

"Screw that," he yelled. "*I'm* goin' up!"

"Well, I guess it's goodbye, then," I said.

"Yeah, I need to get as far away from *you* as I can. She was after *you*, not *me*. I don't want *any* part of what you got going on!" Sirnib began jumping for the platform above his head but it was too high.

I turned and walked to the ledge that led down. "Aren't you going to offer me a boost? It's the *least* you could do, considering *you* brought us here."

I turned to face Sirnib; he looked defeated. "*First* of all," I said, "*I* didn't pick this place. And *second*, if I hadn't grabbed *you*, you'd be toast. Besides, even if I *do* give you a boost, how are you going to get to the next level, and the one after that?"

"You make an excellent point," Sirnib stated. "So why don't you go up with me and we can *both* live?"

"Come on," I said, "you've been here long enough to know that up isn't always up and down isn't always down." My patience was growing thin.

"*Another* excellent point," he said.

"You have two choices: you can stay here until you "jump" or you can come with me." I turned, climbed over the side of the platform, and dropped down. Sirnib paced back and forth on the platform above me.

"All right," he said, "but as soon as we get somewhere else, I'm gone. No offense, Marcus, but you're not the safest person to be around."

"You got *that* right," I said. Sirnib sat down on the ledge and pushed off, landing at my feet.

"Well then, the sooner we get this over with, the better."

We climbed from platform to platform, down through the clouds, to a city below us that Sirnib seemed to recognize. "It's Loo Rin!" he yelled. "Maybe we're *not* so bad off, eh?" From high above the city, I saw what looked like a constantly shifting puzzle. The entire city was in constant motion. Buildings moved, streets suddenly changed direction, I had to stop every now and then to watch. "It's a hell of a good time, buddy, a *hell* of a good time!" Sirnib's excitement mounted; he grew more impatient the lower we got. "Say, can't you do that thing again, get us there a little quicker?"

"Sorry," I said. "I don't want to attract any unwanted attention if I don't have to."

"Smart thinking," Sirnib said as he jumped to the next platform.

The "stairs" eventually took us well outside of the city limits into a vast field of grazing cattle.

"Why don't you run off and get yourself something to eat," I said, "then we can head into the city." Before I could finish my sentence, Sirnib was in the field with a cow shoved halfway down his throat. I watched him eat six of them before the rest of the herd got wise to the boy and ran off. Sirnib wandered back in my direction, sat down next to me, and burped. "I'm gonna' need a few minutes," he said. "Why did I eat so much?" Sirnib bawled. "I'm *sooooo* full." I watched the boy roll around in the grass next to me, clenching his stomach.

"Do you go through this every time you eat?" I asked.

"Shut up," Sirnib bellowed. "I ate too much, that's all. Oh man I am *sooooo* full."

175

"Walk it off," I said as I stood up. "It's time to go."

Sirnib walked a few paces ahead of me, complaining. "Man, I ate too much, I'm *sooooo*... You know what? I think I'm kinda' hungry."

"Shut up and walk," I said. Once among the city streets, it was apparent that the shifting was not confined to the architecture. In Loo Rin, the people shifted at random too. Every time it happened we were left a little disoriented. Sirnib told me that I'd get used to it. We stopped in front of a small open doorway. "Ah, we're here!" the boy excitedly announced. "Let's go in before it moves on us." We descended down a long set of stairs to a large steel door. Sirnib rapped six times on the door and it opened with a thud. "Ah, this is more *like* it." He rubbed his hands together as he walked up to a bar. I followed him and took a seat. "What'll it be?" he asked.

"Nothing for me," I said.

"Suit yourself." Sirnib turned on his stool and called the bartender over. I sat and watched the crowd as the kid ordered his drink. Music blared from a set of speakers mounted on the ceiling over the dance floor. Couples held each other and moved to the beat, which changed with every shift of the building. Somehow, the dancers kept in time as if nothing had ever happened.

"You shhhure you don' want somffffink to drink?" Sirnib had already downed three.

"Slow down there, kid; I ain't carryin' your ass out of here."

Sirnib slammed his glass down on the bar. "Might I have another, kind sir?" he asked the barkeep before looking back at me. "This'll be my last one, I swear. Besides, I'm hungry."

"I'll wait outside," I said. I got up from the stool and started for the door.

"Don't go fffar or you'll never fffind yer way back." Sirnib swayed on the barstool. I was trying not to read the boy, but every time he looked at me I saw things. I didn't think he was *intentionally* being deceitful, but he *was* hiding something. If I hadn't known any better, I might have thought that he knew what I was doing.

I stayed close to the doorway so I wouldn't lose it in a shift, watching as the citizens of Loo Rin went about their lives. I watched them disappear and reappear elsewhere. Occasionally when a crowd shifted, not all of the people were there when the crowd later reappeared. At other times, there might be someone new added to the group. It was fascinating to watch. One of the passersby stopped in front of me with a look of almost recognition on her face, then shook her head and walked away. In the brief moment she looked at me, I saw her life and her death. I also saw her encounter with Elizabeth Patton... Here... in Loo Rin! I took off after the woman, but the crowd had already shifted her away from me. I tried to focus on her eyes as Gabriel had instructed me. I found her two blocks away and shifted to where she was.

"That's odd," someone behind me said.

The woman had apparently heard it, too, and stopped to stare at me. "What?" I asked.

"He just appeared there, out of sync with the rest of us," another voice chimed in.

"That's never happened before," a third person added.

"Hey," I said, "you're in Hell, you expect things to always be the same?" The crowd considered this for a few seconds and then went back to their lives, all but the woman.

"Are... are you her brother?" she asked. I was right; the woman *had* recognized me! What's more, she seemed to know that I was connected to Elizabeth Patton.

"Yes," I lied, "I'm her brother. Do you know where I can find her?" The woman looked scared as she stood there shaking. "She said that she was staying at a hotel down in The Den," the woman said, then turned and ran from me. I'd seen in the woman's eyes that her experience with Elizabeth Patton had not been a good one. I needed to find Elizabeth, but first I needed a guide. I'd noticed a kind of tingling sensation just before the shifts in Hell and I felt another one coming. I saw through Sirnib's eyes that he was still in the bar, ordering another drink. I waited for the next shift and…

"Marcuth, tho good to stheee you," Sirnib slurred, followed by a loud burp. "I ttthhhought you'd nnnnever get back…" He was *trashed*.

"Time to go, little man." I held Sirnib's wobbling head still with both of my hands so that I could look him in the eyes. I needed to know this city; I needed his memories. Regrettably, Sirnib passed out, but before he did, I'd found the district known as The Den. Sirnib had quite a few memories from there. It seemed that he had lied to me about only being in Loo Rin once before. I learned that the Den was Loo Rin's porn district and I learned something else, too. There was a woman in the city, a prophet. Sirnib had been to see her many times during his visits to the city and her visions were *always* right. I figured it couldn't hurt to make a detour to see her on our way to find Elizabeth Patton, so I picked Sirnib up and slung him over my shoulder, waited for the tingling sensation, and shifted.

We stood outside a door where in small black letters the word *seer* was printed. I opened the door and a buzzer sounded. Sirnib began to stir; he must have recognized the sound of the buzzer. A frosted glass window slid open revealing a woman sitting in a chair. She immediately recognized the boy.

"Hey, Nib!" said the woman. "The Madam is with someone right now. Take a seat out in the waiting room and she'll be with you in just a few minutes." I carried the kid out into the waiting room and sat him down in a soft leather chair. I took the seat next to him and we waited. There was absolutely nothing to do in the room but look at the wallpaper. Five-inch wide vertical stripes of green and purple alternated throughout the room, matching the paper in the hallway. Symbols had been painted in various places around the room. Each symbol always had a twin, one on the green stripe with its mate on the purple stripe.

After waiting about twenty minutes I began to wonder why there had been no shifts within this building. A door opened and an elderly black woman with long gray hair hanging down to her waist stepped out. "Is that you, Nib?" she asked.

"Yeah," I answered for him. "He's a little out of it right now. My name's Marcus; I was the one who wanted to see you."

"Well then," she said, "please come in."

I picked the kid up, carried him through the door and placed him down on one end of a waiting couch, then took a seat on the other end. The old woman took a seat in a large chair across from us and began to speak. "How can I help you, Marcus?"

"I'm looking for a woman," I answered.

The Madam sat there and nodded to herself, as if contemplating what I'd said. The woman's chair began vibrating, rising up into the air, slowly moving forward until she levitated directly in front of me. The chair then lowered to the floor and the woman leaned forward.

"Come closer, Marcus," she said, stretching her hands toward me. "Place your forehead against mine and take my... Oh my... Yours are different," she said, "but I have seen eyes like this on another species here... the Ah Me Rah!" It was obvious that my eyes had disturbed her.

"What do you know about them?" I queried nervously. "What do you know about Lilith?"

The Madam took my hands in hers and gently placed her forehead against my own.

I heard a deafening roar and saw a flash of blinding light. It was like watching a supernova. All at once my world went white. *"The Divine Engine has been created."* It was the Madam's voice, but I heard it as a thought inside my head. In the center of the whiteness that could only be seen by the Madam and I, a small black dot appeared and began to slowly grow in size. *"The multiverse is born,"* she chanted. The blackness continued to grow until it encompassed all of my vision. Something was moving about in the blackness now, clouds of gas that spiraled and expanded. The gas separated, forming hundreds of swirling clouds. I began to jump through moments in my life, the speed and intensity increasing as each memory passed. I saw images from my dreams as a child, my visions of today, all of the moments that had led up to this encounter. But the visions didn't stop there. I saw things that were yet to come. The old woman tried to break her contact with my mind; I could hear the fear and panic of her thoughts. Just before she broke away, I saw one last vision. I saw myself die!

The Madam, looking fatigued, fragile even, like she had just completed a marathon, remained in her chair, but it had returned to its original position across the room from me. Sirnib handed the woman a glass of water. She thanked him and turned her attention back to me. "That wasn't supposed to happen. The darkness has a strong hold on you, still."

"What do you mean?" I asked.

"Oh, don't you worry, honeychile, I'm not calling you evil. There are dark forces that are trying to influence you, to control you. Though, perhaps you have seen more than you were meant to see."

"Has this ever happened with anyone else before?" I asked.

"Once," she said, "a long time ago." The Madam was clearly reluctant to talk about her experience.

"Now that I know which side you're on, I suppose it's safe to tell you about it." She placed her glass on a table next to her chair and proceeded to tell me her story. "A young man once came to see me. He, too, sought a girl and, like you, the shadows also had a hold on him. He came to me seeking a town, as well; he was looking for Shadow Lake." The old woman waited for a response. She'd been inside my mind, had seen my visions, and knew that I'd been there.

"Shadow Lake is *here*, in Hell?" I questioned.

"It was, once," she said. "The town was destroyed decades ago."

"But I can still go there," I said. It hadn't been that long ago that I'd dreamed of Shadow Lake. Because I had been there more than once, I knew I could go back. "Did *I* destroy it?" I asked.

"No, no," she said, "it was the boy who done it. You must find a way to get back there; you have unfinished business in that town. But first, you must find the woman you seek. Only then will you learn the answer to your true question."

"Thank you," I said. "May I ask something further of you? Why are there no shifts in your home?"

"The symbols are protection from the shifts," she said, pointing to the wallpaper. "You're not the only one with power, Marcus." The regal woman smiled and then left the room.

"I won't ask you to go any further," I said to Sirnib. "Just point me in the direction of The Den."

The kid's eyes lit up.

"You're going to The Den? Well, hell, why didn't you say so?" He grabbed my arm and pulled me up from the couch. "Just follow me."

BETRAYAL

As Sirnib and I walked the streets of Loo Rin my mind replayed the visit with the Madam. Why was I so surprised to find that I had died in the old woman's vision? If there were seven of me total and only five survived, then it made sense that it would only be a matter of time before I would witness my own demise. "We're almost there!" He'd been saying that every five minutes for the past half hour. I guess it was a whole lot better than *Are we there yet*, but still, it annoyed the shit out of me, nonetheless. We passed through a brick archway and entered the district known as The Den.

All around us neon signs advertised perversity, degradation, and of course, immediate gratification. The Den looked like any other seedy part of any other city. Now, normally, caution would be advised when traversing the streets of a local porn district, but seeing as how *this* particular one just *happened* to be in Hell, extra caution was called for. I realized Sirnib had finally stopped talking to me and had to break into a slow run to keep up with him. He walked with a purpose, though I wasn't sure I wanted to know what that purpose was. It seemed his "little head" was leading the way for us. Sirnib stopped in front of an alley that ran between two buildings. "You might want to check this out."

I followed him through the shadows until we stood before a large wooden door. Sirnib fumbled through his pockets and pulled out a key. He unlocked the door and I followed the kid up a set of stairs, keeping my suspicions to myself. We climbed up six flights before Sirnib said, "Ah, here it is." and opened yet another door. Sirnib ran ahead of me and stopped outside an apartment, waiting for me to catch up. The room number read 666; of course, would it be any other number? He opened the door and there, looking out the window at the city below, was Elizabeth Patton. Elizabeth turned to face us when we entered the room. "Well, it's about *time*," she said with a soft southern drawl, pronouncing the word *tam*.

Sirnib walked into the apartment and quietly slipped into another room. "Sorry," the boy called out, "we took a little detour."

"You little *fuck*!" I screamed. I was *pissed*! The little bastard knew where Elizabeth was the whole time.

Sirnib emerged from the adjoining room with a large bottle of scotch. "Yeah, sorry 'bout that." He pulled the top off of the scotch and held the bottle up to his lips. I was ready to lunge for the little shit and tear him apart myself.

"It's so good to finally meet you, Marcus." Elizabeth turned from the window and walked over to a chair, motioning for me to join her. She wore thick black eyeliner and dark green mascara; this was definitely *not* the same Elizabeth Patton that I had met on the train, though she wasn't wearing much more. This Elizabeth wore a see-through black camisole with a pair of matching panties, and nothing else; she might as well have been nude for all that the clothing did not cover. I took a seat in the chair across from her. "You're the one, aren't you?" she said. "They thought it was me for a while, but they were wrong, it was *you*. You know, they're going to have to kill you." Elizabeth stood and stepped forward, slowly slinking closer to me, her hands exploring her body all the while. One hand found her right breast while the other explored the contents of her panties. "But that doesn't mean we can't have a little fun first."

I pushed my chair back and stood up. "This is just *too* weird in so *very* many ways," I said.

"Come ooonnn," she pleaded in a whine. "I'll bet you're a *great* fuck. And it's not like your *wife's* going to mind." Elizabeth placed her palm on my chest and I grabbed her wrist and yanked her hand away. Then, from the shadows of the room came a voice I recognized.

Lilith stepped out of the darkness and spoke. *"It's so good to see you two getting along."* Elizabeth pulled free of my grasp and silently took a seat. Sirnib watched us from the kitchen still nursing his bottle. Now I knew what he'd had been hiding from me when I looked into his eyes at the bar.

"So," I said, "now that the gang's all here, what happens next?"

"You die!" Lilith said in her best dominatrix bitch voice, *"so, you might as well give me back my heart."* Lilith turned and glared at Sirnib. *"The heart that would still be in my possession if not for* you!"

"I'm sorry, Mistress." Sirnib lowered his head and flashed puppy dog eyes at Lilith, then disappeared into the recesses of the kitchen with the bottle of scotch in tow.

"Why do you want it so bad?" I asked.

"Because her heart belongs to ME!" Lilith screamed, thrusting her hand out vertically, causing Elizabeth and her chair to slam back against the wall.

"Shit!" Elizabeth exclaimed as she rubbed the back of her head where it had impacted with the wall. Lilith stepped forward to where Elizabeth's chair had originally been and held out her hand, palm up. Smoke rose from her fingertips creating a swirling ball, where an image formed within the sphere that hovered above Lilith's outstretched hand. *"My* patience *is wearing thin!"* Lilith snapped.

The image in her hand was from a memory, *my* memory. It was of a visit to Father Stephen's office, one of the bad ones. He had me over the examining table and I was screaming.

"This is what awaits you in Hell, Marcus, now give *me what I* want!" Lilith lowered her hand, but the image continued to hover in the air, taunting me.

"Before you kill me, tell me one thing," I said. "Tell me why you had too kill the other mes and the other Elizabeths."

Lilith smiled viciously at me before she spoke. *"You're to thank for* that *idea, Marcus. When your other began to kill in his realm, his actions created a thinning of the barrier between his reality and yours. Too many of these thin spots between realities can cause them to merge. If this merger happens enough times, the Divine Plan begins to crumble, and everything comes apart. The end of existence for mankind and the multiverse was all* your *idea, Marcus."*

"Yet *you* would live on," I said, "to rule over nothing. What's the point?"

"Having nothing to rule is far better than existing as a pathetic excuse for sentience, such as yourself. You think you know everything, but you're blind. *You humans trap yourselves inside your little worlds, ignoring what goes on around you, and you're* happy! *How can you be happy in* ignorance? *You're a waste of space, you've outlived your usefulness, and it is time to make way for evolution, Marcus."*

"Ha! *You're* the future of mankind?" I laughed in her face; this she-bitch was ridiculous.

"There is no future for mankind!" Lilith screamed. *"It is only a matter of time before humans destroy themselves. The Ah Me Ra are simply speeding up the process, giving evolution a nudge in the right direction, if you will."*

"But you *can't* evolve," I gladly reminded the Ah Me Ra. "You've ascended as high as you possibly can. You'll *never* be as powerful as the Umbra or Chaos, and you'll certainly *never* be as powerful as God!" I could taunt with the best of them. Lilith reached for the image of smoke and pushed it in my direction with all her might, intending to capture me within its reality. My mind reached out to Elizabeth and she shifted to where I had been standing. Just as I shifted away, the image within the smoke made contact with Elizabeth. I could still see through her eyes as I caught a string to retreat; she was laying face down on the examination table in Father Stephen's office as he raped her in my place.

MISDIRECTION

I was back on the train. I saw a body on the floor face down in a pool of blood. I recognized the corpse's clothes; it was the conductor. I rolled the man's body over and found the crushed box that had once contained Elizabeth Patton's heart. Lilith's poem was now pinned to the conductor's left eyeball. Aside from the corpse, the car was empty and all of the doors were locked. I sat down in a seat and waited, knowing that some unspeakable horror was yet to come. I heard a hydraulic hiss and the door behind me opened. I jumped up and ran into the next car, not waiting to see who or what had come to call. This new car *wasn't* empty. Four hideous creatures slumped over the body of a nude woman. The monstrosities appeared to be a cross between a featherless ostrich and a T-Rex. Their back legs were large and muscular, while the front were short and stubby, having large claws on the ends which they used to dig into the flesh of their victims. Large powerful necks rose up nearly two feet from their bodies and were topped by *human* heads. Sensing that I'd entered the car, they lifted their bloody faces from their meal, revealing what was left of a woman's head. She'd had blonde hair so I knew it wasn't Elizabeth. I heard another hiss and the door on the far end of the car opened. I held up my hand gathering light into my palm, shining it outward, temporarily blinding the creatures as they drunkenly lunged at me. I shifted through the open doorway to the dining car just seconds before one of the creatures slammed into the closed door.

The dining car had rows of tables on one side and a bar on the other. Not surprisingly sitting at the bar was Elizabeth, who now wore clothes. She had on a white t-shirt several sizes too large with a pair of pink dress pants that were just a little bit too tight. She turned when I entered and said with disgust in her voice, "You again."

"Yeah, a prophet told me we have unfinished business."

"We do?" she asked, confusion evident in her voice. I sat down two seats away from her at the bar.

"So, you figured out you're dead yet?" she asked.

"Actually, I'm not," I replied. Elizabeth rested her elbow on the bar and placed her chin on her fist, staring at me as I spoke. "Remember what you went through the last few months of your life, how things that just couldn't be happening actually were?" I asked. "Well, I've experienced the same thing."

"Then you've seen her?" Elizabeth questioned with a gasp.

"Yeah, she's an Ah Me Rah. Her name's Lilith."

"A *what*?" Elizabeth clearly had no idea what I was talking about.

"Listen, what you went through was just the beginning and now I have to finish it," I said with conviction.

"What do you mean 'finish it'?" she asked.

"I don't know," I said, "I was hoping you could help me figure that part out."

"Okay," she laughed, "what was your name again?"

"Marcus," I said.

"Okay, Marcus, how do we figure it out? And just what, *precisely*, are we figuring out?"

"Lilith came back and killed the conductor at some point. Did you see what happened?" I assumed that this version of Elizabeth had even fewer answers than I did, but I hoped that maybe she knew something without being aware.

"No," she answered, "the dark woman walked right by me, like she didn't even know I was there. She obviously hadn't come for me, so I ran." Elizabeth started crying. I slid over to the stool next to her and placed my hand on her shoulder. As soon as I touched her we made a connection, and shifted to a new location in Hell.

We arrived in the middle of a large black dome, the home of Elizabeth Patton's singularity. Hovering in front of us was a glowing white sphere wrapped in chains. I turned and faced the tunnel of familiar chains and flames behind us. We watched something move toward us, growing larger. I saw the shadows that made up the creature as it approached, and so did Elizabeth. I turned to her and took her hand. "Try to stay calm," I said. "He can't come through." I stood in front of Elizabeth as Ira rapidly approached. The Umbra's shadowy mass shuttered as it came to a sudden stop. Elizabeth saw this and relaxed, for she knew then that I'd told her the truth; we were safe for now.

"Thank you for bringing her to me, Marcus," said the Umbra. **"For this, I will let you see."**

My head flooded with visions of atrocities that had been committed by my negative self. I saw his power grow, watched him change with his eyes becoming like mine, with a twist. His were sixes. 666, 777. Three numbers, why *three*? The knowledge from the Godivel fruit told me that there was a number for each plane: one for God, another for the multiverse, and still another for Chaos. Contained within this knowledge was that *everyone* has three numbers, although most people's do not match. I learned that, because *my* numbers were aligned, I could occupy all three spaces at the same time. The visions continued, showing me twins being born, a boy and a girl. I watched them grow up and realized that I recognized one of the children. There was no mistaking it; the boy was *me*. It took me a little while to figure out who the girl was, and as the realization hit me, Ira's thoughts came to an abrupt end. In *his* reality, my evil half had a twin sister, a twin named Elizabeth! "You're not getting her that easily," I screamed.

"Watch me." Ira's forms twisted into a face as he spoke the Divine language in reverse. Elizabeth pushed me aside and stepped closer to the creature. I gripped her arm firmly, not wanting her to go to Ira, but once again she pushed me away and reached out to touch the Umbra. The blackness of Ira's shadows moved down Elizabeth's fingers and up her wrists and arms, then spread across her torso and neck. She tried to scream as the darkness entered her mouth and oozed down her throat, but she had no voice. I witnessed her body slowly change forms in front of me, from solid to gas, before being absorbed by the creature. Ira stopped chanting and laughed. *"She is now mine; it is complete."*

"*What's* complete?" I demanded.

"I may now return to Chaos, my home." Ira reared back and pushed forward into the blackness where I stood. The black dome above me shattered. Elizabeth's singularity, once contained within the glowing white sphere, extinguished its light as Ira rose into a murky red sky.

The deep bass tones in my head faded and the high pitches of the multiverse returned. I must have lost consciousness before tuning, because the next thing I knew, I lay in the grass at the bottom of a hill. The ground beneath me was wet and sticky with blood. At the top of the hill I saw three crosses buried in the ground. The sky was dark and black, caused by fires that burned on the far side of the hill. Thick smoke bellowed up into the air blocking out the stars. Someone screamed in the distance and a woman cried inconsolably nearby. The heart of Elizabeth Patton thumped away in my pocket as I climbed Golgotha to meet my savior.

777

BLOODLINES

THE 420

I saw a woman dressed in black sitting on a large stone near the crosses. It had been her grief that had drawn me up the hill. The woman saw me and quickly stood. She wiped the tears from her eyes with a blood-soaked cloth and smiled at me. "He said you would come." She turned to face the man on the center cross that stood slightly higher than the others, her sobs returning. "He is... a great man," she said. "The world will see that one day."

"Yes," I said, "it will."

"He wants to see you." The woman bowed her head, softly whispering a prayer. I looked up at the man's motionless body hanging from the spikes that had been driven through His wrists and feet. He was nude, covered with blood and grime, His hair and beard matted with filth, and His entire body sprinkled with a coat of fine ash that had drifted from the fires. There were deep gashes in His forehead from the crown of thorns thrust upon Him, and there was a spear with its staff broken off hanging from His flesh, wedged in between two ribs. "Is He still alive?" I asked in awe.

"Yes," the woman whispered, "a little."

I stood before Jesus and looked up. The smoke above his head was thick, but somehow stars shone through, three of them in the shape of a triangle above His head. Jesus opened His eyes and His lips parted, but no sound came forth. The tones in my head went crazy, shifting from high to low forming a pattern with the sounds turning to syllables. He was *talking* to me! "You have come far, my son."

"Not as far as you," I said with reverence.

"Not yet," He smiled, the layer of blood and dirt caked to His face cracking and falling away. From a distance He looked dead, even up close the signs of life were scarce, but His eyes were alive and filled with joy. "What would you like to see?" He asked.

"Everything," I said. Jesus opened His mind to me and briefly let me in. I saw too much to comprehend in such a short amount of time, and as His final words to me echoed in my mind, His eyes lost focus.

"With change comes sacrifice," He said. I reached up and pulled the Divine object from His body.

The shaft of the steel spear was imbedded with two jewels. One side held a green gem, the other side, a white. I pushed on the green jewel and the tip of the blade separated into four equal parts, exposing a hidden chamber within. I pressed the gem once more and the spear closed. Next I touched the white gem and the broken staff disengaged and fell to the ground. I turned the spear point down and peered into its hole as I pressed the white gem again. The hole opened up into the chamber I'd already seen inside the spear. I placed the open end to the wound in Christ's chest and filled the chamber with the blood of the Divine being. I pressed the white gem a third time to seal the chamber, and placed the spear in my back pocket as I retreated down the hill. Now, I know people are bound to have questions about my interaction with the so named Son of God, but all I'm willing to say is this: People are going to believe what they want to believe, no matter what proof is provided to support or disprove anything. I wasn't willing then, or even now, to open that particular can of worms. I only wanted to learn what I needed for my quest, but received the rest of Christ's knowledge anyway. I guess that's what I got for asking to know everything.

I tuned back to Anna's Bridge to stash the spear, only to find another me sitting on the platform reading the file on Elizabeth Patton. His eyes held sevens, not sixes, and it wasn't what I saw or felt that told me who the person was; it was what I *knew*. I was in his head and he was in mine. He sat up and placed the papers down to his side. "Hope you don't mind," he said.

"Not at all; it's your life as much as it is mine." I pulled the spear from my back pocket and removed the gold chain from my neck. I placed both of them with the rest of my stash, which had substantially grown since my last visit. I counted twenty-two pieces in all. My other selves had been busy helping me without my realizing it. We were almost halfway finished gathering what we needed to construct the Divine Engine. The other me was laying on the platform looking up at the night sky. At first, his mind was on the stars, but it soon began to wander. He was thinking about the time I... no *he*, had fallen asleep there while watching a meteor shower. How old had we been? The other me answered with a thought, "I was thirteen. Man, mom was *pissed* when I came home the next morning." I sat down next to myself on the platform. The two of us lay there for a while, looking up at the heavens, saying nothing. Our thoughts, however, drifted in very different directions as we watched the Divine Plan play out in the stars above us. I caught a glimpse of his thoughts every now and then, but nothing strong enough to pull me away from my own memories. I was thinking about the night I'd asked Anna to marry me. We'd made love under the stars and I recalled it in graphic detail. "*Hot damn!*" the other me said with a smile. "Thanks for the memory," and he tuned away on his journey.

I sat up and collected the papers the other me had left on the platform. I placed them back into the file and returned them to the stash of Divine items. Things were different when I tuned that time. I saw the other strings around me and felt their vibrations resonating throughout my body. I caught glimpses of other realities as I traveled along the string. I was able to see where each string began, where they led to, and a whole lot more. I caught glimpses of random scenes from each reality. And their songs... I began to hear each individual tone of each individual song at the same time. These were the sounds I'd lived with for most of my life, only now they made sense.

The string spit me out in a dark parking garage, one I'd been in before. I wasn't here to *feel* myself die this time; oh no, *this* time I got to *see*. I was a witness, a witness to the end of a bloodline. Complements of the Godivel fruit, the knowledge within my head told me there were seven bloodlines in all. The reality that I was in was home to an alternate version of me, one of four hundred and twenty individuals that had made up his bloodline. Some members of that line had different colored hair or their facial features were somewhat altered, but they still basically looked like me. The problem with the 420 was that the bloodline was far too diluted. They were still me, but were more like distant cousins. Unfortunately, due to the thinning of the bloodline, most of them were not able to control the thoughts in their heads and had killed themselves or gone mad. The few remaining 420 were easy targets for Lilith.

I did not see what had killed this version of me the first time I'd been there, but I saw it now, and I knew I was too late to save him. The Ah Me Rah stood two feet taller than its victim; its massive legs more horse than human. The creature's black muscles glistened in the dim light of the garage as the beast advanced on the last of the 420. I screamed in vain for the bastard to stop. It lunged at the poor guy and I could do nothing to prevent what was happening. I could only watch and bear witness to the extermination of one of *my* bloodlines. The creature thrust the psycho scissors into its prey and pulled back on the handle. The victim stood for a moment, watching the blades as they opened to form the five-pointed star. He was still alive when gravity took over and the pieces that used to make up his body, *my body*, slid into a pile on the concrete. When he died, a part of me was gone forever, a branch on the cosmic tree that would grow no more. The creature kept its eyes on me as it advanced, the swirling nines within pulsing in time with its heart. I knew I was screwed if it tried to attack, but I also knew I would not die there, as a vision from a prophet in Hell had told me that. The Ah Me Rah stopped about ten feet away from me and thrust the blades into the concrete. The creature began to change, becoming smaller and looking more human, more feminine, more... *Lilith!*

"Crossing time now, are we, Marcus?" she said with a smirk. Lilith walked in a circle around me as she spoke, keeping her distance. Was she afraid of me? *"You have pretty eyes, Seven,"* she said, before stopping to face me. *"The purest of the bloodlines; I shall enjoy killing you."* The dark woman held up her hand and placed all five fingertips together, igniting a flame in the space within her palm. She opened her hand and the flame burned hotter. It grew to approximately the size of a softball as it hovered inches above her palm. Lilith casually tossed the orb over her shoulder where it stopped and floated motionless in the air as she began to circle me once more.

"How many bloodlines have you destroyed?" I demanded of the dark bitch.

"There are four remaining." Lilith purred.

"Why are you *doing* this?" Even I, who had started this journey with a deep hatred for mankind, could not wrap my mind around Lilith's delight in genocide.

"Soon it will be our turn to rule the multiverse," Lilith spat out at me. *"For this to come to fruition the bloodline must die. Only you, Marcus, can undo everything I have set in motion."* Lilith completed her circuit, stopped in front of the blade, and pulled it out of the concrete floor. The fiery orb now floated in the air about twenty feet behind me. Ten feet in front of me stood Lilith and her blades. The orb glowed bright red as Lilith pulled back on the handle and opened the five-pointed star. The orb circled us once and returned to its original position and hovered. Lilith closed the blades and the orb accelerated, following its previous course, but traveling faster and faster around us. The heat created by the circling orb caused engines to explode and vehicles to burst into flames; hell, even the concrete began to melt.

"It will soon be over, Marcus," Lilith cooed over the sound of the chaos around us, *"and you will join the others."*

The parking garage outside of the circle created by Lilith's orb melted and drifted away. The flames from the orb died down and it no longer blazed. The light faded and the empty shell fell to the ground, shattering like glass. *"Are you ready to die, Marcus?"* Lilith slowly walked, dragging the blades on the ground behind her.

"At least answer my question before you kill me. You know the 420 aren't able to activate the Divine Engine, so why are you ending that bloodline?"

"Very well, Marcus; you are correct. The 420 are of no consequence as they were going to die anyway. Most were already dead and the rest were just a bottle or pill away from blowing their brains out or jumping out of a window."

"Then *why* kill them?" The question exploded from me in a burst of rage.

"Everything has a time and a place, Marcus. If the multiverse were to become Chaos, then the balance would tip and our rule becomes eternal! Too bad you won't be around to see it; you have to take this knowledge to the grave.*"* Lilith changed form before my eyes and morphed back into the creature that had killed the last of the 420. It towered over me, smiled, then lunged at me with the blades. In the fraction of a second before they entered my flesh, a single tone sounded in my head and I was pulled to a new reality.

THE 64

I stood on a rocky trail that traversed the foothills of a large mountain. The sky was dark and the stars were beautiful. I saw a cave ahead of me and when I reached it, I realized that I was not the only one enjoying the night sky. I saw a boy in his early teens, sitting against the back wall of the cave staring out at the stars. I stepped on something and looked down; it was a broken statue. I sat down next to it on the path and placed my hands on my lap. "My name is Marcus," I told the child.

"I am Abram," the boy said. "I have been expecting you."

He reached into a small bag that he wore around his neck and pulled something out. Kissing his clenched fist, he tossed the small round object like dice. It rolled across the ground and stopped, hitting the statue in the sand before me. The object looked like a marble made of glass with a strange gold tint. I picked it up and held it in my hands, a soft heat emanating from within. I held it up to one of the brighter stars in the sky and the color changed from gold to blue. I moved it to another star and it turned green.

"Thank you," I said. Returning my attention to the statue beside me, I retrieved the idol from the ground. It was about six inches long and carved from a soft brown stone. The statue was missing its head but I could still tell it was of a goddess by the large, swollen belly. "You know," I commented as I set the idol back down on the ground, "I always thought idolatry was a vain and petty thing for God to consider a sin."

"Worshiping *false* Gods," the boy lectured, "can lead you astray, Marcus. Those who practice idolatry can sometimes cross the boundary between right and wrong, good and evil. There are rules a man must live by if he wishes to be one with God. The Lord does not ask for much and, in return, He gives man *everything!*" A light from the night sky cast a warm glow over the boys face and he closed his eyes. I turned and looked up at the stars to find a bright white light in the sky that looked like a supernova. In a flash, the light increased exponentially and I was temporarily blinded. When my vision returned the boy was gone, all that remained was the child's voice echoing within my head. "Do not stray from the path, Marcus. Do not cross the line." The words faded and a tone grew deafeningly loud inside my skull.

The Boston skyline immediately caught my attention, but on this trip I was in my own body. I waited until I felt the vibration that accompanies another version of me before they arrive. When it came, I quickly moved into the road and grabbed her as she materialized. We then shifted into an alley on the other side of the street, an alley far away from the one she'd died in during my initial visit. She fell to the ground screaming and looked up at me. "Who the *fuck* are *you?*" she spat. This other version of me obviously had not escaped the foul-mouthed part of my personality.

"I'm Marcus," I said, reaching out my hand in friendship, but the woman simply ignored my cue for an introduction and continued speaking.

"You can do it too?" she asked excitedly. "Do you know *why?*"

"Why don't you start by telling me what *you* know," I prompted, not wanting to give away too much information.

"I don't know," she explained, "it started about a week ago. It took me a couple of days to learn how to control the movement."

"Is shifting all you can do?" I asked.

"You can do *more?*" She stood up and brushed the dirt from her jeans. "What else can *you* do?"

"*I* can save *your* life," I snapped back in response.

"Oh big deal! I've appeared in worse places than the middle of the God damned road and I don't owe you jack shit for *that*, pal." It looked like she'd gotten more than my potty mouth, to boot, because she had the same shitty outlook on the world that I'd started out my journey with.

"Just *listen!*" I grabbed her arm to keep her from leaving.

"Do you want me to scream *rape* motherfucker?"

"Go ahead," I said. Knowing me like I do, she would, and she didn't disappoint.

"Let *go* of me, you bastard!" she screamed. "RAPE! Somebody help me, I'm being raped!"

"Okay," I said and shrugged my shoulders. I let go of her and she froze mid scream. I stepped to her side and placed my hand on her shoulder. She stopped screaming and turned her body to face me.

"Yeah, well... *Shit*! Why can't *I* do that?" the woman questioned, wondering how I had moved around her while she remained in place. I let go of her shoulder and walked behind her, placing my hand on her arm. "Stop *doing* that!" she scathingly spat out.

"Fine, if you want me to stop, just hold onto my arm and walk out into the street like you've got some sense." The woman visibly relaxed at that point.

"My name's Jenny," she said as I escorted her to the street.

I knew it was pointless to try and save her; I could see every possible outcome of my actions before I acted and nothing looked good for poor Jenny, so I decided that she should at least know the truth. "Holy *fuck*!" Jenny yelled as we came out of the alley into a sea of frozen pedestrians. She let go of my arm only to become one with crowd. I took hold of her other arm.

"You let go of me, you freeze, just like them. Now listen, there's something you need to know. You're part of something *much* bigger..."

"You mean I'm a pawn," Jenny interrupted.

"We're *all* pawns in *this* game," I replied.

"I've seen things, I've been places... They're alternate realities, aren't they?"

"Yes," I said, "they are."

"I *knew* it!" Jenny took my hand and released my arm. "How many of me *are* there?" she asked.

"Sixty four."

"They don't all look like me, do they?" Jenny had more of a clue than I'd initially thought.

"No."

"Why?" she asked.

"Because yours is not the primary reality," I said.

"Well, then, who's *is*?" she demanded.

The Godivel fruit had shown me that half of Jennifer's bloodline looked like the Jenny I was now talking to, while the other half were variations of her in one way or another, just like with me. But the primary Jenny looked like none of them, *she* looked like Elizabeth Patton. Jenny wouldn't have understood that in the limited amount of time I had left to explain, so I simply said, "Another you." As I answered, a voice slithered inside my head. It was Lilith! *"Playtime is over, Marcus. Now it's* my *turn."*

I stopped walking and looked around to get my bearings. Jenny and I were about three blocks from the alley where Jenny eventually died. I released her hand as time and the world around us returned to normal. *"You cannot stop what has already happened, Marcus,"* Lilith taunted. I sat down on a bench in front of a drug store.

"Is something wrong?" Jenny asked.

"Come find out," Lilith now reached out mentally to Jenny.

"What the hell was *that*?" Jenny sounded freaked.

"What?" I asked.

"That *voice*!"

"You heard that?"

"Yeah, I think it came from over there." Before I could blink, Jenny turned and sprinted down the street, stopping in front of a newspaper stand. I caught up with her and she pointed down to a stack of newspapers with my face on the cover along with the words 'Man found slain in parking garage.' I heard a distant metallic sound that I knew to be Lilith dragging her blades across the asphalt in the alley. Jenny started walking slowly into the shadows. "Don't go in there," I pleaded.

Jenny turned to look at me just as Lilith came into view. The creature was in the form of the male Ah Me Rah again. It stopped, lifted its blade, pointed at me, and spoke. *"Different reality, different alley,"* it said. The Ah Me Rah began to laugh as it stepped back out of sight. Jenny screamed as she was pulled into the alley with an incredible speed. I ran after her. Rounding the back of the building I saw the creature standing there, blades straight out, with Jenny's body impaled and hanging limply. Her eyes were open. She was trying to say *help me,* but no sound came, only a gurgle. The creature pulled back on the handle and the blades separated, splitting Jenny's face into two perfect halves. The left half of her head fell away, splattering on the pavement. Slowly, the other pieces of Jenny separated and slid to the ground with thumps and splats.

"Another one bites the dust, eh, Marcus?" The bastard laughed again.

"Fuck you, Lilith!" I screamed.

"Oh, don't worry, Marcus. We'll have plenty of time for that *later. I'll even keep this form; I bet you'd* like *that!"* Lilith's voice began to fade away, along with her laughter, as a tone slowly grew in my head. This was a tone I'd never heard before; it was like the others, but different. Was it more than one?

"Maybe next time, bitch," I said, turning the tables and taunting Lilith before I left.

The string felt massive, like I was a part of a beam of pure energy. Then came the images… so many visions, so fast, *millions* of realities rushing through my head. I could see and hear everything at once… and then I heard a voice that said, *"The prime Elizabeth Patton is not dead."*

199

With all of the noise in my head it was impossible to know the timing of the song. The old men in the cave had warned me about this but I didn't care, I just *had* to know, so I jumped.

THE 49

I didn't know what to think when the string spit me out on the streets of Shadow Lake. It was morning and the sun was beginning to rise. A thick fog filled the streets and rose into the air, shrouding the sun and casting my surroundings in a dull shade of yellow. I tried to shift to Julia's house but I couldn't. I heard the correct tone in my head, but I could not seem to access it. I couldn't access *any* of the tones in my head, so I walked. What was the connection between Elizabeth Patton and Shadow Lake? I tried to piece the information together. One of my seven original bloodlines, Elizabeth Patton existed in forty-nine realities. I'd met several versions of her already, but suddenly I wasn't so sure which Elizabeth resided in the prime reality. At first, I was sure the prime Elizabeth was deep in the belly of the beast, a shadow slave to the Umbra known as Ira. But soon I began to suspect that the Elizabeth I'd met on the train was no more than a shell, her body taken from the cemetery in Knoxville, Tennessee and reanimated, why? Then there was the Elizabeth I had met in Loo Rin. The knowledge in my head told me she was my "other's" twin sister who was already dead and residing in Hell. So, with the words "the prime Elizabeth Patton is not dead" being voiced as I'd jumped, landing me *here*, of all places, my doubts about the prime Elizabeth grew stronger. I didn't know what help Julia could give me, but I couldn't seem to leave Shadow Lake, and I had nowhere else to go.

I climbed the steps to Julia's house and knocked on the front door. I waited a while, and knocked again. I turned the knob and the door silently opened. "Julia?" I called out and stepped inside. I shut the door behind me and found my way to the kitchen. The inside of the house was as dark as the outside. A light above my head switched on and I turned to face Julia who held a knife in her clenched fist. "Marcus, is that you?" she gasped.

"Yes, Julia," I answered.

"Damn! You scared the *shit* out of me. Look at you, all grown up!" I had aged ten years since the last time I had seen Julia, yet she looked exactly the same. Julia turned and placed the knife on the counter.

"Come," she said. "Sit." Julia walked into the dining room, pulled out a chair and sat at the table.

Julia knew things, had always known things, even if she didn't know what they meant, and I needed answers. "Tell me about the woman of light," I said.

"I only saw her once," Julia paused to decide how much she was going to tell me, "when I was a child. It was a long time ago, Marcus. Memories fade." Julia looked nervous, like she was holding something back.

"No one could forget an encounter with the Ma Hua Ra," I said.

"Is that what the lady of light is called?" Julia asked.

"Her species, yes. Tell me more; tell me where you saw her."

"In the woods," Julia hesitated for a moment. "The hole was not always there. Before the hole there was a statue."

"A statue of a white woman?" I asked.

"Yes. As children, we were told to stay away from that part of the woods, told that the woods were cursed, but there is nothing that can stop the curiosity of a child..." Julia drifted off into her memories. "Groups of us went out there all the time, and one day we found the statue..."

"The other children saw it, too?"

"Oh yes, but she never spoke to anyone but me, and only that one time." Julia's voice changed, becoming more childlike. I had seen her this way before.

"Did you tell your friends she spoke to you?"

"No…" I could tell that Julia wanted to say more, but she continued to remain silent while her eyes grew damp.

"Do you still talk to your friends, the ones who went into the woods with you?" I asked.

Julia's eyes filled to overflowing, leaving trails of tears streaking down each cheek. She held back her sobs at first, but it soon required too much effort. I reached across the table and took her hand.

"It's okay, Julia. You need to tell me; I *need* to know."

"I…" She tried to talk through her sobs, but it was just no use.

"Everything is going to be okay," I tried to reassure her as I gently stroked the back of her hand.

"I… I was eleven." Julia pulled her hand away and reached for a napkin to dry her eyes. "I went into the woods by myself. I went to see the statue…" She took several deep breaths and continued. "I heard her calling to me and when I got there, she was… *different*. She wasn't a statue anymore."

Julia got up and rummaged through the cabinets in the kitchen, no longer speaking in the childlike voice. "She smiled at me and began to glow," Julia said, the memory making her smile a small, sad smile. "You're right, you know… I could *never* forget her." She retrieved a glass from a cabinet above the sink and held it out to me. "You want anything?" she asked. I told her, "No thanks."

"Anyway," Julia continued, "like I told you before, she said that she would send someone to me, that I was to give them something, and then she kissed me on the forehead." Julia ran the tap water for a few seconds before dipping the cup under the stream. She took a sip and placed the cup on the counter behind her. "When she kissed me, I knew… well, I knew that I *would* know. I started knowing a *lot* of things that other people didn't, like why the woods were said to be cursed. Back in the early sixties, a group of teenagers cut a path through the woods to the beaches on the other side of the island. When they came back into town to get some tools, all the teens would say is that they had found something. They packed up what they needed and headed back out into the woods. When they didn't return that night, the boys' fathers went out in search of their children. Their parents found them, but they were too late. All six of the young men lay dead around the statue. Autopsies determined that all of them had died from the same thing, a *heart attack* if you can believe it! But I know it was because the boys had tried to steal the woman's sword; others have tried to do this too, only to suffer the same fate. My friends and I were always too afraid to go near the statue because of those deaths. Several kids were dared to approach the statue, but no one was brave enough in our group. I guess that fear may have saved them all ..."

I knew this was not easy for Julia, so I said nothing for a while, allowing her a short break before I continued my line of questioning. "Tell me what happened after she kissed you," I encouraged with a smile. Julia stared at me for a while before speaking again.

"This... this black stuff started coming out of her mouth and spread across her body, like it was trying to take her over. The white lady fought it, but the ground underneath just started falling away from her. The pedestal, her sword, both lost, but her..."

"The name, do you remember a name on the base of the statue?" I impatiently cut in.

"It was just funny symbols, no one could read them."

"What happened to the woman after the hole opened?" I asked.

"She just floated there for a while, over the hole. Her skin looked like a cow's hide, patches of black and white. She screamed most of the time, but every now and then the lady had moments of awareness."

"Did she speak to you?" I wondered aloud.

"No, she just… cried."

"So what happened to her?" I asked.

"When the earth stopped falling away, the white lady fell into the hole. I never saw her again."

"What happened to the town after the hole opened?" I asked. "You said things changed, *people* changed."

"Only on the inside…" Julia stopped herself.

"What does *that* mean?"

Julia began to sob again. "It means… that once the hole opened, people changed on the inside, but no one ever aged. No one ever got any older, no one… but me…"

"Your friends had to watch *you* age?" I asked.

Julia was crying hysterically at that point. I stood up and she ran to me, burying her head in my shoulder. I held her and let her cry it all out. "They… they don't know who I *am*," Julia sobbed. "Before the woman of light lost the battle with the darkness, she embraced me. Not physically, but in my *mind* somehow. The lady held me in that embrace while the battle for her mind was waged… I felt everything that she felt…"

Julia paused for a moment, hiccupping. "Thank you." She pulled away from me and took a seat back at the table. I retrieved her glass of water from the counter and brought it to her.

"My link with the lady couldn't have lasted more than few seconds," Julia explained, "but I aged seventeen years in that flash of time. When I came out of the woods that day, no one recognized me. At first the townspeople tried to blame my own disappearance on *me*, but once news of the hole in the ground reached the town… Well, let's just say I was cleared of *that*, but held accountable for another incident. They thought I'd had something to do with what happened in the woods, that I'd done something to the statue... and to *them*. I spent two years of my life locked up in a small cell at the police station before everyone realized that the changes going on around them and inside them were not my doing, because the changes continued to happen! Two years locked up, I was only *eleven*! It took two *more* years before everyone realized they no longer aged. The people of Shadow Lake embraced me then, thinking I was some sort of savior or something. They gave me this house and met my every need. I tried not to ask for too much, but they just kept giving and giving, until... Until it became clear that the changes in them were *not* for the better. The more things went south, the more their suspicions returned to me, so I hid. There have always been several empty houses down by the docks. I moved from one place to the next for a long while, but eventually I came back here. I know they didn't just forget about me, but one day they simply stopped caring. I still don't go out much, and when I do, I stick to the woods." Julia reached for her water and held it up. She gazed into the glass for several moments before taking a sip, as if mesmerized by something inside. I took her silence as an opportunity to ask the question.

"Have you ever heard the name Elizabeth Patton?" There was a knock at the door.

THE 210

"You were the first person to knock on that door in over four years," Julia said as she stood, looking around for her knife. I got up and followed her down the hall to the front door. Through the glass of the curtained window we saw the silhouette of a young man. "Is he a local kid?" I whispered.

"No," Julia whispered back. "I've never seen him before."

Although the boy *looked* harmless enough, and I was tempted to tell her not to open the door, something inside told me otherwise. "Open it," I said, ducking into a room off the main hall. Julia looked back at me, shrugged, and opened the door. I watched from the shadows as

Julia stepped out onto the porch and spoke with the teen. "Can I help you?" she asked.

"Um… I thought you'd be a lot older," the boy said.

"Age does *not* equate to wisdom," Julia lectured the boy. "Now tell me what you want or leave."

The kid looked up into the doorway and for the first time I was able to see into his eyes, and into his mind. In that moment, access to the tones in my head returned.

"I… ah… well…" It was painfully obvious that the young man was trying to figure out how to phrase his question. His thoughts came to me faster than he was receiving them, and I couldn't believe it, we sought the answer to the same question! "Um… okay, how do you kill the shadow in the woods, the one in the hole?" Julia was about to slam the door shut. I focused on her eyes and on her mind and made contact. I looked down at the teen through Julia's eyes as she reached for the door. "Wait!" the boy called out.

Julia hesitated. Her thoughts were an open book to me; she was nervous, and scared. So I decided to try something. *"Don't."* I told Julia through her thoughts. *"Tell him to come back in one hour."*

"Come back in an hour?" Julia repeated the phrase more as a question than a statement. She closed the door firmly and engaging the deadbolt, then turned to me and said, "How did you *do* that? You were talking to me in my *head*!" Julia shook her head and walked back into the kitchen.

"Do you *know* him?" she asked.

"Yes and no," I said. Though I'd never met him, I *did* know him. "Listen, Julia, I don't have time to explain everything, but I can give you this…" I reached up and placed my hands on her face, and kissed her forehead. "I must go," I said. "But I'll come back within the hour and I'll have an answer." I didn't transfer much information to Julia, just glimpses of the truth. Enough to let her know whose side I was on, to let her know she wasn't crazy, and enough for her to know the importance of passing on the answer to the question 'How do you kill an Umbra?'

In a flash of light I shifted to the edge of the woods, just beyond the point where everything stopped growing. I walked forward until I saw the earth falling away into the blackness of the pit, and I stopped. The air around me grew thick, like water, distorting my surroundings. I could only see the forest as shadow but it seemed to be moving, rushing toward me in a blur of black and white as the trees filled in the empty land. The darkness grew all around me and my head spun for a moment before subsiding. The image cleared and I stood on a path in the woods, and where the hole should have been, was a young child talking to a statue of a white woman. I read the symbols on the statue's base, the plaque read Dissensio. The white woman bent over and kissed Julia on the forehead, and I watched as the earth beneath the pedestal began to crumble and fall away. Julia turned and ran but only made it about ten yards before something stopped her. She turned around and watched the ground crumble in front of her, stopping just under the tips of her sandals. Julia looked at Dissensio floating over the abyss. As their eyes connected, Julia threw her head back and rose into the air. I walked up to the edge of the pit beside Julia and…

Once more, the world around me began to spin and when it stopped, I stood in a lush forest. It was the same forest, but everything appeared just a little bit greener, and the statue before me was even more magnificent. *"Greetings, Seven,"* the statue said to me.

I bowed my head, "I am honored to meet you, Dissensio." I looked down at eleven-year-old Julia; it seemed she'd made the journey, as well. Julia had attempted to cover her ears with her hands but she never made it. The look of pure terror and incomprehension on the child's face was as frozen as her body, yet time did not completely stand still for her. Julia was slowly aging.

"She cannot see you," said the statue.

"Why have you done this to her?" I asked.

"*The bond I have forced upon the child was necessary,*" explained Dissensio. "*Julia is my link to you.*"

"Link? Then it *was* you," I said, connecting that moment to the voice I'd heard before tuning to Shadow Lake. "Where is Elizabeth Patton?" I asked.

"*She is here, in Shadow Lake,*" said Dissensio.

"How?" I queried. "I saw the last one die! I saw her soul absorbed by the Umbra called Ira."

"*Who you saw was not the last; Lilith tricked Ira. By absorbing the last of a bloodline, the Mille Umbra may gain access to every reality in which that bloodline existed, thus granting the banished Umbra access to Chaos and giving them the power that the Umbra crave.*"

"How did Lilith trick Ira?" I asked.

"*Lilith hid her intentions well. By hiding the prime Elizabeth here, in Shadow Lake, Ira could not sense her.*"

"Because Shadow Lake is in Hell." I deduced. "What will not absorbing the prime Elizabeth do to Ira?"

"*Chaos will deny the Umbra entry.*"

"But won't Ira just find its way back into the multiverse?" I asked.

"*No, Ira's position in the Nexus is now fixed, leaving It exactly where Lilith wants It.*"

"Why the Nexus?"

"*The Umbra must be aligned with the Chimera for the spell to work.*"

"Spell?" I asked. "What spell?"

"There is a spell that, if the incantation is recited properly, a heart removed will continue to beat."

I felt the soft thumping of Elizabeth's heart in my pocket.

"Once that heart's soul has been joined with an Umbra, a bond is formed, unlike the mass of souls that make up the bulk of the creature. This bonding happens only with certain, rare bloodlines, such as yours, Marcus."

"So… what's the importance of the heart?" I still didn't understand.

"If the heart were to be rejoined with its soul, it would unmake the Umbra, destroying It and setting all of Its souls free."

"The living must be reunited with the dead…" I remembered what the young girl had told me at the towers in Hell.

"Yes, Marcus, this is how one destroys an Umbra."

"How would one go about learning this spell?" I asked. This was the answer I'd promised the young boy by way of Julia.

"The knowledge is hidden in the Library of Alexandria."

An image flashed in my head, a map of Egypt on a pumpkin.

"I've got a feeling I'll be heading that direction pretty soon," I said. "One more question: why is there another bloodline in this Shadow Lake?" I referred to the young boy who'd knocked at Julia's door. I now knew the boy's name, and it was a name I'd heard before. His name was Jacob Chant, one of two hundred and ten, and one of my seven bloodlines.

"His task is not important to yours, Marcus. The events unfolding to him are a decade old in your reality. Take comfort in the knowledge that he does not die at the hands of Lilith." The Ma Hua Ra paused for a moment; she looked to be in pain. *"Our time has come to an end, Marcus. Learn all that you can and pass this knowledge on to Jacob. Destroy the Umbra*

and return balance to the multiverse." The world spun around me, and as the spinning stopped, Dissensio screamed. At that same moment in time, the now twenty-eight year old Julia also screamed. Both women fell, Julia to the ground, and Dissensio into the void. As soon as the vision ended I was pulled from Shadow Lake.

THE 21

The difference between my other and I is simple, *he* chooses to kill while *I* do not. The bloodline of the 21 couldn't make this decision; their minds weren't strong enough. The third of my seven bloodlines had two things in common, one: they all looked like me, and two: they all resided in institutions. They had *all* snapped. These 21 were all pretty screwed up in the head, with voices and visions and violence, *oh my*... Most of them tended to act out aggressively when they felt threatened, but who could blame them? To them, the world in their head was their true reality. Our reality, *this* reality, was just a figment of their imaginations. Now, wouldn't *you* freak out just a little bit if the reality inside your head started touching you physically?

Since our brain links us to the Nexus and thus, to the multiverse, it stands to reason that the 21 were actually living in two, and sometimes more, realities at the same time. The human brain is crafty; it learns to adapt, but how does it access these other realities? I finally figured it out. It's all about positive and negative, and it's all about the timing. If a traumatic event happens exactly the same way down to every last detail in the reflected multiverses of the Chimera, the realities can merge, but only to the *person* that this event happens to. Well, *mostly*. Due to the nature of Chaos, some minds gained the ability to cast their visions onto others close by, making those near them or touching them, see what they saw. So, living in more than one reality at once *is* possible.

The string spit me out in a hospital room. I looked down at the man strapped to the bed who looked just like me. His eyes were closed and he appeared to be sleeping. "Are ya here to kill me?" he asked without opening his eyes.

"No," I said, "I'm just here to talk."

I stepped forward and reached for the latch on the straps holding him down.

"No," he said, "leave them. They'll be coming for me soon and I'm afraid I have no fight left."

This version of me seemed much more lucid than the other twenty I felt inside me, but I was not surprised. He was, after all, the prime Marcus of the 21. I pulled up a stool and sat next to the bed; he opened his eyes. "You're really not him?" he asked. "No, I suppose you would have killed me already if you were. Or maybe you're me and I'm him, always with the two's. Two… two…two, two-two…"

Okay, so maybe he was a *little* crazy. The other me began to laugh hysterically. If he hadn't been strapped down, he most certainly would have fallen to the floor. The laughter suddenly stopped and he began to cry. "I… don't want to… be… stuck here," he sobbed. "I'm not… ready… to die."

I heard his thoughts and he knew things that he shouldn't. I learned a lot about the 21 in that moment. In their heads, they could hear everything that I heard, everything that the other six of me heard, but they also heard my evil self's thoughts, and those of *his* others. No wonder the 21 had all gone insane. To have access to all of that knowledge, but to never know what it meant would drive *anyone* crazy. He also knew things that I did not. I found, of all things, the answer to one of the questions that had been haunting me. The question of why Lilith was killing off my bloodlines. For a while, I had thought the Ah Me Rah were just trying to weed out the one who could activate the Divine Engine, but that was before I had known about my others. Once the knowledge of the bloodlines began to creep into my brain, I was aware that Lilith already knew *which* bloodline to search for. So why kill off the others? It seems that, when someone dies before their time, their energy gets trapped at the point where the death occurred. Killing the same person, at the exact same time and place, in multiple realities, creates a tremendous amount of energy. Enough energy to tear a hole between the closest realities: it's the nature of Chaos. Not enough to do any serious damage, mind you, just a little bleed through. Voices, images, even smells, these occurrences are most often mistaken for hauntings.

With most people, there are only two or three branches on a bloodline, but their numbers are in the millions. After all, there are a hell of a lot of realities out there. For some people, their bloodlines are smaller and less diluted. The purer the bloodline, the stronger the energy associated with the spirit. Wipe out an entire branch of one of *those* bloodlines, and the buildup of energy is *enormous*, causing more than just a small hole in the reality and more than a little bleed through. We're talking a complete merger of realities at that point. If this were to happen enough times, in enough places, then the damage becomes irreversible, effectively undoing all of the multiverse. It would seem, for once, that Lilith had told me the truth. The me on the bed stopped laughing. "Thank you," he said.

"For what?" I asked.

"For being here with me when I die. I don't want to be alone."

"I'm sorry," I said, "I have to go." I had another piece of the Divine Engine buzzing around in my brain and knew that I would soon be tuning.

"You'll still be here to me," he said, and closed his eyes as I disappeared.

I stood on a mountaintop. On one side I saw a lush valley filled with vegetation and the sounds of life, on the other, a vast desert, filled with death and a chilling breeze that felt like needles driving into my face. I heard a sound coming from the valley below. It was a song, a lullaby, sung in an Arabic dialect by a strong, deep voice that sent shivers up and down my spine. The voice was mesmerizing, intoxicating, and I needed to hear more, I needed to *see* more. I leaned over the rocky ledge of the mountain and peered down the face of the cliff into the valley below, seeking the maker of that beautiful voice. I saw a path, and a cave, with the melodic, almost dreamy voice echoing from within. This was the prophet Mohamed, and I knew he had something for me. I shifted.

He was quick, his sword was unsheathed and the blade to my throat before I fully appeared.

"I just wanted to hear your song," I said calmly. He looked at me for a while, and I tried not to make eye contact, but his razor sharp blade digging into my throat was rather persuasive. He maneuvered my head with the sword until I had no choice but to look him in the eye.

"Seven," he said, lowering his blade. "Sit with me." Mohamed motioned to the ground. He saw my eyes in his language; this was new information to me.

"Does the number seven mean something to you?" I asked.

Mohamed reached into a sack behind him and pulled out a large white cloth, rolled it out flat on the ground, and placed his sword on the fabric.

"This blade was given to me in the mountains outside Makkan. I was told I could keep the sword, but this," Mohamed said as he unbuckled the scabbard from his waist and handed it across to me, "I was told it belonged to another man. I was told to protect the scabbard at all costs until the day a man appeared before me. I asked how I would recognize this man, and for a reply I was given one word. Seven." Mohamed placed the scabbard in my hands, then wrapped his sword in the cloth and placed it behind him, next to the sack. I looked down at the object in my hands. The piece I held was beautiful, the carvings intricate and painstakingly etched into the strange metal.

"There is one more thing," he said. "I was told how to reactivate the piece."

"What do I do?" I asked.

"Hold the opening up to your mouth and exhale the breath of the Divine."

I did as Mohamed had instructed, and the piece rapidly expanded like a balloon. It maintained it's slightly curved shape and stayed approximately the same length, but it became close to two feet around. I knew instantly what it was. *This* was the shell of The Divine Engine. "Thank you," I said as another tone resounded within my skull. I stood and looked out the mouth of the cave at the fields bellow me. I emptied my head of all thought and listened to the sounds of nature emanating from the valley. The tone in my head mingled with the sounds of life and increased pitch as my vision turned white and I tuned.

I arrived outside the door of a hospital room. Looking in through the glass, I saw that I was back with the last of the 21, but this time he was not alone. Lilith and my *other* were in there with him. I saw Lilith bent over, her face just inches from the man strapped to the bed. She spoke to him, whispering something to speed up his demise, or worse, to prolong his suffering in the darkest depths of Chaos. It was not Lilith's words that caused the last of the 21 to die; she was just having a little fun. No, it was my other who'd delivered the man's death. I watched my negative self methodically carve the flesh from the bone of the man's right leg. He'd made it half way up one thigh before the poor guy had died. Even in death, my evil half continued to carve on the poor man's flesh. Was it punishment for his lack of screams? The victim *must* have felt it, but he just lay there, showing no sign. Part of me wanted to bang on the door, to make my presence known, and part of me wanted to get the hell out of there until I knew what I was getting myself into.

THE 6

I watched as the bastard wiped his bloody knife off on the dead man's hospital gown before sliding the blade into a sheath strapped to his leg. My other stood up and looked at Lilith. I heard a tone rising before they disappeared, I held on to it, and was about to tune…*"Wait."* A soft voice filled my head and I knew where it came from. I opened the door and stepped inside the room. The last of the 21 didn't appear to be breathing. He looked dead, his face completely devoid of emotion. I looked deep into his eyes searching for his fading memories of anything to do with the bloodline of the six. The memories were there, but terribly fragmented. It would take some time to piece them together. I knew the point where our paths had branched and the 6 were born, so I started there, in the early teens of my negative bloodline.

After killing the cat, and then Dusty, my negative half decided to make a hobby out of killing animals. This was when he began to hone his skinning and carving skills. He got a job working for a local butcher, and that helped some, but he still needed the rush from the kill; animals would simply no longer do. Aaron Radcliff and Father Matthews were just the beginning. My other was smart; he knew that if he stayed in such a small town he would eventually get caught. When he turned eighteen, he emptied his bank account, which had grown substantially due to the never-ending supply of rich tourists that flocked to the North East with the turning of the leaves, and moved to Boston. My negative half found it more difficult to kill in such a large city, as there were more people to see and hear, so he waited. He purchased the occasional hamster or rat, and sometimes even brought home a stray cat or dog to pacify his needs. He took his time getting to know the city and how it worked; like I said, he was smart. He got a job at a photo lab; he enjoyed working in the dark. It took more than a year and a half for my other to begin killing people again. He held the same job at the photo lab for six years while he butchered his way through the underbelly of the city. One victim a month was how he started, but soon there were two and three, then one a week. Near the end of his reign of terror on the city of Boston, one victim at a time was no longer enough, and it was only a matter of time before something went wrong. And boy did it ever... Enter Lilith.

Lilith tutored my negative half well, helping him to finish his education first in his class. He graduated as the perfect killer. It has been said that killer's often start with the ones closest to them and my other was no exception. Under Lilith's watchful eye, he wasted no time hunting down and disposing of the other 5 in his direct bloodline. After all, they were weak, and none of them could even *dream* of replacing Lilith's perfect little killer. He picked up the first of his other five at a bar on Lansdowne Street, disguised as a smokin' hot brunette. The first victim took little convincing to escort my other back to his apartment after last call. He was never seen again.

The next to die in the bloodline of six had just taken five hits of some high quality acid, smoked a joint, and started in on a fifth of Southern Comfort. He didn't really need the booze, which was a good thing, because when my other appeared before him, the bottle hit the floor and emptied out into the lime green shag carpet that was presently crawling with worms. *"No need to get the bottle myself,"* the victim thought. *"Why risk it? Make* him *get it."* It didn't even faze him that there was another *him* standing on the other side of the coffee table. *"Must be the acid,"* he thought.

"Good sir, would you mind fetching that bottle for me?" he asked.

My other reached out his arm and the bottle leapt from the floor to his hand; he held it up so the man on acid could see it. The bottle vanished, then reappeared on the table next to him.

"Hey, thanks man, I owe you one." The man on acid reached out for the bottle, but it disappeared before he could grab it. "What the *fuck*? Are they here? Did they finally breach security?" He got up from the chair and ran into the bedroom, dove over the bed, and landed on the floor below a set of windows. His head popped up and he pulled the blinds open with his fingers, pressing his face to the widow as he peered outside. "You'll never get me you *bastards!*" he yelled. "I'm armed; you'll never take me alive!" He ducked down and whispered, "Where the fuck did I put my gun?" The man stood, ran back into the living room, and sat down in his chair where he began to pick the worms from the carpet out of his socks. Lilith appeared in a flash of black light. *"You see, Mark, this is what happens to men who try to be what you have become. They are not worthy, but* you...*"* Lilith slowly licked the side of Mark's face with her soft black tongue, *"you are something special."*

"Should I kill him now?" Mark patiently waited for Lilith's answer. Though lost in another world, their victim heard those words loud and clear. He grabbed the remote control from the table and leapt up onto the chair. "Don't you dare come near me," he shouted. "I know how to use this!"

"Not yet," Lilith said with a Cheshire grin. *"Let him amuse us awhile."*

Their victim reached down and picked up the empty bottle of SoCo, turning it upside down to make sure there was none left. "Just my luck," he said. He'd been looking for an excuse to stay home from work in the morning, but by morning, *this* Mark wouldn't be going anywhere.

Victim number three was in prison; care to place a wager on the charge? He'd placed his order at a local fast food joint, then pulled out a gun and robbed the place. He shot the manager in the forehead for forgetting to give him his receipt. *That* version of my other was serving life with no parole. Killing him would be a mercy and Mark didn't like *that* idea, not one bit. Mark planned to make the con suffer. It's easy to make a man beg for death, but to make them beg for life, *that* was what Mark craved. Complete power. The trick was to make his victims think that there was a chance, a glimmer of hope, that they just might survive the night. Hope would make anyone plead for their life. And Mark was good; he knew how to keep them alive while they slowly grew delirious with the pain; his victims would do *anything* then. Mark had envied the previous one, the acid freak; he envied the man's total lack of sanity. Oh, to live in a world where nothing was real, nothing mattered. But Mark had a job to do, a calling. Yes, he'd envied the last one, but *this* one, lying on the piss and cum stained cot; he would *gladly* kill this one and feel no remorse.

Mark brought along his favorite skinning knife, all polished and shiny. He liked the way his victims' faces looked in the silvery reflection. But as soon as the knife became bloody, the reflection changed, and it was on! Mark looked at the con's reflection in his blade. He looked so peaceful, looked just like *him*. Mark sliced his palm open and slid the knife over the warm blood as it pumped from the wound on his hand. He wasn't worried about leaving his DNA at the crime scene as it would simply match the rest of the blood that would soon cover the cell. Mark preferred to start at the toes of his victims to prolong their suffering, but when he looked into his blood on the knife, it told him to start with the con's face. Mark moved silently to the bed and placed his hands around the sleeping man's neck. The con's eyes sprung open, but it was too late; Mark's grip was too firm. The victim's body relaxed as consciousness left him and he passed out. Mark rolled the con's body onto the floor and stripped the mattress from the bed, exposing the metal frame. He removed the con's clothing and placed the body back on the cot and tied the man to the bed with some heavy nylon rope he'd had the foresight to bring with him. When the con came to he was on his back, his arms and legs were pressed tightly against the metal bars of his bed frame. His head was tied back, he was gagged, and was only able see whatever passed by his narrow field of vision. The con expected this sort of thing to happen in the joint from time to time, but *this* was pretty elaborate, and *very* well planned. It had to be the guards. But the man standing above him had *his* face… and *his* voice!

"I'll bet you're more than a little confused, but don't you worry, only *one* of us will have this face by the end of the hour." Mark held up the knife for his doppelganger to see. He'd wanted to take his time with this one, but the blade had told him no. Mark pulled back on the man's hair and began to cut, tracing the hairline and around the ears, then down, just under the chin. Mark expertly slid the knife under the con's skin and began to peel it back from his chin up to his lips. The con fought, but it was useless; he couldn't move, so the only thing left to do was to lie there and sob. During the moments when the pain wasn't screaming through his body, the con thought he heard a woman's voice in the background. He thought, maybe this *was* some sort of trick; maybe the man peeling off his face really *didn't* look like him. Then he saw the woman. Black as night and cold as ice, and her eyes… her irises were *moving*. Lilith walked into view to witness what was being done to him. *"Look, I think he's* enjoying *it,"* Lilith smirked.

"Shit! What a time to get a boner," the con thought. They said it sometimes happens when you die, so this *must* be the end. He accepted his fate then, and just when he thought it couldn't get any worse…

"Why let such a beautiful thing go to waste." The cold black bitch climbed on top of the con and impaled herself on his traitorous shaft. The con closed his eyes, trying to shut out the pain and the images, but neither would leave him. The fucker carving on him was up to his nose and blood was beginning to seep in, making it hard to breathe. *"I'm getting close,"* Lilith moaned as she slowly moved her hips back and forth. The con felt the metal rails cutting into his back with every thrust. He opened his eyes to see the black woman's breasts bouncing in his face.

Things went fuzzy, breathing was hard, and the con knew he couldn't hold out much longer, so he closed his eyes again. He was only granted darkness for a brief moment before his skin was peeled back over his eyes, taking the lids along with it. Now the con *had* to watch. He watched the man who looked just like him pull out a very large knife. He watched the black bitch masturbate as she bucked and moaned and everything slowly went black. Now the con could only think, and for some reason, his last thought before he died was not a thought at all, it was a prayer. *"Please lord,"* he thought, *"don't let me come."*

Mark numbers four and five shared more of the same brutality as the other victims, but when the time came to separate himself from his bloodline, Mark hesitated. He hadn't expected his final version to have any fight left in him, but he wondered, as *he* grew stronger, maybe *they* did as well. It had been a long time since Mark had made a mistake, and he almost paid for it with his life. The last of his bloodline had somehow managed to get the knife away from him. Lilith had stepped in that time by freezing the moment, but not before the victim had slammed the knife into Mark's back just below his left shoulder blade. Mark stood frozen, with the knife in his back, but he could still see.

"What the fuck was THAT about!" Lilith screamed. Mark's final victim exploded, sending wet chunks of flesh and bone flying in all directions. Lilith walked around Mark and pulled the knife out, prying lose the remains of the severed hand that was still attached to the handle.

"It was close to your heart, my dear, another inch and you would be dead." Lilith spoke softly and then screamed, *"Your heart belongs to ME!"* Lilith stuck her finger into Mark's open wound and pulled down, tearing his flesh. She placed a finger from her other hand into the now widened hole and tugged at the skin until the opening was wide enough to fit her clenched fist in. Lilith reached in, Mark's flesh and bone separating to accommodate her hand, until she was able to reach his heart. Lilith's fingers massaged the muscle. *"I could kill you right now,"* she whispered into his ear, *"but I won't."* Lilith pulled her fist out of Mark's body and the skin began to grow back. The flesh crawled down the cavity leading to his heart, where it stopped, but left a perfect circle in his back, through which his heart could be seen thumping away.

"I'm leaving it open to remind you of my disappointment in you as of late; perhaps I have made the wrong choice?" Lilith pondered aloud.

"No, my love!" Mark fell and groveled at Lilith's feet.

"Very well, come; we have much to do."

THE 7

The visions of the 6 faded and I looked down at the body of the last of the 21. I reached out and closed his eyes. The tone Lilith and Mark had left behind remained, but the others thoughts within my head warned me not to go. They were right, the time would come to follow Mark's string, but it was *not* now. I heard my others in my head most of the time, but their thoughts were random and fragmented. This time was different; my others were working together on this one. I left the hospital room and caught the string back to Anna's Bridge where *my* six waited for me. "We're done," said number three.

"We've got all the pieces," said six.

"Now what do we do?" asked two.

"We *don't* have all of the pieces yet," I said. "There's still a tone left in my head."

"What are *we* supposed to do, sit around on our asses while *you* go…" Before he could finish his statement, all of us froze. We'd all had the same thought at once, but it wasn't one of *our* thoughts. It was one of *his*; Mark had found my girls!

It wasn't difficult to locate my children; after all, there was only *one* reality where Tara and Tori both existed together, *my* reality. I didn't know why I had thought my girls would stay untouched by all of this; it was a delusion that crashed down around me hard. I silently prayed for the power to pull off whatever it was I needed to. No matter, if it came down to it, I would *gladly* die to protect my children. I thought about their eyes; I had looked into them so many times that I could picture every small detail. When I found their tone I tuned.

I landed in a bedroom; the only light came from a night light in the adjoining bathroom, shining through an open door. A large bed was in front of me, and on it, sleeping soundly, were Tara and Tori, my baby girls. I stood there for a moment, watching them sleep, until the tears stung my eyes. I crossed the room to the door and opened it as quietly as I could, then stepped out into the hall. "Stop right there!" Special Agent Mira Stark stood in the middle of the large living room, pointing a gun at someone just out of sight. She turned the gun on me as soon as she saw me, alternating it between our mystery guest and I. "I *knew* you two were twins," she said with great satisfaction in her voice. I continued to walk down the hallway. "Don't even *think* about coming any closer," Agent Stark stated calmly, but firmly. I saw our guest now; he sat on the couch with his legs crossed.

"It's about time you showed up," said Mark.

"You lay one *fucking* finger on my girls and you *will* regret it," I said bitingly.

"Marcus, Marcus, Marcus," he said. "You should know as well as *anyone* that I don't feel regret."

I knew that this was not true; I'd seen his regret myself in the memories from the last of the 21, but Mark didn't need to know this; after all, knowledge is power. Mark uncrossed his legs and started to get up.

"I wouldn't if I were you." Mira swung the gun in his direction, getting a bead on him.

"Well, you're *not* me," Mark said patronizingly, and stood.

Agent Stark fired one shot into Mark's leg; it didn't even faze him. The next shot hit him in the left shoulder. The impact knocked Mark back for a second but he instantly recovered and started advancing on Mira. She fired two more shots in succession, the first hitting him square in the chest, the second dead center in the forehead, and still, he kept walking. "What the *fuck!*" Mira screamed.

Mark was about to attack Agent Stark when another me appeared, and another, and another. The six had located me. Mark stopped advancing and Mira took the opportunity to move into the kitchen, closer to the bedroom, where the children could be heard screaming. "What the hell is going on here?" Mira muttered, more to herself than to get an answer. The seven of us circled around Mark, closing him in. Our thoughts were one as we worked in tandem, but nothing we tried seemed to be having *any* impact on Mark at all. We stopped time, but it had no effect on him. We tried to force him out of this reality, but he would not budge. That could only mean one thing, something was supposed to happen, something that *none* of us could prevent. Then Mark made his move. A flash of silver streaked through the air, followed by red. Number seven fell to his knees clutching his throat. His hands fell away and his head tilted and flopped back, as if on a hinge. I had seen this vision before, shown to me by a prophet in Hell. A stream of blood pulsed out of number seven's neck. It slowed and became a trickle, and then his heart stopped. Now we were six. With the final beat of one heart, the pace of another quickened, giving me an idea. Mark lunged for number four…

I reached into my pocket and pulled out the heart of Elizabeth Patton.

His blade arced back…

I held the heart up into the air and screamed, "Lilith!" She was there before the echo left the room.

"Give me that!" Lilith screamed. Mark became confused; he lowered his blade and stared at Lilith.

"Take the girls to Admiral Forsythe," I yelled to Agent Stark. She was at the end of the hall by the bedroom door, a look of awe and confusion on her face. "I trust him." I said. I randomly pictured every place that I had ever been throughout my life, marking each tone, writing my *own* song. When my song was complete, I let myself go, following this new series of strings. The song I had written had no pattern; it was simply random noise to the uninitiated. When I chose a note, I chose it by memory or image, not by the tone. I hoped that this would make things a little more difficult for Lilith and Mark to follow me, as I had no doubt they would do. Lilith, because she wanted Elizabeth's heart, and Mark, because he couldn't stand the thought of *me* having something *she* wanted. Ain't jealousy a bitch?

There were seven hundred and seventy seven of me when this had all started; now we were down to eight. Six remained in *my* bloodline, including me. I felt the void where the seventh should be, and so could my others. One Elizabeth Patton was left, who should be dead; there *would* be consequences. And that left Mark... Part of me hoped *I* would be the one to kill him. He'd taken a lot of lives, a lot of people who were close to me. It wasn't the lives that I missed the most, it was the love... the love that I'd never again share with my wife and children. I knew that I was being selfish but I couldn't help it.

8̲8̲8̲
INFINITY TO THE THIRD POWER

AN UNEXPECTED GUEST

The song abruptly stopped and was replaced by a single tone, and it was beautiful! The tone was like the sweet spot on a violin, the kind of note that gives you the shivers in an oh-so-good way. I caught the string and my head exploded with images laid out over every inch of my mind, images of my life that shifted and turned. I'd seen these images before, in a vision I'd had when this all started. I remembered the lines that stayed fixed, the lines that created the larger image. And now that I *saw* the image, I realized it was *not* an image at all. The lines made up a mathematical equation.

At first I had no idea what the symbols I was looking at meant, but the more I looked, the more I understood. This equation had been imbedded somewhere deep in my mind. The Godivel fruit had released this information to my conscious mind so that the symbols, letters, numbers, they suddenly made sense. I was looking at the Divine Plan. The pieces of the Divine Engine were there, each piece representing a thought of God. I followed the equation from beginning to end, from the dawn of time until the end of time, and what *did* I find at the end of the equation? I found... the answer.

∞
∞
∞

The answer to man's ultimate question is God: infinity to the third power. In the words of a woman named Julia, *God is the Chimera, God is three.* Positive, neutral, negative. Heaven, the multiverse, Hell. Three separate entities that exist as one.

The final string spit me out in the middle of an intersection, cars screaming by in both directions at incredible speeds. There was no traffic light but the timing of the vehicles was perfect, missing each other, and *me*, by mere inches in all directions. I shifted to the sidewalk and joined the crowd of pedestrians who moved as efficiently as the cars. I looked at the buildings and the architecture, everything had a pattern, everything made sense. I ducked into the first alley I spotted and heard a woman's voice. "Hello, Marcus," she said. "I've been waiting for you." The woman was attractive, in her late forties, with long jet-black hair that swayed from side to side. "My name is Claudia Spencer," she said.

"As in Andrew's wife?" I asked.

"Yes," she said. "You must come. There is something you need to see." Claudia turned and I followed her deeper into the alley that came to a dead end. "Well," Claudia said. "Go on, open it."

"Open what?" I asked. "There's nothing there."

"Marcus, you of *all* people should know to never trust what you see, now go on." I reached for the wall. "A little to your left," Claudia directed. My fingers touched some sort of doorknob. "Now turn and push," she said. I pushed the door open and a soft blue light filled the alley. "This way." Claudia stepped ahead of me and entered the door. The light radiated from every surface of the hall, turning Mrs. Spencer into a silhouette before me. She stopped at another blank wall and waited for me to catch up before opening the door.

Every surface but one in the room radiated a yellow light, from the chairs in the corner, to the table in the middle of the room. And on that table was the one thing not illuminated, the body of Dr. Andrew Spencer. "Is that really him?" I asked. Claudia placed her hand on my shoulder.

"You're wondering how an Umbra can be in Heaven," she said. "Yes, Marcus, I know what he was, what he *is*. That is why he is here, waiting for God to decide what to do with him. Andrew Spencer never hurt me or anyone else," she paused and laughed. "Andrew couldn't even kill a mosquito; he'd just sit there, letting it suck him dry. He was a *good* man and he led a *good* life. He helped others, Marcus, just like he helped you, though you may not see it yet. Andrew Spencer and Animus are not entirely one and the same. If the Umbra had chosen someone else, Andrew would have grown up to live the same life, which is why he was chosen. Animus was tired of death, It wanted to *live*! Do you believe in such a thing as atonement for your sins, Marcus?"

I wasn't sure what to say. I knew that *my* time was short; thanks to the fruit I knew that I would *not* be one of the five old men writing my gospel up on a hill. I'd committed a lot of sins, and I knew the tainting of my soul was far from over, but the thought *had* crossed my mind. Would the slate be wiped clean? Or would I have to suffer for my sins and be cast into the heart of the beast?

"Yes," I said, "what he did *does* matter."

"I hope so," Claudia sighed. "Andrew deserves to be in heaven with *me*." Mrs. Spencer paused to pull a handkerchief from her pocket and dry her eyes. "Go ahead," she said, nudging me toward his body, "Animus has something to show you."

I looked into Andrew's eyes and his pupils dilated. *"We meet again, Marcus Quincy,"* a voice boomed from within my head. "Animus," I said aloud. *"Yes,"* the creature answered.

"Where is Andrew Spencer?" I asked. *"He is here, but he is weak. Ira took much more from him than meat. If judgment is not passed soon it will be too late for him."*

"What will happen?" *"His soul will be trapped in this place forever."*

"What *is* this place?" *"God's loophole, a piece of Heaven He never completed, a place where anything is possible. Chaos is unpredictable, Marcus; God comes prepared."*

"So do the Mille Umbra," I shot back. "Why am I here?"

"I must ask you to do something for me... for Andrew and Claudia ... and maybe even for yourself. I ask you to allow me to leave this place with you. Leaving this body will allow Andrew Spencer to enter unto Heaven, and I can help you, Marcus."

"What happens to me, do I become part of your collection?" I asked suspiciously.

"Unlike my brethren, I have no collection of souls. I have only Andrew Spencer and he is far from my prisoner. For an Umbra to enter a human, the host must be willing. Andrew Spencer has a very old soul, Marcus, and he has lived many lives. I offered him a chance to make a difference in his world and he accepted." "And if *I* accept, you'll help *me*?"

"Yes, Marcus. Destroying Ira will not be easy. It would benefit you to have my knowledge of the Mille Umbra." Animus was right, I would need his help. And besides, I already carried the burden of sin, so what was a little more baggage? "What do I need to do?" I asked. *"It is done."*

I felt the Umbra inside my head. I looked down into Andrew Spencer's eyes as they lost focus and he... blinked? Andrew sat up and looked at his wife who began to cry.

"Claudia?" he questioned, confused.

"Yes, darling, I'm here." She rushed into his embrace.

"Where... where is he?"

"He's gone," said Claudia.

"Where?"

"Here." I said as I stepped forward.

"Marcus? Yes, it *is* you." Andrew reached out and pulled me into his arms. "I will mourn the loss of his presence," he said, "but I thank him for reuniting me with my precious Claudia." Andrew's attention quickly returned to his wife. It had been just over twenty-five years, a quarter of a century, since Andrew had last held Claudia. For Animus, this amount of time meant nothing, but for Andrew it had been an eternity.

"We must go," I said. "And Andrew, Animus thanks *you* as well." When I tuned, I left behind a man who had done so much to help me, knowing that *his* had been a happy ending.

I appeared on top of a large sphere, looking down at the city miles below me. I could see everything. I saw the entire layout of the city, the circles and lines, geometric patterns and shapes, like a massive crop circle. The sky around me was scattered with spheres, like the one I stood on. The colors within them shifted with the clouds, purple to gold, just like the buildings in Eden. Animus whispered softly in my head all the while. It told me of Its past, long before Andrew.

Animus was born some time after the multiverse, a few million years perhaps. By "born", I mean Animus became *aware* of Its surroundings and of Itself. Several million years passed by with nothing to accompany the silence but the Umbra's own thoughts, and then... life. At last, something to break the silence, because with life comes thought. Even the simplest of thoughts were comforting at first, but soon many species evolved, their brains growing in new and wondrous ways. Thoughts of these new organisms moved from the simple to the profound. Animus had watched as civilizations and cultures grew, and It waited until the time was right, when mankind needed something to believe in, when we needed a *God*. Animus had been more than willing to take the role, and he did a wonderful job until one day, a thousand voices appeared in Its thoughts. There were others like Animus; they were the Mille Umbra.

The first of the Umbra to become aware was Angere, the oldest and the cruelest of the Ancient Ones. Angere united the Umbra in Its hatred for all things living and set out to destroy all that God had created.

There were seven that had defied Angere, seven Umbra that had grown a little too fond of humanity, who took just a little too much pleasure in influencing our lives. These are the seven Umbra: Invidia, representing envy; Desideo, representing sloth; Edax, representing greed; Edacitas, representing gluttony; Ira, representing wrath; Salax, representing lust; and finally, Animus, who represented pride.

Thinking they would die, Angere banished the seven deadly sins from Chaos, sending them into the Nexus. Somehow, they survived. Such is the nature of Chaos. Angere was furious when he learned that the seven Umbra where alive and could still influence, though no longer control, the multiverse. Angere vowed that the Umbra would never be allowed to return to Chaos. I wondered then, what would have happened if Ira had succeeded in his plans to return to Hell?

Although the Umbra could no longer fully control their respective universes, most found that influence over the multiverse was more than enough, for their influence had found its way into the world of men, who once again treated them like Gods. The Umbra craved the adulation, all but Animus, who had chosen a different path. Animus simply wanted to *live*. His desire to live was still no different at this moment; I could sense the Umbra's will to survive, feel Its yearning for more of life's wonders as It told me these things, but not everything. "Why are you holding knowledge back?" I asked.

"You have eaten from the Tree of Knowledge, Marcus. If you needed to know these things, then you would know them." I guess I couldn't argue with that. *"Do not worry, Marcus. God would not have let this happen if it were not a part of His plan. Do you think He would let an Umbra roam freely through Heaven if He did not deem it necessary? I can show you things, Marcus; I can help you find what remains to be found."* I still didn't fully trust Animus and It knew that, but at least It didn't seem to care. *"Your kind has forgotten that thoughts and emotions are linked, that one cannot find the truth by searching for it, only by feeling it. Trust your feelings, Marcus. When you find the truth, you will know."*

A tone rose in my head, jarring the world around me. When the motion stopped, we stood on a hillside just below a layer of clouds in a place that seemed vaguely familiar to me. Below us, I saw a large walled city. The wall formed an oval, with enormous towers that reached up into the sky every few hundred yards. Within the walls there were even more towers and spires and turrets, but none as grand or as tall as the palace at the city's center. The palace shone white and gold in the light from the setting sun, making it nearly impossible to see what lay beyond. *"If you do not wish to die here, Marcus,"* Animus cautioned, *"then you must do as I tell you"* "Where *is* here?" I asked. *"Welcome to Avalon."*

A NEW QUEST

The truth flowed through my mind as we descended the hillside; I knew it, I *felt* it. This was the knowledge that countless men had died for as they protected secrets that the masses must never know. Until the first century, all of the knowledge from around the world and beyond had been housed in the Library of Alexandria. A wealth of knowledge thought to be gone forever, but not all was lost when the library was destroyed. When the rubble was cleared, they found them in pristine condition, the Eight Books of Knowledge. The books were taken to Jerusalem, where they were hidden beneath the Temple Mount, only to be discovered by a group of knights on a Crusade over a thousand years later. The knights read the books and used this knowledge to their advantage. They forged copies of the books before turning over the fakes to the Vatican as commanded, hiding the *true* books in a grave behind a church they had built on a hillside in southern France. Several centuries later, a young king began *his* quest for this knowledge, his quest for the Holy Grail.

The city of Avalon was built on a ledge jutting out of the mountain, with only one side facing the hills we traversed. I saw no gate or door or even a window in the wall, leaving us no option but to take the narrow path on the north side of the city. Large sections of the path crumbled away as I walked, dirt and grass plummeted to the grassy plateau far below. I cautiously made my way around the wall to the east side of the city, where the rocky ledge reached out over the land. *"You feel it, don't you, Marcus?"*

Yes, I'd been there before. I saw the valley below, and the giant grassy steps leading up to the mountain. I'd climbed those steps in a dream, to find my fair maiden waiting for me in the tower. The path ended before a small wooden bridge extending out over a deep fissure in the rocky ledge. I crossed the bridge to the city wall but there was nothing there, no entrance. *"Wait for it,"* Animus whispered.

Flames leapt from twin cauldrons on each side of the ledge, and as the sun set and the shadows lengthened, a door appeared. I knocked seven times on the large wooden door, just like the last time I was there. Nothing happened. *"Once more,"* Animus prompted. I knocked a final time and the door rumbled open.

The courtyard was full of people; rows of stalls lined the walls and the crowds gathered in a frenzy of commerce. The smell of fresh fruit and smoked meat filled the air. I crossed the courtyard, weaving in and out of the crowd, until I stood before the door to the tower. I entered the door and shifted to the top. *"Why do you think you had to knock eight times Marcus?"* Animus, ever vigilant, was trying to tell me something but I ignored him. Julia was asleep on the sofa.

"Julia… Anna?" I called out. The woman's eyes opened and her face filled with fear.

"Thou must be mistaken," she said and sat up.

It hit me then, what Animus was trying to tell me, I was in a different reality. This Julia looked at me like she'd seen me before, but couldn't quite place where. She looked into my eyes and I looked back at hers. "Oh my," she said when she saw my eyes. "Is thou certain thou art in the proper place?"

"Yes and no," I said. "The wrong place for the person I mistook you for, but the right place for why I'm here. I need to see your king, I need to see Arthur." When I looked into her eyes, the knowledge from the Godivel fruit told me that the woman's name was Bethany. She was part of Julia's bloodline, which also made her part of *Anna's* bloodline. Now I knew the connection.

Bethany's eyes revealed that she remembered living several past lives, but had forgotten where she was. She'd been in Avalon a long time. Bethany's life cycle had been in its infancy when the Ah Me Rah murdered her nearly five centuries ago. Her next cycle was slated to begin in three months, provided I complete and activate the Divine Engine within the hour.

"What is it thou seeketh from my King?" Bethany asked.

"His wisdom." I answered truthfully.

"Thou art blessed!" she stated joyously. "My King hath *much* wisdom."

"Will you take me to him?" I requested.

"Yes, m'lord… yes, I shall." I reached out my hand; she hesitated at first, but grabbed hold.

"I wouldn't…" Animus whispered in the back of my skull.

"Think of the palace," I said. Bethany closed her eyes and we shifted. We appeared just inside the palace doors, she opened her eyes and jerked her hand away. "What manner of deceit hast thou wrought?"

"I warned you, Marcus." Animus gloated. Her cries had alerted the guards.

There were six guards, all in shining gold armor, and all were heading my way. *"Stay calm, Marcus."* Animus cautioned from within. One guard descended from each of the four staircases that rose along the outside walls of the room, and two more came through the doors just beyond the grand staircase that rose in the center of the massive hall. *"Just stand still and wait."* The guards surrounded us, each with his sword drawn and pointed at my face. They noticed my eyes and hesitated. I saw enough in their eyes to know that they would kill me if their king gave them the word. A figure appeared at the top of the grand staircase and slowly descended. He wore no crown, but I knew that this was the king. He drew his sword and advanced. *"Drop to your knees!"* Animus hissed and I obeyed. *"Tell him..."* I followed the instructions that Animus poured into my head, trusting him for the first time.

"It would be an honor to taste your steel, my king," I said.

Arthur raised his sword, stopped, and lowered the blade to my neck.

"What sort of trickery is this?" he demanded.

"I used to bring Andrew here in his dreams," Animus explained. *"He and the king became friends and this is how they met. I will tell you more at a later time, but first, tell him..."*

"The time of which Animus foretold has come," I said. "We are here for the books."

"Is he *in* you?" asked the King, sensing that Animus was with me.

"Yes," I answered.

"How can this be?"

"Andrew Spencer is dead," I told him. "Animus left him so Andrew's soul could enter Heaven."

"Andrew is here? Ha! Perhaps we *will* meet again." Arthur lowered his sword. "You must come with me."

I bid farewell to Bethany and followed the king up the staircase and into a large room. In the center of the room was a circle of eight pillars that rose up into the darkness. The floor within the circle was illuminated light blue. "You say you saw Andrew here, in Heaven?" Arthur asked.

"Yes," I said. "He was with his wife."

"Good, good." Arthur pushed in on a plaque set into one of the pillars. A panel opened, causing the floor to turn from blue to red, and then to white. The changing of the floor color was not the only change that took place; we were now in a completely different room. "This is the top of the tower," Arthur explained, "where I keep my most valued secrets. Very few men have seen its contents, and fewer still have lived to tell of it." I looked around the spherical room. It was much smaller than the one we'd just left, and there were doors all around it, at least two dozen.

"Don't worry," I said. "I'm only interested in the books,"

"Through here." Arthur led me to one of the doors. "On the other side, you will find the objects you seek. Good luck, my new friend, and God speed." Arthur reached out and firmly grasped my hand.

"Andrew told me this was the proper gentleman's goodbye."

"Farewell, my friend," I said, and reached for the door.

KNOWLEDGE

On a pedestal in the center of the room sat a large gold box. Two beautiful Cherubs were carved into the lid, their wings and hair connecting in a spiral at the center where there was a five-pointed slot. It seemed that the "psycho scissors" were the key to opening the Arc of the Covenant. Luckily, there was a pair of them leaning against the wall in the corner of the room.

At the base of the Arc sat the Eight Books of Knowledge in two piles of four. Each book was bound in a different manner; some had locks, while others didn't seem to open at all. That was okay; I didn't need to open them to know what was inside, because just running my hand over each book was enough. Like some kind of psychic brail, the knowledge contained within flowed up through my fingertips, into my blood and into my brain. *"Enough, Marcus, each of the books has a name and a purpose, and each book must be read in the correct order."* Animus was doing his best to keep me on task. I spaced the eight books out on the floor in two rows of four and stood over them. The four books on the top row had locks, while three of the books on the bottom row did not seem to open, and the fourth had no locking mechanism at all. "Well, what's the first book?" I asked. *"The Book of Balance,"* said Animus. *"Do you know which one it is?"* *"No."*

One of the locked books caught my eye. It was bound in black and white leather with a seam sewn into the center of the binding, making one cover black and the other white. The book was bound with a leather strap stitched into the binding that encircled the book, this strap also held the means to unlock the secrets of the ages. The lock was on the white half, flat and round, about the size of a quarter. I reached down, picked up the book, and placed my thumb on the circle of metal. The lock turned from white to black and clicked open.

A strange light temporarily blinded me as I opened the book. There were no pages inside, as the book was more like a box. The light emanating from within was gray, half white and half black, the balance of the two colors. It washed over my face, crawling up into the pores of my skin. I felt the light as it entered my blood, making its way to my brain, and with it came the knowledge from the Book of Balance. The knowledge embraced me, drawing me into its stories and passages. It was too much all at once, so I shut down most of my senses and simply *felt* the information as it fought for room in my rapidly crowding mind. It was far too much information to try and explain, so I'll simply say this: do *not* underestimate the importance and the power of balance in your daily life, for without it, *nothing* can exist. I found *my* balance, between sanity and insanity; maybe that's why I was chosen to seek out the Divine Engine and restore balance to the multiverse. "What's next?" I asked Animus. *"The Book of Time."*

I looked down at the seven remaining books. I studied the books carefully until I made a startling observation. One of the books on the bottom row that did not appear to open seemed to be made out of several different materials ranging from a thick copper-like metal to a soft velvety cloth. I watched as the materials seemed to crawl across the cover of the book. I picked up the tome and turned it over in my hands, and upon further inspection I realized the soft material was not a part of the cover, but some sort of mold. The binding of the book crumbled in my hand, exposing a sharp piece of metal that I cut my thumb on. I pulled my hand away and looked at the wound, which was about half an inch wide and a quarter inch deep. My blood streamed from parts of the wound while the rest of it shifted from various stages of healing and then back to open wound again. The decay on the cover of the book in my other hand did the same thing at the same time. *"If it is the correct book,"* Animus said. *"It will open for you."* Things were the same upon opening the book, except this time the light was white. It seeped into my skin and held me like before, while around me, time sped by and stood still all at the same time. I relaxed and let myself go; concentrating only on the feelings the information gave me.

Time is a funny thing; invented by man to give meaning to God's world, yet mankind had *no* idea that time was so much more. Time is everything from beginning to end; time *is* God… or part of God anyway. Time, thought of as a dimension unto itself, is something that has always been here and always will be. Does this not describe God? Time is not a line or a circle or a wave, time is a *mass*. Time encompasses everything and everything is connected by time and by God. Time is God before his division into positive and negative, the imprint left behind, what was there *before* the "big bang". I closed the cover and looked at the remaining six books. Animus had anticipated my question. *"The Book of Wisdom,"* he said.

A wise man would put a lock on this book and Animus agreed. I inspected the three remaining books on the top row, immediately ruled one of them out, and focused on the other two. The one on the far right looked like an ordinary, leather bound book with a dark crimson cover. The other book was bound in a soft, flesh colored fabric like silk, much too delicate for a book containing the wisdom of the multiverse. No, the Book of Wisdom would be a no frills, no shit, ordinary book. Again, Animus agreed with my thoughts, so I picked up the crimson bound book, placed my thumb to the lock, and waited for the click. This time, the light emitted was green.

Here was man's *true* book of knowledge. It contained the wisdom of the wisest men throughout the centuries: prophets, scholars, astronomers, mathematicians, and engineers. There was knowledge of technology in those texts that is still far beyond our grasp. Here was the proof that there was technology and knowledge lost with the destruction of the Library of Alexandria, technology used to build the ancient temples and cities, technology the church tried to hide. Yes, the church lied to us, but its intentions were good; look what today's technology is doing to our species, good and bad. Technology is going to change us entirely; with every passing day we become less human. Technology *will* cause our next evolution. I let the knowledge have its way with me and closed the book a wiser man. Animus encouraged me to continue. *"The Book of Awakening,"* he said.

There remained two locked books, two books that wouldn't open and one unlocked book. One of the locked books was sure to be the Book of the Dead in one form or another, the human face on the cover told me so. Was the other the Book of Power? My guess was that the Book of Power was one of the two that would not open, so it was down to the unlocked book and the flesh colored book on the top row. The unlocked book was bound in faded black leather, with no markings at all. Nothing about that book screamed "awakening", but the soft flesh colored cover of the locked book intrigued me; it reminded me of a newborn's skin. *"I concur,"* said Animus. I opened the Book of Awakening to a soft glow of yellow light.

The Book of Awakening was all about learning to put two and two together, looking for signs, and trying to determine outcomes. So how *do* we recognize signs? When we see something out of the corner of our eye that's not there, when we first notice some random object that we've passed by a million times, that unsettled feeling we get when we ask 'was it ever there before now?' *That* is a sign. The next time this happens, remember what you were thinking about, and think about it more. Think about it long and hard, because in one way or another it involves a major decision coming up in your life. All that said and done, the book I held was a map to the Divine Plan. Like I *needed* another map! I placed the book on the ground at the foot of the Arc with the other books I'd already opened. Four remained. *"The Book of Enlightenment,"* Animus whispered. One of the books that did not open caught my attention, the one on the far left. The symbols that adorned the cover were definitely Eastern in origin, as I remembered seeing one of the symbols carved on a bridge in India. Buddha… Enlightenment. I picked up the book and opened it to a soft red glow.

What *is* enlightenment? Is it the knowledge of all things known? It couldn't be, I still had three books to go. Yes, enlightenment *is* knowledge, but it is also the ability to realize that there are reasons for everything that happens, good *and* bad, and all we can truly do about it is smile and say "Oh, okay", and move on with our lives. Now, seeing as how things happen for a reason, we are once again forced to ask why? I did not know the answer to that question at the time but I knew this: While we have no preordained destiny we *do* have choices, and these choices dictate the outcome of our reality. In each reality, every individual choice is part of what dictates the future for that universe. We must remember that we are in control of our destinies, and above all else, we must remember that Chaos does *not* have to be a bad thing. Patterns can trap us, they can destroy our lives, patterns can destroy *everything*! Death and rebirth, a fundamental Hindu belief, is nothing more than a pattern and patterns can be broken. *That* is why we need Chaos in our lives, to break the patterns. Since one random choice can change your life forever, take the time, make the effort, and put some thought into the choices you make. Every choice makes you who you are and who you're going to become. The knowledge in the Book of Enlightenment is available to all, scattered throughout the religious texts of all cultures, the fundamental belief that if you live a good life, you will be rewarded in the next.

Animus urged me to continue the journey. *"The Book of Death,"* he said. I already knew which book Death would be; it was the book bound in the face of a human man. I picked up the book and placed my thumb on the lock; it clicked and opened. The black light burned my senses, dulling them to prepare me for the knowledge of the dead, a knowledge that has been forgotten for centuries. The Egyptian Book of the Dead, Lovecraft's Necronimicon, both only contain diluted passages from the text I held in my hand, the translations forgotten or lost with time. Here were the laws of the afterlife, and within its text were ways to break the rules, ways to cheat death, ways to resurrect the dead, and a way for me to bring Anna back. It was hard to push the feelings aside and the book knew it, becoming less and less forthright with its contents. *"One's*

intentions must be pure if they wish to obtain the knowledge of Death,"
Animus reminded me. I focused on my goal until the dam finally broke
and the knowledge came flooding into my mind.

Why do we fear death? We fear death because it is so easy for us
to cling to what we know, and unfortunately, what we know is what
we see. It is not death that we fear it is change, because change makes
us uncomfortable. *God* is order, but Chaos, being the opposite of God,
has its own patterns, and even bad patterns are more comfortable than
change. Death *should* be feared, as it too has its own patterns and we can
get caught in them just as easily. Yes, we *must* embrace Chaos, for Chaos
is choice, and choice can break the patterns. As soon as this thought
filtered through, the book released me. *"The Book of Rebirth,"* Animus
demanded. I'd figured that birth had to follow death.

Now I was left with the unlocked book and the book that would
not open. They sat side by side on the bottom row. The book on
the left, the one that would not open, was bound in gold leaf and
just screamed power, but... There was something tempting about the
unlocked book, the way it just lay there, taunting me with its secrets,
vulnerable. All I had to do was reach down and open the cover, and it
was *that* temptation that made my choice easy, for man has *always* been
tempted by power. I picked up the gold book, shiny and new, knowing
it was the correct book, and it opened.

I pulled the cover back to a brilliant orange glow, the combination
of red and yellow, combining the colors of the Books of Awakening
and Enlightenment. The Book of Rebirth was an extension of the
Book of Death, an extended guide to the afterlife, telling of what lies
beyond death. That book went more into depth about the importance
of patterns and cycles, how even though a pattern can be broken, the
original pattern will still remain in its own realm. Breaking the pattern
merely causes the birth of a new reality. But what happens when the
cycle is complete, when the multiverse no longer expands, and things
begin to die? Patterns remain, imprints left behind that can never be
destroyed. When the multiverse is no more, when everything dies and
all realities come to an end, what happens then? A new cycle, a new
multiverse is formed, following the imprint of the last. Not exactly the

same, just the basic patterns, but once life takes hold, choices dictate evolution, and we are reborn the same, but different. There are no guarantees. One day a multiverse may form that never produces life and what happens then? What happens to us as we await the next cycle and the next chance to be reborn? We, like God, are energy. We become part of His collective, part of time; we watch, we wait, and we learn. But how do we retain this knowledge once we come back reborn into the multiverse?

Why is that, when we get into a bind, we almost *always* go with our gut feelings, our instincts, no matter *what* anyone else tells us? It is because, a lot of the time, we are right. If we listen to our minds *and* our conscience, we will usually make the right choice. That is because our instinct is a part of us that remembers what we've learned in our travels throughout the multiverse. Patterns are not the only things that leave an imprint; we do, as well. Look at how many traces of our lives we leave around us when we die. Log in names, passwords, pin numbers, screen names, the initials you leave when you get high score on a video game, even your music and movie collection tells a little bit about you. All of the things you purchase throughout your lifetime, everywhere you go, everything you do leaves an imprint in some way. Not all of these things will be repeated the next time around, due to the choices you make throughout each lifetime, but the imprint will still be there. So that leaves the answer to the question 'what happens to us when we die?' We are not reborn as soon as we die, as I'd learned from the Book of Death. We spend time in the reflected multiverses of God or Chaos, depending on how we lived. Time in Chaos is dictated by the life you lead, but your time in Heaven is not. The amount of time you spend in God is equivalent to the time you spent on earth, then you are reborn into another body, another life, and you repeat this over and over until the cycle is complete and it is time to start again. I closed the cover, leaving only the Book of Power, my hands trembling as I picked it up.

To have knowledge is to have power, yet to have power is *not* to have knowledge. One must first obtain knowledge before one can obtain power. The balance becomes tipped; yin and yang are not equal, exceptions to the rules are made when it comes to the wielding of power, they *must* be. *"You have done well, Marcus,"* Animus said with slight satisfaction, *"This book can only be read last. Power without knowledge is useless; you have avoided temptation now reap the rewards."* Was this the Umbra's way of telling me how he planned to right the wrongs he had committed? I opened the final book and the light was all colors at once, like the rainbow reflections in the buildings of Eden. I wasn't sure how much more knowledge my head would contain. It hurt like hell already, and now, with the opening of the final book, my head was pounding, feeling like it was growing to a massive size, threatening to explode at any time… "Damnit Cap'n, she c'nt take any mo're."

POWER

What *is* power? Is it something that can be seen, something to be held and coveted? No, power cannot be physically held. No man can control power, *power* controls *man*. Is God power? I knew God is energy, but is God *power*, that was the question. We call God a *higher* power; is *that* the truth, is God *more* than power? From my previous readings, I already knew the answer. *Knowledge* is power, but it's more than that. We *must* know how to use it, for it is much more difficult to use power than it is to use knowledge. The use of knowledge alone requires years of training; wielding power without the knowledge to use it has *always* been a fatal error. Remember Hiroshima and Nagasaki? Abusing power with the knowledge to use it correctly is the same as using power with no knowledge at all. If power is not used for its true purpose, then it can *not* be controlled. There are a lot of things that we can do that should not be done, and with the advent of new technologies, the list just continues to grow larger by the day. What will the future hold for us if man is able to figure out the complexities of time? What if man is able to somehow master time, to master time travel? Knowing what you now know, what does this do to the Divine Plan and what will this do to God? Change is the nature of Chaos, it is needed for balance, but just look at what the introduction of the seven deadly sins did to us. Imagine how much the balance of power would be tipped if man had *more* of a say in what direction the Divine Plan took. The consequences could be devastating! Unless we learn how to properly use power, or more correctly, how to let power use *us*, we are in danger of contaminating the patterns, diluting them more and more with each cycle, until there will not be enough left to follow, voiding the Divine Plan. What happens then? That, my friend, is when we can truly say that God is dead, and *WE* will have been responsible.

I know it's hard to believe in things that cannot be seen, but it shouldn't be that way. We know that to believe in a higher power you don't have to see it, we take it on faith. Scientists don't have to see results to believe in a theory, so is seeing *truly* believing? Simply put, no. If God is power, and knowledge is power, then you don't need to *see* God to believe, you have to *know* God, and there *is* a difference. So how does one go about knowing God? How does one correctly follow God's Divine Plan? We have to look for the signs. This is where the patterns come into play. The patterns in life are not only reflections of *us*, pieces of *us*, they are also pieces of *God*. You have to put together the pieces to get the whole picture. You need to learn to read the things that go on around you, because that is *your* Divine Plan. *You* need to learn to see the signs that tell you when you're heading down the wrong path. That is a power we have all been given; we just need to remember how to use it. Power is everywhere in everything. Objects have power, words have power, but when you combine the two, words made real become objects of *unlimited power*. The Book of Power had told me about the pieces of the Divine Engine, and basically, when all of the pieces of the Divine Engine were brought together, they would tell me how to build it. I placed the last book down on the floor and stood before the final piece, the Arc of the Covenant.

I retrieved the psycho scissors from the corner of the room and brushed away the dust and cobwebs as best I could. I placed the blades into the slot and turned. The mechanism whirred and clicked as the locks disengaged. I dropped the five-pointed star to the ground and returned my attention to the Arc. I pried open the lid, letting it fall to the floor behind the relic with a loud metallic clank. The box was solid inside, except for a space two feet long and one foot wide. Inside this space was a box made of a familiar metal. I pulled that smaller box out and held it in my hand. It was only about six inches wide, had a handle, and opened like a briefcase. There were ten pieces inside. Those pieces formed two plates, two tablets, each made up five parts. Both plates were positively charged, and in the forces that would be created within the Divine Engine their power would be limitless. I closed the box. A tone in my head reached out and I shifted.

"Where are we going?" I asked Animus. "*We have time, and you have unfinished business,*" was his reply. "And what might that be?" I questioned, anxious to complete my task of building the Divine Engine. "*You must find the last Elizabeth Patton, and quickly.*"

"How am I supposed to do *that* when I'm in Heaven and she's in Hell?"

"*There is always a way, Marcus.*" "And that is?" I inquired. "*They are called the Amen Ra. Eight hundred and eighty eight reflections of God. Like the Umbra, each its own entity yet it thinks as one, for it is still part of the whole. They will help us if we ask the right questions.*"

THE GODS

The knowledge was there, coming from the Book of Enlightenment. I only got bits and pieces of it but from what I could tell, when God divided forming the Chimera and the multiverse, the gods were born. Just as Chaos is the opposite of God, the Amen Ra are the opposites of the Mille Umbra. When the multiverse was formed, there was no one "Big Bang", though there *was* a first. The first galaxy to be formed was born in all three dimensions, one in Chaos, one in what would eventually become the multiverse, and one in God. The collision of positive and negative tore a hole in God, tearing out a piece and dividing it into three. One piece was released at the center of the galaxy in God, another in Chaos, and the third piece of God was scattered throughout the galaxy surrounding the Nexus, planting the seeds for life in the first reality. These pieces of God still contained his thoughts, but they were each their own entity, a new consciousness that was born from the old. The one in Chaos took the name Angere, while the one in God was called Osiris. These demigods soon learned they were not alone. The chain reaction started by the birth of the multiverse resulted in nine hundred and ninety nine original galaxies. One hundred of these realities made up the beginnings of the multiverse and eight hundred and eighty eight of them were formed within God. Chaos, however, was granted its version of all nine hundred and ninety nine realities, eleven of which were exclusive to Chaos. Eleven realities where life was never allowed to take hold. *"These are the deepest levels of Hell,"* Animus told me, *"with no possible way out, and meant only for the worst humanity has to offer."*

When we arrived at our destination, I stood in a vast field of chest high grass that was dark red, the color of rusting copper. I saw mountains in the distance made black by a white-hot sun shining through the peaks. *"I am attracted to my opposite,"* explained Animus. The sun grew brighter as it rose over the tops of the mountains. *"It knows we are here."* I realized then that there was no sun above us, just a vast ball of light almost the size of the mountain it rose above.

"What's its name?" I asked. *"It is called Serapis."* The light was taking form as it drew closer, growing vast wings, with a long neck and tail. The great beast swooped down, an immense dragon of white light. As it hovered above me, the downdraft of its thumping wings flattened the grass around me for miles.

"What is it you seek, Marcus Quincy?" Serapis boomed. The words bellowed from its gaping maw, the heat of its breath blistered my skin, which then instantly healed.

"How do I find the Shadow Lake in Heaven?" I cried out to the beast.

"You do not," the creature replied.

"What happened to it?" I asked. Within my head, Animus told me.

"When Salax found a way to merge Dissensio with the Ah Me Ra, all of the Shadow Lakes in all realities merged, even the ones here in Heaven."

"How could God let that happen?" I asked.

"It was a small price to pay for what God was given in return," the creature bellowed as it came to rest on the solid ground, folding its massive wings.

"What did God get in return?" I called to the beast towering over me.

Animus answered in my head. *"A Rive."*

"A what?" I asked, puzzled.

"A Rive is a passage between dimensions, a passage from Heaven into Hell."

"Where do we find the Rive?" I asked Serapis.

"Osiris possesses the Amenti Rive. You will find Osiris here..." I heard the tone, but just barely. The tones of heaven were too high for even a dog to hear and I could only hear them when I needed to. "Thank you," I said.

"It was a pleasure to play my part in the great plan." The beast nodded and turned, spreading its massive wings with the speed and force of a god. The dragon of light took to the skies and disappeared behind the mountains like the setting sun. The sky remained a soft violet, almost lavender, and after a while the stars began to shine through. *"Are we ready?"* the creature inside my skull asked. I focused on the new tone and caught the string.

I arrived on a road that wound its way through the peeks of a white mountain. Everything around me looked to be carved from great pillars of salt. Even the stone walls that lined the roadside were white and corroded. Before me I saw a vast bridge stretching over a deep cavern leading to a massive white castle carved into the mountains on the other side. I shifted to the entranceway. The hall inside invoked feelings of meekness and futility, making me feel inferior with its vastness and complexity of patterns and shapes. I walked deeper into the castle, the passageway narrowing and ending at a single door. I stepped through and stood on a large rock on the edge of a waterfall of molten earth, the air thick with smoke and burning ash. I closed the door behind me and it vanished. An endless see of lava rushed toward the falls. There was no place to go. I looked down at the endless pit that swallowed the rush of magma pouring over the edge. Was there something down there?

I saw it glowing in the darkness just out of sight, was it getting bigger, or was it getting *closer*? The light grew more intense, shining a soft blue. It stopped in the darkness of the shadows beneath the stones protruding from the ledge that I stood upon. At first, all I saw was a glowing orb the size of a tire you might find on an eighteen-wheeler. A brighter light swam within the depths of the orb like an iris, watching me. It stayed there for several seconds and then thrust upward until the creature towered above me. It was huge, a giant black worm with gray markings, spirals, like a tribal tattoo. The head consisted of a large gaping mouth that opened and closed as if sucking in the putrid air around it. The creature had two protrusions under its mouth that were more like feelers or arms. Above the mouth, on the top of its head, was the glowing blue eye. It leaned in close; its huge mouth just yards away. *"It is…"* Animus began… "Osiris," I said.

"Marcus Quincy." It answered back. The creature had two voices, one that thundered and rumbled in the low octaves of a nowhere near human voice, the other a soft feminine voice, a voice that was, dare I say… sexy? **"We have been watching your progress, Marcus. And you, Animus, we have been watching you as well. Your actions continue to surprise us."** Osiris reared up, the creature's eye just feet away, its inner light focused on me.

"Follow the path and you will find the key," Osiris bellowed, then withdrew and fell away into the darkness of the abyss below.

From the same darkness came a rumble and a cloud of smoke. The molten rock shot up like a geyser from the pit. It rose into the air about a hundred yards out, towering above me. Something seemed to be forming within the magma as it reached its maximum height, causing it to spread out to the ledge I stood upon. I watched the lava slowly pour down from the top in a six-foot wide strip until it was just yards away. And as suddenly as it had begun the flow stopped and hardened, forming a vast staircase leading up into the darkness.

The staircase led to a narrow opening on the face of a cliff. I stepped inside and followed the caves twists and turns until I came to a large cavern with no visible exit. It was a dead end. I stopped at the wall of rock that blocked my path and reached up to run my fingers across the cold stone. "What now?" I asked. *"Follow the path."* Animus repeated Osiris's words.

"How? It's not like I can walk through solid rock."

"Can you not?" I hadn't even thought about it. I could do a hell of a lot of things that I could never do before, so why not? I pulled my hand back and placed my fingertips to the stone. I felt the rock grow soft and I pushed, watching my arm sink in up to the elbow! I pressed forward and entered the wall. On the other side was a cavernous room with a great pool the size of a small lake. The water was held in a massive stone bowl surrounded by six columns rising up into the darkness, each the size of a skyscraper. Ahead of me I saw a pier leading to the waters edge. I followed until I could go no further, thinking, why not, if I can walk through stone why can't I walk on water? I stepped onto the lake and began to cross. When I reached the center of the massive bowl of water I saw an old brass skeleton key floating in the air before me. "Is it?" I inquired. *"Yes, Marcus, it is the Amenti Rive."*

"How does it work?" I asked and Animus told me. I reached up, extracting the key from the air. I held the Rive in my clenched fist and said, "Take me to Hell!"

THE AMENTI RIVE

I stood before an old dilapidated church. Beyond the structure I saw a rusty iron gate beneath a sign that read 'Shadow Lake Cemetery'. The door to the church was locked so I slid the key I held in my hand into the slot and the bolt gave. I pushed the door open with my shoulder and entered the church. The air was cold and damp, filled with the smells that accompany decades of mold and rot. Half of the pews were overturned or smashed to bits, the pieces used for kindling in a long dead fire now reduced to piles of ash that filled a circle of black carbon on the floor. The only thing in the church that was not in a state of disrepair was the altar. The stone had been kept shiny and clean, and there was a cloth draped over the altar that was white, free of dirt and rot. I saw the remnants of candles scattered about the room, some no more than small pools of wax while others looked recently burned. I walked across the chapel to the altar and studied the intricate designs adorning the cloth. I saw various religious symbols from many different cultures that had been painstakingly embroidered into the fabric. A loud thump drew my attention to a large wooden cabinet with two doors, and as I approached I heard the distinct sounds of a man sobbing.

I opened the door to the confessional and entered. The sobbing continued from the other side of the wall, beyond a solid wood panel that covered the window between the stalls. I waited a couple of minutes until the sobs died down. The man coughed and sniffled and the wooden panel slid open. The screen was missing and I saw the man's face, half of it at least; he looked down at the floor as he spoke.

"You used the key!" the priest demanded. "Where did you get it?"

"That's not important," I said, "Tell me what you know about the Rive."

"I will tell you *nothing*!" he screamed. The man looked at me for the first time, his eyes filled with terror. "Your eyes!" he screamed. "Did *she* send you? Is this another test?" The man sprang from his seat and cowered in the corner of the small space.

"I'm not here to hurt you," I tried to reassure the man. "Please, just tell me what you know about the key."

"*NO!*" the priest screamed as he stood and lunged for the door, just about tearing it from the hinges. His shouts continued from outside the confessional. "I will take that key *now*!" The man demanded as he wrenched the door to my stall open. "Give it to me!" He waved a knife through the air. The priest lunged at me and I shifted outside the confessional and pushed the door shut. I placed both of my hands where the door met the wall, one high and one low. The wood instantly began to soften beneath my palms, melting together until door and wall became one. I backed away as the man inside threw himself against the tightly sealed door.

"Let me *out* of here you bastard!" he screamed as he thrashed about the small room. When the noises stopped I entered the door on the right and saw the man trying to wedge himself through the open window. He appeared to be stuck, as only one of his arms and his head had made it through.

"Please, get me out of here," the man pleaded.

"Tell me what I want to know," I demanded.

"All right, all right, I'll tell. Just let me out of here."

"You want out of that window you gotta' tell me first." I grabbed the man by the hair and lifted his head so he had no choice but to look me in the eyes. He still had the knife in his hand, and he raised it behind my back, ready to lunge the blade into my flesh. With a single thought the man froze.

"I can't move!" he screamed. "Why can't I move?"

"Come now," I said, "Should a man of the cloth be trying to kill somebody?"

"God abandoned me *long* ago," he said with a hint of distaste.

"You lie," I said. I could see the truth in his eyes, it was not God who had abandoned the man, it was the priest who had abandoned his faith. I turned and pulled the knife from the man's hand and released control, his body relaxed. "She promised me everything," he sobbed.

"More lies," I said. "You should have known better, coming to you as she did, telling you what you wanted to hear. Would a creature like *that* be sent by God?" It had been Dissensio, sent by Salax to seduce the priest.

"Part of her was," he sobbed. The priest knew more than I initially suspected, so I probed deeper into his mind and deeper into his past.

"That was a sign Father," I said, "seeing the part of her that was good, *that* was a gift from God, your clue to make the right choice but you chose not to."

"But she… all she wanted was the key." His sobs grew louder as his body trembled, shaking the walls around us.

"And for that, you condemned your town to Hell?"

"I had *no* idea!" he screamed.

"*Wrong*!" I shouted back. "You refused to see the signs, you suspected what you were doing was wrong but you did it anyway. When the time came, you didn't listen to your conscience, you handed over the key." He knew I was right. I knew the truth that *he* was still not ready to acknowledge. I pushed in on the man's wedged shoulder and he tumbled back into the other room, crashing to the floor. "Well," I said, "I've got unfinished business to tend to. I'll be seeing you around Father." I turned and left the confessional, closing the door behind me.

"You can't leave me here," he screamed. "You said you would get me out!"

I stopped and approached the melted door to his stall.

"I said I would get you out of the *window*." I turned and walked away.

"You *bastard*! I'll get you for this!" His screams echoed throughout the old church as I closed the doors and stepped out into the crisp night air.

I shifted through town wondering two things, was I in the correct Shadow Lake, and if not, how in the hell did I get to the right one? Animus didn't seem to have any answers; in fact, he wasn't saying anything at all. I went to the obvious place, I went to Julia's, but when I got there the house was gone! All I saw before me was a smoldering pile of rubble. *"Focus on the Julia you know, Marcus. See through her eyes."*

Animus was back. I slipped into a memory so I could feel her close to me. I held that feeling in and reached out in search of her mind. I felt the current flowing through my blood, the charge building slowly at first and then...

I looked out the front window of Julia's house. I could hear her thoughts like before and she was wondering where I was. I had told her I would be back by then. I knew then that Julia was still alive, and this was not *my* Shadow Lake. This was the reality the *key* had come from. I slipped the key into my pocket, focused on Julia, and tuned.

The door burst open as soon as I appeared. Julia lunged down the steps and into my arms. "I thought you were never coming back," she wailed, almost in tears.

"Are you all right?" I asked. "Has anyone else been here?"

"No, no... I'm fine, everything's fine. Did you get your answer?"

"Yes," I said as she pulled away, yanking my arm to follow her into the house. Once inside, she turned and locked the door. I followed her to the kitchen where there was a kettle of water cooling on the stove. I entered the dining room and sat down at the table while Julia made her who knows how many'th cup of coffee. I watched her, she was calming down before the caffeine even hit her system. I pulled the key from my pocket and placed it on the table. "Do you know what this is?" I asked.

"It's a key," she said as she sat down in the chair next to me placing her mug on the table in front of her.

"It's a way out of here for whoever holds it," I explained.

"Really?" Julia sat up, looking hard at the object. "That name you gave me," she said. "Elizabeth Patton. I asked around and," Her eyes stayed on the key as she spoke. "Billy Darien said he overheard Old Mrs. Crawford talking about a houseguest of hers by the name of Elizabeth, said she was giving her a hard time." *Sounds like Elizabeth Patton to me,* I thought to myself.

"Where can I find Old Mrs. Crawford?" I asked.

"Come on, I'll take you." Julia rose from her chair and grabbed my arm, hauling me up with her.

"No Julia," I said as I slipped the key into my pocket. "You need to be here when the boy comes back." I took Julia's face in my hands and looked into her eyes. "Think about where Mrs. Crawford lives," I instructed. I followed the map Julia was making in her mind and marked the location. Then I left *her* with something. I left her with the answer that Jacob Chant would be returning for. I told her everything she would need to know and a little more. I figured the truth was the least I could give her, I owed her that much for all of the help she had given me. "I need to go, Julia. Time is growing short and I have *my* part to play now."

"Yes, Marcus," Julia let go of my hand. "Go and do your part, and thank you, thank you for coming into my life and making it such a wonderful place."

ENDING THE LINE

I looked up at the sign above the gate that read: Shadow Lake Cemetery. I pushed the gate open and headed up the path. The house on the hill was a silhouette in the light of the full moon, casting its shadows through the nameless graves, their markings eroded by time. I stayed in the shadows until I reached the edge of a large, open yard leading to the front steps of the house. I shifted to a darkened corner of the porch; the boards creaked and moaned from my sudden weight. I peered through a window and saw the room was empty. With a single thought, I was inside. I found no signs of life as I quietly crept through each room on the first floor of the house. I remembered seeing a staircase in the front hall so I returned there and climbed the steps to the second floor. The east wing of the house was empty, all of the rooms unlocked, but when I reached the back of the house I found the door to the west wing locked. I placed my hands on the solid oak door; the wood faded and I saw the hall on the other side. A man stood halfway down the hall, his back to me. A door opened across from him and a woman stepped out. She was old, dressed in period clothes, like she'd purchased her wardrobe from the set of a bad gothic horror film. This must be old Mrs. Crawford. The couple spoke for a while until talking escalated to arguing. The woman turned and walked away. The man threw his hands up into the air and yelled something before entering the door the woman had initially emerged from, slamming the door shut behind him. I waited until old Mrs. Crawford entered the door at the end of the hall and then shifted.

I placed my hand on the door the man had disappeared behind and saw a staircase. I heard a scream from somewhere above so I shifted up before the man could reach the top of the stairs. I ducked into an empty room just as the door at the end of the hall opened. The man walked down the hall and entered the room where Elizabeth was being held captive and spoke to someone new. They argued about something and then both left. I waited for the door to shut, then crossed the hall and entered the room.

Elizabeth Patton sat in a large wooden chair with her arms and legs bound tightly. She looked bad, like someone had been carving the flesh from her arms; long strips of skin were missing, leaving the meat and veins exposed. She looked up at me quickly and then hid her face again. Slowly, she turned my way, and with almost a look of recognition on her face, she asked, "Do I know you?"

"In a way," I said.

"Are you here to kill me or rescue me?"

"I'm not sure yet, you weren't supposed to live." I had debated this with Animus on a couple of occasions but neither of us could come up with a solution.

"You had better think fast," Animus cautioned, *"they are returning."*

I locked the door and started to untie Elizabeth. When the men reached the door, the knob would not turn so they started pounding on the door. I heard more footsteps and the jiggling of keys.

"Let me through." It was Mrs. Crawford. The key slid into the lock and the door pushed open, Elizabeth stood, I had to think...

I pulled Elizabeth into my arms and grabbed a knife from the table. I held the blade to her throat as Elizabeth's captors tumbled into the room. "Come any closer and she dies," I said. The old woman laughed. "She is going to die anyway," she said. "Can we not make her suffering last a little bit longer?"

"I'd rather kill her than let *you* carve her up," I hissed.

"What are you *doing?*" Elizabeth was sobbing now. She had no fight left; she just stood there, slumped in my arms. The two men advanced and I pushed the knife deeper into Elizabeth's throat, drawing blood. The old woman put up her hand and the men backed off. "All right!" she screamed. "What do you want?"

"*Well Marcus,* Animus whispered, *where* are *you going with this?*" I didn't know myself, what the hell was I doing? I raised my hand up above my head and drove the knife into Elizabeth's heart. A look of panic and terror filled her eyes as I sat her back down in the chair. I got down on my knees in front of her and pulled the key from my pocket. I placed the Rive in Elizabeth's hands and wrapped mine around hers.

"I'm *so* sorry Elizabeth," I said "But it had to be done. You have to do something for me now, when I let go of your hands you have to squeeze this key tightly and say, *I want to go to Heaven.* Can you do that for me?" She looked at me, confused at first, and then smiled. She nodded and I let go of her hands.

"I want to go to Heaven," Elizabeth whispered and disappeared in a flash of light. The men attacked me from behind, hitting me hard on the head, and then everything went black.

CAPTIVE

When I came to, *I* was tied to the chair. One of the men had taken the metal box from the Arc of the Covenant from me. It was open and he was taking apart the tablets and putting them back together again. "What the hell are these?" he asked the other man.

"Beats the hell out me." The second man sat at a small sharpening wheel. Sparks flew from the grinding stone as he passed a large knife over the spinning disk of stone. The other man threw the pieces of the tablets back in the case and tossed the box onto the table. "Gotta' take a leak," he said. "Want anything?"

"No," grumbled the man at the wheel. The other man left and shut the door.

"Let's give *this* a try." The man said as he switched off the wheel and rose, stumbling in my direction. "Nice and sharp now... you won't feel any pain at all." He sat in the chair next to me and placed his free hand on my right arm. He took the tip of the blade and placed it between his open fingers that gripped my arm, and slowly pushed the knife into my skin. The man watched my face, but I did not respond. I made no sign of pain or discomfort, like what he was doing was not effecting me at all. He began to get angry, twisting the blade, grinding it into my flesh. I looked him in the eyes, concentrating only on him. Slowly my vision went blurry and things began to spin. When my sight came back, I was standing *over* my body strapped to the chair. I was more than simply *seeing* through his eyes, I had complete control of his body! I twisted the knife and watched my body scream out in pain but it was he who felt it, not me. *I* was in him and *he* was in me. "Nice and sharp," I said with his voice and smiled, "You won't feel any pain at all."

The door behind me opened and I let go. I was pulled back into my body, and he to his. In the confusion, the man let go of the knife still embedded in my flesh and stumbled into the second man when he entered the room. The first man, now frightened, turned and ran down the hall. The remaining man looked at me. "What was *that* all about?" he asked. "Never mind. We have more pressing things to discuss. Like who you are and why you're here." The man ran the tips of his fingers across my forehead and over my eyes, then took three of his fingers and pressed them to my eye socket. "I should take them out. I bet *she* would reward me well for these."

"Or Lilith will kill you for interfering," I said. He removed his hand; by the look on his face *that* thought had never even crossed his mind. The door opened and old Mrs. Crawford arrived.

"What happened up here?" she demanded. "And take that *thing* out of him." Old Mrs. Crawford pointed to the knife. The man grabbed the handle, twisting the blade a little bit but I gave him no reaction. He grumbled something to himself and then pulled the knife out. "Now leave us," Mrs. Crawford demanded.

"But…"

"*NOW!*" she screamed.

"Yes, Ma'am." The man turned, wiping the knife on a bloodstained handkerchief. He placed both on a table and left the room without saying another word.

The woman stood there looking at me. "I take it you're Old Mrs. Crawford." I said.

"*Miss…*" she hissed angrily.

"A little touchy there grandma?" I asked sarcastically.

"*Silence*, I will *not* stand for this insolence!" She calmed herself and continued. "You know who I am, now I am simply asking that you be so kind as to return the favor."

"See Granny, all you had to do was ask nicely. My name's Marcus Quincy."

"Well now," her face lit up. "I've heard quite a bit about *you*." She began to pace the room, anxious, as if waiting for something to happen. "Tell me what you did with Elizabeth Patten, what did you give her," she asked.

"I didn't *do* anything to her," I said. "I just gave her the key." The woman stopped, turned and lunged for the chair, leaning down in front of me as she spoke.

"A key you say? Was it the Amenti Rive? Was it *here*?"

"Yeah," I said, "sorry you missed it."

"You *fool*!" she screamed. "The key is our salvation. Where did you send her with it?"

"I didn't *send* her anywhere. The *key* took her to Heaven."

"Is that how it works?" she asked curiously. "It is just as I had suspected, we can save this town and once more ascend to Heaven."

"I hate to burst your bubble, Granny," I said, "but making deals with Lilith and Salax, well that's *not* the way to be getting on God's good side now is it?"

"What do *you* know about *God*?" she screamed. "*God* is the one who destroys. *God* is the one who murders. Paradise is coming yet *He* sends *you* to try and stop it! Ask yourself why."

"What are you talking about?" I asked Animus as well, but he remained silent.

"You don't know? God didn't tell you? Big surprise, they call Lucifer the Prince of Lies, but just read the Bible; it's full of God's lies and empty promises. He has abandoned us in the past and He is doing it again. The Day of Judgment is upon us and Eden will descend from the sky and open Its gates. Why do you wish to stop this Mr. Quincy? Why?"

257

"Because we're not ready," I said.

Even without the help of Animus, I was beginning to put things together. Once the seed was planted there was no longer a reason for the Godivel fruit to keep the knowledge from me. The upcoming celestial alignment marks the end of a cycle and the end of life as we know it. This will be the End of Days as foretold in Revelations. By activating the Divine Engine before the start of the alignment I could stop this from happening, giving mankind... how many chances *has* God given us? Our species has survived a lot in the past, too many times to merely call it luck or coincidence, so just take a chance and believe in Divine Intervention. I would love to see the gates of Eden open once more and all of humanity welcomed inside but we're not ready; too many would be left behind. Be happy that God still sees our potential and is willing to give us another chance. With my actions we'd have several billion more years to grow up and learn how to get along. I had completed what I had gone there to do, and that was to free Elizabeth Patton. It was time to get down to business. "Sorry Granny," I said. "I need to get going." The knots in the ropes that bound me to the chair untangled and fell to the ground. I stood and walked past her. She fell to the floor and curled up into a ball. "Please don't hurt me," she pleaded. I picked up the box from the Arc of the Covenant and opened it to make sure all of the pieces were inside. I looked down at old Mrs. Crawford and smiled. "Don't worry," I said. "There's nothing I could do to you that would be worse than the fate you have already chosen for yourself." I closed the box containing the final pieces to the Divine Engine and tuned to Anna's Bridge.

The Five were waiting for me when I returned with the Commandments. They had all of the pieces scattered atop the wooden platform and were standing around talking and puffing away on cigarettes. I opened the box that I retrieved from the Arc and assembled the plates before I placed them among the other objects laying about. It happened instantly. The pieces began to levitate, twisting and shifting position to fit inside Mohamed's scabbard. A soft humming was heard from within the scabbard as the parts continued to connect. The Divine Engine ignited in a brilliant display of color and light and descended to the platform. All of the pieces we had collected were used but one.

"*The Spear is the key,*" Animus told me. Filled with the blood of Christ, the Spear of Destiny was the key to starting the Divine Engine. The Spear hovered in the air before us and I reached for it... There was a pop of static behind me and someone grabbed my arm. *It was Mark!* He grabbed the Spear out of the air and disappeared.

9⁹9
CHAOS

FORGIVENESS

I stood there for a moment, wondering what to do next. The five around me seemed just as perplexed. Was it all for nothing? Was this how it was going to end? No. I knew what had to be done. It was time to go to Hell and take back what was mine and if all else failed, the beating heart in my pocket told me that I would at least take *something* out with me.

"I'm going," I said to the others. "I'm killing Ira and finding the key."

The five simultaneously held up their left wrists to examine the time, even though only two of my others wore watches. "Don't worry," I said. "I'll have it back in time."

"Are you ready for this?" asked Animus.

"As ready as I'll ever be." The Umbra conjured up a tone from Hell for me and I caught the string.

"So, where *do* you take off to?" I asked Animus as we tuned. "Where are you when you're not digging around inside my memories, violating my mind and fucking my brain?" The Umbra was not amused. *"Like the Amen-Ra,"* Animus explained, *"the Mille Umbra are one collective mind,*

260

and we are very good at hiding our thoughts from the Others. Sometimes, however, we have no choice but to let our guards down, and when we do, the Umbra listen. That, Marcus, is what I am doing. I am listening."

"Anything I can use?" I asked. *"He knows we are here."*

"Who?" *"Angere,"* the Umbra whispered. I'd dealt with Umbra in the past, but none as powerful as Angere, pure evil, pure hatred. "Is it here?"

"No," the Umbra answered. *"It is... waiting."* "Let him wait," I said. "But keep listening. I'm gonna take a look around."

I stood in a gully on a steep hillside, carved into a mountain from years of water runoff in the spring. It was nighttime and the sky was clear, a black moon shone high above casting rays of black light through the silhouettes of the tree branches above me. I was trying to decide which way to go, up the mountain or down, when I heard a scream that sounded like a young child coming from the hills below me. I shifted and found the child trapped within a cage suspended in the air from the trees above by a thick rope. The cage was spherical in shape and constructed of tree limbs and twine tied tightly together with only a small window to look out. The boy saw me and started to smile but thought better of it. Instead, he retreated into the darkness of the cage. "Well Sirnib," I called out. "What have you gotten yourself into now?" I waited but received no answer. "Okay," I called out. "I'll be seeing ya." I walked beneath the boy's suspended cell and continued down the gully. When I got about a hundred yards away he began to scream, "Come back, Marcus. Please, come back..."

I shifted into the sphere, which rocked with the extra weight and the startled jolt from Sirnib when I appeared. He sat down, crossing his arms and legs. "What are *you* doing here?" he asked sheepishly.

"I'm not sure," I answered honestly, "but it looks like I'm here to see you."

"Why, to pay me back for what I did to you? Fuck you, you're in Hell buddy, get used to being screwed!"

"How about this," I said. "You do *one* thing for me and all is forgiven."

"What is it?" the boy asked suspiciously.

"No, answer first."

"Fine," Sirnib said reluctantly. "I'll do it. What do you want me to do?"

"Hold on," I said with a smile. I thought about the rope holding the cage, it snapped and the sphere fell, bounced, and began to roll down the gully into the valley below.

We were thrown all around the cage as we bounced and rolled and jolted our way down the mountain. We hit something hard and the sphere bounced high into the air, sending both Sirnib and I tumbling uncontrollably until we returned to solid ground with a bone-crunching jolt. The cage hit a tree, and then another, and we came to a stop. Wood splintered and cracked, flying in all directions. The globe was split almost in two. I looked up through the crack and watched the black light from the moon filter down through the branches of the tree that had stopped our descent. I climbed out and fell to the ground laughing. "What's so funny?" Sirnib demanded.

"Come on," I said through a fit of laughter, "that was a *blast!*"

"No fucking way man, you'd never get me to do it again, not in a *million* years!"

I just laughed some more. "So, where are we?" I asked.

"Not where we want to be," the boy answered nervously. "Can you get us out of here?"

"Sure," I said, "but I don't think you'll like where I'm going any better."

The boy just stood there looking at me for a moment. "Do you want out of here or not?" I asked.

"You are *such* an asshole. Fine, let's go."" Sirnib waddled over and wrapped his arms around my legs.

"I warned you," I said, and we shifted,

REDEMPTION

Sirnib stepped away from me, stretched out his arms, and yawned. "Where are we?" he asked.

"Beats the hell out of me. You said you wanted out, I didn't hear you offering up any suggestions."

"All right, all right, here is fine. Now let's go find out where *here* is." Sirnib started off across the field of orange wheat-like grass, his head barely showing above the top of the stalks. I followed closely behind as we descended the hillside to the city. "Do you know it?" I asked. He shook his head from side to side.

Clouds of thick black smoke hovered over the small city. Each building on the horizon had several smokestacks protruding from their rooftops and each chimney pumped as much black smoke into the sky as the next. There were smaller structures strewn throughout the cluster of factories, houses, and shops. I saw a woman hanging out what I first mistook to be laundry in the back yard of one of the nearby dwellings. As we drew closer I saw that the laundry was actually human skins hanging out to dry in the hot evening breeze. "You think this is a good idea?" I asked.

"I think I know where we are," Sirnib said. "I've never actually been here myself but I've heard rumors about it." He stopped and watched the woman hanging out her skins. She glanced up at us, then went back to her work, pulling the next skin from her basket and draping it over the line.

"This is one of the cities on the outermost rim of the eleven forbidden realities," Sirnib explained. "There's no need for a body in *there,* them poor bastards." the boy hung his head for a moment and then continued. "They ship the bodies out here to be recycled for meat, meat for the beasts that guard the inner realms." The words sounded funny coming from the lips of a child.

"So why are we here?" Sirnib asked nervously.

"Because I'm going in." I said.

"*In*? Are you crazy?" the boy shouted.

"Yes, in. Into the depths of the inner realms, into the heart of the beast."

"No fuckin' way man." Sirnib stopped and threw his hands up in the air. "I'm not having nothin' to do with this!"

"Don't worry," I cut in. "I'm not asking you to come along, just help me find someone who can get me in."

"All right," the boy shook his head and let out a deep sigh. "But then I'm finding my own way outta' here."

I put out my hand. "So it's a deal?"

"It's a deal," the boy said as we shook. "Say, Marcus, what were you doing back there, back where you found me?"

"You going to tell me what got you into that mess?" I asked.

"You first," he said.

"I bet you mine's better," I taunted.

"Fine! I was caught trying to steal a horse." I just looked at him. "What?" He threw up his hands. "Fine, I got caught stealing a horse from the stables of the mayor."

"*And?*"

"...after I got caught sleeping with his wife. Happy now?"

"Yes, Sirnib, I like your newfound honesty." I looked at him and smiled.

"So how did you do it," he asked. "How did you find me?"

"I didn't," I said. "*He* did,"

"*He*, who the fuck is *He?*"

"Animus," I said.

"An *Umbra?*" Sirnib stopped and turned quickly, his eyes darting in all directions. "Where? Is it here?"

"Sort of," I said.

"Where, I don't see no Umbra," Sirnib said with a sneer.

"It's in here." I pointed to my head.

"You have an Umbra *inside* you?" Sirnib began to laugh hysterically. I grabbed hold of the boy and held him still, forcing the child to look into my eyes while Animus made his presence known.

"Enough! That's creeping me out, man." Sirnib shivered and started to twitch. I let him go. He ran up ahead to a cluster of small shacks and began talking to a group of children playing with the partially decomposed carcass of a large animal. When I had crossed half the distance Sirnib turned and made his way back to me. "There's a church a couple of blocks away," the boy explained. "You might find help there." Sirnib led me through a cluster of factories and run-down shacks until we came to the church. The structure wasn't much better than that of the surrounding dwellings, the only distinguishing feature being a large wooden cross nailed to the roof. We climbed the stairs and entered the building and my nose was instantly filled with the smell of burning incense, sandalwood maybe. A short and *very* old man in a robe shuffled through the tight spaces between the pews and made his way to the front to greet us. "Welcome, my friends," he said. "I am Father Machuelle. How may I guide your spirits?"

Sirnib tugged on my pant leg saying, "Let me do the talking." He turned to the priest and said, "My friend here wishes to find a way into the forbidden realms."

"Stop right *there*! I will have *no* part in this!" The old man shook his head and waved us away.

"Hear me out." Sirnib ran to the old man's side. "Ask me who this is, that's all I ask." Sirnib pulled on the man's robe, turning him in my direction.

"Fine, who is *this*?" the old man reluctantly inquired.

"Why, this is Marcus Quincy," Sirnib said proudly.

"*The* Marcus Quincy?" The priest sounded overjoyed. "The one from the scriptures?"

"Sure enough," Sirnib gloated. "Will you help us now?"

"Yes, I will help you. Come, come with me." The old man stumbled through the pews, leading us into a back room. He stopped and whispered something to a young woman, turned to us, and said, "Wait here, please. I'll only be a moment." The two disappeared down a narrow flight of stairs.

"So, Sirnib, exactly *whose* side are you on?" I asked.

"I'm sorry," the boy said. "I have to play both sides to get the information I get."

I laughed and ran my fingers through his hair. "That's all right."

266

"Quit it!" the boy yelled. "You're messing it up."

"So it was you who left Elizabeth's heart on the train for me to find." I said.

"Yeah well, *somebody* needed to give you a push in the right direction." I laughed some more and we waited, until finally the woman returned. "This way," she motioned for us to follow.

We descended down a narrow flight of stairs into a cramped basement where the old man was strapping equipment to a partially skinned cadaver. "Over here," he said. "Sit down." The old man pointed to a chair next to the table with the corpse. I crossed the small room and took a seat. Sirnib hung out near the stairs and watched as the priest dabbed oil on my head and placed some kind of electrodes there. "Just relax." He flicked a switch on a strange looking machine and the equipment came to life. The electronics beeped and LED's flickered as the equipment booted up, filling the room with a soft hum.

"So what exactly does this *do*?" I asked.

"This will connect you with the deceased man beside you. Show you where he was before his body was shipped out here. Now relax, you might feel a little sting." It was more than a *little* sting, more like someone had just driven a knife into my brain, then I saw the tone.

I focused on the tone, remembering its location. The old man shut down the equipment and pulled the electrodes from my head. He neatly wrapped them and placed the wires on a bench beside the table. I sat up and Sirnib slowly made his way over to me. "So we're good now?" he asked.

"Yes," I said. "We're good." Sirnib looked at me and said nothing more, then turned and climbed the stairs. I heard a scream and a crash from above and Sirnib came tumbling back down.

"Go, Marcus," the boy screamed. "She's found us." As Sirnib said this, *she* stepped around the corner, tall and black and pure evil. "Lilith," I said.

"Give me the heart, Marcus," she hissed, *"and I will let the child live."*

Sirnib sat up behind her. "Just go," he screamed. Lilith reached into her stomach and started pulling something out. Hand over hand she pulled the blades out until they were complete. She raised the five-pointed star into the air and extended the sword in my direction. I saw Sirnib sitting on the floor behind the dark bitch; he stood and charged at Lilith screaming, "Get out of here, Marcus, *go!*" I had no choice but to listen to the child so I tuned, and the last thing I saw as the string carried me away was Lilith lunging at Sirnib with the blades.

THE INNER REALMS

I arrived somewhere in the sixth realm of Chaos, not quite where I needed to be but close enough. I stood on a beach of red sand. The tide was low, the ground wet beneath my feet. I saw some sort of streetlight on the pier ahead; the globe was a human head. Bright white light spilled from the mouth, nose, eyes, and ears. The head was bald and the skin was illuminated an eerie, bright red. The pole it rested atop was constructed from bones, some human and some not, and at the base of the lamp was a ring of ribcages. In the glow of the light I saw my feet were red from walking through the wet sand. I walked out onto the pier and spotted some fishermen out on the ocean of blood. I knew the light was now behind me making me extremely visible to them, but I didn't care. I began to walk down the pier, listening to the water churning around me as the tide came in.

I saw three men on the boat. They were huge, like body builders or wrestlers. The boat turned out to be not much of a boat at all, more like a raft made from long rotting planks of wood set atop rusty old barrels. One of the men appeared to be guiding the raft with a pole. Another of the men chopped away at something on the side of the raft with some sort of weapon and the third was hunched over a large sack. The boat started to tilt and jerk wildly when the men stopped what they were doing and stood staring at me. All of them wore rags for clothes, legs and sleeves missing, smeared and drenched with blood. I saw their faces or lack thereof. Each face was flat and void of all features but a mouth;

they had no eyes but still they stood and stared. The man examining the bundle waved to me and then the fishermen returned to their work.

When I reached the end of the pier the men were no more than twenty yards away. I saw then that the sea around the boat was filled with people! They were somehow held just below the surface, so if they struggled they could displace enough water to catch a breath of air every now and then, until they grew tired. The man with the pole steered the boat through the throng of bodies thrashing about in the bloody waters around them, while the man with a large roughly fashioned blade whacked away at limbs that clung to the boat for support. When the third man had finished his work he hauled a nude woman from the sack and threw her over his shoulder. She had been unconscious up until that point, and when she came to she started screaming violently. The man steering the raft stopped and placed the pole into a notch cut into the floor. A piece of wood was nailed into the plank with a single spike; the large man pushed it around with his foot until it locked the pole into place. He then turned and picked up a large round hunk of metal like a cannonball, and tossed it into the sea of blood and bodies. There was a chain attached to it; the woman screamed even louder when she realized the other half of the chain was attached to the collar around her neck. The chain pulled tight and yanked the woman off of the man's shoulder and into the sea. The woman screamed at first but soon stopped when she realized she needed to keep her mouth shut if she wanted to live.

There it was before me, the perfect example of a human's will to survive. Not realizing she was already dead, the woman fought to live. Even when large faceless men put a collar around her neck, tied it to a weight, and tossed her into a sea of blood, even *then* she still fought to survive. I looked out into the ocean and saw nothing but miles and miles of bodies thrashing about in the blood, doomed to forever fight for life and air. When they drown they are hauled out, brought back to life and then tossed in once again to join the struggle to survive. But while they were out... *that's* when the creatures had a little fun, making them not want to drown again that much more. The man returned to the pole and steered the raft back toward the pier, the remaining men picking up weapons and hacking at the limbs of those unlucky enough to grab on.

I turned and retreated down the pier, back to the beach and the head on the pole of bones. "So, where to from here?" I asked Animus.

"There is a shack on the beach to the north. Go there," he instructed. I began walking.

Animus was silent until I reached the small, single roomed hut. *"He is expecting us. Go in."*

"Who is he?" I asked.

"He is a merchant, a dealer of goods, a trader of secret, and an old friend." I opened the door to an empty room containing nothing but dirt and cobwebs. When I stepped inside and closed the door things changed. In the dark I saw objects forming in the shadows, while the walls seem to move away from me in all directions.

I instantly found myself standing in a large room filled with test equipment of all kinds. There were heat chambers, ovens, several thermal freezers, and large fans exhausting fumes from even larger boxes that were suspended in the air. I crossed the room and entered an open doorway. There was some*thing* sitting behind a large oak desk. It had dark green skin with brown markings like a boa or python, sort of human shaped, with arms and legs but several of each. A half arm shaped like an elephant's trunk protruded from the back of the thing's neck. The trunk had "fingers" that it was using to scratch its forehead. The creature's head had a thick brow, thin cheeks, small mouth and nose, but large black eyes. It sat forward and spoke.

"Welcome, Marcus. Animus has told me much about you. He tells me you need to find a way into the first realm to Angere." The creature sat back and put his four arms behind his head. "I can help you with this for a small fee."

"I have nothing to give you," I protested.

"What I want you have plenty of. I simply ask for one single drop of your blood. What do you say?" He put his arms back down on the table and waited for my response. I pondered his proposal. Why would he want my blood? *"Remember, Marcus. The blood of the Divine flows through you,"* Animus whispered. *"Here in Hell your blood is priceless. Many would kill for less than a drop. The fewer that know you are here the better."*

"What can *my* blood possibly be good for?" I asked.

"The blood of the Divine can kill what cannot be killed."

"Okay," I finally said. "You want a drop of my blood, that sounds fair. But no more than a drop, got it?"

"Yes, Mr. Quincy, no more than a drop." The creature stood and squeezed out from behind his desk. "Follow me and we will complete our transaction."

We entered yet another large room full of spare parts; this time everything was radio related. Receivers, speakers, wiring and microphones all scattered about in piles on tables. We crossed the room to another door. "In here," he said, ushering me through the open door. "Sit, Mr. Quincy, sit." The creature pushed me toward what resembled a dentist's chair. I sat down and waited as he fumbled with the instruments and gauges on a large machine.

"So, how do you know where to find Angere?" I asked.

"Oh, I don't," he said. "I will simply get you to the first realm. If Angere wishes to see you, *you* will not have to worry about finding *Him*."

"Sounds good to me," I said as I sat back in the chair. The creature turned on the machine. He pulled out a small needle and stuck it into the side of my leg, extracting one single droplet of blood. He then moved to my side and placed the required electrodes on my head, examined a couple of monitors, and opened the cover to a switch.

"Are you ready?" he asked.

"I'm ready," I said.

"This is going to sting just a little bit," he said as he laughed and flicked the switch.

ANGERE

Nothing happens in Hell without the blessings of Angere. If I wished to find Ira and get the key back I needed to see the creature. It *knew* that, and it expected as much. And punishment for not seeing Angere first, well, I'd rather not go into that. Angere is one sick bastard. The innermost realm of Chaos is a bizarre mix of seduction, temptation, torture, rape, even murder, but never your own. There was no dying there, not for the prisoner anyway, and there was *no* escape. When a soul is sent there it is final, left to suffer in one way or another for eternity, without *any* chance of ever getting out. The inner realms contain enough atrocities to make anyone sick to their stomach no matter how strong they think they are. All of your worst fears and nightmares can be found in the ten outlying realities, but the innermost realm… The innermost realm of Chaos is reserved for the worst of the worst, the sinners who will *never* stop, no matter how many chances they're given. Now, I'm not talking about the petty sin repeat offenders, that's what the nine hundred and eighty-eight outermost realms are for. I'm talking about the power seekers who will do *anything* to get their next fix, the violent sinners, and the murderers. The most creative tortures are reserved for *them* in the inner realms. None more so than in the domain of Angere. On occasion, others are sent to the first realm, those who have pissed off the forces of darkness one too many times, or committed sin in the name of the righteous as they 'fight the good fight'. Those who have sinned in the name of the righteous, they offend Angere more than anything, because they mock him with their sins in the name of God. I am one such sinner, and I fear that my fate will lie here in the innermost realm of Chaos, with an anti-god named Angere.

Everything around me was black and silent, not a flicker of light nor the faintest hint of sound, just the overwhelming feeling of darkness pressing in on me. Then there were the thoughts. I couldn't tell where they were coming from but they were in my head nonetheless. Finally, someone who hated mankind more than me. At least *I* could see man's potential, but Angere, his was a hatred that went far beyond loathing and contempt. On the other hand, the Umbra got a slight amount of amusement from watching the tortures going on around him. Yes, his hatred for all things living was far worse than mine ever could be. There was a time when Angere actively pursued the means to the end of existence, but not if it meant the end of the Umbra, for *He* wanted to live. Sounds like someone else was just a little bit guilty of the sin of Pride. Maybe that's why Angere let Animus in here with me.

Over the millennia Angere had tired of the game, and had come to the realization that for him to survive, there must always be balance. There would always be good and there will always be life, so Angere left the plotting of the destruction of mankind up to his brethren and took refuge in his realm. He disconnected from the rest of the collective; he was older and he knew how. There was only one voice that Angere could not block out, the true negative God, the One Thousandth Shadow… Chaos itself.

"It's here." Animus whispered in my head. "Where?" I asked. All I saw was darkness. *"Do you not feel him?"* I felt the pressure around me, the thoughts in my head. *"The Umbra in Hell are not like the ones you have encountered thus far."* Animus continued. *"They feed off your nightmares, taking any shape or form they desire. Angere does not wish to be seen. It has no mass of souls to pose as a physical body, It is only thought, only presence."*

"AND YOU ARE ONLY HERE BECAUSE I ALLOW IT." The voice boomed in my head leaving an echo that seemed to last an eternity.

"Then I guess a thank you is in order," I said. The creature said nothing; I guess the ruler of Hell doesn't have a sense of humor. "I'm here to…"

"I KNOW WHY YOU ARE HERE!" It boomed. ***"YOU ARE HERE FOR IRA AND YOUR DARK HALF. I CARE NOT FOR THEIR PLANS OF DESTRUCTION AND DOMINATION. THE***

LESS CHAOS HAS TO DO WITH THE MULTIVERSE, THE BETTER. YOU, ANIMUS, YOU HAVE PAID YOUR DUES. YOU DO NOT WISH TO RETURN TO CHAOS AND YOU HAVE NO DESIRE TO ALTER THE BALANCE, THEREFORE I FORGIVE YOU OF YOUR SIN OF PRIDE. YOU ARE NO LONGER BANNISHED AND MAY RETURN ONE DAY IF YOU SO DESIRE. AS FOR YOU, MARCUS, I WILL ALLOW YOU ACCESS TO IRA. FOR ATTEMPTING TO KILL ANIMUS ALONE, IRA MUST SUFFER, AND FOR PUTTING THE BALANCE IN JEOPERDY, IRA MUST DIE!"

"Thank you," I said. "Where can I find him?"

"IRA IS HERE, WHERE THE THREE POINTS ALLIGN." The information flooded in and another spot was marked on the map. I'd been to this place before; it was in the twenty-second realm of Chaos and I knew I could find it again. "Thank you," I said, but Angere remained silent. I focused on the tone the Umbra had given me and departed for the twenty-second realm.

STRIPPING THE SHADOWS

I gazed down upon the steel platform below me, the towers looked even taller than I remembered them. The chains and rings glistened in the light from the crimson sky as they hung suspended by some unseen force. I walked down the hill and climbed the stairs to the platform, only to find someone awaiting my arrival. It was the young girl with the British accent that I had encountered in the field of orbs on my initial visit to the towers. "Didn't expect to see you again," I said.

"And I did not expect you to have company. Tell me, how does it feel to have one inside of you?" she asked curiously.

"Crowded," was my answer.

"I'm sorry," she said. "I could not stay away. There are some things that *must* be witnessed." I still had no idea who this girl was, and if

Animus knew he stayed silent. "I am taking a great risk being here," she said. "But I must see, I must know that it *can* be done."

"Well then," I said. "Let's get on with it."

The girl scurried off into the shadows of one of the towers and sat in the darkness watching me. I saw a control panel to my right that had two buttons, one labeled *chains* and the other labeled *power*. I pressed the power button and somewhere below the platform a generator kicked in. I pressed the button labeled chains next and the air filled with the sounds of gears grinding and chains tightening. The shackles pulled taut against the rings that hovered in the air as they slowly began to rise. The gears stopped moving when both of the rings were horizontal. I heard a relay engage from within the control panel and a new motor kicked in. The machinery moaned and the chains began to move once more. They no longer moved up, only out, slowly spreading the rings until they were approximately twelve feet apart. Arcs of electricity shot out from the suspended rings, the air filled with a deafening roar and a flash of light. A spark ignited in the center of the current that crossed between the rings, growing larger and brighter by the second until it encompassed the entire area between the towers. There was a sudden explosion, followed by another deafening roar, and the Umbra began to take shape.

I saw a huge black shadow between the towers, but soon the shadow grew shapes, like smoke swirling through light in a darkened room. The shadows shifted and writhed as they screamed out in pain, awaiting their return to one reality. When the screaming stopped, the souls sobbed. The two rings were now imbedded into the twisting flesh of the beast. The towers didn't move at all as the creature struggled in protest of its captivity. I looked up at Ira; it knew I was there. The Umbra also knew that Animus was there, and the girl, but it was more perplexed about Animus. Ira couldn't understand what had happened, why Animus was still alive, and above all else, why Ira could no longer hear his thoughts. Or mine. Ira was weak, being stretched out between the Chimera had taken its toll on the creature, and it soon lost its fight and just hovered in the air. The creature's thoughts raced. It was looking for a way out, but the Umbra knew the device and it knew there were no weaknesses, for the towers had been designed by Chaos itself. The heart in my pocket began to beat faster as the creature had finally broken.

"Do you want to see what you've been missing while you were gone?" I called out to the beast. Ira said nothing so I opened up my mind and let it see. I listened to its thoughts as it learned of Lilith's betrayal and the beating heart of Elizabeth Patton just inches from my fingers. The Umbra's hatred boiled but it would not give away its secrets, not just yet. But it *was* ready to speak.

"It looks like I have lost and you have won. Do you feel the pride my brethren?"

"Yes," I said, "and by the way, Angere has forgiven Animus for his sin of pride, and did I mention he gave me permission to use *this*?" I pulled the heart from my pocket and held it up for the creature to see. The beast was close to exploding. It knew all was lost and for the first time in its extremely long life it felt fear. **"Do it,"** the creature sighed. **"Get it over with and be God's good little puppet."** Ira *wanted* to die now. "Oh, no-no-no, it's not going to be *that* easy. I think I'd rather let you sweat it a while, let you feel what it's like to have *your* life go to Hell, then maybe you'll know how *I* feel. You took *everything* from me, my wife, my kids, my *life*! There's *nothing* I could do to make you suffer enough for that! The only thing I can do is this…"

I walked beneath Ira and jumped up, shoving the heart into the creature with my fist. I hung from the Umbra as it floated above the platform. The shadows around me screamed in agony as they began to come undone. The outer shadows that made up the "skin" of the creature were the first to break away and float up into the red sky, followed by the flesh and muscle, and then the entrails and finally, the bones. The final shadow to detach from the Umbra's consciousness lowered and hovered before me. It took me a few seconds too see beyond the twisted and contorted features of her face but I knew it was her, I knew it was Elizabeth Patton. She smiled for a moment and then turned, joining the others as they ascended into the heavens.

The last of the shadows were gone, the last of the Umbra's souls set free. Ira had nothing now but consciousness and a growing fear of the end. Slowly, its awareness began to fade and fear turned to terror and panic. I felt Animus growing restless inside me, what was he up to? My head was thrown back and my mouth opened wide. A shadow tentacle sprang forth and devoured the last remaining thoughts of Ira before he disappeared forever. Animus reeled his line back in and released control as I fell to the metal flooring of the platform. I stood and Ira's thoughts began rushing into my head. Animus was playing them for me, skipping through them randomly. What was he looking for? There were thousands of thoughts, some about events involving me, most of them not. We were starting to get to the good stuff, the memories of Lilith and my evil self. I watched Mark beg to be given the order to kill Anna and the children. And I watched Ira *give* that order without one single shred of emotion. The thoughts went on and mine drifted. Ira was gone, that was one down. Now I had to find that bastard *me* and get the key back so I could return and activate the Divine Engine. Images raced through my mind, images of the things I would I do when I caught up with Mark. I had learned a lot about torture in my travels through Hell and it would soon be time to put these new skills to the test. A single word brought me back from my thoughts to Ira's. The word was Trinity. I remembered the picture the Admiral had shown me, the black and white photograph of me at the testing site called Trinity. Ira's thoughts told me that my negative self had gone back and taken the bomb, the Umbra instructing Mark what to do with the weapon if all plans had failed. He was to take the bomb to the Nexus point in the center of our galaxy and detonate it.

What is a black hole but pure dark matter? But a super massive black hole like the one at the center of *our* galaxy, it is comprised of both positive and negative Dark Materials, both Dark Matter *and* Energy. Detonating the bomb within these dark materials would cause another Big Bang, overlapping this reality and wiping out all of existence. If I was successful in stopping Mark I could still get the key back in time to activate the Divine Engine. If not, I might as well let him blow the whole thing sky high, because without that key all but a very select few of us were going to be thoroughly screwed.

I stood alone on the platform. The girl was gone and Ira was dead. "What happens to an Umbra when it dies?" I asked Animus. "*I do not know,*" It replied. "What do you mean you don't know? What would have happened if you hadn't left Andrew's body?" I asked.

"*There is a difference,*" the Umbra answered. "That *was not death. Angere had thought he killed us once, the seven of us; however, we were simply banished, sent out into the Nexus and eventually the multiverse. To answer your question, Marcus, God could have decided to let Andrew's fate be the same as mine and suffer the consequences of returning to Hell. Or he could have killed me.*"

"But what happens to you when you die?"

"*Simply put, I do not know. This is the first time it has ever been done. Only time will tell us what happened to Ira, weather or not he is truly dead.*"

Angere sanctioning the death of an Umbra? This was contradictory to what I knew about the code of ethics followed by the Mille Umbra. Killing another is the same as killing a part of oneself. The Umbra are one consciousness, separate but the same, and so are we, each his own individual consciousness yet part of a collective. We are all made up the same stuff and science has already *proven* that this smaller stuff is all connected, so why can't we believe that we are all one? Like the Umbra, with each murder committed *by* our species, *to* our species, we become just a little bit less than we once were. Violence creates fear, which leads to distrust and eventually, hatred. We move closer and closer to Chaos with each passing day. Soon our reality will be completely inside Chaos and there will be *no* return. The Divine Engine *must* be activated. The cycle must not be allowed to restart, not with things the way they are, not like this. All of the violence and hatred will be carried over into the next developing realities as it follows the imprint left by the last. There is only one way to stop this from happening. We must learn to loose our hatred and embrace love. The purest of the emotions, love can overcome everything! We must stop blaming everyone else for our problems, take control of our own lives and embrace love. We must choose to make the right choice when faced with a moral dilemma, or things will be *much* worse the next time around. The chances of someone else finding the Divine Engine and activating it without being stopped by Chaos are growing smaller with each second that passes. It must be done here and it must be done now!

THE BACK UP PLAN

With the remnants of Ira inside me I felt my other, and I knew Mark was near. I heard the crackle of static and he appeared before me on the platform. "You're too late," I said. "But don't worry, Ira didn't suffer like *Anna* did." I saw the anger growing on Mark's face when he looked up at the chains as they came to life, returning to their original position. I lunged at Mark but he was too fast. He shifted off to the side dealing me a severe blow to the back as I passed him by. I hit the floor hard and my lungs hurt like hell when I tried to refill them with air. I placed my hand to my side and felt a broken rib sticking up through the skin. I pushed it back in place and stood. "Where is it?" I asked. "Where's the key?" Mark just laughed. I shifted behind him and ripped off the back of his shirt, ready to lunge in and tear out his heart through the hole Lilith had made, but… The hole was *gone*! Mark's head spun around on his shoulders to face me, and he spoke. "You idiot! Do you really think Lilith would leave me that vulnerable this close to the end?" In the blink of an eye, his body was facing the same direction as his head. Mark grabbed me and pushed me back hard, slamming me into the side of one of the towers, once more taking my breath away. I looked up at the bastard as he laughed some more. "Don't worry," he said. "This is *far* from over," and he disappeared.

"Fuck!" I screamed and pounded my fist into the steel beam of the tower.

"Calm down, Marcus," Animus demanded from somewhere in the back of my mind.

"Easy for *you* to say," I hissed angrily. "You know, you could have helped out a little bit. You have no problem taking me over for a little snack on Ira, but then you just sit around watching me get my ass kicked all over the place? Thanks a lot!"

"This is your battle, Marcus, and as for my 'little snack', you will benefit from it more than you will ever know."

"Yeah, we'll just see about that." I stood, brushing the dirt from my clothes. "Well, what now?" I asked. *"Follow him,"* Animus said.

I focused on the tone Mark had left behind, separating it out from the rest before I tuned. I arrived inside the old slaughterhouse in my hometown; the sun had just set and the shadows were quickly falling. The canopy of trees outside the smashed windows grew dark and the room went black. I heard Mark whistling a song I thought I knew. The sound was coming from the office up on the catwalks. I shifted up and ducked down below the broken windows just around the corner from the open door. Mark stopped whistling. I waited for something to happen but nothing did. He taunted me with his melody once more and I stretched myself around the corner to look down the walkway. Except for the bomb the room was empty. I felt a blow to the back of my head and my face hit the rusted metal catwalk, hard, cutting it deep. I rolled over to face Mark as he held out the blades of the five-pointed star in front of my face.

"Sit. Up." Mark stuck the tip of the blades into the soft tissue of my nose, slicing into my left nostril. There was no turning back now the blades had tasted blood. "Where is your God now, you *fuck*!" Mark screamed.

"Animus, a little help here?"

"Ha…" Mark laughed again. "You think that *thing* can save you? When the Umbra are in you, it is *you* who controls the power yet you, Marcus refuse to use it. You're fucking weak!"

"At least I got to have what you couldn't," I taunted. "Even if you *did* take her away. I know how much you hated Anna and the kids and what they represented, and I know how you envy me for having the one thing you could never hang on to... love."

"You know *nothing* about me!" Mark screamed as he drove the blades into my stomach. "How do you like me *now* you *fuck*?" he yelled. Mark's yell turned to a howl, a call to the moon. He laughed out loud as he placed his hand on the end of the handle of the blades. "See, you piece of shit..." he hocked up the best lougie he could muster and spit. I was lucky; it missed my face but hit my shoulder and began sliding down my shirt. "There's no God here to save you," Mark continued, "no divine intervention, you're totally and thoroughly *screwed*!" Mark twisted the blades a little bit to let the blood flow more freely from my wounds. "And yeah, maybe I envy you a little bit but I didn't *hate* Anna. I showed her more love than you could *ever* imagine. I could read her thoughts as she was dying, Marcus. Do you know what she was thinking? I'll tell you. Your precious wife wanted to know how you could do that to her. She died thinking I was *you*. Her last thoughts were of the one she loved *cutting out her heart*!" I pushed up against the blades, trying to stand, but the action only made my wounds more severe. The bastard laughed. "It's over shithead! Who knows, maybe next time around *I'll* be the one doing the 'right thing', oh wait, there won't *be* a next time. See, me and my little friend in there," Mark pointed to the bomb in the office, "gotta' take a little trip. So there ain't no point in trying to activate some stupid fucking piece of shit Engine that's supposed to magically fix everything. You're done and your God no longer needs you! That's why *He* does nothing and *I* do this." Mark began to pull out the handle of the five-pointed star. I felt the blades inside me, eager for more flesh. "Oh, and about that key. I have no fucking idea what you're talking about. See ya'." Mark cocked the handle and opened the blades.

Consciousness came back to me with a vengeance. I looked down at my body, amazed it was still in one piece, but I hurt like a *motherfucker*! Small red lines followed the path of the blades where they had separated my flesh. I looked around, both the bomb and the bastard were gone, and so was Animus! There was no trace of him in my head at all but there were memories. Was that his way of leaving me a message, his way of saying goodbye? The Book of Death holds the knowledge to raise the dead, and there were several means to do so, provided the correct spells are used. No *one* life can be traded for another but *many* may be traded for *one*. Unfortunately, by *many* we're talking about millions of lives, a disaster of biblical proportions. No one had ever tried trading a life for that of an Umbra, it could *never* be done, but a *sacrifice... that's* another story. And obviously it had worked. I stood, wondering what to do next when a new wave of 'memories' hit. *The blood of the Divine has power, the power to kill what cannot be killed.* I remembered these words spoken to me in Hell, and now I knew what they meant. The blood of the Divine is harmless if it's your own for this blood already flows through you and can do you no harm. But the blood from *another* Divine bloodline... now were talking! Mark had no idea what I was talking about when I had mentioned the key, so he was not the one who had taken it... it had been me!

I tuned to Anna's Bridge, grabbed the key out of my own hand, and returned to the slaughterhouse. I held the Spear of Destiny in my hands, the blood of Christ contained inside its reservoir, the blood that could kill Mark. I now had the means to stop that bastard once and for all. I caught Mark's tone and tuned but when the string spit me out I saw nothing but black. I was in the Nexus. Mark began to whistle his song again and when my vision grew accustom to the darkness I saw him. My other had attached some sort of panel to the bomb he had stolen from Trinity. He put down his tools and started punching numbers into the keypad; he was arming it! His whistling turned to singing when he reached the chorus of the Porcupine Tree song... "Give me the freedom to destroy... Give me a radioactive toy..."

"Give me a *break*," I said.

"You're alone." Mark sounded surprised, then he laughed. "So It *did* save you. No matter, all I've got to do is place my hand on this panel and *boom*!" I shifted places with the bomb just as Mark reached up for the control panel. When I appeared, he placed his hand on my chest and I drove the spear into his gut as hard as I could. "This... isn't... over," Mark whispered through the blinding pain. "It was promised... that I would be the one... to choose your Hell. Just you wait, Marcus Quincy. I have quite... the surprise in store for you." I pressed the gem on the spear, injecting the blood of the Lamb. Mark started to convulse in my arms as *his* blood poured from all openings. I let him go and he fell back into the darkness, growing smaller and smaller in his descent until finally, he was gone.

Even though the Umbra within my head was now gone, it was time for another wave of memories from Animus. *This* was his thank you. I learned that, in cases where sins are committed for a just cause the sentence is limited by time. Sometimes even the vilest of sins, even *murder* is deemed necessary by God, but all sinners must still be punished. One of *these* souls will only spend a certain amount of time in the inner realm and would one day be released and allowed to enter Heaven. I smiled. Now I knew that I would see my Anna again. I turned to the bomb and wondered what to do with it, because if *his* touch would activate it then so would *mine*. I immediately shifted back to the platform with the bomb to once and for all activate the Divine Engine.

REALIGNMENT

The five turned to me when I reappeared. "What the hell is *that*?" two asked.

"Just a bomb," I said. "Oh, and if you touch it, it'll go off."

"Guess we won't touch it," they all said.

"Do you have the spear?" asked four. I held it up. The 'me' closest reached out and took it. "Shit, it's empty," he said.

"That's not a problem." I retrieved the spear and held out my arm. I made a nice wide gash in my forearm and filled the reservoir with my blood.

"Is that going to work?" they asked.

"Yes," I said, "it'll work." When the spear was full, I placed it into the slot in the shell of the Divine Engine, the slot that was once the opening of Mohamed's scabbard.

"What time is it?" I asked.

"We've got ten seconds," they answered. I pushed the spear in with the palm of my hand and injected the blood. The light emanating from the machine grew brighter and a whistling sound filled the midnight air. "Six, five, four, three, two, one..."

It is done. The Divine Engine had been activated and the cycle had been stopped. The Engine would shield us from the effects of the alignment and in turn, realign our reality closer to the center of the Nexus, further away from Chaos. All of the choices made from here on out will decide which direction our reality moves next. Closer to God or back to Chaos, the choice is up to *us*. Chose wisely because next time, we my not be able to stop it. Even as you read this, the Divine Engine is rewriting the Divine Plan, and from now on the great plan will be written by *us*. The imprint we leave will last forever, repeated over and over again by new realities for millions of millennia to come. Now more than ever *we* control our destiny. Use this knowledge wisely and maybe one day there will no longer be a need for Chaos and we will truly be one with God. Maybe one day we will finally put aside our problems and work together toward a better life for all and a better future for our children. I wish I could be there to see it. I know I will not live to see that day but I will always hold on to the hope that it *will* come. The day we realize that we are all one, and violence and hatred have brought us nothing but pain and suffering. It must be *love* that we seek and not power, for love is a power more intense than the mightiest of weapons. Love can conquer *anything*! I will die having known such love, and one day we *will* be together again. Yes, one day I will know how it feels to be near my beloved once more, when our minds connect and we are complete, and when the love between us overcomes everything and I... I finally make it home.

I had one more thing to do, one more task to take care of. People say that bad things always come in threes and for Chaos this *will* be true. I looked at the Five, they were all enjoying the moment in their own way, talking and laughing. Not me; I had my *own* destiny. It was time for me to part ways with the Five, to say my goodbyes, and complete the final act. I still had one more sin to commit; I still had to kill Lilith. I turned to my others and yelled to get their attention; they stopped what they were doing and looked my way. "I've gotta' go," I said.

"We know," they replied in unison. One by one we embraced and said goodbye, knowing this would be the last time that we met. I stepped away from them and nodded one last time. "Hey," they said, "don't forget your bomb." I smiled, caught the correct string, and tuned.

I had no idea how to find Lilith. I was hopping I wouldn't have to. I was hoping *she* would find *me* and I could end this thing once and for all. I had a plan, hatched from the memories given to me by Animus, plotted from the Books of Knowledge. I now had the means and the power to kill an Ah Me Rah. At first I had planned on trying to find Sirnib, to see if he was still alive and to see if he could lead me to Lilith, but my trip was interrupted. I was pulled from the tone back into the Nexus, stopping with a terrible jolt. When the stars stopped spinning around my head and I could see again, much to my surprise, I gazed upon my Ma Hua Ra. "Gabriel," I said.

"Yes, Marcus. You have done well. The task is complete and your destiny is fulfilled. Thank you for showing me that there is still hope for mankind, that God was not wrong in putting his faith in your species... and *for opening up my eyes."*

"You're welcome," I said, shocked, "but I'm not quite finished yet."

"Yes, I am aware of your intentions."

"It won't add any time to my sentence will it?" I asked with a smile.

"No, Marcus, You're actions will add no time."

"Good," I said. "Oh yeah, while I'm thinking about it, who was that little girl I kept running into while I was in Hell?"

"Do not worry about her, Marcus. She is your daughter's problem."

285

"My daughters problem, huh? Guess they've got their *own* part to play in the Divine Plan." Gabriel laughed his angelic laugh and smiled.

"Yes Marcus, as do we all. And for your part I am offering you one wish before you go... anything within my power."

"I'm guessing my wife is not among them," I said.

"I'm sorry, Marcus, she is not."

"Then I want to see the girls."

"They are no longer together," Gabriel explained, *"but if you wish, you may choose one."*

"You're going to make me *choose* between my children?"

"I am truly sorry, but this is how it must be." I knew there was no point in arguing, but I wanted to anyway. I was pissed, why should I have to choose? After all I've done, why couldn't I have this one simple thing? Then I realized that it was *not* about me and the choice became clear. I knew that Anna no longer thought that I was the one who killed her, but Tori... I could not allow her to grow up thinking her father had tried to kill her, thinking I'd murdered her mother. I would *not* let that happen.

"Then the choice is made?" asked Gabriel.

"Yes," I said. "I wish to see Tori."

GOODBYE

The string dumped me in a dark bedroom and there she was, curled up into a ball under the covers, her arms wrapped tightly around her favorite teddy bear. She smiled as she slept occasionally giggling and snorting. I fell to my knees beside the bed and began to cry. It had been so long since I had seen her, I wanted to touch her and I wanted to hold her. I began to doubt myself. Would it be better if she never knew I was there? Had I already done too much damage to my child's fragile mind? Gabriel had said that it was not possible to see both of the girls, which led me to believe they had been separated and placed in different foster homes. I wondered if my baby girl was dreaming of her mother. It had been a long time since *I'd* slept but when I did, my mind was dominated by dreams of Anna and dreams of the girls. I saw the girls as teenagers, sometimes arguing. And I had a dream of the two becoming one beautiful perfect child. But the dreams of Anna… sometimes I was lucky and the dreams would be kind, but most… most were haunted by Anna's murder at the hands of the man I myself had just killed. I dreamed that I was him, as Mark methodically and yes, even *lovingly*, carried out the act that took Anna away from the girls. Was I any better than him? "Why are you crying, daddy?"

Tori sat up in bed looking at me. She was a lot bigger than I had expected; had it been that long since I'd seen her? She held out her bear for me. Tori used to bring him to me when I was sad, she said he was a good listener and his fur was soft and nice to cry into. I took the bear, cradled it to my face, and sobbed quietly. She was right. Tori tugged at her nightgown and climbed out of bed. My child ran to me and threw her arms around me, softly sobbing with me.

"I love you, daddy," Tori whispered in my ear.

I had to push my face into the bear to keep from sobbing too loudly and waking up her new family.

"Do you like it here?" I asked.

"It's okay," she said sadly, "but I miss you and mommy, and I miss Tara."

"I know, honey. I miss you all so very much."

"Will you get to see Tara?" she asked. I held back the sobs and answered.

287

"No, honey. I could only see you."

"That's too bad," Tori said. "Tara is always so sad when I see her."

"You get to see her?" I asked.

"All the time," she said sadly. Tori's arms tightened around me and she put her lips to my ear. Her breath was soft and warm and seemed to fill my body with electricity, every nerve tingled with the delicious current. "I know it wasn't you, daddy," she whispered.

I felt the tears starting to come again. I closed my eyes and pulled her face to mine as she continued.

"I know it wasn't you who choked me in the hospital," she said. "And I know it wasn't you who killed mom." I opened my eyes.

"*Wow*, cooool!" Tori yelled just a little too loudly. I put my finger to my lips.

"Sorry," she whispered. "Will I have eyes like that someday?"

"I don't know, honey. I think your eyes are just fine the way they are."

"I don't." Tori crossed her arms and pouted.

"Listen honey," I pulled her close again, "I'll see what I can do to get you some new eyes." I hated lying to her, but I could not let her be sad the last time she saw her father. "Thank you Tori," I said. "Thank you for believing in me." I kissed her on the forehead.

"Do you have to go?" she asked.

"Soon," I said through my tears.

"Can we play a game first, please?" she pleaded.

"Sure," I said. "What do you want to play?"

"We can't play a video game, *that* would be too loud. I know; wait right here! I have some board games in the closet." Tori tiptoed across the room and slowly opened her closet door. She stepped inside for a few seconds before emerging with an armful of boxes. "Which one do you want to play? You probably don't have much time do you?" She sounded disappointed.

"Any one you want, honey," I said. Tori shuffled through the boxes a few times, then made her choice, picking the game that would take the longest to play. It was some sort of combination card and board game with cartoon monsters. I had trouble keeping up with the rules but Tori didn't seem to mind. Sometime into the game she started yawning and struggling to keep her eyes open. Her head began to tilt and then she jolted herself awake.

"Maybe it's time you climb back in bed baby girl," I said, my voice filled with sorrow.

"Okay, dad, you probably need to go," Tori said with a yawn. She hugged me tightly and kissed me on the cheek. "Thank you, Daddy." Tori let go of me and climbed back into bed. I kissed her on the forehead, and she smiled, then began to softly snore.

I stood up and stepped back, everything around me going black. The black slowly turned to gray and Gabriel appeared before me leaning against the bomb I had stolen from Mark. "Where are we?" I asked.

"We are sill in the Nexus," he answered.

"What happened?"

"You," said Gabriel. *"In the beginning, the Nexus was white. It was tainted by the seven shadows and over time was turned black. The activation of the Divine Engine is returning the Nexus to what it once was."* Gabriel paused to let the Godivel fruit do its thing. With our reality having shifted closer to the center of the Nexus, Chaos no longer had such a powerful hold on us and the darkness slowly began to fade. This darkness will not be gone forever, not unless we fight to move

in the right direction, to move closer to Heaven and closer to God. It does not matter what faith we are or what we believe, just as long as we believe there is a paradise that awaits us in the next life. So why wait? Only by making the world around us a paradise will we truly earn the right to enter Heaven. Stop waiting and wishing for the end to make things better, stop bitching about things and *DO* something, make a difference and *make* the world a better place. Heaven is there for the taking, embrace it, and make it part of your life and the lives of those around you. See the good in man, see the good in the world and most importantly, *never* forget to love. We have a chance to rewrite our future, to become something new, something better, to *evolve!* Take this chance, this gift from God, and use it to make your life better, to make *all* of our lives better, to truly be at peace, and to become one with the Creator. *"Are you ready, Marcus?"* Gabriel asked.

"Let's get this over with," I said. Gabriel smiled. He spread his legs apart and opened his arms, forming the five-pointed star with his body. "Thank you," I said, "and goodbye."

Gabriel wrapped his arms around me. *"Goodbye, Marcus."*

SACRIFICE

I stood in a small hallway; the entrance to what was the chapel where a blind priest named Anderson Clark had once found sanctuary. I left the bomb in the hall and searched the back room only to find the trap door closed. I opened it and climbed down into the hallway leading to the single basement room. The boxes of ID's had been overturned and spread throughout the room, making it impossible to see the floor, or anything else buried underneath. I saw a door on one of the walls that had been hidden, covered over with stacks of boxes until now. I climbed over the pile of ID's until I reached the door. I ascended a narrow set of stairs that led into a shed behind the church. The small shack had no door which allowed me to see what was going on outside.

I saw a large fire burning. Its flames were bright red and the smoke blocked out the stars in the night sky. On the other side of the fire I saw

Father Clark; he was lying on his stomach atop a woodpile. Although my vision was obstructed I knew Lilith was there. I had the knowledge and the means to kill an Ah Me Rah but could I pull it off? Could I be convincing enough to fool Lilith? I changed the numbers in my eyes from sevens to sixes and stepped out into the warm night air. The scent of the ocean mixed with the smell of smoke as I walked toward the fire. I had to think like my negative self. I had to make Lilith believe I was Mark, so I opened up my mind and let the ruse begin.

I could now see what Lilith was doing to Father Clark. She had taken the form of a large male with the legs of a beast, and unfortunately, the cock of one, too. The priest's pants were down around his ankles, which dangled above the ground as he lay slumped over the woodpile. The beast was having its way with the man as he lay there sobbing. When Lilith saw me she stopped and turned, the beast's cock slid out and slapped against its knee. My ass hurt just thinking about what had been done to the poor man.

"What are you doing here?" the beast demanded. *"You have a job to do."*

I filled my mind with lies, and some truth… I showed Lilith the events leading up to Marcus's death at the hands of Mark. How I had stolen the key, preventing Marcus from activating the Engine, and how I had killed the last Elizabeth Patton, casting the spell and removing her heart as a sign of devotion to my one true love. So far Lilith was buying it. I reached into my pocket and placed my hand around the fruit from the Tree of Life. I felt it transform within my fingers, beginning to swell and beginning to *beat*! I pulled the forgery from my pocket and held it out for the creature to see. Lilith looked confused for a moment and then smiled. *"Yes, the timelines are changing; no wonder I did not see. Then Ira is still alive?"*

"Yes my love," I lied.

"Not for long," Lilith hissed. *"Give me the heart."* The creature transformed, growing smaller and feminine. Lilith reached out and took the heart into her hand, placed it to her nose, and drew in the scent of Elizabeth Patton. A small drop of blood ran from one of the severed

veins and down onto Lilith's finger. She slowly licked the blood from her hand and smiled. *"The last is* always *the sweetest."* Lilith took a bite, savored the flesh for a moment, and then swallowed.

Father Clark's sobbing turned to laughter. "Shut up!" Lilith hissed, but her voice was different. She no longer spoke with the voice of a god, just a simple, feminine voice. Lilith looked up at me and her face filled with terror as she watched my eyes change back to sevens. She looked down at her hand to find the heart was no longer there. Instead, she held the glowing white fruit from the Tree of Life. Lilith dropped the fruit to the ground and backed away. She held out her arms and watched as her skin slowly lost its shine and her color began to dull, first turning gray, then brown, and then tan. The only thing to remain black was her hair. Lilith screamed as her transformation competed and she became human. Father Clark pulled up his pants and stumbled over to my side. "It's good to see you again, Marcus."

"Good one," I said to the blind man.

"Yes," he said. "That was a pretty clever bit of acting on your part. I'm proud of you, my son."

"Ah, but you've yet to see the final act," I said with a smile.

"I can't wait." The Father cocked his head, listening for something. He turned and punched Lilith directly in the face. She fell to the ground landing on her ass, blood pouring from her nose and tears from her eyes.

"Why did you have to do this?" Lilith sobbed.

"Sorry sweetheart," I said sarcastically, "but all good things must come to an end. Speaking of which, I have a little surprise for you." I took the Fathers hand and turned to him. So much had happened since this all began. So much had changed, *I* had changed. I'm not the same person I was in the beginning and I'm proud of that. Like Gabriel, my eyes had been opened and I had finally learned to see the good in man and the good in the world. Yes, I had found my balance and I had at last found piece. I was ready to move on, to take the next step in my evolution and become what all saviors must become, a martyr. And like all martyrs I do this not because I have to, but because I *choose* to. The Divine Engine had been activated and my task was complete but my journey was not over, not yet. Lilith *must* die!

"Are you ready to leave this place?" I asked Father Clark.

"As ready as I'll ever be," he answered. I shifted the bomb from the hallway and watched Lilith's reaction when it appeared and hovered in the air before me.

"No, Marcus, please," Lilith whimpered. "Don't let it end like this."

I ignored Lilith and squeezed the father's hand. "It's time to go," I said as I placed my free hand on the control panel and detonated the bomb. The last sound I heard before I died was Lilith screaming and Father Anderson Clark laughing.

EPILOGUE

GENESIS

Admiral Robert Forsythe turned and closed the car door. He waited for his assistant, Lieutenant Amanda Briggs, as she pulled her skirt down trying to cover her long tanned legs. The two walked up to the automatic doors of the hospital and entered.

"So, do you think Mr. Quincy might be telling the truth?" asked Lt. Briggs.

"I believe some of it," the Admiral said with a face of stone. "I think it's worth looking into." He pressed the button for the elevator and waited.

"Would it be possible for *me* to interview him?" the woman asked. "On my own, I mean."

"I'm sorry, Amanda," the Admiral said, "but he's too dangerous." The elevator doors opened and they stepped inside. "How about this: I let you sit in on any interview you wish, once we get him back to the facility, but today you must stay in the control room and watch."

"Fine," Amanda sighed with obvious disappointment. The doors opened and the pair stepped out into a brightly lit hallway, both nearly getting run over by three large men racing down the hall toward a crowd of screaming nurses. The staff was gathered around the door leading to the psychiatric ward. Admiral Forsythe sprinted down the hall and caught the door before it closed behind the men who had rushed inside. The Admiral waited for Lt. Briggs to catch up and left her with the duty of explaining to the nurses who they were and why they were there.

The Admiral saw a hoard of nurses gathered around Marcus Quincy's room. One of the large orderlies pushed his way through the crowd and looked into the window of Marcus's room. He closed the shutter and turned, making his way out of the crowd, rejoining his two partners. "I don't know what the hell they expect *us* to do about this," said one large man to another. The Admiral moved past them and made his way through the mob. "What's going on?" he asked the nurse closest to the door.

"I have no idea," she said. "He started screaming and convulsing and then… *that* happened!" The nurse turned with the rest of the staff as they went back to their stations. The crowd slowly dispersed, leaving the Admiral alone at the door. He opened the shutter and looked inside. Admiral Forsythe stepped back from the window as his brain struggled to comprehend what he had seen. In the middle of the room was a pile of objects. The Admiral saw a scabbard, a bowl, a set of gears that looked like they belonged in a grandfather clock, and many other items. This however, was *not* what unnerved the admiral the most. Sitting in the room, in a circle around the objects, were five identical men and *all* were Marcus Quincy. Was this a last ditch effort by the forces of darkness to tip the balance or was this God's work? Admiral Forsythe stepped away from the room and shook his head. He reached for his phone, dialed a number, and said, "I need a transport team."

Sirnib sat at the bar. He downed his latest bottle of beer and placed it with the rest of the empties. There were at least two-dozen. He looked at his watch anxiously and then ordered another beer. As the door to the bar opened, Sirnib turned to look, and she was finally there. He saw the most beautiful woman he had ever set eyes upon in his long, long life. '*That lucky bastard,*' he thought. The woman walked over to the bar and took the stool next to him. Sirnib glanced down at her legs as the soft material of her skirt slid aside. '*Man, the things I would do for a piece of that!*' The woman looked at him and smiled.

"So, did you find it?" she asked.

"Yup," Sirnib slurred. "He's most definitely being held in the innermost realm. You know what that means right?" The woman grabbed the beer from his hand and drank, draining the mostly full bottle. "Yeah," she said, "I know what that means." Sirnib placed the bottle with the others and called the bartender over.

"You want one?" Sirnib asked. The woman said no.

"Look," he said. "I helped him get there once but I can't make any promises. Besides, I didn't even get him half way there; he did the rest on his own."

"Don't worry; I can get there." The woman rose from the stool, leaned down, and kissed Sirnib on the cheek. "Thank you," she said, and left the bar.

The darkness surrounded her as the force closed in, pressing down on her skin and filling her lungs with putrid air. It was hard to keep the fear away, but she was strong, she *had* to be. Her husband had made the ultimate sacrifice to ensure a future for mankind; the least she could do was show a little courage in the face of darkness. So Anna Quincy waited. The air around her grew cold and filled with the awful smell of rotting corpses. Anna closed her eyes and held her breath. She exhaled. "Are you here?"

"YES," the Umbra boomed.

"I'm here for my husband," Anna called out. Angere did not reply, instead, he let Anna wait, to stew in her doubts and fears; oh how he loved the way it felt. "Well?" she called out.

"YOU MAY TAKE HIM." The Umbra finally answered. *"I GROW TIRED OF HIS THOUGHTS OF LOVE, HIS THOUGHTS OF YOU. IT SICKENS ME TO MY VERY CORE. TAKE THE WRETCHED CREATURE AND LEAVE HERE FOREVER."*

The darkness and pressure faded and Anna found herself standing in front of a familiar door, the door to the bedroom she shared with her husband so many years ago, so many lifetimes ago. Three to be exact. Anna had returned to the world of the living three times since the events that had torn her family apart. She had lived three lonely lives never wishing to find love, never wanting anything but the embrace of her sweet, sweet Marcus. Soon she would have him, *hold* him once more, but first… first she had to open the door.

Marcus held the knife in his hand, mesmerized by his reflection in the blood-streaked blade. The body lay splayed out before him just like a million times before, just like the next one would when he'd finished with this one. Over the years, Marcus had learned to take his time. The longer each one lasted, the longer it was before he had to see her whole again, only to start things over and once more destroy what he loved the most. Marcus looked down at the beautiful face of his wife. He cut off a piece of her shirt and dabbed at the blood that streaked her cheek. He didn't like to touch her face, *anything* but her face. Marcus had to see her as she truly was, even as her body lay torn to pieces, scattered throughout every inch of the room. Anna's face always remained the same, just as he remembered it from a past life that felt so long ago. It would be time soon, time for the body to disappear and a new one to walk through the door. Marcus sobbed as he went back to work, sliding the knife into the last remaining bits of flesh on his wife's body. The door opened.

Marcus looked down at the shredded corpse on the bed, then at the woman who stood in the doorway. It wasn't time yet, he wasn't finished. Marcus held the knife out in front of him and jumped from the bed, charging the woman. When he was within a few feet something made him stop, something that felt familiar, something that felt *right*. Marcus remembered this feeling from long ago; it was one he had sworn he would never forget. Of all of the women who had walked through the door, none had *ever* given him this feeling, as they were *not* his Anna, they were simply vessels. This is what Marcus had told himself over the years. He'd come close to losing the memories of how she'd felt in the past, but it would not go quietly, not without a fight. And here it was again, standing right in front of him. There was no escaping it. There was no doubt… It was *her*!

Marcus dropped his knife. "Is it… Is it you?" he stuttered.

"Yes, Marcus, it's me. It's Anna." Tears filled her eyes as she watched the confusion grow on her husband's face.

"How… how long have I been here?" Marcus finally asked.

"Seven hundred and seventy seven years," Anna answered as the tears began to roll down her face. She reached out her hand. Marcus looked at it for a moment and then smiled. Anna smiled back as her husband took her hand. "You've suffered long enough Marcus," she said. "It's time to come home…"

The End

ABOUT THE AUTHOR

Michael Williams is an accomplished author, artist, and musician. His first novel, The Divine Engine, combines science, religion, and fantasy to craft a dark and at times, horrific narrative. As an author, his roots lie in the worlds of H.P. Lovecraft, Philip K. Dick, and Clive Barker. Worlds where science and religion are one and the same, drawn together as opposing forces should be.